FLEU

Cynthia Harrod-Eagles, author of over thirty successful novels, including *The Orange Tree Plot* and the
best-selling *Dynasty* series, won the Young Writer's
Award in 1972 with her first novel, *The Waiting Game*.
She studied English and History at the University of
Edinburgh and University College London, and had
a variety of jobs in the commercial world before becoming a full-time writer in 1978.

Also by Cynthia Harrod-Eagles in Pan Books

ANNA

Cynthia Harrod-Eagles

FLEUR

PART TWO OF
THE KIROV SAGA

PAN BOOKS
LONDON, SYDNEY AND AUCKLAND

First published in 1991 by Sidgwick & Jackson Limited

This edition published 1992 by Pan Books Ltd,
a division of Pan Macmillan Limited,
Cavaye Place, London SW10 9PG
Associated companies throughout the world

1 3 5 7 9 8 6 4 2

ISBN 0 330 31791 1

Typeset by Florencetype Ltd, Kewstoke, Avon
Printed in England by Clays Ltd, St Ives plc

FOR MY HUSBAND

The Kirov Family

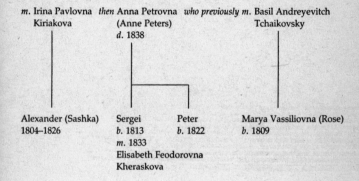

Nikolai Sergeyevitch Kirov
d. 1828

m. Irina Pavlovna   *then* Anna Petrovna   *who previously m.* Basil Andreyevitch
   Kiriakova   (Anne Peters)   Tchaikovsky
                   d. 1838

Alexander (Sashka)   Sergei   Peter   Marya Vassiliovna (Rose)
1804–1826   *b.* 1813   *b.* 1822   *b.* 1809
                     m. 1833
                     Elisabeth Feodorovna
                     Kheraskova

BOOK ONE

English Rose

Chapter One

Once the carriage had passed the village green at Shepherd's Bush, the open fields and little farms were left behind. Despite the midsummer heat, Fleur leaned forward and put the window up. Buckley, the Hamiltons, coachman, believed in 'driving good horses at a good speed', as he put it, and once he got onto the pike road, he raised an uncomfortable dust.

Besides, from here almost all the way to Tyburn Corner there was building going on on both sides of the road. Holding onto the strap as the carriage swayed and rattled towards London, Fleur gazed out of the window, with the endless internal monologue of the solitary person for company. In fields where lately cows had grazed, men were pegging out plots and gouging brown furrows in the green turf; where once market gardens had sported rows of beans and cabbages, there were rows of identical houses in various stages of completion.

It was all progress, noise and bustle – all change. Nothing was immune. Behind the Kensington gravel-pits, the Hippodrome racecourse had disappeared, its track commemorated only in the crescent shape of the terraces which covered it; while on the site of the Grandstand now stood a church, in the ornate and fantastic new Gothic style. Soon, she thought, the villages along the north side of the Uxbridge pike – Knolton Hill, Bayswater, Westbourne Green, Paddington – would all be joined together in one endless sea of stucco, and it would be impossible to tell any more where London ended and the country began.

Of course, it was a good thing, proof that England was prosperous again. Fleur was twenty-four, too young to remember the French Wars which had drained the country of its life-blood for twenty long years; but she had grown up with the aftermath, the terrible depression of the 'thirties and 'forties.

Some of her earliest childhood memories were of men 'on the tramp' – labourers without money or work begging at the door. Many were discharged soldiers: Peninsula veterans with their feet wrapped in rags, peasant-style; Waterloo survivors bearing the stigmata of their courage – horrible scars, missing fingers, arms, eyes. They had frightened her mother, and if they came to the front asking for work like honourable men, the standing order was to drive them away; but when they crept like beaten dogs to the back door, the lower servants, torn between fear and pity, would smuggle out parcels of food and clothes, whatever might not be missed by the housekeeper.

They had frightened young Fleur, too, but she could not ignore them, or run away from them. One day she hid behind a bush in the garden to watch an old man hobble away from the back door, with a dole of bread and onions stuffed into the pockets of his baggy and threadbare army greatcoat. His face was gaunt, and blackened down one side with a powder-scar, and there was a silver stubble of beard over his chin and jaw. He had a foot missing, but he went along nimbly enough on one sound leg and a crutch.

She mustn't have been well-enough hidden, for as he passed her bush he stopped and looked at her quizzically, and then smiled.

'Come on out then, missy,' he said. 'Come on, I won't hurt you.'

Fleur revealed herself slowly and cautiously, ready to run at the first sudden movement; but the soldier continued only to look at her and smile. He was the thinnest man she had ever seen. His nose and cheekbones were so close under the skin that they made it look shiny; his cheeks were seamed and his eyes were sunken, and she knew with some close-to-the-earth instinct of the child that he was starving to death. Yet she saw now with a kind of fascination that he was not an old man at all. He was probably not more than thirty-five or forty.

He said, 'By God, you're a pretty one! It does me good, the sight of a little lass so pretty! I had a little daughter myself once – only she was dark, not fair like you.'

It was on the tip of Fleur's tongue to ask where she was, but as she looked into his eyes she knew somehow that his little girl was dead. She felt strangely drawn to him, and wanted desperately to do something for him, to give him something. She thrust her hand into the pocket of her apron, and brought out the only thing it contained – a white handkerchief. She knew it was a poor gift, and she held it out to him hesitantly, unsure if it would be acceptable.

He shifted his balance on his crutch and held out his hand. It was all knuckles, and seemed too big for his wrist. He took the handkerchief and looked at it wonderingly for a long time; and then he looked at Fleur, and she saw to her horror that he was crying.

'I used to be an ostler,' he said. The tears ran down his seamed cheeks very slowly, as if they, too, were close to death. His fingers closed round the scrap of white linen, and he nodded to her, pulling his lip in under his teeth, and hobbled away. She watched him until he was out of sight, and then crawled in under the bush and stayed there for a long time, hugging her knees for comfort and rocking back and forth.

It was not until years later that she came to understand why he had said what he said. 'I used to be an ostler.' As she grew up, a lonely girl in a large house, the servants had been much more her companions than they ought, and she had learned a great deal about them and their ways. She learned that amongst male servants, those who cared for horses were an elite. To be a groom, stableman or ostler was a matter for great pride.

The soldier had been telling her he had not always been as she saw him then; but what could a man on a crutch do around horses? Exiled from his trade and his pride, he could only beg for bread. Year by year she had teased out her memory of the episode, worrying at it, wondering over it. She was afraid that in offering him her handkerchief she had somehow hurt him. She was afraid he had thought she pitied him in the wrong way, despised him for his weakness.

He had not cried until *after* she gave it to him, she was sure of that. Sure of it. He had been hopping along nimbly, pleased with his bread and onions, until he had met her; he had left her grieving, and she knew she would never be able to rid herself of the feeling that she had somehow made his suffering worse. 'I used to be an ostler.' It was like a tiny thorn in her mind – grown over, but still prickling at any incautious movement.

Well, that was long ago. The scars of war had healed, times had changed. The currency had stabilised, business had picked up, the railways had come. The empty workshops and silent factories sprang to life again, the chimneys darkened the skies as before, and now in 1850 England was flourishing, with industry growing by leaps and bounds, and trade expanding everywhere.

People were flooding from all over the country into London, the largest industrial city in the world, and people had to have somewhere to live. Fleur gazed at the ant-hill activity which rendered the familiar increasingly unfamiliar every time she performed this journey. This was the spoor of the new kind of builder, like Mr Cubitt who sometimes dined with Papa at home at Grove Park. Instead of being commissioned in the old way to build a house for a particular person, these new men borrowed large sums of money, bought up great pieces of land on which they built streets and streets of houses, and paid back the investors and made their profit from the rents. It was a good thing, of course – an excellent thing! Fleur only wished there were room in the system for a little more variety. There would come a time, she thought, when you might wander about those identical streets and have no idea where you were.

But England – and London particularly – was an exciting place to be in 1850. She was glad to be going to visit her Aunt Venus and Uncle Frederick, to catch up on the gossip and see some fresh faces. It wasn't that she was unhappy at home in Chiswick – she had plenty to occupy her – but everyone liked a change now and then, and it did get rather lonely sometimes, with Papa away so much, and Richard at school. He was in his last year at Eton, making the right friends, playing a great deal of cricket, and learning to hold his liquor like a gentleman. He was a handsome and popular boy with, as Aunt Venus said mordantly, no more abilities, as eventual heir to Papa's property, than he was ever likely to need.

The carriage reached Tyburn Corner. It still presented an unfamiliar sight to Fleur, with the public gibbet removed at last: it was now to be, much more grandly, the site of Nash's Marble Arch, which was in the process of being moved from its original position in front of Buckingham Palace. Once past the scaffolding, they plunged into the tunnel of Oxford Street. The traffic was a solid mass as usual, and they were forced to a halt.

It was hot and stuffy inside the carriage. Fleur cautiously opened the window again. The inevitable smell of horses, a smell she always associated with London, was spiced today with a pungent whiff of pigs. Somewhere up ahead of them a herd of swine – evidently the immediate cause of the hold-up – was squealing, after the manner of their kind, as though they were being butchered there and then.

Something ought to be done about the driving of animals to market through London's busy thoroughfares, she thought. At least it should be restricted to the early hours of the morning when the streets were empty. It was hard enough to get through the mass of vehicles, without the added hazards of flocks of sheep, pigs and geese – quite leaving aside the nuisance of all the extra manure, which made it sometimes impossible to find a crossing-sweeper. One day a couple of drays would interlock themselves at a crossroads, and the traffic of London would simply grind to a halt. She envisaged the scene with an inward smile. They would have to dismantle all the carriages on the spot, one by one, and take them away in pieces.

For the moment, however, Buckley was a man of long experience, and from his vantage point up on the box decided there was no future in staying where they were. The hint of a gap opened up on the right where a determined hackney-driver was edging his hansom out of North Audley Street, and with a fearsome cracking of his whip Buckley swung the horses right across the road, under the fretting noses of a dray, two growlers and an overloaded knifeboard 'bus.

The 'bus horses flung up their heads, the driver let loose a chilling stream of abuse, and one of the outside passengers threw a lump of orange-peel at them. Fleur hastily put up the window as Buckley, who was a Londoner born, returned the abuse with interest; but they were into North Audley Street, free and clear, and a few minutes later they were pulling up outside her aunt's house in Hanover Square.

On her way up the steps, Fleur paused to look back at the coachman with mock severity. 'I didn't know you knew such words, Buckley. I'm shocked.'

Buckley was not deceived. 'You shouldn't of had the window down, Miss Flora, not in London! And if you've not heard them words before, what with all them pauper orspitals you visit, then I'm a Dutchman.'

He and Fleur were old friends. They exchanged smiles of perfect understanding, and she gathered her skirts and went on up the steps.

'My dear Fleur,' sighed Aunt Venus, 'nobody in London talks of anything but this Great Exhibition.' She was a thin and upright elderly lady, her greying fair hair dressed in a false front of curls after the manner of her youth. She still had an incomparably graceful way of wearing a shawl, like Madame Recamier, but otherwise she was a stern, hard and angular aunt. 'By the time it happens – if it ever does – we shall all be sick of it.'

'But of course it will happen,' Aunt Ercy said earnestly. She was a plump and downy aunt, with shy, myopic eyes, which made her look like a sleepy bird. 'The dear Queen has quite set her heart on it. You know that whatever the dear Prince wishes—'

'But your father will have told you about it, of course,' Aunt Venus interrupted ruthlessly. She regarded Ercy as a twittering fool, and usually ignored anything she said, unless it was to argue with her. The two sisters were little alike in looks, but

16

inside they were almost equally self-absorbed, though their selfishness manifested itself in different ways.

'Papa has mentioned it, but he isn't one of the Commissioners, you know,' Fleur said.

'He's a member of the Royal Society, and a prominent one at that. He's bound to know all about it,' Venus pronounced. 'Where is he, by the way? He should at least have called in to pay his respects.'

'He's in Derbyshire,' Fleur said. 'He's coming back by train this afternoon, so I'm sure he'll call.'

'If he recollects where he is,' Aunt Venus said drily. 'I suppose he's visiting Chatsworth? I wonder that having Devonshire so near a neighbour in Chiswick, he needs to pursue the poor man into the country.'

'You know perfectly well, Aunt, that he doesn't go to Chatsworth to see the Duke. He goes to consult with Mr Paxton.'

Aunt Venus nodded coolly. 'Yes, that's Ranulph's style – consorting with servants. He never troubles himself to make eligible connections. My poor child, if it weren't for Frederick and me, you'd have grown up a savage!'

'Mr Paxton isn't a servant, he's a great expert. And Papa has such a particular interest in the lily—'

Aunt Ercy, who had been only half attending, fixed eagerly on this. 'Lily? Who can you mean, dear? Is there a lady in the case? Don't tell me your dear father is contemplating a second marriage at last? After all the times we've tried—'

'Nonsensical woman!' Venus rounded on her. 'Go back to sleep! A lady in the case, indeed!'

Fleur saw her junior aunt's lip tremble, and intervened. 'I was talking about the water-lily, Aunt Ercy – the rare tropical lily Mr Paxton's growing at Chatsworth.' Ercy still looked confused, and Fleur went on patiently, 'Don't you remember, it was Papa who suggested giving him a seedling, because the one at Kew wasn't flourishing, and they were afraid of losing it altogether?'

'Well, I recall something about it,' Aunt Ercy said, applying the corner of a handkerchief to her eyes, and looking at her sister reproachfully over it. 'But there's no need for Vee to be so unkind. I can't be remembering everything all the time!'

Aunt Venus growled, and Fleur went on hastily, anxious to keep the peace. 'It's astonishing how it's grown. The leaves are quite five feet across now, Papa says, and so strong – you'll hardly believe this, Aunt – that Mr Paxton's little girl Annie, who's seven years old and quite solid, can stand upright on them! It's outgrowing its tank, and Mr Paxton's talking of enlarging the lily-house. Well, he loves to be building—'

'Building?' Aunt Ercy said, her mind hopping nimbly. 'Talking of building, my dear, have you heard about the plan the Committee's put forward for the pavilion to house the Prince's Exhibition? Everyone says it will never do. Twenty million bricks, and to cost a hundred thousand pounds – or was it the other way round? Poor Lord Brougham is quite beside himself about it—'

'That's what we were talking about ten minutes ago, you idiotic creature!' Venus said wrathfully. She turned to Fleur. 'Brougham is a prosy old fool, but the Committee has put up such a hotchpotch, nonsensical design: a great ugly thing like a railway shed, with a dome half as big again as St Paul's, all made of brick and iron and stone, as solid as Buckingham Palace! Once it was up – and that would take for ever – it would have to stay up, a permanent eyesore right in the middle of London.'

'Oh no,' Ercy said earnestly. 'The dear Queen has *promised* that whatever they build, it will certainly be taken down again within the year. Otherwise it would never – but there are the trees to consider, of course, which—'

'Trees, Aunt?'

'Half a dozen old elms would have to be cut down to make room for the building,' Venus said briskly. 'By the uproar in the House you'd think it was six members of the Royal Family going to the guillotine!'

Ercy shuddered theatrically. 'Oh, don't say that horrid word, Vee, I beg you! When I think of poor Gran'père—'

'Then don't think,' Venus said brutally, and went on talking to her niece. 'But it's not just the building – the whole scheme is misguided! London to be flooded by countless thousands of foreigners? Can you imagine the dangers, the dirt, the diseases – to say nothing of turning every lodging-house in Knightsbridge into a—' She snapped her lips shut to prevent herself from saying the word 'brothel', but her sister knew quite well what she hadn't said.

'Oh, Vee!' she cried faintly.

'And Richard Mayne has the gravest doubts that the Police Force could cope with such a gathering of vagabonds and pickpockets as would converge on Hyde Park.'

'You make it sound like an invasion,' Fleur said, amused. 'I thought it was supposed to be a celebration of Universal Peace?'

'The Free-Traders would have it so. But the Protectionists think differently – and I don't know that they're wrong. If the Prince wants an exhibition of *English* art and industry, let him go ahead, but why invite the rest of the world? Why should we put our hands in our pockets to help foreigners and revolutionaries show off their wares – and probably steal our trade into the bargain?'

'Oh, but Vee—' Ercy began a protest at this near-heretical criticism of her hero, and then stopped of her own accord. It was only two years since revolution erupted all over Europe, and France had for a second time exchanged its monarchy for a republic. For those who grew up before 1815, and particularly for two elderly French ladies, it was hard to accept with equanimity that Paris was again ruled by a Bonaparte – Louis Napoleon, the Tyrant's own nephew.

After a brief pause, Venus changed the subject. 'But what about you, Fleur? What have you been doing with yourself? Have the young men of Chiswick come to their senses yet?'

Fleur smiled. 'Rather I haven't yet left mine! No, Aunt, there is no young man in the offing, if that's what you're asking – nor likely to be.'

'But Fleur, dear,' Aunt Ercy protested, understanding this at least, 'you must get married some time.'

'What for, Aunt?'

'What for? What for?' The question perplexed Ercy 'Well

19

dear, a woman must do something. She needs some occupation.'

'But I'm always busy,' Fleur said. 'I have the house to run. And there are the neighbours to visit, and my horse to ride – no one can ever want for amusement when there are horses.'

'Still you must marry at last,' Venus said stiffly, not liking to have to agree with Ercy about anything. 'You're four-and-twenty, and your father won't live for ever.'

Fleur felt the familiar resistance hardening inside her. 'I have been provided for, Aunt. I shall have a sufficient income of my own to set up house and live comfortably.'

'Not alone. In the first place it isn't proper, and in the second place, it's eccentric. You would grow peculiar. No one would receive you.'

'I thought you despised a slavish adherence to fashion,' Fleur said stubbornly. 'I thought you wanted me to be independent.'

'You mistake me. I've encouraged you to have independent opinions, but not to put yourself outside society. There is no place for a gently-born woman who remains unmarried. You'd be forced to go and live with Richard and his wife, and believe me, none of you would enjoy that!'

'It's such a waste, Fleur dear,' Aunt Ercy broke in. 'So lovely and clever as you are, to leave all your talents unused!'

'But I shouldn't be idle, Aunt,' Fleur replied persuasively, watching Aunt Venus out of the corner of her eye. 'I would still have my works of benevolence to occupy me.'

'Yes, dear, visiting the sick and the poor, I know,' Ercy fluttered anxiously, 'and very good in its way, of course, but I hardly think it's the same thing as—'

'Works of benevolence!' Venus exploded, successfully distracted. 'Depend upon it, you do more harm than good when you interfere in these cases! Why should you be supposed to know better how to run a man's life than the man himself? I've told you before, you should let them alone.'

'But some of them are in great distress.' Fleur joined the argument happily, glad to have turned attention for the moment from the particular to the general. 'I'm willing to let alone the strong and healthy, but what of those who are sick or famished or in trouble?'

'I dare say the Almighty means them to be,' Aunt Venus said robustly. 'It's not for you to interfere.'

'You take care of your servants when they're sick,' Fleur pointed out. 'And when they grow too old to work, you give them pensions and gifts of all sorts.'

'Of course you take care of your dependants, for the very reason that they *are* dependent. When you take them into service you take away their ability to look after themselves. That's your business. The rest are not.'

'But the poor—'

'You can't help the poor, Fleur, and that's the truth of it. Ten to one but you simply make things worse. Much better let 'em get by as best they can. If they can't find a way to live, they'll die, and that will be that.'

'I can't quite agree with you, Aunt. When I see a man – or a woman or child – in some distress which I know I can alleviate—'

'There it is, you see!' Venus said triumphantly. 'It comes down to your personal vanity. Beware the sin of pride, Fleur! Is it to be by *your* hand, and not God's, that their fate is decided? Are *you* to come between a man and the exercise of his own free will? If God means him to face certain trials in order to temper his soul, who are you to interfere?'

'Oh, come, Aunt, how can it endanger the soul to lend a suit of baby clothes to a poor woman who's just given birth . . . ?'

The discussion continued, broadening and deepening satisfactorily, wandering through theology and philanthropy via philosophy to the craggy landscape of anthropology and ancient cultures. When they got to the Spartans exposing unwanted babies, Aunt Ercy slid from bored incomprehension quite gently and naturally into sleep.

Fleur and her Aunt Venus enjoyed nothing more than a cut-and-thrust argument which exercised the intellect, though their views differed on many – perhaps most – subjects. It was an exercise they had enjoyed for many years: Venus had had a great deal to do with Fleur's upbringing.

Fleur's mother had been the youngest of three daughters born to the exiled Count and Countess de Vries, who had fled Revolutionary France in 1793 with nothing but the clothes they stood up in – and the considerable fortune in jewels they managed to carry away with them in two large cloak-bags.

The Countess had been heavily pregnant at the time, and Venus, whose vanities were few but complex, was proud that she had actually been conceived in France, which she felt made her more genuinely French than her siblings. Other babies followed, but the boys all died, leaving only Venus, Aricie, born in 1801, and Phèdre, born in 1806.

Venus had been her father's favourite. She was the first-born, and he had seen her as a last link with his homeland. In consequence he had lavished a good deal of education as well as attention on her, before creeping melancholy at the events in France had turned him into a recluse. His was not a happy temperament, and while he had taught Venus to think, and initiated her into many subjects in those days thought unsuitable for a female to study, he had had no tenderness for her. Papa's library had not been a place for laughter or games. Venus had grown up a solemn little girl, and as her father grew more embittered and introspective, he had infected his protégée with a strain of hardness and intellectual arrogance.

Aricie and Phèdre, brought up entirely by their mother, had developed into just the sort of pretty fools society expected them to be; and in time, despite their father's increasing withdrawal from the world, all three girls had made good marriages. Venus married Sir Frederick Hoare, the banker's son; Aricie – who had long since anglicised her name into Ercy – took Lord Markby; and Phèdre married Sir Ranulph Hamilton, a baronet of private means who was already making a name for himself as a botanist.

Despite the difficulties of the times, the husbands of the de Vries girls were successful. Sir Frederick, finding his father's bank too restricting, went into Parliament, survived the Reforms of '32, became a friend of the unpopular Edwin

Chadwick and interested himself in public health and public works.

Lord Markby also had the skills of survival, though in his case it was not brilliance but the lack of it which was his strength. He had never been known to quarrel with anyone, nor to express an original idea: he was a natural courtier. Having got along well enough under the affable regime of Sailor William, he did even better under the new young Queen. He survived the Court's move from St James's to Buckingham Palace, and the successive Household purges of Lord Melbourne and Prince Albert, and became at last Master of the Robes, largely because he was one of the few courtiers of his seniority whose character was unimpeachable. Ercy was made Lady-in-Waiting to the Queen, and her gratitude and admiration for the Royal couple was secured for ever.

Sir Ranulph, dedicating himself to his chosen field, became a noted authority on orchids, published several books and monographs, and received honorary degrees at Cambridge and Edinburgh, as well as a fellowship of the Horticultural Society. He was made special adviser on orchids to the Royal Garden at Kew, and in 1840 he was appointed Chairman to the Botanical Committee of the Royal Society, of which Prince Albert became President five years later.

The marriages of the elder sisters remained childless, but Phèdre bore Sir Ranulph – despite his long absences abroad on botanical expeditions – a boy and a girl: Fleur in 1826 and Richard in 1832. Two years later, after a long decline, Phèdre died.

It had not been a particularly happy marriage, though probably neither of the principals recognised the fact very clearly. Ranulph was regarded by his large acquaintance as a pleasant-tempered, easy-going man, erring in his relationships, if at all, on the side of indulgence. The truth was that his considerable intellect was so completely channelled that he simply did not care enough about anything else ever to be angered or offended, or to wish to change it.

He married Phèdre because she was a pretty girl of the right age and of good family. He installed her in his house, made her a generous allowance, and never afterwards gave her a thought. He pursued his career, spent long periods away from home, and even when he was at home, was usually shut up in his study or hothouses, living on a plane too far removed from his wife to notice, far less to care, that she was lonely and bored. Phèdre, a weak, nervous, rather silly woman, not having the intellect to understand what was wrong with her life or to do anything about it, took to fancying herself ill to fill the emptiness.

It was a sad fact that Venus, strongly independent and with a keen intelligence, would have made an excellent wife for Ranulph, and would probably have been very happy with him; while Sir Frederick, a genuinely warm-hearted and sympathetic man, would have been far happier with Phèdre, whom he could have cared for and cosseted, and who would have given him the children he longed for. Children played no part in Sir Ranulph's desires. He knew he needed a son to inherit his property, but if it had been possible to buy one full-grown and ready for use, he would have seen nothing wrong with the notion.

Fleur was born during one of her father's longer absences, a circumstance which prejudiced Phèdre against her – she had a difficult delivery, and felt lonely and ill-used. Venus, who gave up the pleasures of the Season to nurse her, was cross and unsympathetic: if only Ranulph had been there, everything would have been all right, Phèdre thought.

In honour of her husband, and thinking it wonderfully clever and apposite – combining her nationality with his obsession – Phèdre named the baby Fleur. Ranulph returned after an absence of more than a year, having gone away with no idea that his wife was even *enceinte*. He greeted the fact of a daughter with no interest, but when Phèdre proudly told him of her stroke of genius in choosing a name, he roared with derisive laughter, wounding his wife's feelings and fatally compromising any possibility of a relationship between mother and daughter.

Venus, who by that time had given up expectation of having children of her own, took over responsibility for the baby,

24

albeit from a distance. Phèdre had no interest in the matter, and was easily influenced by her sister, so it was Venus who chose Fleur's nurses and later her governesses, who directed her education, chose her books and toys, and decreed whom she might play with and what she might do for recreation. When Fleur grew old enough to be conversable, Venus took a more direct interest in her. She actually spent time with her, having her to stay, and taking her on trips to places of educational interest.

It was only Fleur's mental development that interested her, however. She had no human warmth to give; and believing, as people do, that the way she had been reared was the best, she perpetuated her father's mistakes with her niece. Fleur was brought up to study, to think and to be good, but not to laugh, or romp, or to be cuddled or petted. Her aunt was too stern, her father too absent, and her mother too fretful and sickly, to nourish the flame of affection that was in her.

But children are adaptable, and love, where it exists, will out in some form. She might not have love from her own family; but there were the servants, and there were animals, and from those sources Fleur acquired the minimum to survive. When baby Richard arrived, Fleur might easily have loved him, but his birth signalled the beginning of Phèdre's final decline. She retired into semi-invalidism, taking the baby with her. In her suite of rooms at the back of the house she brooded over him, and languished in an atmosphere of lavender-water, smelling-salts, baby clothes, and genteel sickness, into which Fleur was introduced briefly and formally once a day.

Fleur hated those visits. She hated the close smell and the claustrophobic atmosphere of the overheated, over-decorated rooms. Her mother, a cascade of lace and ribbon, finest white lawn, gauze scarves and cashmere shawls, would be in bed or on the chaise-longue, reclining against a heap of lace-trimmed pillows, a handkerchief and vinaigrette in her hand. Her white face and blue-ringed eyes reminded Fleur always, painfully, of a trapped bird, and she looked at her daughter with a faint resentment which grew stronger as Fleur grew prettier year by year.

Hustled into the Presence by the hard hand of a housemaid, Fleur would present herself, hands behind her back, feet together and stomach well out, tucking down her chin in the effort not to cry. She knew it was wicked not to love her mother, but she wanted only to get away as quickly as possible. Sometimes in the night she would wake and cry out in terror as the uncontrollable thought came to her that she wished Mama would hurry up and die. God knew all your thoughts, as she had often been told, and she would be punished for it, sure as fate.

Having inspected her appearance, Phèdre would subject her to a brief catechism. She was asked if she had been good, if she had done her practice, if she had said her prayers; after which she was told she might kiss her Mama and leave her to rest. This was the moment Fleur dreaded. Close to, her mother smelled of lavender, but under that there was a sad, sour, stagnant smell like dying flowers in a vase. And the texture of her mother's cheek to the lips was unnaturally soft, as though it might crumble at a touch like curd cheese.

Fleur would hesitate, tears of fear and disgust rising in her throat, until the hint of a pinch from the attendant maid drove her to do her duty. Then she would be allowed to go; and when outside the door her tears came in a scalding flood the servants thought she was crying because she loved her Mama, and called her a good girl. But one day, she knew, she would be unable to bring herself to perform that kiss; one day she would burst into tears before she got out of the room, and her dreadful secret would be discovered.

Phèdre died in the end without fuss, quietly in her sleep, while Sir Ranulph was in South America. Fleur was woken one morning by a housemaid with an unnaturally grave face, who told her that she must put on a black dress, because her Mama had gone to be with the angels. The information confused Fleur a little, firstly because she knew she had no black dress – her mourning clothes had been made for her in anticipation, but without her knowledge – and secondly because she would have thought being with the angels a cause for celebration rather than gloom.

She did not properly understand that her mother was dead, and her confusion was perpetuated when Uncle Frederick arrived, with Aunt Venus, to see to all the arrangements in his brother-in-law's absence. Fleur loved Uncle Frederick and associated him with pleasure. She waited for some indication as to what form the party would take and whether she would be allowed to join in.

Enlightenment came the next morning when she was taken down to breakfast. Her aunt and uncle were in the breakfast parlour alone, and she caught the end of their conversation before they realised she was there.

'It's a merciful release,' Frederick was saying.

Venus was standing by the window with her back to the door, a handkerchief crumpled tightly in her hand. 'It's a mercy for the boy,' she said harshly. 'Two years old and he can hardly walk or talk! She was ruining him. Thank God she's dead, that's what I say! If she'd lived another year we'd have had an idiot on our hands.'

Frederick had seen Fleur, wide-eyed at the door. 'Hush, Vee!' he said imperatively.

Venus turned, and Fleur flinched from that terrible face. There was pain in it, but not a pain she could comprehend; and a kind of vengeful anger. It was as though the eye of a primitive and powerful goddess had fallen on her. Fleur shrank down into herself, knowing something terrible was to happen, waiting through a short but ghastly silence for the blow to fall.

'You had better come upstairs and see your Mama,' Venus said at last.

'Oh Vee,' Frederick protested, but feebly. 'Can't it wait? After breakfast perhaps—'

'Come, child,' Venus said implacably, ignoring him. She stepped forward, holding out her hand. Fleur placed hers in it, as a victim places her head on the block. The fingers closed like a vice, and Venus led her out of the room and up the stairs. She walked fast, almost dragging Fleur with her, up the broad, oak stairs, along the passage carpeted with dust-coloured drugget, and up to the closed white door of Mama's suite.

The house seemed unnaturally silent. The longcase clock on the landing ceased to tick; the sunlight falling through the small window held its breath, and the dust hung motionless in it, suspended. The tall white door swung open, and the familiar stuffy odour closed around them. But there was another smell, too, like the dead-flower smell of Mama, but intensified, and infinitely worse – false-sweet, dirty, loathsome!

And there was Mama, lying in bed as usual, but, oh, not as usual – lying down, not propped high, and with the sheet drawn up to her chest and her hands folded on top; still, so very still. Venus led Fleur towards the bed, and Fleur's body cringed back, her feet dragging, knowing before her mind had understood that she didn't want to be here.

They stopped beside the bed. 'Your mother is dead, Fleur,' said Venus. 'You must kiss her goodbye for the last time.'

'No,' said Fleur, her mouth drying. 'Please no.'

But, 'You must,' said Aunt Venus. The iron grip hardened, and Fleur was thrust implacably forward. There could be no argument.

Afterwards Fleur ran downstairs alone, blindly sobbing, and cannoned into Uncle Frederick, who was standing anxiously at the foot of the stairs, awaiting events.

'Fleur, my dear,' he said, catching her and setting her gently on her feet. She lifted a wild face to him, seeing the comprehension of everything in his eyes, her mother's death, her aunt's pain and anger, her own previously unperceived loneliness. It frightened her almost more than the death-chamber had.

'Please,' was all she managed to say; but Uncle Frederick seemed to understand. He hurried her out into the garden and held her head while she was sick into the wallflowers; and then, far from rejecting a wicked girl who had wished her mother's death on her, he led her to a wooden bench in a sunny corner of the garden, and took her onto his lap. He sat like that for a long time while the sun moved slowly round behind the cherry tree – not saying anything, just holding her.

Afterwards, when Sir Ranulph returned, and it was plain he

would not have time to be interested in a small baby, Ercy took Richard home with her. He was a pretty baby, and the disadvantages of his first two years soon dropped from him, and he developed into a normal, chubby little boy, high-spirited and noisy. Ercy doted on him, smothering him with indulgence and sugarplums until he was old enough to be sent to school. She almost broke her heart at having to part with him, but she never baulked at the necessity; nor, once Markby had pointed it out to her, at the propriety of his spending his school holidays mostly in his father's house.

Fleur remained at home, under the charge of her latest governess. Frederick would have liked to have taken her home, as Ercy had taken Richard, but Venus would not have agreed to it, even had it been proper, in view of Fleur's greater age, to suggest it. Venus continued to interest herself in Fleur's upbringing, and had her to stay when Ranulph was away from home, and if her influence was not entirely benign, it was at least consistent.

At eighteen, with her aunt's approval and her father's indifference, Fleur had dismissed her governess and taken up the reins of the household, which she had governed ever since. Though she had grown up into an extremely pretty young woman, she had reached the age of twenty-four without ever having formed a romantic attachment, and Aunt Ercy, brought up to think that nineteen was on the shelf, regularly deplored the excess of education which had unfitted her niece for a woman's vocation.

But it was not the education, nor the amount of it, which had made Fleur so different from other young women of her rank. All she knew of love was the affection one felt for servants and dogs and horses, and perhaps the pity for those in trouble. The scenes she had witnessed in childhood at the back door had left their mark on her – she occupied much of her spare time in those works of benevolence which Aunt Venus so condemned, interesting herself in the poor and sick of the parish.

She had grown used to a great degree of solitude, enjoyed her independence, and on the whole was content with her life, and had no wish to change it. Marriage she saw as admitting someone else to a position of authority over her, and she did not see what there was to attract in the prospect. As for an intimate and loving relationship with someone of her own rank – well, she had never seen it done, and did not know how it could be done.

Aunt Venus looked on with wry amusement as Fleur's almost startling eligibility attracted, like moths to a lighted window, innumerable young men; who then, like the moths, proceeded to knock their infatuated heads senseless against the window-pane. They found it impossible to reconcile Miss Hamilton's extreme prettiness – the golden ringlets, the cerulean blue eyes, the English rose complexion – with the strength and independence of her mind.

Venus knew that Fleur must marry sooner or later, and since she knew nothing of love and cared less, she assumed that Fleur would eventually come to her senses and contract an alliance with some suitable person, probably introduced by Venus herself. She was not aware that deep inside Fleur there was a sleeping self whose needs, though unrecognised, would not be denied.

Though Fleur did not as yet understand it consciously, she felt that there was another kind of life to lead, as well as that of the mind. If it came to her, she would recognise it and seize it; and if chance never sent it her way, she would at least never compromise it by entombing herself in the kind of lifeless marriage that her father and her aunt had contracted.

Chapter Two

Aunt Ercy woke refreshed from her doze and took herself off, yawning, to the Markbys' apartment in Catherine Wheel Yard, St James's Palace, to begin the lengthy process of dressing for dinner. Hardly had she left when the drawing-room door opened again, and Sir Ranulph came in.

'Well, I've got something to tell that will amuse you!'

he chuckled. 'Joe Paxton is going to knock them all for six!'

He was a tall man in the prime of life, and though exposure to harsh climates in the course of his expeditions had weathered him, he still had a great deal of the golden, blue-eyed beauty he had passed on to his children. If there was something a little inhuman about the beauty, something cool and distant about those bright blue eyes, few women, at least, noticed it. Many had been attracted to him, but short indeed was the time he had spent with any of them. He liked male company, and disliked emotional entanglements. His passions were aroused only by his work; and his essential needs, now as when his wife was alive, were satisfied by discreet ladies to whom it was a business transaction, who made demands on nothing but his purse.

'I suppose it's too much to expect you to enter a room in the conventional manner,' Venus greeted him sternly. 'Sit down, Ranulph, and stop bobbing about in that uncomfortable way.'

He winked at his daughter and said, 'Your Aunt don't like enthusiasm of any sort. Smacks too much of Jacobinism for her taste.'

'Don't talk such nonsense,' Venus said. 'What is this news of yours?'

'Joe Paxton is to build the pavilion for the Great Exhibition, that's what!'

'Nonsense, how can he?' Venus was scathing. 'He didn't even submit a plan – and the Building Committee's put forward its own design, in any case.'

'Ah, but you know quite well *that* will never be accepted. Listen, I'll tell you how it came about. We were standing in the lily-house, and Paxton was telling me about his plans for extending it. I said I supposed it would be a lengthy job, and he said not at all: the way in which it's constructed makes it the easiest thing in the world to alter, extend, or even take down completely. I laughed and said it was just the opposite to the Brick Carbuncle they were planning for the Exhibition; and then the same idea struck us both simultaneously!'

'You don't mean Mr Paxton proposes a glasshouse for the Exhibition?' Fleur said.

'Yes! There, I knew it would surprise you! But it's the very thing, don't you see? Firstly it will be so much cheaper, and secondly it will do away with all Brougham's objections to solid bricks-and-mortar. It will be so obviously temporary that no one will be afraid of it: up in a trice, and down in a trice! And what could be more appropriate to a great garden, like Hyde Park, than a great glasshouse?'

Fleur's imagination was at work. 'It would look so pretty – light and airy, like a cloud-castle! Imagine it glittering in the sun, and the colours of the sky and the trees seen through it! But it would have to be huge, Papa. Can anything so big be made of glass? Would it be safe?'

'Paxton says so. The engineering principles are the same, you know, whether it's a—'

'That's all very well,' Venus interrupted, 'but it's far too late. The Committee's already put its own plan out to tender. They won't consider an alternative now.'

Sir Ranulph waved a hand. 'Trifling, trifling! That can be got over. If necessary I can talk to Buccleuch and Cole – they'll see reason.'

'And the Building Committee won't like having their noses put out of joint – even by the most eminent gardener in the world.'

Ranulph shook his head. 'You misjudge them, Vee. They're good men – activated by the most disinterested feelings. Oh well,' he conceded with a rueful smile, 'human nature being what it is, there may be one or two who'll find it hard to swallow their pride. But Stephenson is the best of men, and Brunel will see the sense of it, and they'll carry the rest of them along.' He jumped up restlessly. 'Is Fred still in the House? I might just step up and consult him about it—'

'Oh sit down, you intolerable jack-in-the-box!' Venus cried. 'Frederick's too busy now to listen to your nonsense: there's to be a division on the Papal Disabilities, and Russell has sent out the whips. You can talk to him at dinner – nothing can be done today, in any case.'

'True enough. Paxton said he's coming up to Town tomorrow to see Ellis, so he can step across to the Board of Trade

32

afterwards and speak to Granville about it then. He'll be his own best advocate – everyone likes Paxton.'

Sir Frederick's return from the House was the signal for dinner to be put on the table. During the first course he initiated most of the conversation, and he was an entertaining talker. He was from a long line of bankers, but had followed his father into the family business more from duty than by desire. He had not that single-minded passion for money which alone enables a man to understand its mysterious moods and predict its behaviour as if it were a lovely but capricious mistress.

Parliament was much more to his taste, giving an outlet to both his sociability and his benevolence. He was a Benthamite and a pragmatist, and enjoyed the solid, earthy business of getting things done, whether it was Railways, Catholic Relief or the Banning of Cesspools; but his practicality was tempered by an easy-going generosity which often provoked his wife sorely. When he tossed a handful of coins to a beggar or promised to put a tramping man in the way of work, she would scold him fiercely and call him sentimental.

The conversation over dinner was wide ranging. All four of them had enquiring minds, and on occasions it was easy to forget the differences between them in age and sex. The discussion of Paxton's notion of housing the Exhibition in a giant greenhouse led on to the topic of architecture in general. Frederick, mounting a familiar hobby-horse, bewailed the loss of the arcading in Regent Street, which had been pulled down recently by public order.

'I walked up through Regent Street on my way home this evening, deep in thought, not noticing my surroundings; and when I came to myself suddenly, I couldn't tell for a moment where I was!' He shook his head sadly. 'It was an appalling act of vandalism. Nash's Grand Design – all those lovely Doric columns – the whole spectacular sweep of the Quadrant – all destroyed for the sake of a few miserable shopkeepers who complained that the Cyprians kept away their business! Did you ever hear such nonsense?'

Venus tapped an admonitory forefinger on the table, and Sir Ranulph grinned at his brother-in-law. 'Not up to your usual standard of tact tonight, Freddy!'

Fleur smiled. 'It's quite all right, Papa, you needn't worry. I know perfectly well what a Cyprian is. And after all, if I didn't, there'd be no harm done, would there?'

Frederick looked from one to the other, startled. 'Lord, Flo! Did I really say –? I'm sorry, m'dear. Deuced if I don't forget sometimes how young and innocent you are! You seem so much like one of us, I forget to mind my tongue.'

'I think he means that for a compliment!'

'But Uncle,' Fleur said gravely, 'has pulling down the arcades answered, do you think? It seemed to me that when I was last in the Quadrant there were just as many painted faces as ever.'

Frederick shook his head at her. 'Now you have shocked me! It's bad enough for you to know what a Cyprian is, but to recognise one when you see one!'

'My Aunt might feel the same way about you, sir!' she parried.

Venus interrupted and firmly changed the subject. When they retired to the drawing-room, Fleur was persuaded to indulge her uncle in a game of backgammon, and Venus beckoned Ranulph to the other end of the room. A long, low-pitched conversation followed, which the two players observed in the intervals of play, exchanging glances of amused complicity with each other.

'Vee's giving poor Ralph toco about something,' Frederick murmured gleefully at one point. 'I'm always glad when I see it, simply that it ain't me!'

'It should have been you,' Fleur said. 'I don't know why my aunt is blaming Papa for your mentioning *filles de joie* in front of me.'

'Your fault was worse than mine,' Frederick protested. 'You ought to have swooned away, or at least had the vapours!'

'No, nonsense, why should I be shocked?' Fleur laughed. 'My charitable works bring me all the time up against both the causes and effects of prostitution.'

'Ah, but you wouldn't even have pretended a suitable embarrassment if we'd been in conventional company,' he said shrewdly. 'That sort of unfeminine self-possession will put you at a disadvantage in the marriage-mart, Flo my dear!'

Fleur was not entirely surprised when a tap at her door as she was preparing for bed heralded a visit from her father.

'Can I sit with you a moment, love? I want to talk to you.'

'Yes Papa,' she said, and he laughed.

'Lord, don't look so blue! I haven't come to tear you off a strip!'

'But Aunt Venus has been talking to you about me, hasn't she?'

'Yes, my love, but it was nothing bad. She thinks you are too isolated down in Chiswick, and that you ought to mix more with society so that you don't become eccentric.' Fleur smiled at that, but he frowned and went on, 'She has a point, you know. Too much independence makes one impatient and intolerant—'

'Am I so?' Fleur asked, mortified.

'Oh, Lord, no! I don't suffer fools gladly, either. But you are just a little inclined to let people know what you think of them, by a look if not always in words.'

She felt her cheeks grow warm. This was the most intimate conversation she had had with her father in years, and it was almost a telling-off. Her pride as well as her feelings were wounded. 'I'm sorry I've disappointed you, Papa,' she said stiffly.

'Oh, you've not disappointed *me*,' he said cheerfully. 'I don't mind in the least what you do! But I tell you what, Fleur – you must get married some time, and your aunt is right – you'll never find another man who'll let you run on in the way your uncle and I do.'

She had nothing to say to any of that, and after a moment he went on, looking at her intently, 'Isn't there anyone you fancy at all, love? You're uncommonly pretty, after all. What about the Scott boy? I saw you dancing with him for ever last Christmas.'

'Teddy?'

'Oh, Teddy, is it? Well, you evidently like him, and he seems a decent enough sort of young man. Can't you marry him?'

'Teddy and I grew up together. I've known him all my life, but I don't want to marry him.' She regarded her father shrewdly. 'Teddy isn't the eldest, you know – that's Harry.'

'Oh, well that's no use then,' Ranulph said easily. 'The Scotts ain't so very plump in the pocket. I expect Harry will get everything.' With a grim sort of amusement, Fleur watched the thoughts process across her father's face. 'He'd be the better match for you, after all. You must try if you can't fancy him.'

'Yes, Papa,' she said colourlessly, and looked down at her hands. She knew that her father was not really interested in the question, but had been driven to take it up with her by her aunt. She had merely to endure in silence, and it would soon be over: he wouldn't say more than enough to be able to assure Venus he had 'talked to' his daughter.

So it proved. 'Anyway, Richard will be back soon,' Ranulph said as the happy thought came to him. 'He can take you about, and introduce his friends to you. You'll soon find someone you like.'

She looked up. 'Richard won't be home for long, though, will he?'

'Where else would he be?' Ranulph looked perplexed. 'He can't be thinking of Cambridge, surely? The last time I mentioned it – taking it for granted he'd be going, you know, or what else was he a Tug for? – he almost bit my head off. Said he wasn't an inky grind or a damned cleric, thank you very much!'

Fleur smiled at this accurate representation of her brother's style, glad that the attention had turned away from her at last. 'Ah, then he hasn't spoken to you about it? I wondered if that might be the case, from the tone of his letter. No, his idea now is to join the army. He wants you to buy him a commission.'

'What?' Ranulph said explosively.

'Yes, Papa, and on the whole, I think it might be just the right thing for him,' she said seriously. 'After all, he isn't

36

clever, poor darling, but he's a good rider and he dances beautifully, and he'd look very handsome in uniform.'

Ranulph laughed. 'That certainly comprehends everything Wellington ever asked of an officer! But, Lord, Flo, have you any idea how much it costs to keep a man in a good regiment? And knowing Richard, it would have to be a fashionable one. To say nothing of buying the commission in the first place!'

'A fortune, I should think,' Fleur said calmly. 'But after all, whatever he does, he'll be expensive. The army will keep him out of mischief, and I dare say he'd spend just as much at Cambridge, on much more vulgar pursuits. At least with a commission he'd only run up a gentleman's debts.'

'That, my love, is very cold comfort!'

One chilly day in September Fleur was riding up Sutton Lane, about half a mile from home, on her good bay gelding Oberon, with the faithful but silently disapproving Buckley riding behind her. Richard had gone off for a day's fishing with some friends, and she was taking the opportunity to pay a visit which she was aware was long overdue.

At the end of the lane was a terrace of four sixteenth-century cottages, known as Sutton Row. Halting Oberon before them she thought sadly that lovers of the Picturesque would have gone into ecstasies over them, and reached eagerly for a sketching-book.

The terrace was long and low, the walls patchily whitewashed, the oak beams faded almost to silver. The roof was buckled like a stormy sea, its tiles decorated with lichen; the chimneys leaned alarmingly, and the small, crooked windows were lattice-paned with ancient glass that was greenish and almost opaque. Under the windows a little strip of earth had been dug, which was crammed with marigolds and pansies. It looked enchanting – everything the Romantic School admired.

Unfortunately, as she was only too well aware, they had been built without foundations onto bare earth, and inside they were dark, damp and insanitary. The windows admitted little light and, since they were not made to open, no air at all. The earth floor sweated, and the walls ran water in damp weather. Rats lived in the roof-space, and the ancient lath-and-plaster was a haven for bugs.

There was only one privy for the whole Row – an earth-closet which, when it rained a great deal, did not drain properly, but seeped noxiously under the walls of the end cottage. And all water had to be fetched from the public pump a quarter of a mile away, so washing of persons or clothes was a luxury rarely indulged in by the residents.

Buckley dismounted and came to hold Oberon's head while Fleur jumped down. In the end cottage lived a family named Black, who combined poverty, fertility and consumption to a distressing degree. She had visited them many times, always with Buckley's disapproval, and without making any discernible improvement to any of the conditions.

'No smoke from the chimney,' she commented. 'They've let the fire out again.'

'Yes, miss,' Buckley said, and gathered himself for one last assault. 'Best let me go in, Miss Flora. T'ain't fitting—'

'Now don't!' Fleur said quickly. 'We've been through all that already.'

'But the dirt, Miss Flora! The disease! You might catch something.'

'It's consumption they suffer from, Buckley. You get that from living in those conditions, not from a short visit.' She began to unbuckle the bag from the dees, knowing he hadn't yet delivered himself of his worst fear. Out of the corner of her eye, she saw it gestating in his face.

'But miss,' he cried at last in an urgent undertone, 'the – the *little visitors*!'

She turned to him, trying not to smile, for she knew he felt very strongly about it. 'I promise you I shan't come out of that door with anything that has more than two legs! There now, does that satisfy you? Tie up the horses, there's a dear man, and then come and help me kindle the fire. I'm sure to want hot water at the least.'

Before they reached it, the door was opened by a girl of eight, who stood rubbing the sole of one bare, dirty foot on the top of the other and grinning shyly at the visitors.

'Hello, Betty,' Fleur said. 'How are you today?' She observed with dismay the brilliant, painted colour in the child's cheeks and the brightness of her dark eyes. She was acquainted by now with all the kinds of consumption, and this, she thought, was the worst. The sufferer burned up like a piece of paper, was quickly consumed, and then suddenly snuffed out.

'All right, miss. Have you come to see Ma?'

Buckley gave the child a malevolent look of disapproval for her familiarity, which Betty entirely ignored. She backed into the house, and Fleur, taking a good deep breath, followed.

The doorway was so low that, though she was not a tall woman, Fleur had to bow her head to pass under the lintel. The darkness inside took a while to adjust to, but the smell was instantaneous – a mixture of old sweat and dirty bodies, of ammonia, sewage and sickness, a disturbing whiff of putrefaction, and the sweetish smell of lice. It seemed to thicken the air almost to soup, coating the inside of her nose and mouth. Fleur breathed shallowly and fought the desire to spit: her mouth was full of saliva, but she didn't want to swallow it.

The earth floor under her feet was slippery, and the dampness inside the house made it seem penetratingly cold. There was no fire in the hearth of the single downstairs room, which was not only the sole source of heat in the house, but was also used for cooking. On the bed to one side of the room, the two younger children sat, playing with a small puppy, and an even smaller kitten whose eyes and nose were crusted yellow.

Buckley came in behind her with an armful of wood he had collected from the pile under the eaves. He glared at Betty, who had begun leisurely to scratch her head, and with massive disapproval went across to kindle the fire.

Betty turned to Fleur, big with news. 'Ma's in bed, miss,' she said importantly, and laid both hands on her belly. 'She's got a pain *here*.'

Fleur felt a twinge of consternation. It might only be the gripes, but Mrs Black's latest delivery had been a hard one, and it was those, in her experience, which most often led to childbed fever.

39

'I'll go up and see her. Now, my love, I've got some calves'-foot jelly here for you. I want you to have a spoonful now, and then put it up on the chimney-shelf out of the way. When your father comes home, tell him you and Jackie are to have a spoonful twice a day. It's not for anyone else. Do you understand?'

'Yes, miss,' Betty said. Fleur could only hope her instructions would be followed, though she feared the jelly might just as easily be given to the new baby, or even the puppy.

The stairway in the corner of the room opened at the top directly into the bedroom, which contained nothing but a bed. The whiff of corruption seemed stronger up here. Fleur noted the broad green stain on the ceiling above the bed, over the head of the mother, who lay against the pillows suckling the new baby. The sheets, the pillow covers, and the woman's clothing were all horribly dirty and worn. Only the baby clothes, which Fleur had provided a week ago, were of good quality, and even they, she noted, were now grubby.

Despite her debilitating illness, Mrs Black was horribly fertile, and she had already borne eleven children. She was only five or six years older than Fleur herself, but with her sunken cheeks, hollow eyes and missing teeth, she looked nearer fifty. Black was a poor provider, not lazy or dishonest, but too stupid and inept for any but the most basic of labours, frequently laying himself up with injuries, and always the first to be laid off when work was scarce. All he seemed good for was to breed a string of consumptives from his unhealthy wife. They had buried four already, and now the eldest boy, Jack, had the bistred eyes and slow, careful cough that spelt his ultimate doom.

The symptoms of the mother's consumption usually disappeared during her frequent gestations, perhaps one of the reasons that she did nothing to avoid conception. Today, however, she was looking flushed and unwell, and there was a preoccupied look about her eyes, which suggested that she was in pain. A step nearer the bed, and Fleur caught the sweet-sick odour of pus, and her heart sank. Childbed fever was almost always fatal.

She placed a firm restraining hand over her feelings, and dredged up a reassuring smile for her face.

'Hello, Mrs Black. How are you today?' she said pleasantly.

The following morning the wind went round to the south. The mild, golden day was perfect for galloping, and since he was eager to get his chestnut mare, Pearl, fit before the cubbing started, and since he hated to ride alone, Richard nobly offered to escort his sister on a long ride.

They went by Turnham Green and over the Back Common, galloped over the plough, skirted Starch Green, and then ran all the way out to Wormholt Farm before turning back – what Richard rather grandly called 'a three-mile point'. The speed and freedom brought a fine colour to his face and a brightness to his blue eyes, and he was at his most agreeable.

Fleur always hated to return by the same route she went, so they came back via Chiswick, meaning to cross the grounds of Chiswick House, which shared a boundary with Grove Park. The Duke of Devonshire, being not only a neighbour but a friend of Papa's, had always encouraged the young Hamiltons to regard his grounds as an extension of their own garden.

As they passed through the village, however, Richard's pride took a fall. Pearl was still very fresh and rather nappy, and at the corner of Church Street she took exception to the Rector's gig, which was just coming out of its own gate. Resisting Richard's urgings to pass it, she kicked out, catching the Rector's horse square in the chest and cutting it slightly. Since the Rector was driving himself, Richard was obliged to listen to a blistering lecture about his and his horse's manners without being able to say a word in his defence, though plenty had suggested themselves to him. They rode on at last, but Richard had been brooding ever since.

Now, as they neared the wicket into their lane and the end of their ride, Fleur glanced at her brother and said, 'Do stop sulking! It was entirely your own fault, you know. You ought to manage Pearl better than that.'

Richard bristled. 'How can I help it if she's fresh? Anyway,

I'd sooner have a horse with some spirit than a deuced old slug like that whiskery grey thing of Rector's!'

'Spirit is all very well, if you can control it; but you get Pearl lathered up, and then you can't hold her.' Fleur grinned. 'Oh, but you should have seen your face when he called you a cow-handed young thruster! If looks could kill . . . !'

'He'd no business saying that,' Richard growled. 'And all that pi-jaw about *Eton manners*. I bet he went to some beastly Doctor Floggem's Academy or other! I tell you, I had the deuce of a job not to knock him down. If he hadn't been a man of the cloth—'

'Very likely,' Fleur said, not at all soothingly, 'but you know in your heart he was right. You were being heavy-handed, pulling Pearl's mouth about so, it's no wonder she kicked out.'

Richard hated to be in the wrong, and looked about for an excuse. 'I'm not far off thinking she's too light for me, you know – more of a woman's ride, really. If only Pa weren't so deuced tight-fisted, he'd have bought me something up to weight by now. I can't see myself hunting Pearl if the going's heavy this season. She'd never stand a long point.'

His sister glanced at him shrewdly. 'What you're really complaining about is that he hasn't bought you the commission you wanted. But it isn't meanness, you know. He just forgets.'

'Forgets!' he growled.

'Anyway, why such a hurry? I should have thought you'd like to spend a little time at home. I was hoping you'd escort me to a few parties and balls this winter, before you go away and leave me all alone.'

'Much you care about being alone,' Richard retorted. 'And if you mean you want me to parade my friends for you to take your pick of, I can tell you I don't mean to do it. I haven't forgotten last Christmas, when I brought Wilkins and Tommy Gander home! You're a damned sight too satirical, and I don't care to have my friends laughed at.'

'I don't laugh at them.'

'Much you don't! Well anyway, they think you do, which comes to the same thing. And besides, if you wanted to get married, you wouldn't need my help to do it, so don't humbug me, Flo my girl. I never knew a female more able to get her own way than you.'

'What a pretty picture you paint of me. I only wish it were the truth! But here we are at the wicket, and I'm female enough to need you to get down and open it. What a pity it is women can't ride astride.'

'Deuced good thing, if you ask me,' Richard said, preparing to dismount. 'You're enough of an embarrassment to me as it is. Hullo! Here's a piece of luck – there's a Cit at the gate, all ready to open it for us! It's worth a tip of the hat to me,' he added, giving himself away, 'not to have to remount when Pearl's in this mood.'

'Hush! It's not a Cit,' Fleur said hastily. 'It's Teddy Scott. Now do be civil, Dick!'

'Not I, by Jove!' Richard said hastily. 'You can entertain your lovers yourself. Hulloa, Scott! Good day to you! Sorry I can't stay and talk – my mare won't stand, you know.'

The young man in plain country clothes had civilly opened the wicket for the riders, and was able to do no more than raise a startled hand in salute as Pearl shot past him, flinging up mud, and disappeared at a butcher's trot up the lane towards the stables. Fleur made an exasperated face at Richard's back, then walked Oberon sedately through the gate and halted him while Scott fastened it behind her.

'Thank you,' she said. 'You must forgive Richard – he's suffering from a severe attack of wounded vanity! Mr Copthall called him cow-handed for letting Pearl kick his cob.'

Scott approached her stirrup and looked up at her with a familiar mixture of old affection and new longing. The Scotts' home, Elmwood, was next door to Grove Park on the other side from Chiswick House; a pleasant old house, but without the benefit of a river frontage. All the young Scotts, in consequence, had haunted Grove Park's pleasure-grounds for the sake of the fishing and bathing, and since Teddy and Fleur were of an age, they had been friends all their lives. On his return from Oxford, he had discovered that his former playmate had become a beautiful young woman, and everything had changed for him. That it had not for her was his tragedy.

43

'Poor Dick!' he said. 'Feelings are so tender at his age.'

'At his age? Oh Methuselah!' Fleur laughed at him. 'But I didn't know you were back.'

'I only came last night, too late to walk up and call on you.'

'And how was Leicestershire? You are a strange one, Teddy, coming away just when anyone else would be going there.'

'Ah, but I didn't go for the hunting,' he said lightly. 'Have you finished your ride?'

'Yes. Where were you off to?'

'Home, but I'm in no hurry.'

'Walk with me to the stables, then,' Fleur invited cordially. 'Mind, while I jump down.'

'Let me help you. It's muddy here.'

Fleur allowed him to jump her down, unaware of the pleasure it gave him, since to her the touch of his hands on her waist was no more exciting than Buckley's. He hooked Oberon's bridle over his arm and offered his other arm to her, and they walked up the lane together.

'I haven't seen you since you came back from London the last time,' he said. 'How's the what-you-may-call coming along – what was it *Punch* called it?'

'The Crystal Palace? Oh, at a great rate! And everyone in London is glass-mad! You wouldn't believe what they're predicting will be built of it in the future – houses, railway stations, waiting rooms – anything you like! It'll be glass cathedrals and glass factories next.'

'I can see the advantages, of course,' Scott said. 'It's light and strong, and iron and glass are cheap. But this Exhibition Hall – surely in the summer the sunlight will be blinding, and the heat unbearable?'

'Unbleached calico,' Fleur said promptly. 'The roof and the south elevation are to have blinds across them. Oh, Mr Paxton's thought of everything, I promise you – drainage, ventilation, even a patent dust-free floor!'

'I see you know all about it,' Teddy smiled.

'I've heard nothing else these months past,' Fleur said. 'My aunt hates the whole thing, but I like Mr Paxton, and of course there's a sort of family interest in all his works.'

'So the enemies of the Exhibition have been routed, have they?'

'Well, they've found a way to placate Colonel Sibthorpe over the elm trees, at least. They're not to be cut down after all: there's to be a transept across the centre of the building with an arched roof to accommodate them. The trees will live actually inside, like part of the Exhibition.'

'And very pretty they'll look, too, when the leaves are out.'

'Ah, but they've forgotten one thing,' Fleur said wickedly. 'What about the birds that nest in them? I should think the exhibitors might find flocks of sparrows flying to and fro over their treasures something of a disadvantage.'

Teddy laughed. 'Shame on you, Miss Hamilton, for your ungoverned imagination! I dare say Mr Paxton will invent a patent bird-scarer—'

'All made of iron and glass, no doubt, and powered by steam! I'd put nothing past him. But now, Mr Scott, I want to talk to you about something serious. I went to visit some of your father's tenants yesterday.'

'The Blacks, Sutton Row. You needn't have – I meant to go myself tomorrow,' he said shortly.

'How did you know?'

'Your housekeeper's niece told our housemaid.'

'The new baby's arrived,' Fleur sighed, 'I'm almost certain Mrs Black has puerperal fever, and you know what that means. I've arranged for Dr Walker to see her today, but there's little enough he'll be able to do. The poor woman was terrified she was going to be sent to hospital. It took all my powers to persuade her to let me call Dr Walker at all.'

'Well, you know why,' Scott said. 'When they go into hospital, it's a thousand to one they'll never come out. People of her order only go to hospital to die, and she knows it.'

'In a few days, a week at the most, she'll almost certainly be dead anyway.'

'Well at least she'll die in her own bed.'

'Yes, but that's small comfort. Teddy, the roof's still leaking, right over her bed. There was actually moss growing on the bedroom ceiling! It's a great deal too bad of your father. I've asked him at least four times to have it seen to.'

'Have you, by George? Perhaps that accounts for his foul temper these last few days!'

'Don't joke, Teddy – the whole family is consumptive, and that cottage is as damp as the bottom of a well. It's killing them. I wish you would speak to your father. Surely he could spare a man for the job? I don't suppose it would take more than an hour or two.'

'Look, Fleur, the rent of those cottages doesn't go near to paying for the repairs they need. And the Blacks hardly ever pay their rent anyway. They should be grateful my father lets them stay at all, when anyone else would have thrown them out long ago.'

'How can you talk like that? Have you any idea what it's like inside that cottage?'

'Of course I have – but you shouldn't! There's no need for you to visit the Blacks. They aren't your responsibility.'

'The poor are everyone's responsibility!'

'Oh—' He looked exasperated. 'But why must you go yourself? Other ladies send a servant with a bowl of soup – why must you always be different?'

She rounded on him. 'Because I *am* different! And I shan't give up what I see to be my duty, even at the risk of shocking you!'

'I'm not shocked. I just worry about you, going into places like that. You're a lady – you're tender and delicate. You shouldn't be exposed to dirt and disease and—'

'Will you speak to your father or not?'

'I can't interfere with my father's business decisions.'

'How can it be a business decision, when there are lives at stake? Is profit more important than people?'

'Rents are business. And if businessmen don't make a profit, everyone will starve.'

'That was your father talking, not you! You aren't like that, Teddy!'

They had halted in the lane, the better to continue the quarrel, and now he paused before answering, looking down into her lovely face, and thinking how she was more beautiful than ever when her eyes and cheeks were bright with animation. If only he could ever be the cause of it!

'No,' he said more quietly, 'I'm not like that. But you must believe me, Fleur – I have no influence over my father. Now less than ever.'

'Why, what have you done?'

He looked wry. 'I didn't tell you what I went into Leicestershire for. I was sent to stay with my cousins and make my fortune, but I came back unsuccessful, and it's put both my parents out of temper.'

'What can you mean?'

'I failed to secure the hand of Miss Marlow.'

Fleur laughed at him. 'What, the rich Miss Emily Marlow, your cousin's friend? Wouldn't she have you, Ted?'

'Worse than that,' said Scott, his eyes fixed on hers. 'I wouldn't offer.'

'Oh.' She faltered, and felt her cheeks grow warm. Scott plunged recklessly on, seizing both her hands to ensure her attention.

'You know why. Oh Fleur, can't you, won't you marry me? You know how I feel about you! We could be so comfortable, and Father and Mother would like it of anything! I can't love anyone else, and it makes everyone so mad with me.'

Fleur couldn't prevent herself from laughing. 'Teddy Scott, you are a fool! Am I to marry you simply to stop your parents scolding you?'

He coloured. 'No, of course not. I suppose I expressed myself badly, but you know what I mean.'

'Yes, I know. You think you're in love with me, and your parents want you to make a good match so that they needn't provide for you out of Harry's patrimony. Oh, don't look at me like that! I know *you* aren't mercenary. But this being in love with me is all fudge, you know. We played spillikins together when we were children, that's all. There's nothing more to it than that.'

He dropped her hands. 'You really are a heartless girl. A fellow talks of love to you, and you dance a mazurka on his tenderest feelings.'

'No I don't, Ted. I'm very fond of you, but as a brother, and I couldn't possibly marry you. Now don't say any more about it, please, or we shan't be comfortable together. There are plenty of other girls, you know.'

'I'm not interested in other girls.' He sighed and stared gloomily at the ground. 'However, if you won't have me, I may even be driven into Miss Marlow's arms. There's another plan afoot which I like even less: Father's talking of sending me into the army.'

'No, really? But it wouldn't be so bad, would it? It's what Richard wants above anything – a life of luxury, with nothing to do but appear on parade once a week.'

Scott looked grim. 'That isn't quite what Father has in mind. I'd be expected to live on my pay.'

'But there'd still be the commission to buy, and that could come to thousands. I wonder your father hasn't thought about the expense.'

'He has. I'm to go to Woolwich,' he said bitterly.

Fleur stared a moment, and then began to laugh. 'For a moment I thought you were serious!'

'I am serious. It's a genuine, imminent threat.'

'But Teddy, you an Engineer? You can't even draw a straight line! Remember when your papa gave you that corner of the garden for yourself, and you tried to mark out a flower-bed with pegs and string?'

Oberon, growing bored with standing still, blew at Scott's hair and tentatively nibbled his ear, but he didn't even notice. His face was very serious, and Fleur thought he looked suddenly rather handsome.

'Don't laugh at me,' he said quietly. 'Father means it. He says I'm idle and luxurious, and I'm to go to Woolwich immediately after Christmas. That's all the future I have to look forward to – an Engineer officer. A grease monkey. A grind.'

Fleur looked at him levelly, perfectly well aware of what was in his mind. 'Perhaps you'll like it. An Engineer officer is still a gentleman, you know, and your companions will at least be more intelligent than Richard's.'

'How can I be a soldier? The idea of war makes me sick!'

'We haven't had a war for thirty-five years. At worst you may be sent to India or Ireland, and even Lord Wellington survived that!'

'Fleur, please! You know I'd hate it! Won't you please marry me, and let us be happy together?'

'It's no good, Teddy, I can't marry you just to keep you from being an Engineer.'

'Not just for that! It would be so comfortable—'

'Oh, comfortable! I'm comfortable now. I should need a great deal more than that to tempt me to change my condition.'

'What sort of more?' he demanded.

She looked at him sadly. 'Something I don't think you could give me,' she said.

'And that's your last word?' He turned away abruptly so that she shouldn't see his face. 'Very well,' he said, rather muffled. 'I wish you may not regret it.'

'I hope not, too. Let's walk on – Oberon's getting cold.'

Chapter Three

Normally Kensington Road was a quiet enough street, its traffic enlivened by nothing more out of the ordinary than a squadron of cavalry posting back to the Knightsbridge Barracks, or a glimpse of the Duke of Wellington passing in his carriage on his way to Apsley House.

Not so in April 1851. From all over the country, from all over the world, came the exhibits for the Great Exhibition of the Works of Industry of All Nations. Great waggons, loaded high with packing-cases, trundled along at snail's pace, drawn by teams of straining horses. They converged on Kensington, rumbling over the cobbles with a noise like thunder, keeping to the kerbside of the road, so that, in theory, the normal traffic – carts, gigs, hackneys, drays and 'buses – could clatter past down the centre.

The pavements were crowded day and night with a densely packed, slowly moving mass of sightseers. There were Londoners, sharp-featured and sharp-voiced, thrusting through the crowds with the impatient authority of the native; and country folk in plain flannel and heavy boots, bewildered as cattle, staring about them as though they had been lightly stunned. There were families from the industrial north, pinch-faced women in plaid shawls, clutching their children tight by the hand, and cave-chested men, determined to stand their ground against exploitation, but ready to be taken in by any genial rogue who would give them a kind word and a friendly smile in this alien place.

And there were foreigners of all sorts, strangely dressed and strangely complected, with beards, with pantaloons, with funny hats, chattering in two dozen different tongues, waving their arms like windmills. If the newspapers were to be believed, they were also secretly plotting to overthrow their own and everybody else's governments, and to impose on freedom-loving peoples the evils of Communism, Socialism, Chartism, and every other terrible modern 'ism', not to mention Popery and Anarchy into the bargain.

And to add to the glorious confusion there were pedlars with trays of souvenirs, gold- and silver-coloured medals, paper panoramas and gelatine views; hawkers with baskets of oranges and coconuts and barrows stacked high with bottles of ginger-beer; jugglers and street musicians and card-sharpers and puppeteers; touts of every sort offering forged season tickets, blank Exhibition guides and non-existent accommodation; pickpockets, drunks, pugilists, urchins and beggars. The street was a bedlam of shouts, whistles, catcalls and curses, of dogs barking and whips cracking, of dust, mud, carriage-wheels and horse dung, of nutshells, orange-peel, bones, and all manner of lost property trampled underfoot.

The focus of everyone's attention was, of course, the Park; and, behind the railings against which the milling crowds pressed, the great Crystal Palace itself. Messrs Fox and Henderson had brought it into being in record time. The upper portion rose majestic and glittering in the spring sunshine from the hoardings which concealed the works. Everyone pointed out to everyone else the magnificent arch of the Transept, and told and retold the wonderful story of the reprieved elm trees, which were coming into bud under its shelter.

There were still ladders sloping against the sides, and tiny figures picked their delicate way over the glass roof like ants. Inside, five hundred decorators were busy painting the iron-work in shades of pale blue, yellow and scarlet. *The Times* had criticised these primary colours as vulgar, but the consensus of the crowd was that it was pleasant, light, gay, and altogether the very thing. When the flags of all nations were flying from the rooftop, the effect would be magnificent.

On the other side of the Building, between it and the Serpentine, ran Rotten Row, where polite society exercised its horses. Fleur was cantering Oberon there, enjoying his smooth, even pace, and the soft drumming of his hooves in the tan, and stealing a glance from time to time at the astonishing structure which seven months ago had existed only in the mind of the Duke of Devonshire's head gardener.

The method of construction was so novel and intriguing that applications to be admitted to the site had multiplied week by week, and a reprehensible trade in forged workmen's passes had flourished outside the Park gates. The contractors had relented at last and allowed a limited number of observers inside the hoardings each day, charging them five shillings each, the proceeds going into an accident fund for the workers. The Queen herself had already been eight times; though Fleur remembered with a smile that Mr Fox had com-plained to Uncle Frederick that every time Her Majesty visited, she got the workers so excited that it cost him twenty pounds in lost time.

With a week to go before the opening, the excitement was rising to fever pitch, and even Aunt Venus had been so far infected as sometimes to forget that she disapproved of the whole thing. Fleur and her father were fixed in London for as long as they wished. She smiled as she remembered how they had been invited. Aunt Venus and Uncle Frederick had come to stay for Christmas as usual, and over the Christmas dinner the conversation had turned once again, as it so often did, to the Exhibition.

For once Venus hadn't objected; instead, with an indulgent smile, she said, 'You and Fleur must come and stay for the whole summer. You won't want to have to travel up every time you visit the Exhibition. And besides, there will be bound to be lots of other things going on in London. Yes, you shall stay in Hanover Square, and I shall see to it that you are well entertained.'

The effect of her munificence was immediately spoiled, however, by Frederick, who, on his third glass of claret, winked at his niece and said, 'Don't be too grateful, love. She's acting out of the purest self-interest, you know.'

'Frederick!' Venus said awfully.

'Oh, no, Uncle, I'm sure it's not so.'

'I assure you! Ever since it was known the Exhibition was to take place, we've been bombarded with requests from relatives we've never seen before, who all discover they can't survive another year without making our better acquaintance. There won't be a bed to spare in the whole of London next summer, and so your aunt is planning to forestall the people she don't like, by installing those she does before opening day!'

Whatever the reason for the invitation, Fleur was very happy to accept. Christmas had also been marked by the announcement that negotiations were concluded on Richard's commission. He was to join his regiment in January, and she had anticipated another solitary year.

Having resigned himself to the inevitable, Sir Ranulph had come up to scratch handsomely, buying Richard a cornetcy not just in a fashionable regiment, but in *the* fashionable regiment, the 11th Hussars.

'The Cherrypickers – Prince Albert's Own!' Richard said breathlessly after his interview in Papa's study on Christmas Eve. His face was flushed and his eyes bright and he looked, Fleur thought affectionately, no more than fifteen in his excitement. 'It's everything I could have wished for!'

'Good God! It must have cost Papa a fortune!'

'I suppose so. Of course, the price of the commission is fixed, but then there were the bribes—'

'Which probably came to twice as much again!' Fleur said. 'But you're not supposed to use that word, love. They're *douceurs*, didn't you know?'

'Oh really? Well, the cornet who was selling was waiting for a lieutenancy in the 17th Lancers, which depended on the retirement of a captain of the 8th. The captain wasn't willing to sell out unless he could be sure of a comfortable income, and so there were *douceurs* to be administered all the way up the line. Pa wouldn't tell me the "demmed total" but I believe it was several thousand pounds.'

'But will the purchase be approved? I mean, the 11th, you know – the smartest, most fashionable regiment in the Light Brigade!'

'Already has been. Pa asked Uncle Markby, and he spoke to the Queen, and she spoke to the colonel of the 11th, Lord Cardigan, who's a great favourite of hers, and so it was settled.'

Later, when Fleur spoke to Uncle Frederick about it, he added to her information. 'Of course, Cardigan don't spend much time with the regiment nowadays, which is all to the good, because he's quite mad, you know.'

Fleur laughed. 'Oh come!'

'It's true. The stories I could tell you, you'd hardly believe!'

'I've heard say he's a very handsome and affable man.'

'Handsome, certainly. And as splendid as a peacock. In the old days, whenever he went up to Town he would send half a dozen of his best troopers on leave, and pay them a shilling each to station themselves all along St James's Street and salute him as he went past.'

'And this is the manner of man who commands our crack cavalry?'

'Oh, Richard will like it beyond anything! He'll be ready to swoon over the uniform – the Cherrypickers have the tightest pants, the shortest jackets, and the most irrational headgear in the world!'

'He'll become a tremendous swell.'

'The most tremendous. He'll grow his moustaches and say "vewwy" and "sowwy", affect a terrible boredom and secretly long for a pell-mell battle to prove himself.'

'Too cruel, Uncle!'

'Do you think so? I'd say he was perfectly suited to being a cavalry officer. He's a neck-or-nothing rider, and if ever there should be a war, he'd lead the charge in the coolest possible manner, and never show a particle of fear.'

'That sounds a little kinder. But, seriously, is that really all that's needed in a battle?'

'My dear Flo, an officer's duty is simply to get his men into position, and keep them there by displaying his indifference to danger. Only bring an English soldier face to face with the enemy, and he'll do the rest. I have *that* from the Duke himself.'

'The Duke?' Fleur raised her eyebrows. 'What does he know about war?'

'Don't be mischievous. You know perfectly well that "the Duke" in a military context means Lord Wellington, and in a botanical context Lord Devonshire.'

'Well, there's not likely to be a war in any case. Richard will either fry in India, or grow moss in Ireland.'

'Not Richard. If his regiment goes abroad, he'll go onto half-pay until it comes back!'

Her mind was called back from recollection by a familiar voice.

'Hulloa, Fleur! I say! Over here!'

She reined Oberon in, looked about her, and saw Richard and a fellow cavalryman on their horses under a budding chestnut tree a little way off. From any distance, it was not possible to mistake the 11th Hussars. The tight crimson over-alls with the double gold stripe, the fur-trimmed, gold-frogged pelisse worn off one shoulder, the red and gold barrel-sash, the fur cap with the white and crimson plume . . . all Hussars were splendid, but the Cherrypickers were quite dazzling!

'Hullo Richard! I was just thinking about you!'

'Strordin'ry coincidence – I was just talkin' about you,'

Richard drawled in his new Hussar accent from behind his even newer cavalry whiskers. They were not yet very convincing, but his soldier-servant anointed them with mysterious nostrums at night, which he swore would have them flourishing in no time.

'I thought you were in Hounslow. What are you doing here?' said Fleur.

'Oh, nothin' much. My particular friend, Brooke.'

'Good day to you, Mr Brooke.'

'How d'e do?' Brooke murmured with fashionable languor and raised his fingers to his cap as though with an effort. That he was a tremendous swell was evident: his whiskers must have been longer and glossier, and his wasp-waisted corsets tighter than anyone else's in the regiment.

'Have you come to see the Crystal Palace?' Fleur asked innocently.

'Lord, no! On duty, ma'am. On our way from takin' a message to Horse Guards,' Brooke said, raising his eyebrows at the idea that they might be interested in a Sight. 'Just thinkin', matter of fact, good thing when it's all over. Feahful crush. Too dashed many Cits and wowdies, Miss Hamilton, for my taste.'

'That's true,' Richard said. 'You shouldn't be riding alone, Fleur. I wonder my aunt allows it. T'ain't safe.'

Fleur knew perfectly well that what really worried him was the lack of consequence she was displaying to his new friend. The newest cornet in the regiment had his dignity to consider, and unconventional behaviour by any member of his family undermined it.

'Oh rot!' she said mildly. 'I've been riding alone these six years, as you very well know.'

'At home – that's different. This is a public place. You should have Buckley with you.'

'Buckley's got other things to do. Besides, what could possibly happen to me in such a public place?'

Richard looked stubborn. 'It don't look right. And there are a lot of ugly customers about. These aren't the usual sort of people you find in the Park, you know.'

'Same in the Clubs,' Brooke agreed. 'Full of Country members one's never seen before. Give you my word!' He opened his eyes slightly wider. 'And just the other day, Johnson – the porter, you know – had to chuck a howwid fellow off the front steps! Labourer or some-such, sittin' there eatin' a beef sandwich – with mustard oozin' out of the side!' He shuddered.

'How appalling!' Fleur said sympathetically.

Richard intervened hastily. 'How do you think Pearl's looking?'

'Very fit – and you needn't have worried about the crimson shabraque clashing with her coat. It sets it off to perfection!'

It was the right thing to say. Richard looked pleased. 'Major Forster said last week he wished he might buy her from me, she's so neat and sure-footed.'

'But don't you wonder if she isn't a bit light for you? If there was a battle and the going was at all heavy—' Fleur began solemnly, and Richard reddened and made a face at her.

'She's good enough for the 11th, and the 11th is the best regiment in the cavalry, so there! And when we do go into battle, I can tell you we'll ride straight over the enemy without stopping for anything!'

Fleur smiled provocatively and pointed with her whip-stock towards the Crystal Palace. 'There stands the greatest monument to Universal Peace ever built! There won't be any more battles. We don't need war any more: any little differences between nations will be settled with calm talk and diplomacy.'

'Oh fudge!' Richard said hotly. 'How can you say so, when there's trouble brewing everywhere – Austria crushing Hungary, Poles in exile, this new man in France brimful of ambition, Russia just waiting to seize Turkey! It's only a matter of time before we're called on to sort it all out.'

'A prospect you plainly relish! But I think your ambitions are colouring your judgement.'

'Fact is, ma'am,' Brooke said politely, lightening her ignorance, 'that it ain't the thing for a nation to go too long in a state of peace. Slackens the moral fibre. Makes us weak and luxurious. War – war in a good cause, that is – is good for us. A sort of – of—'

'Catharsis?' Fleur offered.

'Purge. Like the Cwusades. Come back feelin' all right with the world.'

'Thank you for explaining it to me, Mr Brooke. I had no idea war was so good for the health.'

The young man looked awkward, not sure whether she was laughing at him or not. Richard knew which it was, and hastened to intervene again. 'Never mind all that, Flo. What's the news? How's Pa?'

'Enjoying himself. He's fascinated by the Exhibition. He's been inside the Building to see the works twice. Uncle Frederick's been three times: I'm afraid it's the plumbing that fascinates *him*, though. Pipes and ducts and fountains and fire-cocks – he took the knees out of a pair of trousers crawling about the floorboards to see where the pipes went.'

'Shockin'!' Brooke cried feelingly, and then blushed, realising he had been impertinent.

Fleur, however, only smiled. 'Quite reprehensible! It makes Aunt Venus so cross. She's banned all mention of the Exhibition or the Crystal Palace at the dinner-table, but they just seem to come creeping in, in spite of everyone's good resolutions. The whole thing's so exciting, don't you think?'

Brooke coughed a little, and said, 'Are you goin' to the Duchess of Alderney's ball next week, Miss Hamilton?'

'Yes, indeed, Mr Brooke. We dine with the Duke first, so I dare say we shan't get there until late, though. You know what he's like.'

This casual mention of the Commander-in-Chief winded the subaltern slightly, but he showed a courage and determination worthy of a Hussar officer by plunging ahead anyway. 'May I hope for the honour of a dance, ma'am?'

'I'm most flattered, Mr Brooke; but I must beg you to ask me at the ball itself. I never engage beforehand. It makes for a dull evening to know exactly what's going to happen, don't you think?'

Feeling his sister was getting out of hand, Richard said that they should really be riding on now, and goodbyes were exchanged, probably with equal relief on both sides. Pearl, however, was most indignant at being torn from the side of her old stable-companion, whose acquaintance she had been happily renewing. She resisted, and squealed most embarrassingly, and at last Fleur, suppressing her laughter for her brother's sake, bid him remain where he was while *she* rode away.

This worked rather better. Oberon turned obediently to her hand and heel, and to save Pearl anguish she rode him away from the tan and through the trees, so that they would be out of sight as soon as possible. She meant to circle back, but found it so pleasantly quiet away from the main route that she lingered amongst the trees, going further and further from the track, walking Oberon on a free rein and thinking with pleasant anticipation of the Duchess's ball. Strong-minded and independent she might be, but she was not so unfeminine that she didn't enjoy wearing a beautiful gown and being flirted with by agreeable young men.

She didn't at first notice the three men lounging against the tree up ahead of her, smoking the traditional short clay pipes of the 'navvies' who had built England's canals and railways. Oberon saw them first, pricked his ears, and then snorted a little as he spied the three terriers they had with them. Fleur's daydream was rudely interrupted a moment later when one of the men slipped the terriers' leashes, and the dogs raced forward, barking shrilly.

Oberon was not particularly nervous, but no horse likes a trio of curs baying at him and nipping at his heels. He snorted and half reared, and began waltzing against Fleur's restraining hand, trying to get away from the noisy tormentors.

Fleur, more annoyed than alarmed, held him and shouted at the men, 'Fetch your dogs off! They're frightening my horse!'

The men only laughed, clearly enjoying her predicament. Oberon span round, trying to face the dogs, which were growing more excited all the time. She tried to ride him away from them, but they worked as a team, circling him, keeping him hemmed in. She was afraid he might bolt, which amongst the trees would be very dangerous. She called out to the men again, trying to keep her voice calm and level, though it seemed to her to waver alarmingly.

'Very well, you've had your fun. Now call them off, before there's an accident.'

The only response was more laughter. One of the men 'sicced' the dogs on, and the barking rose to new heights of frenzy. Glancing down at them, Fleur began to be afraid, for they looked like fighting-dogs, trained to the pits, bull-baiters, perhaps. She knew that such bestial sports were still popular amongst a certain section of the population. Now they were attacking in earnest, and one of them, leaping high, succeeded in biting Oberon just above the hock. The gelding lashed out, and then reared right up; the combination loosened Fleur's hold, and with a cry of dismay she came off, hitting the ground with a jarring thud which jerked the reins out of her hand. Oberon leapt away, swerved to avoid the navvies, and disappeared between the trees with the terriers yelping after him.

Fleur struggled to sit up. She was shocked by the incident and shaken by the fall. Her hat was off, her hair was coming down, her teeth were jammed together, and she was fighting furiously with tears of rage and humiliation. That the men had deliberately set their dogs on her, and laughed at her struggles, filled her with helpless fury; but she did not immediately anticipate any actual danger.

She was feeling about her on the grass for her hat and whip when she saw one of the men detach himself from the tree against which they were all leaning. He exchanged a look with his companions, glanced warily about him, and then began to walk towards her. Fleur felt as though she had been dropped into icy water. Her tears sank instantly, and she became suddenly and shockingly aware of her predicament. She had deliberately strayed from the main riding track into the seclusion of the trees, and she was alone – one slight female at the mercy of three powerful labourers.

Robbery from the person was the first thing that jumped to her mind. She hadn't much about her to steal, no purse and little jewellery, only her gold stock-pin and her watch.

However, there was always her clothing – of good quality, worth pounds in the second-hand market – and her boots and whip. Her whip! Her fingers closed about it gratefully. Well, she was only one against three, but she would give a good account of herself, by God! She would not submit tamely to being robbed.

These thoughts flashed through her mind in an instant, even as she was struggling to disentangle her feet from the heavy folds of her skirt in order to get up. She was aware that the other two had also pushed themselves upright and were strolling towards her; but her eyes were fixed on the first man.

He was short and broad, like most navvies, hugely muscular in the shoulders and arms, his face extremely weathered and battered-looking. He must have taken a tremendous blow to the side of the head at some time, for his nose and right cheekbone had been smashed, making that side of his face misshapen, and there were two scars across his forehead which cut his right eyebrow into a nonsense of tufts growing in three directions. His lips were parted, and she could see he had teeth only in the left side of his head. He had been gripping the pipe stem between them; his gums on the right side were naked.

Then in an access of acute and hideous understanding she realised that it was not robbery he had in mind. His eyes fixed on her face, he had drawn his hands out of his pockets, removed his pipe from between his teeth, and stuffed it into his pocket, and these deliberate movements were to her as clearly preparatory as if he had begun unbuckling his belt. Shock and fear made her legs weak, even though her mind remained quite appallingly clear. He was going to rape her. His scarred, blackened hands would touch her body. His loathsome flesh would violate hers.

That he would certainly kill her, too, for the moment was of secondary importance; in that instant she understood with piercing and unwelcome clarity the meaning of the common expression 'a fate worse than death'. Despite her activities amongst the underclasses, she was in ignorance of precisely what rape entailed. She knew that prostitutes performed the carnal act for money, and as a result often became *enceinte* or contracted terrible diseases; but she knew only very hazily what the carnal act was. However she didn't need to be able to visualise it to know that she was facing a situation of the most extreme and horrible danger.

She felt the air dry on her eyeballs as her eyelids stretched wider. There was no drop of spittle in her mouth – her tongue stuck to the inside of her cheeks, making it impossible for her to cry out. Worse – yes, the worst thing of all – was that, still struggling to get up, she was staring into his eyes, and she read in them the awareness that she knew what it was he wanted. Knowing, and knowing that he knew she knew, somehow seemed to make her a party to it. They were locked together in a loathsome complicity of thought.

Seconds only had passed. Her numb fingers, tugging at the twisted folds of her riding-skirt, suddenly pulled them loose. Her feet were under her, she was up on her legs, and with no thought now of fighting back, only of escape, she was desperately turning away. She took a step. Her knees were so weak that she stumbled as she tried to break into a run. He was close behind her. Her clothes hung about her in a deadweight of worsted, her boots were leaden. She could not run, she could not breathe – the tightness of her stock about her neck was choking the air from her.

One more step only, and then he had her. His hand closed like a vice about her upper arm, and he swung her round towards him. His hideous face was only inches from hers, his warm, putrid breath was in her nostrils. A single despairing shriek tore itself loose from her throat before he clapped a hand hard as leather over her mouth and pulled her against him with muscles like iron bands. She struggled wildly, fighting to breathe past his stifling hand, but there were black spots before her eyes and she felt her small strength slipping from her. Now there was no escape. She knew what it was to die.

And as suddenly as it had all begun, it was ended. She saw a flurry of movement behind her attacker; her arm was first wrenched agonisingly and then released, and the violence of the movements flung her to the ground. A tall man – a gentleman – had seized the navvy by the shoulder and pulled him away from her. The navvy had turned to grapple with him and the newcomer was raising his arm to break the man's head with his whip-stock.

There were shouts – someone else was there behind them – and the other two took to their heels. Her assailant flung up his arm to protect himself, reaching with his other hand for the stranger's throat. They swayed to and fro on the spot, struggling in terrible silence; but the shouting of the second-comer had attracted attention, and more people appeared, running from between the trees, calling out. Suddenly the navvy seemed to think better of it, tore himself out of the tall man's grasp, and ran.

Fleur was shaking all over in reaction to the shock and fear, and sobs were catching at her breath, though she struggled against them. Her rescuer bent over her. Through a mist that came and went, she saw his dark, handsome face looming towards her.

'How is it with you? Are you hurt?' he asked her. His hands were tender on her shoulders, his breath sweet that touched her face. He spoke to her in French, and she answered automatically in the same language, without at once realising she had done so.

'Not – not hurt. Only shaken.'

The mist began to clear. She found herself looking into a pair of hazel eyes of quite remarkable beauty. There was a dark, smoky-blue rim around the gold-green irises which made them look somehow wild, like a mountain cat's. There was something fantastic about noticing such a thing, she thought vaguely, when her entire body was jangling with distress.

'Can you stand up?' he asked.

'I – I think so.'

'Try, then.' He took her hand and placed his other hand under her elbow and raised her gently to her feet. She swayed and was obliged to clutch at him for balance, and he passed an arm round her waist, allowing her to lean against him. The deranged tumult of her nerves sank a little: it felt so safe in the circle of his arm, so natural. She felt the fine wool of his coat-sleeve under her fingers, and smelled – roses? Cloves? No, clove pinks, that was it. He had them in his buttonhole.

Over his shoulder she saw a groom standing a little way off holding two horses, and at once her mind leapt to Oberon.

'My horse—!'

'It's all right, my man will go after him. He won't have gone far,' said the stranger, still in French, though his accent, she decided now, was not quite that of a Frenchman: there was something more exotic and rolling in his pronunciation. 'How did it happen? Did that man drag you from the saddle?'

'No, I was thrown. They set their dogs on me, and my horse reared.'

Quite an audience had gathered. Some of the first-comers had run after the three men, and were now returning to say that they had lost them. A debate began as to whether a search should be made, or the Peelers fetched, or whether in fact it was hopeless, since the ruffians seemed to have got clean away.

Fleur began to feel horribly exposed, the object of vulgar curiosity. Still clutching her rescuer's arm, she pressed it anxiously and looked up pleadingly at him, longing to be taken away from this place.

'I think, mademoiselle, we should—' he began, but was interrupted by a shout. Someone came running through the trees leading Oberon at a trot.

'Where is she? Is she hurt? Oh God, what's happened?'

Plenty of voices were ready to answer him.

'Young lady here . . .'

'Taken a tumble, poor precious!'

'No, she were set upon by a gang o' thieves!'

'Nah, anarchists, weren't it?'

'Taken up for dead by that gemmun there . . .'

'Nick o' time . . . desperate ruffians . . . screamed fit to bust . . .'

Oberon's reins were thrust into someone's grasp, and the newcomer had caught Fleur away from her rescuer with strong and hasty hands, startling her. But here was a familiar

63

face, a familiar voice, made strange only by the unfamiliar plain blue uniform and cap of the Royal Engineers.

'Teddy? You?'

'Fleur! Are you all right? I found Oberon running loose back there. What happened?'

'Do you know this lady?' the stranger asked, in English.

'Known her all my life,' Scott replied shortly. 'What's *happened* here?'

The stranger bowed, ignoring the frantic question. 'Then I think I may safely leave you, mademoiselle,' he said to Fleur in French, but with a slight note of interrogation.

Fleur was beginning to feel both confused and exhausted. 'Oh – yes,' she said vaguely. 'Mr Scott will take care of me. Oh sir, wait, I must thank you—'

But he had already turned away, and Scott was urgently repeating his request for information and reassurance. By the time she had explained the circumstances briefly to him, the stranger had retrieved his horse and servant and quietly disappeared. It seemed the last straw. Without knowing clearly why, Fleur burst into tears.

'Oh Lord!' Teddy said in alarm, holding her against his shoulder and patting her vaguely.

'It's the shock, sir,' said a sensible-looking woman standing nearby. 'I should get her home if I was you.'

'Yes, of course,' he said, looked doubtfully at Oberon, and added, 'In a hackney, I think.'

'S'right, sir,' said the man who was holding Oberon. 'If you take the 'oss and start a-walkin' the young lady towards the gate, I'll run on ahead an' get a cab for you.'

'Peelers did oughter be told about them murderers,' said a toothless crone with relish. 'Nobody's not safe in their beds with this 'ere Exerbissun fetchin' all them foreigners and riffraff. Didn't oughter be allowed.'

'Give over, Ma! They'll be long gone be now,' said someone else. 'Took orf like 'ares.'

'Best get the young lady home, sir,' the sensible woman intervened. 'She's starting to tremble like an aspring, and no wonder, poor soul.'

'I'm all right,' Fleur gasped between sobs. 'I j-just don't seem to be able to s-stop.'

Fleur woke to the sound of the dawn chorus, and after a moment of confusion, remembered the events of the previous day. Having been put to bed very early in a state of nervous collapse, she had slept soundly through the evening and night, and now, of course, had woken well before her normal time.

She turned over onto her back and stared up at the tester, investigating her inner sensations. She could feel the stiffness of bruising, particularly on her left upper arm where the navvy had grabbed her, and on her hip and shoulder where she had struck the ground when she fell from the saddle. Otherwise she had sustained no physical damage; but the strain had left her with a curiously lethargic feeling. It was not entirely unpleasant: it was a little like the warm exhaustion one felt when reclining in the bath after a day's hunting.

Shock had mercifully blunted her memory of the attack itself. The worst thing she could remember about yesterday was the ride home in the hansom, jolting over the potholes, sobbing uncontrollably and feeling horribly sick. Poor Teddy, riding Oberon for her, had had an uncomfortable time too, across her side-saddle; but he had been very understanding when they arrived at Hanover Square. Fortunately everyone had been out, so there was no outcry to endure. Teddy had taken charge, paid the cab, dealt with the servants, supported her up to her room and sent up a maid to help her undress, bathe, and anoint her bruises with arnica and witch-hazel.

He had also waited until her aunt and uncle came home, in order to explain everything to them. Fleur was glad to have been spared the inevitable examinations and post-mortem. She fully realised her folly in riding alone so far from the beaten track and had no desire to be told of it again, and Teddy must have spoken long and earnestly to her anxious relatives, for when Aunt Venus came in to see her later, when she was just drifting off to sleep, she said nothing about it. She merely enquired – astonishingly gently, for her – how Fleur was feeling, and told her that Uncle Frederick had gone with Teddy to make a full report to the magistrates on the incident.

'I don't suppose there's any chance of catching them now,' she said, 'but it's the proper thing to do. And now, Fleur, dear, if there's nothing you want—?'

'Nothing, thank you,' Fleur murmured sleepily.

'I'll leave you to rest. Mr Scott sends his regards and will call tomorrow to see how you are.'

And that was the last thing Fleur remembered. Now, lying against the pillows in this strange languor, she thought about the man who had saved her life. Who was he? A gentleman, of course – his clothes, his voice, his actions all proclaimed it. A foreigner – he had addressed her automatically in French, but with that unusual accent. Probably he had come for the Exhibition. He seemed distinguished – perhaps he was a delegate from one of the overseas governments.

And what of him as a person? His age, she thought, was in the middle to late thirties. A handsome man, in a dark and saturnine sort of way. Not ill-tempered, that face, but somehow sad. There had been some trouble in his life, perhaps. Fastidious, yes – his coat was of the finest, his appearance everything that was neat, his hands – she remembered his hands – beautifully kept. And the flowers in his buttonhole – that was a touch of the individual. She recalled very clearly the smell of the clove pinks, and also – she shut her eyes, smiling a little – underneath that, the sweet, clean smell of *him*, of his skin, his person.

She had been that close to him. She had rested against him, feeling so safe, so safe! It was a strange thing, how in that moment of danger and fear, there had been such a sensation of intimacy with him, as though she had known him always; his arm around her had not been the intrusive touch of a stranger, but something known and welcome, something good.

She felt a vague tremor of excitement and happiness, the sort of feeling she had known as a child when she woke on Christmas morning to the anticipation of some special pleasure. She had been in deadly danger yesterday, and out of that had come a feeling of newness, as though she had been reborn.

She wished she knew who he was. It was like him, she thought absurdly, not to wait to be thanked, but to remove himself discreetly from the scene once it was sure she was safe. But she wished she knew his name, so that she could think of him by it. Who *was* he? Well, no matter, if he was in London for the Exhibition, she would see him again. He was a gentleman, probably a distinguished foreign delegate, and the circle of polite society was small: they were bound to meet sooner or later.

She stretched luxuriously, and then snuggled back into the pillows. The birds were singing madly, and through the bed-curtains she could see the glow of a fine sunny day beginning outside. It was good to be alive! Somewhere out there, perhaps just waking too, perhaps thinking about her, was her tall stranger, bound to her now by intangible cords of circumstance. They had shared a moment of perfect intimacy which had changed everything, for ever, and when they met the next time, it would not be as strangers.

And they would meet again, she knew it: it was fated.

Chapter Four

'How are you feeling today, Fleur? I must say, you don't look any the worse for your adventure,' said Teddy Scott.

'I'm a little tired, and a little bruised, but otherwise very well, thank you.'

'Bruised? From the fall?'

'Yes – nothing that shows, but I shan't be riding today, at all events.'

'I hope you won't be riding alone at any time, after what happened. You should never—'

'Thank you, Mr Scott! I've already had a peal rung over me by Aunt Venus – I don't want another.'

'Oh – no. I beg your pardon.' He coughed and fiddled with his gloves. 'That's a very becoming gown you're wearing. What do you call that colour?'

'*I* don't call it anything. It's called lilac-rose,' Fleur smiled. 'Did you come all this way to talk about clothes?'

'Well, you won't let me lecture you—'

'Certainly not. That's a very charming uniform you're wearing, Mr Scott. Plain and modest – none of the gaudiness of Richard's Hussars about it.'

'Engineers aren't obliged to frighten the enemy by their magnificence. Have you seen Richard lately?'

'Yesterday, in the Park – *and* he warned me not to ride alone, so I am well chastened, I assure you!'

'What was he doing in the Park? Is he happy in his regiment?'

'As a lark. He'd come to look at the Crystal Palace, pretending madly all the while that he wasn't interested in it at all! And what about you? What are you doing in London for the second day running? I thought you were fixed at Woolwich?'

'As a matter of fact, I came to look at the Crystal Palace, too – not for myself, though. I was sent to study the building technique, in case there should be anything that could be adapted for our use.'

'Our use?'

'Oh, building bridges and so forth,' he said vaguely.

'It sounds as though you're settling in. Do you like it after all?'

'It's quite interesting,' he admitted. 'Father would be amazed – he was always sure I had no brains at all, because I was awkward in company. People are so unpredictable, but machines – well, you always know what they're going to do, and if they go wrong, there's a simple reason. You can put them right again. It's very soothing.'

'Soothing!' Fleur was amused at the adjective. 'But yes, people are a great deal more troublesome and unregulated. Like those tiresome Blacks, for instance. I don't suppose you've any more news of them?'

'Not since Easter, when I was home on furlough. I went to

see how they were managing without their mother. The eldest girl's come back home out of service to take care of the little ones, but of course that means less money coming in. And Black was laid up with a cut hand that had gone septic.'

'That's just like him! I suppose he neglected it.' She hesitated. 'And what about Jackie?'

'Sinking fast, I'm afraid. I don't think it will be very long.'

'Ah,' she said, and bit her lip.

Scott longed to comfort her, but could think of nothing to say except, 'He's better off out of it, perhaps. When you think of the sort of life—'

'Yes,' she said, cutting him off. The echo of words came to her from long ago: *it's a merciful release* . . . It was a thing people said. Well, she had known how it would be for Jack. She remembered little Betty, and Maria before her, and all the others going back down the years; a procession of coffins, pathetic both for their size and their cheapness. She roused herself, for Teddy's sake. 'I'm glad you went to them – I'm sure you did them good. I suppose you parted with some guineas, from your slender purse?'

'Oh, well, I could hardly do less. I got Walker in to look at Black's hand, too. He said he thought he could save it.'

'You're a good man,' Fleur said. 'But didn't you mean to tell me all this? Easter's long past. You might have written to me.'

He smirked a little. 'I did hope I might have the opportunity to tell you face to face,' he admitted. 'In fact, when I'd finished at the Crystal Palace, I was going to walk across to Hanover Square to see if you were at home. You can't imagine my shock when old Oberon came cantering up to me with no one on his back. Frightened me to death.'

'I'm very glad you happened to be there. Though my stranger was being everything that was kind. I wish I'd had the chance to thank him.'

'A gentleman doesn't need thanking for a service of that sort,' Teddy pronounced. 'He looked like a wealthy man. He had the largest diamond I've ever seen in his stock-pin.'

'I didn't notice that. There was so little time . . . I wonder if I'll see him again?'

'I expect you're bound to – at the Exhibition, sooner or later. Will you be well enough to go to the opening ceremony? It would be a shame to miss it. It sounds as though it'll be splendid.'

'I'm not ill, Teddy,' Fleur said patiently. 'Of course I'll be there.'

'Oh good. Did you know there's to be a detachment from our regiment present, along with the Sappers and Miners? Why, I'm not sure. One of the Sappers is to raise the Royal Standard when the Queen arrives, but anyone could have done that. However, I don't complain. The officers drew lots for the privilege of attending, and my name came out, so I shall be there too.'

'How democratic you are in the Engineers! In any other regiment it would have been the Colonel's nephew who was chosen, automatically.'

He grinned. 'There are advantages, you see, to not being fashionable. But talking of being fashionable, I really don't think you should ride alone any more, not with so many rough characters about. Now, don't look mulish at me! You know I'm right. I wonder your Papa should allow it.'

'Papa never worries about me. And I'd have been quite safe yesterday if I'd stayed on the tan, which I fully meant to do, and which I shall certainly do in future. I can't endure being followed about by servants who would sooner be anywhere else but there.'

'Very well – but would you allow me to escort you, when I'm in London? I quite often have a few hours free in the morning or the afternoon, and you know I'd like nothing better.'

'I always enjoy your company,' she said hesitantly, seeing the eagerness he was trying to conceal. 'But, Teddy, you do understand, don't you, that I'm not likely to change my mind?'

'I'm not such a coxcomb,' Scott said with dignity, 'as to pester you with attentions that aren't welcome. Of course I meant it just as a friend.'

'Then, just as a friend, I should be glad to accept.'

Entering the morning-room and finding his daughter there, Sir Ranulph greeted her vaguely, as if he only just remembered who she was.

'Ah, Fleur.' She looked up from the letter she was writing, and he stood where he was, apparently stranded by the unexpected encounter.

'Yes, Papa?' she prompted. 'Have you been somewhere agreeable?'

'Only the Club.' He chuckled suddenly, and pulled out the chair opposite her at the table. 'Yes, I've something to tell you, too! What a stew the Prince has stirred up now, to be sure!'

She laid down her pen expectantly.

'I've just had the whole thing from Sydney Herbert,' he said. 'He has a lively sense of the ridiculous, though I've always found him a trifle too *point devise* for my taste. And that wife of his – however,' he caught himself up and returned to the point, 'it seems that the Prince had the idea of asking the Belgian Ambassador, as senior member of the Diplomatic Corps, to read an Address on behalf of all the ambassadors at the opening ceremony of the Exhibition.'

'That sounds like a good idea. Was it well taken?'

'It seemed so at first. But then a furious letter from Brunnow, the Russian Ambassador, arrived on Palmerston's desk saying that the whole idea was outrageous. He said no diplomat could speak for any country but his own, and that in any case the proposal should have gone through proper Foreign Office channels. So Palmerston wrote an icy letter to Russell demanding explanation, and Russell wrote a sharp rebuke to the Prince. All the diplomats decided to have no part of it, and recriminations started to fly back and forth. What a joke!'

'But what did the Prince say?'

'Oh, he stuck to it that since half the exhibits were from foreign countries, it was appropriate to have some kind of official participation by the Diplomatic Corps. But wait, there's more! In the meantime, the Belgian Ambassador had gone down to Windsor to report to the Queen, and he brought back a message for his colleagues, to the effect that the Queen had intended the whole thing as a particular compliment to the Diplomatic Corps, but that she had no way of forcing them to accept a mark of politeness, which anyone else would have regarded as an honour.'

'Oh dear! They must have been very embarrassed.'

'Yes, all except Brunnow, who apparently feared for his life if he let anyone else claim to speak for Russia! By now, of course, they were all eager to go along with the Address after all, but it seems Palmerston's grown tired of the whole thing, and he's now decreed that the ambassadors may attend the opening ceremony, but only as spectators, without any official status. It's all highly diverting, don't you think?'

'The poor Prince! He does mean well.'

'Don't let your Aunt Ercy hear you speak like that! Oh, he's a good man, but he can be high-handed as well as high-minded. The fact is that he should have gone through the proper channels. But he would never have got the idea past Brunnow, even then. The Russians have had the deepest suspicions of the Exhibition from the beginning.'

'But they are taking part, aren't they?'

'They've sent cases of goods along, but their government's refused passports for any Russian citizens to come to it. They think England is crawling with conspirators and assassins just waiting for the chance to murder the Tsar and overthrow the regime.'

The door opened and Sir Frederick put an enquiring head around it.

'Ah, there you are. Good – I wanted to talk to you both.'

'Hullo, Fred! I've just been telling Fleur about the Address of the Diplomats. I suppose you've heard all about it?'

'Yes, I had it from poor Brunnow this afternoon at St James's. He had to put a stop to it – he was in the deuce of a pickle! On the one hand, he couldn't let the thing go ahead with himself alone excluded, because that would be an insult to the Tsar, who regards himself as the Doyen of Monarchs; but on the other hand he couldn't let anyone else claim even indirectly to speak for the Russian people, or the Tsar would never trust him again.'

'You sound as though you have his case at heart,' said Fleur.

'I've got a lot of sympathy for Brunnow. He's an excellent man, and a first-class diplomat – studied under Nesselrode, you know, the Old Master. And Nicholas must be the devil of a man to work for.'

'Unpredictable, I imagine,' Sir Ranulph said. 'Charming you one minute, and sending you off to Siberia the next. You met him when he came to London back in '44, didn't you?'

'Yes. Strange man – though I suppose being an autocrat is bound to make you a little mad in the end. The Queen and the Prince got quite to like him, though.'

'What was he like, Uncle?' Fleur asked.

'Very tall, extremely handsome. Charming to talk to, very good with children – but there was something about him, all the same . . . Rather frightening in a way, I thought.'

'Palmerston couldn't stand him at any price. Said the charm was all a put-on and that underneath he was a ruthless b— a ruthless chap.'

'I don't think it's that,' Frederick said slowly, frowning in thought. 'I think the Queen summed him up when she said she thought he was "not clever". Very sincere, she said, and very anxious to be believed, but "not clever". Well, add to that unlimited personal power, and a quite justifiable fear of being assassinated, and you've a recipe for unpredictability.'

'I was telling Fleur the Russian government refused permission for anyone to come to the Exhibition – is that right?' Ranulph asked.

Sir Frederick looked unaccountably embarrassed. 'Well, yes, they did, though there's a party of official observers, and the exhibitors of course. As a matter of fact, that's a subject rather close to home. I've got a confession to make, and I want your support when I tell Venus about it.'

'This sounds exciting. What have you done?' Fleur asked, her eyes dancing. 'If it's something Aunt Venus will disapprove of, it promises to be entertaining for the rest of us.'

'Yes, you'd like to see me chewed out, wouldn't you! Well,

Ralph, you'll support me, at least? A man has the right to invite anyone he likes into his own home, hasn't he?'

Sir Ranulph nodded. 'Oh, I have you! You've been waylaid by one of the relatives from the country, and badgered into inviting them to stay for the Exhibition.'

'Aunt Venus will be furious. That's why she invited Papa and me. You know how she hates rustics!'

'Oh, he's not a rustic, precisely, though he is a little odd,' Frederick said, adopting an air of insouciance. 'I'm sure you'll both find him amusing. I'm just not sure where he'll fit into Vee's scheme of prejudices. One's never precisely sure with her what she'll object to.'

'More and more intriguing! Well, who is it, Uncle? What reprobate have you invited to stay?'

'He's not a reprobate, he's a Russian,' Frederick said, trying to look unconcerned. 'One of the exhibitors. Brunnow asked me to invite him, and I could hardly refuse, could I? Anyway, his name's Polotski, and he's a highly respectable merchant.'

Sir Ranulph gave a shout of laughter. 'By God, Fred, you've done it now! Why on earth did you agree to it?'

Sir Frederick looked a little sheepish. 'Well, you know what it's like trying to find accommodation in London this close to the opening! The Embassy rooms are all spoken for, the hotels are all full, and every leading hostess has her parties made up for the whole summer. It's Vee's own fault, really, for having empty rooms.'

'I don't think she'll agree to take the blame. But in any case, it was Brunnow's problem, not yours. Why should he ask you?'

'As a matter of fact,' Frederick said, looking ever more sheepish, 'I think it was because Polotski and I have interests in common. What he particularly wants to study at the Exhibition are the new kinds of water-closet.'

This revelation left his audience too delirious for further comment.

Once Aunt Venus's worst fear, that the guest foisted upon her would turn out to be bearded, proved groundless, she was on the way to forgiving her husband the rest of his folly.

'I could not for anything have sat down at table opposite a bearded man. I should never have been able to eat a morsel,' she said.

'Now, Vee, would I have brought home a bearded man?' Frederick said, though it had not occurred to him until that moment to wonder. 'And he speaks French quite well, so you'll have no trouble making yourself understood.'

His wife's eyes flashed. 'I have never in my life had trouble making myself understood. But what does he eat? And what about his religion? Will he insist on sleeping on the floor, or having his bed face due east? Will he keep us awake all night with chanting and burning incense?'

'Good lord, no! They're Christians over there – well, of a sort, anyway. And as for eating – whatever your cook sends up, my love, is good enough for anyone, wherever they come from.'

'I was not concerned about good enough – I was wondering about strange enough,' she retorted snappishly.

Mr Polotski was a little strange-looking, but that was more to do with nature than nationality. He was a short man, with considerable *embonpoint* which, added to a rather muscular frame, and a singular lack of neck, made him appear almost circular. He was surprisingly nimble, however, moving about quickly and lightly on the balls of his feet, rather like a sailor, and since he wore soft leather boots, he was as soundless about the house as a cat.

To Venus's surprise he was fair. She had always imagined Russians, as far as she had ever bothered to imagine them at all, as being dark-haired and swarthy, but Mr Polotski had fair skin, blue eyes, and light brown hair with just a hint of copper in it. He had obviously been handsome in his youth, and his smile was rather boyish. Altogether he was not nearly so alarming as she had expected.

His immediate peculiarities were confined to eating enormously, and to wearing a fur coat indoors. It was a rather chilly evening, which made Venus glad of her shawl when she left the circle of the fire, but wearing a coat was going rather too far, she thought. However he smiled most charmingly and explained in fair French that it was not so much the cold that troubled him as the draughts.

'In Russia, you see, we fit double windows in the winter. We have a Dutch stove in each room, and the rooms lead one into the next, without any of your English corridors. So the temperature is everywhere the same, and there is never the least draught. Dear madame, our ladies wear their summer gowns all through the year!'

'How very singular,' Venus replied crushingly.

Fleur yielded without struggle to his charm. Polotski told her at once that she reminded him of his dear wife, and as she translated this correctly as the highest compliment he could pay her, they hit it off splendidly.

Apart from his wife, his great passions seemed to be cooking and jewellery. 'Cooking is man's most truly creative art,' he told Fleur in the course of their first long conversation. 'It is the most aesthetic. All other art is contaminated by materialism. But with cooking, the end product is utterly ephemeral, and unique. It is an art which exists for its own sake alone.'

'I hadn't quite thought of it like that,' Fleur said.

'Of course not! What has a young lady like you to do with cooking? It is a passion for man's middle years, when other passions have cooled. You, so slender, so beautiful, may only sense it dimly. What can you know of the poetry of spices, of soured cream, of truffles? How can you appreciate the triumph of man over the forces of nature, as represented by the perfect soufflé?'

Fleur struggled for a moment, and then laughed. 'You're roasting me!'

'Of course I am,' Polotski said, his blue eyes twinkling. 'Just a little! But truly, I hope it will be many years, mademoiselle, before food becomes a passion with you. My other great love you may appreciate already. I am a jeweller by profession, though my fortune now comes largely from merchantile trade. But I am, of course, the finder of the Polotski Emerald. That, officially, is why I'm here.'

'Of course! How stupid of me not to have realised. I'm looking forward very much to seeing it. Is it very beautiful?'

'Yes, it is beautiful – it is beauty's self. But of course there is more than one sort of beauty. Yours, for instance, mademoiselle, is quite different. I should like to have the privilege of designing a jewel for you – something exquisite. Sapphires, I think. No one understands sapphires like we Russians! If ever you wish a parure of sapphires, promise me you will come to me to create it.'

'I can promise that with the greatest of confidence,' Fleur laughed.

'Yes, you may mock me, with those laughing eyes! But one day you will make a fine marriage, and your husband, fortunate man, will wish to give you jewels to match your beauty. I'm afraid like most young men – for of course you will marry a young man – he will want to load you with diamonds and gold.' He sighed and shook his head. 'Like spreading a heavy sauce over a delicate fillet of sole! You will not let him, however. You will remember your conversation with old Father Polotski, and say "No, my lord, I will have sapphires, nothing but sapphires!" '

'He is to be a lord, then?'

'A lord or a great man. Or both. You cannot marry a commoner.'

Fleur shook her head. 'I don't think I shall ever marry.'

Polotski only smiled. 'You will marry,' he said confidently, 'because beauty such as yours demands its homage. You must have a lover; and since you are both practical and romantic – a rare combination, I may say, and quite enchanting – you will marry him.'

'If he is a great man, perhaps it would be more exciting to be his mistress. Don't mistresses have all the fun?'

'By no means,' Polotski said, unruffled. 'There can be no greater happiness, mademoiselle, than in having your lover for your spouse. You'll learn one day.'

May Day was declared a public holiday in honour of the opening of the Exhibition. It dawned bright but chilly, with a definite nip in the air, but the swathes of mist over the parks and public gardens were soon sucked up by the rising sun, promising a fair day.

Mr Polotski was away early, leaving just after six o'clock for the Crystal Palace where, with the other exhibitors, he would indulge himself in a final frenzy of rearranging and dusting. A great many of the Russian exhibits were not yet on show: a hundred and thirteen cases of goods had turned up at last after being held up by ice-bound seas in the Baltic, but little had been unpacked. Sir Frederick went with him, promising to be back for breakfast.

Breakfast was to be at eight, for Sir Frederick said they must leave early to be sure of good seats. The sale of season tickets – three guineas for gentlemen and two guineas for ladies – had soared to more than twenty thousand once it had been announced that all holders would be allowed in to the opening ceremony. Venus grumbled at being expected to keep country hours for the sake of a mere exhibition, but she was ready, dressed to the last detail, and seated at the table when Fleur came in to the breakfast parlour at eight o'clock.

'Ah, there you are, child,' she said, looking remarkably pleased with herself. 'What have you got on? Yes, very suitable. I must say you have good taste.'

Fleur had chosen a gown of spring-green *gros d'orient* with three-quarter sleeves and a three-flounced skirt, all trimmed with darker green ribbon. Under it she wore a high-necked embroidered cambric chemisette, whose sleeves ended at the wrist in a neat double cuff. She glanced down at herself and then at her aunt with amusement.

'I should thank you for the compliment, Aunt, except that since you formed my taste, you are only complimenting yourself.'

'A touch, Venus!' Sir Ranulph murmured. 'She has you there.'

'Nonsense. I may have guided her as a child, but she has made up her own mind any time these ten years. You'll wear your sea-green bonnet with it, of course,' she decreed. 'The *gros de Tours* with the pleated pink satin lining.'

'Yes, Aunt,' Fleur said meekly, taking her seat and smiling thanks at Dickens who came up to fill her coffee cup. 'No, nothing to eat, thank you. I'll just have a little toast.'

'Finicking nonsense. I hope you may not feel faint later,' Venus said, and applied herself once more to ham, kidneys and buttered eggs. She would never subscribe to the fashion which said that ladies must eat like birds. 'You never know with these grand occasions when you may eat next.'

'But there are refreshments on sale at the Exhibition, aren't there?'

'Pooh! Pastries and Seltzer-water,' Venus dismissed the idea. 'You should make sure of your ground before you advance, as the Duke says.'

Sir Frederick walked in at a quarter to nine and said, 'It's all right, you needn't rush. I've managed to bespeak some seats – and a good thing I did, for I don't know how we'd manage otherwise. There was already a crowd at the three main entrances when I left. But one of the ushers used to be a porter at the House, and he remembers how I used to slip him a half-crown now and then. He's going to rope off four chairs for us.'

'Is that allowed, Uncle?'

'Not at all,' he replied genially, 'but what's the use of being a Prominent Person if you can't get preference from time to time? However I think we had better go soon, for I don't know how long my personal Cerberus will be able to hold the multitudes at bay.'

The Queen was not due to arrive until noon, but by ten o'clock every seat was filled, and the Transept, naves and galleries were banked with pink faces under tall hats and silk bonnets. A murmur of conversation rose on the air like the sound of summer bees as the spectators gazed around, in most cases for the first time, at the most fabulous scene the world had ever witnessed.

Even though prepared for it in imagination and by what she had been told, Fleur felt dazed. Under the ribs of the transparent roof, immeasurably far above her head, there seemed to have been created the magic of a world of warmth and brightness, where perpetual summer reigned. The soft, radiant quality of the sunlight filtering in through the glass roof and walls, the haze of distance, the iridescent colours expanding on the lambent air, all combined to produce an impression of sheer immensity that was almost overpowering.

There was an extraordinary luminosity which was a mixture of light and air and space, contained and yet endless; and at the heart of it all, at the very centre of the Transept, was a great fountain carved out of pure transparent crystal, which threw dazzling skeins of water into a lacework of spray fifty feet into the air. Facing the fountain on the north side of the Transept was the royal dais under a gold-fringed canopy decorated with plumes of white feathers. All around were statues, looking curiously dead-white against the strong red of the Turkey cloth which everywhere draped and framed and supported the exhibits. Tall palms trembled in the rainbow air, and ferns and flowers and greenery were massed and banked in pots at every angle. And above them all rose the great elm trees in their full summer verdure, towering up into the curved transparent spaces of the transept roof, like mysterious, silent captives from another world.

For a little while, it was not possible to speak. Fleur could only look and look, and remember with an inward shake of the head those like Richard's friend, Mr Brooke, who had feigned boredom, or mocked, and sworn that nothing would drag them here. She watched the airy dance of the fountain prisming the light into dazzle, and could only feel glad and honoured to be present.

Some time later Sir Ranulph, who had slipped away to talk to some of his friends, returned to his seat saying, 'Paxton says that Mayne told him there are half a million people in the crowd outside. Can you imagine? They're all remarkably well behaved, though. Ah, here come the notables at last. That will give us all something to stare at.'

Gradually the official places were filling. Fleur watched the Duke of Wellington, silver-haired and bent with age now, walk in to a burst of applause which he acknowledged by not so much as a lift of the hand. There were stern Lord Anglesea and kindly Lord Raglan, two more Waterloo veterans, one who had lost a leg and the other an arm at that famous battle. Sir Frederick nudged Fleur to point out Lord Cardigan, Richard's commanding officer, tall, still handsome, and magnificent in full dress uniform. Fleur was more interested, however, to spot the detachment from the Royal Engineers, and to be able to pick out Teddy Scott, standing at his ease and whispering to the Sapper officer beside him.

Then the politicians came in, many of them, like Lord John Russell and Lord Palmerston, familiar figures to Fleur; and the diplomats, who, though they had no official place in the proceedings, made up for it by the gorgeousness of their apparel. They were gaudy in chocolate-coloured court dress with filigree buttons over long white silk waistcoats; in gold lace and decorations, plumed hats, ribbons and stars; in uniforms of blue and silver, green and gold, sky and scarlet and the old Imperial white.

Then came the English Court officials in all their splendid variety of uniforms, from the beefeaters in their red frocks and the heralds in their gold tabards to the gentlemen-at-arms in their shining brass helmets with the drooping white feathers.

'There's your Uncle Markby,' Frederick said suddenly, 'over there, look, talking to Garter King-at-Arms. Look at his face! This is meat and drink to him!' He chuckled. 'Your Aunt Ercy comes later, of course, with the Queen's procession. I wonder if—'

'Oh look!' Fleur cried suddenly, grasping his arm. 'There's the man who rescued me in the Park!'

'Really? Where?'

'Over beyond the fountain, to the left of the statue with the sword. I'm sure it's him – the tall man in the green uniform coat.'

'Where? I don't see – you don't mean the cove with the white moustaches?'

'No, no, not him! To the left, and behind the – oh, now he's moved, and you can't see him! Oh, how vexing! But I'm sure it was him.'

'He's probably attached to one of the embassies,' Frederick said with interest. 'They're all diplomats in that corner.'

Fleur continued to stare, but the man had presumably moved right away, for when the bodies parted, there was no sign of him. 'I wish you'd seen him – you might have been able to tell me who he is,' she said.

'You're bound to see him again,' said Frederick. He glanced at her disappointed face and said, 'You can wear that bonnet to the Exhibition every day, you know. He's sure to see you in it sooner or later.'

The frown disappeared. 'Really, Uncle—!' she laughed.

But at that moment there was a stir in the crowd as a blur of bright colour passed the northern entrance, marking the arrival of the Royal party with its escort of Life Guards. Every head turned; the volume of talk rose and then fell to an expectant hush; and after a brief delay the trumpets suddenly flourished, ringing loudly in the echoing spaces and making several people jump. The appointed Sapper stepped forward and ceremoniously hauled on the lanyard that raised the Royal Standard from the pole on the summit of the Transept roof. The tall, wrought-iron gates across the north nave were flung back by the guardian beefeaters, and the Royal party appeared, preceded backwards by various chamberlains.

The crowd broke into a roar of approval which was not even drowned by the tones of the massive organ beginning the national anthem, and continued cheering as the small figure of the Queen, in pink silk brocaded with silver, the Garter ribbon, and a diamond tiara, walked up onto the dais. With her were Prince Albert, and the two eldest children, the Princess Royal and the Prince of Wales – 'Vicky' in white lace with a wreath of roses, and 'Bertie' in Highland dress.

When the last notes had died away, the Prince left the Queen's side and went to stand at the foot of the steps with the other Commissioners, and read an Address to the Queen, describing briefly how and why the Exhibition had come into existence. The Queen replied briefly, her small voice as clear as a bell in the soft summer air of the great greenhouse. Then the Archbishop of Canterbury, looking like a mediaeval angel in his tightly curled wig and billowing lawn sleeves, invoked the blessing of God on the enterprise.

It was a prayer of thanksgiving, Fleur thought, as much as an invocation: humble and heartfelt thanks from a people who had known no war on their own soil in living memory, no famine, plague, invasion or revolution. In England there was peace and plenty; no sword was lifted against any man, no dictator's heel was on any neck. Men travelled freely to and fro, spoke their minds without fear, and went about their lawful business unhindered; and everywhere knowledge grew, industry expanded, and everything progressed ever towards greater liberality and prosperity.

And the symbol of it all was that small, slight woman standing quietly under the canopy, unafraid and unguarded at the heart of her own people. This was real freedom, Fleur thought. Let other nations proclaim their republics and cut each other's throats in the name of liberty: England, even if it was at the prompting of a German-born prince, celebrated freedom in a peaceful exhibition of Art, Industry and Free Trade, through which the monarch could walk safely without a bodyguard.

A deeply moved silence followed the Archbishop's prayer; and then the great Willis organ, two hundred musicians, and six hundred choristers burst suddenly into the 'Hallelujah Chorus', and Fleur bit her tongue.

The official procession, which was to accompany the Queen on a brief inspection of the Exhibition, began to form up while the singing was going on, headed by Mr Paxton, Mr Fox and Mr Henderson, with various members of the Committee behind them.

Sir Ranulph leaned across Fleur to say to Sir Frederick, 'I say, Fred, who the deuce is the Chinaman? I thought China refused to take part?'

'It did. There's no official representation,' Sir Frederick said, watching the mandarin in his gaudy silk coat with some surprise. 'Splendid-looking beggar, isn't he? Seems quite at home, too – look at him chatting to the Duke! Shaking hands with Anglesea too. I suppose they must know all about him.'

A moment later the mandarin caused a commotion by thrusting his way through the crowds, mounting the dais in front of the Queen, and flinging himself on his face in obeisance at her feet.

'Good God! That's not in the programme!' Frederick cried. 'What can he mean by it? Why don't the rods take him away?'

No one seemed to know what to do about him. It was the Queen herself who saved the situation, for though evidently put out, she smiled fairly graciously and indicated to the Committee that the Chinaman should be allowed to join the procession as a representative of the absent Empire, immediately behind the ambassadors.

The procession took three-quarters of an hour to walk up one nave and down another, though it was doubtful whether any of the members of it could have seen anything of the exhibits. Then the Queen returned to the dais and gave the order to Lord Breadalbane to declare the Exhibition open. The trumpets flourished again, and the renewed cheering was echoed by a hundred-gun salute outside in the Park; after which the Royal party left, and the ushers began to take down the barriers to allow free access to the exhibits.

'Best stay here for a few moments, until the crowd disperses a little,' Sir Frederick said to his ladies.

'I'm just going to try to get a word with Cole,' Sir Ranulph said. 'See if I can find out about that Chinee.'

Ten minutes later he was back, chuckling. 'The man's a hoaxster! It's a great joke!'

'You mean he isn't a Chinaman at all?' Venus asked.

'Oh yes, he's a mandarin, all right, but he wasn't sent by the Emperor! Far from it – he's the proprietor of that Chinese junk moored on the Thames at Temple Pier. He shows people over it for a shilling a time.'

'Good God! But what was he up to? Making fun of our ceremonials?' Frederick asked.

'Apparently he said he just wanted to pay his respects to the Queen along with everyone else,' Ranulph said with a grin, 'but between you and me, I don't think this little show of his will do his trade any harm!'

'You mean he did it to attract customers? It's outrageous! He should be clapped up!' Venus said indignantly.

'Oh come,' Ranulph laughed, 'this is a celebration of Free Trade and enterprise, isn't it? I'd say he was being very enterprising indeed. He ought to be congratulated!'

Teddy Scott appeared, edging through the crowds with his cap under his arm, and made his bows.

'Wasn't it all splendid?' he said. 'I've heard people saying it was even better than the coronation.'

'Yes – and with the mandarin for comic relief, too!' Sir Ranulph said.

'Redbridge of the Life Guards said they all had a very bad moment or two, thinking he was an assassin,' Scott told them. 'But Her Majesty was wonderfully cool, don't you think?' He turned to Fleur. 'What a ravishing bonnet! We're off duty now – might I offer you my arm, if you're going round the exhibits? I promise you you'll need one. The crowds are beyond anything.'

Venus nodded approvingly. 'Yes, do go with Mr Scott, Fleur my love. One needs a man to make a passage through crowds like this.'

'Thank you,' Fleur said gravely, knowing quite well what she was up to, 'but Papa is to escort me. I shouldn't like to offend him.'

'Your father won't want to be bothered with you. He's longing to get away by himself and talk to his friends – aren't you, Ranulph?'

'Quite true,' Sir Ranulph said cheerfully. 'Go with young Scott, Fleur, there's a good girl! Joe Paxton has promised to show me the system for controlling temperature and humidity: it's just what I need for my new orchid-house. You'd only be in the way.' He began to walk off, to make his escape certain, turning back only to say, 'Be sure and visit one of the conveniences in the rest areas, my love. I'm told they're a marvel – and the very first public ones in the world! The Prince thinks we shall have them in the parks next, and on every street corner one day.'

He strolled away, leaving Venus looking scandalised, and

Frederick laughing. 'I think that was a pass at me! Your papa is an original, Flo!'

Scott turned to Venus to say politely, 'Where would you like to go first, Lady Hoare?'

Venus waved him away. 'You two must go off on your own. We're bound to want to move at a different pace. In any case, in such a crowd it will be impossible for us all to keep together. I'm sure I can trust Mr Scott to take care of you, Fleur.' She smiled graciously at Teddy. 'I hope we shall see you in Hanover Square for dinner, Mr Scott?'

'Thank you indeed, Lady Hoare!' Teddy bowed, gave Fleur his arm, and led her away.

'Aunt Venus is as subtle as the toothache,' she complained. 'You see how blatantly she pushed us together.'

'I'm extremely flattered!'

'You've heard of the expression "a sprat to catch a mackerel"? Well, you're the sprat. She hopes that seeing me on your arm will encourage other suitors.'

'I'm not so proud— I'll accept any encouragement that's offered,' Teddy grinned. 'What would you like to see first? The conveniences?' Fleur gave him a look. 'Well, perhaps you would like a little luncheon, or coffee and ices, before we look at the exhibits?'

Fleur freed a hand to glance at her watch. 'I rather think the rest areas will be crowded at twenty minutes past one, don't you?' she said gravely. 'Let's go and see the Koh-i-noor.'

'Is that your idea of avoiding the crowds?' Teddy hooted. 'My dear girl, you haven't an idea . . .'

Chapter Five

'Well, mademoiselle, are you going to the Exhibition this morning? How do you like it now?' said Mr Polotski, resuming his seat at the breakfast table as Fleur took hers. From the virgin state of the covers, it was plain that they were the first two down.

'Oh, it surpasses all my expectations,' Fleur said. Before the opening she had expected to want to go several times, but like almost everyone else in London she had completely underestimated the extent and fascination of the exhibits. She had been five times already in the first week, and didn't believe she had seen a tenth of it; and she knew there were things, like the Machine Court, that she would want to visit again and again. The sight of so many moving machines – designed to perform tasks as disparate as punching holes in thick iron sheeting, and folding envelopes – was something she could watch by the hour.

'I never tire of looking at those levers and wheels all working away so rhythmically,' she said, remembering. 'It's – beautiful.'

He smiled understandingly. 'Yes – like a very skilled man with a scythe mowing a hayfield. It's a kind of ballet.'

'Have you been able to see any of it yourself?'

'Oh yes. I have an assistant I can leave in charge. Also a nice English policeman in a tall hat to guard the Polotski Emerald! My fellow countrymen are very surprised that there are no soldiers with muskets on duty inside the Building, even when your Queen visits. But I tell them, this is England! Here men pride themselves on their honesty.'

'Oh, everyone is so pleased and proud of the Exhibition, they wouldn't misbehave for worlds!' Fleur said, and then caught up with what he had said. 'But don't Russians pride themselves on their honesty?'

Polotski twinkled at her over his fork. 'In Russia a man may be honest, or successful – not both.'

His plate sported several chops, some burnished brown sausages, and a considerable wedge of cold game pie. A portion of the latter was on its way to his mouth, well daubed with mustard, and he paused to regard it fondly for an instant. 'I must tell you that your English mustard I like very much! I am in love with it, truly. I mean to purchase a great quantity to take with me when I go back to Russia. And I have already thought of some recipes to—'

'But you can't mean that Russians are deliberately dishonest?' Fleur persisted with a frown, ignoring his divagation.

'Do you know the expression *caveat emptor*? Let the buyer beware! If a man can sell a bale of wool weighted with a rock, he is not dishonest, but cunning; and if the buyer can repay him with a sack of grain that is half sand, he will be pleased with his own sharpness. Your English manufacturers, who pride themselves in selling first-quality goods at a fair price, I find enchanting! It is so refreshing to do business in such an atmosphere of trust.'

'But how dreadful your alternative must be,' Fleur said.

'You must remember we are a different people. The Eastern bazaar is our natural habitat, and the thrill of bargaining is in our blood.' He observed her doubtful expression. 'Russia is more different than you can imagine.'

'I think it must be. But I think also you are teasing me.'

He smiled, neither confirming nor denying. 'You have not been to see the Russian Court, yet. You have not seen my emerald.'

Fleur looked rueful. 'I mean to, of course, but there is so much—'

'Of course, of course. We shall be here all summer; and later it will be better, when more of our goods have arrived. Have you seen the great Koh-i-noor? How did you find it?'

'Disappointing.'

He laughed. 'Yes, I thought you would. It is not much to look at, is it? A dull grey egg in a golden cage.'

'To tell the truth, I found Mr Chubb's safety device more interesting than the diamond,' Fleur said. 'The policeman guarding it told us that if anyone tried to steal it, at the first touch a spring would be released and the diamond would drop instantly into the strongbox underneath. But Teddy said he couldn't believe anyone would want to steal such an ugly thing anyway.'

'Teddy? Is that the earnest young man who accompanies you?'

'Yes, Mr Scott.'

'What a nice thing it is, to be an officer. So much leisure, so few duties!' Polotski observed. 'And does he accompany you today?'

'No, I'm going with Uncle Frederick this morning. We thought we'd go early, before it gets too crowded.'

'So you will take your ride this afternoon?'

'Yes, I suppose so,' Fleur said. She had been varying the time of her ride in the Park day by day in the hope of seeing her rescuer again. She reasoned that if he had been riding there that day, he would surely ride there again, so she must meet him some time. So far she had been unlucky. Indeed, she began to wonder if he had left London, for she had not seen him at the Exhibition or at any of their evening engagements, either.

'I wonder if I might ask you a very great favour,' Polotski said, breaking into her thoughts. 'I have been two weeks shut up inside the Russian Court with the packing-cases and straw and dust. I long for some fresh air. Even more, I long for some feminine company! Your kind aunt has put her carriage at my disposal this afternoon, and I should count it a great honour if you would take the air with me for an hour or two.'

Fleur was taken aback: she had not finished blinking at the description of Aunt Venus as 'kind', and the revelation that this high-stickler had offered a mere merchant the use of her treasured new barouche, when she found herself solicited to promenade publicly with a middle-aged married man with no neck and no waist and a tendency to fur collars on his coats.

On no fine day, in any case, would she willingly exchange riding Oberon for driving in a carriage, and she hesitated; but Polotski was looking at her with such a humorous expression of hope mingled with expectation of disappointment that she found she couldn't deny him.

'I should be pleased to,' she said.

Everyone who visited the Crystal Palace had their own favourite exhibits. Aunt Venus spent a surprising amount of time in the French section. It was the largest after the English – clear evidence that France had recovered from the terrible depredations of the Napoleonic Wars as completely as the country which had conquered her.

In less than sixty years she had been successively republic, empire, restored Bourbonist monarchy, Orleanist monarchy, and now republic again; but as Venus said to Fleur, perhaps a little wistfully, no matter who ruled at the Tuileries, the spirit of France remained the same – and the silks and gauzes from Paris were still the best in the world.

Even Richard had risked the scorn of his friend Brooke and spent two hours at the Exhibition on each of two consecutive days, though he had not managed to get much beyond the Carriage Court, where the sight of so many stylish phaetons, gigs and sulkies reduced him to dumb envy. The dumbness was only temporary, however: he called at Hanover Square afterwards, cornered his sister, and expatiated at length on the virtues of each.

'And when I said I'd had enough of carriages,' Fleur complained indignantly to Sir Frederick as they entered the Exhibition a little later, 'he began all over again with Colonel Colt's repeating firearms!'

'Ah yes, they can fire ten bullets without the need to reload, can't they? Just think what that would mean in a battle!'

'Six. I assure you I know all about it,' Fleur said drily.

'At the risk of maddening you, I must say I'd like to see those myself. Shall we start with the American section today?'

'If you like.' They showed their tickets and passed through. 'But it's becoming a regular hazard at social engagements. Everyone you meet says "Have you seen so-and-so?" and before you can say yes or no, they plunge on and describe it to you in the minutest detail! The only defence is to get in first with your own dissertation. I'm working up a very pretty speech about the patent envelope-making machine which I shall recite, with or without provocation, to everyone I meet.'

'They won't hear a word,' Sir Frederick laughed. 'Where's your lovesick swain today? I must say, I'm getting quite used to tripping over him in every doorway.'

'I don't know,' Fleur said indifferently. 'We had a disagreement yesterday over the statue of the Greek Slave.'

'Ah yes. Nauseating piece of work, isn't it? Sentimental and prurient at the same time.'

The catalogue described it as 'a young and beautiful Greek girl, deprived of her clothing, and exposed for sale to some wealthy Eastern barbarian'. The nude creature languished artistically, a length of chain from between her shackled wrists draped carefully where her modesty most required it. It had already become, astonishingly, the most popular exhibit in the Crystal Palace.

'So I said, but Teddy said it was nice. Nice, of all things!'

Frederick raised an eyebrow. 'And that was enough to cause you to quarrel?'

'Oh, we didn't exactly quarrel, but I'm afraid I teased him rather. When he said he thought it was beautiful, I said I hadn't realised his taste ran to simpering ninnies—'

'Cruel, Fleur!'

'And I asked him to explain why a mere girl, conspicuously naked in a public market place, needed to be restrained with chains and shackles. I'm afraid he thought I was being unwomanly and coarse.'

'And so you were,' Frederick grinned. 'Shame on you! No wonder he's punishing you by staying away.'

'Oh, as to that, I expect it's just that he's on duty today.'

'Not before time, judging by the amount of time he's spent in London this last week. I thought Engineer officers were different, but it seems they're just as idle as the rest.'

Fleur said nothing. It had occurred to her to wonder why Teddy had so much time off duty, but he was a very accommodating person to go round the Exhibition with, so she had not enquired too closely.

Frederick glanced at her and said, 'I've been thinking, Fleur, that you may just have to hint that young man away, unless you mean anything serious by him.'

'Teddy knows how I feel. I've told him I won't marry him, and that we can never be more than friends.'

'Yes, love, but it's in the nature of the malady not to believe in *never*. A man in love is an optimist, as long as there's anything he can interpret as encouragement. It's so much easier to think that the apple will drop into your hand, if you just go on shaking the tree long enough.'

Fleur coloured. 'It's all such nonsense!'

'Is it?' he said, looking at her thoughtfully. 'Well, perhaps – but persuasive nonsense, all the same. I think your Teddy is more smitten than you like to believe, and it would be a kindness in you to keep him a little more at arm's length.'

Aunt Venus's new barouche was a smart one, and the pair of bays harnessed to it met even with Buckley's approval, so having resigned herself to not riding, Fleur took her place beside her unlikely companion with a pleasant smile. She was wearing a killing new *Barèges* carriage-gown, which had only just come back from the mantuamakers, and the sea-green bonnet with the pink satin lining, and knew she was looking her best. As they were conducted at a sober pace by her aunt's elderly coachman along the fashionable drive, she was aware of heads turning as they passed.

'Ah, how they all envy me!' Mr Polotski chuckled. 'It makes me feel young again. My Sophie was such a one as you, when she was your age. Not so truly beautiful, but she had that certain something. You do me so much good, mademoiselle – I cannot tell you how grateful I am.'

'You've no need to be grateful, sir,' Fleur said, embarrassed.

'And green of all colours suits you,' he went on, eyeing her approvingly. 'It is the colour of life. I could wish the Polotski Emerald were mine, so that I could set it for you. It is too beautiful never to be worn.'

'Who does it belong to?'

'To the Emperor, of course. He has merely lent it for the Exhibition.' Polotski told her the story of how he had found it quite by chance, many years ago, in a river in India. He was on a journey to Katmandu to buy silk rugs, and had stopped to water his horse. The animal had pawed at the riverbed, as horses do, and the emerald had simply rolled to Polotski's feet. It was too big ever to be able to sell to an individual, so he had given it to the Tsar.

'That was very generous of you,' Fleur remarked. 'I wonder you could bear to part with it.'

'I was repaid in favours,' Polotski told her. 'Licences and monopolies. That is how I've risen to my present eminence. But yes, it was hard to part with it, knowing it would spend its life in a strongroom, unseen. And after I had put so much of myself into it! The cutting and polishing took me many months, you know. But when it was finished, it was like everything green in the world, distilled into that one stone. I always knew that it would be the best thing I had ever done.'

'So you worked it, too? I didn't realise.'

'I would not have trusted anyone else. Even then, I was so afraid that I would do something wrong. One slip! With such a stone, there is no second chance. But when it is something very important, it is better to live with your own mistakes than someone else's, don't you agree?'

'I haven't thought about it – I suppose so.'

'However, I made no mistakes. To tell the truth, I think I was under guidance from a surer hand than mine,' he smiled.

'But you sound as though you enjoyed doing it.'

'I was a good jewelsmith, and it made me happy to do what I was good at. A man should know what he is good for – and a woman, too, of course. Even now, when I feel restless, or have a problem to think out, I go to my little workroom and try my hand at something. Besides,' he chuckled, 'it's as well to keep in practice. The Emperor has raised me high, but you never know in my country when you might fall from favour and have to begin again.'

'It seems that Russia is a dangerous place,' she said doubtfully.

'Not for you. When you come—'

'*When* I come?'

'But of course you will! You and your father and your aunt and uncle must all come. You have all been so kind to me, and Russians are very hospitable. You must come and stay in my house in Petersburg. And you most especially, Mademoiselle Fleur! I want so much for Sophie to meet you.'

'I cannot think it will ever be in my power,' Fleur began.

'Would you like to?'

'Yes, very much.'

93

He nodded as if that were all it took. 'Then you will come. You will like Russia. It is very beautiful and very romantic.' He eyed her consideringly. 'Yes, and Russia will like you. We admire the English , but they are sometimes stiff and haughty, and that does not suit us. We like to laugh, you see, and to dance, and to play foolish games; and when we fall in love – ah!' He laid a hand on his heart and rolled his eyes up to heaven. Fleur laughed. 'Yes I think we must find you a Russian husband. Nothing less will do – a passionate Russian husband who will adore you and buy you sapphires and sing to you.'

'How do you know he will sing to me?' Fleur asked, enjoying his nonsense.

'All Russians sing when they are in love. That is how I won my Sophie. I sang her a song about a maiden who refused her lover: he went away to war and was killed in battle, and she was so heartbroken she pined away and died. A wonderful song, and it made Sophie cry very much, so of course she fell in love with me. Shall I sing it to you now?'

'Please do!'

Polotski began to sing. He had a fine basso voice surprisingly deep and powerful for such a small, stout man, and eyeing her sideways, he drew out the tragic phrases more lugubriously the more Fleur laughed. He was quite unselfconscious, and though Fleur could see the coachman's ears standing out almost at right angles with surprise and disapproval, she derived a wicked enjoyment from the situation, and from the astonished stares they were drawing from the passing carriages.

The last heartbreaking note died away. Polotski turned upon Fleur and said severely, 'It is a very sad song. You are not supposed to laugh, mademoiselle!'

And then there was a flurry of movement and Teddy Scott appeared on horseback beside the carriage, looking hot and flustered.

'What the deuce is going on, Fleur?' he cried, reining his horse too hard and making it start and fling its head about 'Everyone's staring at you!'

'Hullo, Teddy,' Fleur said. Her first feeling on seeing him was a faint irritation. Must he intrude himself just when she was enjoying herself? And now he was going to bombast about propriety and feminine reserve. But he was an old friend, and she tried for a neutral tone of voice. 'I'm surprised to see you here.'

'Surprised? You're surprising the whole of Hyde Park!' He turned impetuously on Polotski. 'Don't you realise, sir, that you're making Miss Hamilton conspicuous with that damned row?'

'No, I didn't realise,' said Polotski pleasantly. 'I was only singing. Do not the English sing?'

'Not in public, they don't. Damn it, don't you see how everyone's staring? Do you mean to make her a figure of fun?'

'Mr Scott,' Fleur said sharply, 'that's enough.'

'Don't you care what people think?' he rounded on her.

'Not in the least. I had much sooner enjoy myself.'

'Even if it means making yourself a spectacle?'

'It's you who are making us conspicuous,' she said, angry now. 'Lower your voice, and stop scowling at me like that!'

'No, dash it, Fleur—!'

'I won't have you quarrel with me in public, as though you had rights over me!'

'Anyone who cares about you—'

'And you have been unforgivably rude to my guest! You will apologise to Mr Polotski at once.'

'No, I'm damned if I will!'

'How dare you!'

'Peace, peace, children,' Polotski chuckled. 'I am too old to be the subject of a squabble. I think Mr Scott has some other cause of anguish besides my singing – am I right?' He looked at Teddy shrewdly. 'I think perhaps he wishes it was him in the carriage beside you, mademoiselle. Ah, but I should cut a poor figure on your horse, sir, and so I cannot oblige you by exchanging!'

Scott scowled so horribly that Fleur knew Polotski had struck the truth, and her anger dissolved instantly. Controlling her desire to laugh, which she knew would hurt

95

Teddy's already wounded feelings, she said seriously, 'What *are* you doing here, Mr Scott? Shouldn't you be at Woolwich?'

'I managed to get a few hours' release, so I thought I'd come and take you riding. You *said* you wanted to ride this afternoon,' he said reproachfully. 'Then they told me at Hanover Square you'd gone out in the carriage, so I came after you, but I never thought I'd find you with this – this person, making such a – what I mean is – oh *damn*!'

In the face of Polotski's unrepentant amusement, it was impossible for him to go on being righteously angry. His ears scarlet, he turned his head away and faced forward, staring between his horse's ears as it paced beside the carriage, concentrating on breathing deeply and trying to repress his hurt and jealous fury. Fleur didn't care enough about the conventions, that was the truth of it, he thought. It was all very well being high-spirited, but she never thought how it looked to other people; and as for preferring queer birds like this Russky merchant to the company of a proper English gentleman . . .

Polotski remembered well enough what it was to be young and in love, and said meekly, 'Perhaps I did sing rather too loudly, mademoiselle. I forgot that we are in England, not Russia, and that such things will not do. I beg your pardon. And yours, sir. You were quite right to point it out.'

'Oh well, no, that's all right,' Teddy muttered, a little mollified. 'It's just that – I just thought – by Jove!' Something caught his eye and he abandoned the utterance with relief. He stared a moment, and then turned to Fleur. 'If I don't mistake, there's your tall stranger at last! Your rescuer.'

'No, where?' Fleur cried excitedly.

'In that barouche coming towards us. No, not that one, the second one. Don't you see him, sitting beside the little dark fellow with the scrap of a beard and the fuzzy hair? I'm sure it's him.'

'Yes! It is him! So he is still in London. Oh, I'm so glad!'

Polotski, who had heard the story, craned round with interest to look. 'That little dark fellow, as you call him,' he said, much amused, 'is His Excellency Mikhail Khamensky, the Imperial Commissioner to the Great Exhibition!'

'Then my stranger must be Russian too! I should have guessed it!'

'He is tall, handsome and brave: of course you should have guessed it,' Polotski agreed.

'He sees you, Fleur,' Teddy said.

'Oh sir, do you know him? What's his name?' Fleur murmured to Polotski, her eyes fixed on the approaching barouche.

Polotski glanced at her. Under her green bonnet, framed by the fluted pink satin of the lining with its edging of tiny white silk roses, her face was flushed, and her eyes were very bright. Her hands were clasped tightly together in her lap, and he felt he could almost hear her heart beating. She was very lovely, and it made him feel pleasantly, richly sad, which was how beautiful things always affected a true Russian.

'Yes, I know him,' he said. 'His name is Kirov. Count Kirov.'

The two carriages drew opposite each other. The tall stranger's eyes were fixed on Fleur's, and in a graceful gesture he did not merely lift his hat, but removed it, baring his head in the sunlight as though to a sovereign. His companion Khamensky, who had been talking to him, turned to see who Kirov was saluting, his hand going automatically to his hat. Fleur bowed her head slightly in polite acknowledgement of his compliment, but could spare little more than a glance for him, for her eyes would not leave her rescuer's face.

Too soon the moment was past. The carriages drew apart. Fleur knew better than to look back, however much she wanted to; but Teddy did, to see Kirov, resuming his hat, turn for one keen, snatched glance as Khamensky evidently questioned him about the incident. Then Teddy looked at Fleur, and saw the brightness of her eyes, the colour in her cheeks, the excitement of her slightly parted lips, and misinterpreted them.

Fleur had got herself a great deal too upset about the whole thing, he thought. He meant to tell her the next time they were alone that she might be sure the man did not want or expect any more thanks than she had already given him. He was obviously a gentleman, and would certainly not be feeling in any way offended that she had not managed to discover his identity before this. She might put the whole thing from her mind and be easy.

Polotski accounted to himself for Fleur's agitation in a very different way from Teddy Scott; but then the idea that a man of nearly forty was too old to be attractive to a young woman of Fleur's age never occurred to him.

The Duchess of Alderney's ball at Hardiway House in Grosvenor Square that evening was the most important social event of the first week of the Exhibition. Fleur dined with her aunt and uncle at Apsley House beforehand, but without her father, who had a Royal Society dinner to attend. The Duke of Wellington had known Sir Frederick's father through the bank, and was well acquainted with Sir Frederick in the House. He had, moreover, been one of Venus's mother's many public admirers, and on several occasions in the past Venus had acted as hostess for him; so he and the Hoares were on terms of some intimacy.

As a host he was always kind and affable, and he had never lost his appreciation for a pretty young woman, so Fleur's greeting from the Commander-in-Chief of the Armed Forces was everything that was kind. As she took her comparatively lowly place at the long table in the vast state dining-room, she reflected that her pleasure in dining at Apsley House must come from contemplation of the distinction of being invited. In her experience, on any occasion when there were more than twenty at the table, the sheer number of dishes to be laid out meant that they would all be cold before they could be tasted.

'And I've never been able to relish eating cold something that ought to be hot,' she remarked to her left-hand neighbour, with whom she had struck up cordial relations. He was a Captain of the Staff from Headquarters, a handsome young cavalryman named Jerome, who plainly admired Fleur. Her right-hand companion was a very stiff civilian of middle years, who seemed to think he had been placed too far down the table. He addressed two commonplace remarks to Fleur, and then, evidently regarding his duty as done, spent his time craning towards the head of the table and trying to overhear the conversations further up.

'Yes, it's a great pity the Duke still clings to the old way of serving dinner,' said Captain Jerome. 'In Russia they manage these things much better. Instead of laying everything out on the table, each dish is served separately. No matter how many guests there are, each one has a footman standing behind his chair, and everyone has the same thing served at the same instant from an individual bowl or salver. It's quite a thing to see at the Imperial banquets – five hundred soup tureens advancing as one!'

'Oh, have you been to Russia?' Fleur asked, trying to sound no more than normally interested. Since discovering her rescuer was a Russian, the word had a special resonance for her. It leapt out at her instantly from a page of print; she could pick it out of an inaudible conversation on the other side of a room. It was a word particularly hers.

She had been frustrated in her desire to question Mr Polotski, firstly by the presence of Teddy Scott, who insisted on riding beside the barouche all the way back to Hanover Square, and then by Mr Polotski's being summoned back to the Exhibition by an urgent message from his assistant. She had gone up to dress before he returned, and as he was not dining at the Duke's she would not see him until tomorrow morning. So still all she knew about her rescuer was his name.

'Yes, I was there with Seymour three years ago,' Jerome said. 'It's a fascinating place, though some of their ways take some getting used to! It seems shocking to us, but everyone there takes bribes, and getting anything done at all is a long and frustrating process. But Petersburg is the most beautiful city in the world, and the ballet and opera are beyond comparison. Do you care for the ballet, Miss Hamilton?'

'Yes, very much,' she said vaguely. She didn't want to talk about the ballet, and was wondering how to intrude the question she wanted to ask. She took a first step. 'You must have made many friends while you were in Russia?'

'Oh, yes. They're a wonderfully friendly people. And I firmly believe the Russian officers' mess is the most hospitable in Europe. I never met with more kindness anywhere.'

Fleur was working hard. 'It must have been sad for you to leave, with no knowing when you might see your friends again. In the normal way there are so few opportunities for our two nations to meet. But there are a number of Russians in London for the Exhibition, I believe – perhaps some of your particular friends may be amongst them?'

If Jerome thought her line of questioning odd, he didn't show it. 'No, none of my particular friends, though I am acquainted with some of the people who are here.'

'Do you know Count Kirov?' she asked as casually as she knew how.

Jerome glanced at her. 'Kirov? Yes, I know him slightly. Are you acquainted with him, ma'am?'

Fleur felt herself blushing and fought it. 'A nodding acquaintance only,' she said casually. 'He seems a very – pleasant gentleman. I really know very little about him, however.'

'He's from an interesting family,' Jerome said easily, leaning back a little and studying Miss Hamilton's face as he spoke. 'His mother, so the story goes, was an English governess. I don't know whether that's true or not; but his father was an eminent diplomat and stood very high with the previous Tsar, Alexander: he was one of the prime architects of the Tilsit agreement, and was Alexander's chief man in Paris for many years. Unfortunately the family suffered a reverse back in '25 – that business of the Decembrists. I expect you've read about it?'

'No. I know very little Rusian history, I'm sorry to say.'

'Well, when Tsar Alexander died there was some confusion over which of his brothers was to succeed him, and a group of army officers known as the Decembrists took advantage of the confusion to raise a rebellion, hoping for liberal reforms. It was quickly put down and came to nothing, but those involved were punished rather harshly.'

Fleur remembered stories about the way the present Tsar

had put down the Polish rebellion twenty years ago. Harshness was taken to be a normal part of Russian government, but she had never before had a personal interest in a story. 'I see. And was – did the Count—?'

'The present Count Kirov's elder brother was one of the conspirators. He was arrested and sent to Siberia, and died there a year later.'

'How horrible!'

'Yes, it must have been. From what I gathered when I was in Petersburg, the present Count wasn't implicated – well, he'd only have been a boy at the time, not more than twelve or fourteen years old, I suppose – but it was bound to cast a shadow over the whole family.'

'To see one's brother exiled to his death!' Fleur said. The sadness she had seen in his face – the marks of old sorrow: it was no wonder! 'It must have affected him deeply.'

'I believe he's regarded in Petersburg as something of a recluse. As I said, I know him only slightly – though I knew his younger brother, Petya, quite well. He was in the Preobrazhensky Guards – their crack regiment. He was a very jolly fellow.'

'Perhaps he was too young to remember the tragedy,' Fleur mused.

'Perhaps,' said Captain Jerome, with such evident indifference that Fleur felt obliged to take the hint and change the subject. She longed to ask more, but it would have looked peculiar to press the Captain further.

'If the Duke runs true to form, we shall be very late at the ball,' she remarked. 'We shall hardly arrive before the supper interval.'

'We shan't need dancing to work up an appetite, at any rate,' Jerome smiled, glancing at her empty plate. 'But Lady Alderney's suppers are famous! May I have the honour of escorting you to the supper-room, Miss Hamilton? And of the first dance afterwards?'

It was in fact after the first supper interval that the Duke's guests arrived at the ball, and Jerome was quick to re-engage

Fleur for the second supper, before being summoned to the Duke's side and disappearing with him into an ante-room.

Uncle Frederick went immediately to the card-room, and Aunt Venus, escorting Fleur to the ballroom, said she would wait only to see her with a partner before going there herself. 'A pity young Jerome has to dance attendance on the Duke – he's just the sort of young man for you. However, I don't suppose you will be long without a partner,' she added, surveying her. 'Indeed, Fleur, I've never seen you look better.'

'Thank you, Aunt,' Fleur said, surprised.

Venus continued to look at her rather searchingly, and went on, 'In fact, you are one of those women who seem to improve as they get older. Certainly you have a sort of something that you didn't have at eighteen. And a blonde must be a true beauty to wear white. Your mother couldn't. She was a pretty woman, but white made her look sickly.'

'Thank you again, Aunt.' Fleur hesitated. 'I wonder why it is that compliments from you make me feel uneasily like a prize exhibit at an Agricultural Show.'

'You are a prize exhibit, and you had better understand it, Fleur, and know your worth. I don't want you to waste yourself on the likes of young Scott.'

'And Mr Polotski?'

'Yes, Polotski too. He is a harmless enough creature – indeed, I quite like him, now I've got used to him – but to go riding with him in the Park is the outside of enough. I wouldn't have offered him the barouche if I'd known you meant to accompany him.'

'I didn't intend—'

'It's not at all the thing. People will say you keep queer company. I don't want to hear you talked of as an eccentric.'

Fleur was hurt. 'Very well, Aunt. I shall dance every dance tonight, and flirt madly with every eligible man who comes near me. That should put your mind at rest,' she said.

Venus frowned and opened her mouth to rebuke her, when they were interrupted. Lord James Paget, long one of Fleur's admirers, was beside them, making his bow.

'I see I have beat them all to it! First on the field and last off it, like the Fighting 95th, you know! May I have the honour of the next dance, Miss Hamilton?'

Flicking a glance at her aunt, Fleur turned the full force of a charming smile on the cheerful young man. 'Thank you, Lord James. I should be delighted.'

'The pleasure, ma'am, is *all* mine,' said Paget. 'Servant, Lady Hoare!' He bowed again, and whisked Fleur away for the waltz.

'You've done my aunt a great service, you know,' Fleur said as they stood waiting for the music to begin. 'You have reassured her that I am not entirely beyond redemption.'

'Beyond redemption?' Paget looked at her, puzzled. 'Why, what can she find amiss with you, Miss Hamilton?'

'I'm afraid she finds me unfeminine,' Fleur said demurely.

'You?' It was a simple and heartfelt tribute. He gazed at her in open admiration. 'But you're the most beautiful woman in the room, ma'am!'

Her gown was deceptively simple, white gauze embroidered all over with tiny white flowers, worn over an undergown of stiffened white silk. Her hair was knotted behind with blush roses, and narrow white satin ribbon threaded the long ringlets that brushed her bare shoulders.

She seemed to him the essence of womanhood, delicate, exquisite, like a porcelain figurine lovingly painted with the most skilled hand and the finest brush. Simply looking at her made him want to gather her up tenderly, and protect her from the rough realities of a harsh world.

'You have such a beautiful colour in your cheeks, Miss Hamilton,' he went on, much moved by his own perceptions, 'and your eyes are shining like stars.'

'It's this tight lacing,' she said confidingly. 'I can hardly breathe. Oh, what we suffer for fashion! Yes, it's true, Lord James! Don't laugh at me! You don't think God gives any woman a waist this small, do you?'

Fleur had always been popular at balls, being not only beautiful and a graceful dancer, but a lively conversationalist. She was never in danger of sitting out a dance, and indeed was so well supplied with partners that she was happily able to refuse Lieutenant Brooke's obliging invitation when he and Richard finally arrived.

Richard sought her out in a pause between dances to tell her that he was glad she was so popular, but that he didn't entirely approve her choice of partners.

'There's no need for you to stand up with all these old men – married men, too, some of 'em!'

'What on earth do you mean?' Fleur asked, fanning herself discreetly. Heat and lacing had given her rather too brilliant a colour.

'Well, Norrie, for instance – he's thirty-five if he's a day, and old Colonel Fawcett's antique! And Calthorpe's married, and so is Herbert. Why do that sort always want to dance with you? It ain't flattering.'

'It's because I don't flirt and languish. They know they can have a sensible conversation with me.'

'Well it doesn't do you any good, does it? You ought to start flirting, before it's too late,' Richard said wisely. 'Who's taking you in to supper?'

'Captain Jerome,' Fleur said, amused by his solicitude.

'Jerome of the Staff? Oh he's a capital fellow! Right age, good family, decent property – and a place in Leicestershire! Now if you could fix *him*, I should be quite happy.'

'Thank you, Richard,' she said gravely. 'But it would mean turning down Mr Brooke, you know.'

Richard flushed. 'Don't make fun of me. Brooke's my friend, but I know he wouldn't do for you. Damn it, Fleur, if you can't make a go of it this summer, with London full to the brim of eligible men, what's to become of you? How do you think I shall feel, if you dwindle into being a spinster and a figure of fun?'

'Much obliged to you! I shall please myself, however.'

'Do!' he retorted. 'But you can't really want to go back to Chiswick and spend the rest of your life there, visiting sick paupers and being ogled by the curate once a week.'

Fleur closed her fan with a snap. 'There's my partner looking for me. Don't worry about me, Dick, I know what I'm about,' she said sharply, and moved away.

It was the last dance before supper, and her partner, a rising star of the Foreign Office named Buckhurst, had looked forward to a lively chat with the unconventional Miss Hamilton, and even cherished hopes of cutting out Jerome and taking her in to supper on his arm. He found her unaccountably preoccupied, however, and when his best sallies had fallen flat, and his most provocative openings had been answered with bland smiles, he relapsed into a baffled silence.

Fleur was unaware of how she had disappointed her partner. Richard's words had given her pause. She had always been quite content before, wanting only to retain her independence, and to be allowed to go on pursuing her own interests without interference.

But the past week had been so full of novelty and amusement that the idea of going back to Chiswick and her usual routines had made her heart sink. This glimpse of a larger world had made her old life seem very confining; lonely and monochrome. It made her feel restless. She wanted to travel, to see strange places, to meet new people. If it were true that she had been spoiled for normal life, her future in Chiswick would be very uncomfortable.

When the dance finished Mr Buckhurst was quite happy to relinquish his place at Miss Hamilton's side; but etiquette demanded that he stay with her until her supper-companion claimed her, and at that moment Captain Jerome was nowhere in sight.

Fleur was just as eager as Buckhurst for them to part, and after a moment she said, 'Please don't feel you need to stay any longer. Your own partner will be waiting for you, and Captain Jerome will be here in a moment. I expect he's still talking to the Duke.'

'I couldn't think of leaving you, ma'am,' Buckhurst said hopefully.

'Do think of it,' she urged him, and gave him a little, friendly shove. 'Go on now, what can possibly happen to me? Do you think I shall be abducted and sold to an Eastern barbarian, like that preposterous Greek Slave? Someone is waiting for your arm to go in to supper, and you had better abandon me than offend her!'

Buckhurst grinned, remembering why he had wanted to dance with Miss Hamilton in the first place. 'If you're sure, ma'am . . .'

'I'm sure. If a white-slaver approaches me, I'll give the view halloo and you can come and rescue me.'

Everyone was in motion now, streaming towards the supper-room. Fleur decided to make her way towards the ante-room where the Duke had been holding court, to find Jerome. The crowd passing through the ballroom doors onto the staircase-hall was large and crushing, and once through the doorway Fleur extracted herself from the flood and stood aside to wait until it abated a little.

She was standing to one side of the door, inspecting the gauze of her skirt for damage, when a voice at her side said in French, 'Ah, my God, is it really you? At last, at last!'

Fleur felt the hair rise on the nape of her neck. She turned her head and looked up, but could not think of anything to say. Her tall stranger was there beside her, looking down at her with an expression in his strange and beautiful eyes which made her feel suddenly light-headed.

'I've looked everywhere for you, and until that moment in the Park when I passed your carriage, I thought I must have dreamed you! But you are real. I see now my poor imagination could never have invented you.'

He possessed himself of her hand, and pressed his lips to it. It was a gesture quite devastating, and wholly foreign. No English gentleman could or would have kissed her hand like that. Her heart seemed to be doing erratic things inside her, which made it quite difficult to breathe.

'I've remembered your face perfectly these two weeks, but still I do not know your name,' he went on. 'Please allow me to present myself. I am Count Sergei Nikolayevitch Kirov, most entirely yours to command!'

'Yes, I know,' she said foolishly.

Chapter Six

'You know?' he said, raising his brows. They were very fine brows, she noticed, delicately marked in a good arch. She imagined running her finger over them, and shocked herself into a blush.

'I mean, I know you are Count Kirov. Not the rest, of course.' I'm babbling, she observed in surprise. What is wrong with me?

He smiled sympathetically, as if he knew what she was thinking. 'We can't talk here. Come, give me your hand.'

He presented his sleeve to her, and without understanding how it had happened, she found herself walking with him in the opposite direction from the supper-room. A moment later they stepped back into the fast-emptying ballroom by the small door at the end, next to the dais on which the musicians had been sitting. The musicians had left in search of refreshment, and this end of the ballroom was empty. There was a bank of greenery, including some well-grown parlour palms in great pots, marking the corner of the dais, and in the shelter of this the Count stopped and faced Fleur again.

'This will do for the moment. Tell me at once,' he said, 'you took no harm from those ruffians?'

'No, none at all. I was shaken and angry more than hurt.'

'Thank God! I've been so worried. I was afraid of the reaction you might suffer afterwards. But you have spirit – you wouldn't let it devastate you.'

Looking up at him, Fleur found that she had not remembered anything about him except for his eyes – and even there she had remembered only a shadow of the reality. They were extraordinary, luminous, and that strangely beautiful rim around the irises gave him the look of something untamed.

The rest of his face was in accord with his eyes. There was nothing of the English gentleman in his looks: it was a long face, foreign from the high cheekbones to the strong, indented chin; dark without being swarthy, powerful without being coarse. His mouth was long, sensitive, expressive, but marked at the corners with lines of deep unhappiness. His hair was fine and thick, almost straight, the colour a dark gold-brown, like old bronze.

It was a face so unfamiliar, so wild, it might have come out of a dream; yet she felt as though she had always known it. I knew you in some other place, long ago, she thought involuntarily. That was foolish; yet she felt no restraint with him, no need of formality between them.

'Why did you go away so suddenly that day?' she asked. 'I wanted to thank you. I didn't even know your name—'

'But you know it now?'

'Someone told me. Why did you go away?'

'I felt there were already too many people around you. The young man, your friend, was there to take care of you, and the sooner you were removed from the insult of those staring eyes, the better.'

'Yes, that's what I wanted most of all, to get away from them.'

'I know. And if I had stayed it would only have delayed matters. Your friend would have felt obliged to thank me.' He smiled suddenly, 'But I didn't think it would be so hard to find you again.'

'Have you really tried to?'

'Do you need to ask?' he said. Since she was sixteen, she had been accustomed to being flirted with, and from an Englishman she would have known this for flirtation. But with him she was unsure. She felt a little dizzy; though perhaps that was only because she had to tilt her head so far back to look at him.

'I enquired everywhere, I described you to everyone, but no one seemed to know who I meant,' he went on. 'I began to think I must have been dreaming – and then when I did see you again at last, there was nothing I could do about it! I couldn't ask Khamensky to stop the carriage, not there, blocking the drive. I was wild with frustration – and then he told me that he didn't even know who you were!

"No," he said, "I cannot put a name to your elusive flower"—'

'That's my name,' she said faintly. 'Fleur.'

'But how astonishing! Since the moment I first saw you, that is how I have thought of you. I said to Khamensky: "She is like a flower", and we always referred to you that way. But quickly, let me know your other name, so that I don't lose you again.'

'Hamilton,' she said, feeling suddenly self-conscious. She wished it had been a less sturdy, more euphonious name. 'I am Miss Fleur Hamilton.'

He was puzzled. 'Hamilton? But that is an English name. Are you not French?'

'No,' she said.

They had been speaking in French; now he dropped into English as if it were equally easy to him. 'Then it's no wonder I couldn't find you!' he said, smiling. 'I've been asking everywhere for the beautiful French girl with the golden hair who looks like a wild rose! But why did you speak to me in French that day?'

'You spoke to me in French, so naturally I answered in French.' He didn't seem to find this an adequate answer, so she went on, 'I am English, my father is English, but my mother was French. We spoke both at home.'

'I see. Well, I am Russian, my Russian father usually spoke French, and my mother was English. We spoke all three at home, with a little German thrown in for good measure!'

'Then it's true that your mother was an English governess?'

He looked at her with interest. 'Who told you that?'

Before she could answer there was the sound of boot-heels on the echoing floor, and Captain Jerome's voice, level, but perhaps admonitory, said, 'Miss Hamilton!'

She turned guiltily. The ballroom was now empty except for them and the approaching Jerome. She flung a distracted look in his direction, and said to the Count, 'It's my supper-partner. I'd forgotten all about him.'

'I'm flattered,' Kirov murmured with a slow smile.

'But we shouldn't be standing here like this, all alone,' Fleur said, with palpable regret in her voice.

He continued to smile. 'Don't worry, I shan't disgrace you. The proprieties shall be observed. I must go and join my party, but may I dance with you later? Tell me when I may come to you.'

'The second after supper,' she said quickly, and turned as Jerome reached them.

'I beg your pardon, Miss Hamilton, for being so late,' he said gravely. 'The Duke detained me, and then I went first to the supper-room, thinking you must have grown tired of waiting for me and gone ahead.'

Before Fleur could say anything, the Count bowed to Jerome and said, 'Now you are here, sir, I shall feel no apprehension in leaving Miss Hamilton to your care. Please excuse me, ma'am: I am waited for by the Ambassador's party.' He bowed to her, too, with an air of calm civility, and left them. It was well done, Fleur thought, placing her hand on Jerome's offered arm; he could not think there was anything untoward in the situation.

Jerome, leading the way towards the supper-room, seemed to be frowning in thought. A moment later he said in a strange, flat voice, 'A curious coincidence, ma'am, that we had just been talking about Count Kirov. I had no idea you knew him so well.'

'It is only a slight acquaintance, Captain, as I told you,' Fleur said. But of course, he had seen them standing very close together, alone in an empty ballroom, and talking without restraint or formality. The arm beneath her hand was stiff with disapproval, and all at once she had a rather heartening sense that adventure, excitement and mystery had entered her mundane life at last. She decided that she didn't mind shocking people when it was something worth shocking them over, and walked beside Jerome with her head up and a small, pleased smile hovering about her lips.

She did her best during the supper interval to respond to Captain Jerome's conversation and to refrain from looking towards the door, but her mind was elsewhere, and the interval seemed long and weary. Why must people eat so much? What sickening things oyster patties were! How nauseating cold tongue, and cold duck like strips of grey, greased leather! Out of the corner of an eye she watched a woman eat a creamed-chicken basket and then smile fascinatingly at her companion, unaware that a flake of pastry was stuck to her upper lip.

It was hot and she was thirsty and Jerome brought her a glass of champagne, which she drank rather quickly. She realised she had been answering him almost at random, and tried to make amends by being vivacious. Some other young officers, including Paget and two more of her former partners, drifted across to join them, and she laughed and chattered brightly to them, plying her fan vigorously to cool her burning cheeks. Jerome looked at her strangely and refrained from offering her more champagne; and when he replaced the glass in her hand with a dish of iced sherbet, she barely noticed the substitution. *He* had not come into the supper-room at all. The Ambassador's party must be in some ante-room having deep and important discussions, she thought. Would the interval never be over?

When everyone was in motion again, back to the ballroom, Jerome offered her his arm and said to her quietly, 'Are you feeling ill, Miss Hamilton? You look flushed, almost feverish.'

Fleur turned to him, grateful for the excuse to escape. 'I am finding the heat rather trying,' she said. 'If you would be so kind as to excuse me our dance, I would like to retire for a few minutes.'

He bowed gravely. 'Of course. Can I send anyone to you, or tell anyone?'

'No, thank you. I am quite well, I assure you, only a little hot and breathless.'

He escorted her to the foot of the stairs and she thanked him again and almost ran up to the retiring-room. There, under the curious gaze of the attendant, she sat before the mirror and looked at the reflection of her brilliant eyes and cheeks. She looked somehow different to herself, more vivid, more alive. What has happened to me? she thought.

Sergei Nikolayevitch . . . What wonderful sounds the Russian names make! *Sergei* . . . He said I was like a wild rose! How foolish it would sound from the lips of a Captain Jerome; but from him, in his voice, with his accent . . . His voice – almost tangible. I love the sound of his voice. I almost feel it on my skin . . .

'Are you all right, miss?' the attendant asked. 'Shall I get you some water? Only you look quite uncomfortable.'

'No thank you. I'm quite all right,' Fleur said absently, examining her reflection critically. She tweaked a curl into place and bit her lips to redden them.

'P'raps you'd like to lay down a bit, miss? P'raps you're laced a bit too tight—?'

'No, no, it's just that it's very hot in the ballroom. Would you powder my shoulders, please.'

It must be time to go back now. Where would he come to her? If she lingered a little on the stair, in the corridor, perhaps she would meet him looking for her . . . He had looked for her, he said, everywhere . . .

She was accosted before she reached the ballroom, but not by the Count.

'Hsst! Fleur! There you are!'

She started and turned. 'Teddy! What on earth are you doing here? I didn't know you were invited.'

'I wasn't, but it doesn't matter. There are so many people here, no one will notice an extra face.'

'But how did you get in? Why is your jacket twisted like that? And you've snagged your overalls. You look as though you've been climbing trees.'

He straightened his jacket quickly and brushed himself down. 'Only one – up it and over the garden wall. But there was a bit of a drop the other side.'

She began at last to take in what he was saying. 'You don't mean to tell me – Teddy, are you mad? You must go at once, before anyone sees you!'

'What, before I've had a dance with you? That would be poor sport!' he said, catching at her hand.

She pulled it away sharply. 'Don't be a fool! The ballroom's

112

full of military people. Good God, the Duke's here! You're not unknown, nor invisible. Don't you realise the trouble you'll be in if you're recognised?'

'I'm in trouble already,' he said lightly. 'I might as well be hung for a sheep as a lamb.'

'Oh God, what else have you done?'

'I'm here without leave. I'm supposed to be duty officer. Oh, don't worry – nobody saw me go. I went over the wall there, too. I'm getting quite good at walls.'

She stared at him, perplexed. 'But – I don't understand. Why did you do it?'

'To have a dance with you, of course.'

'Oh, don't be an ass!'

He looked taken aback at her reaction. 'I mean it. Don't you know the hero dares all for love? Well, I risked everything just for one dance with you – and it'll be worth it!'

'Oh Teddy!' she cried, exasperated. 'How could you be such an idiot! Go back at once, before anyone sees you! How could you think I'd want to dance with you on such terms? You could be court-martialled for this! Oh really, you are too tiresome!'

He looked utterly crestfallen. 'But – but I did it for you! To make you see how – to make you love me. I thought if I showed you how much I love you and – how I'm adventurous and – and everything – that you'd marry me.' He reached involuntarily for her hand, his next words blurted out from the heart. 'Oh Fleur, please won't you? I can't get used to the army!'

She put her hands behind her. 'I thought you were beginning to like it.'

'I like building bridges all right, but it's the drills and manoeuvres I can't get used to. I can never remember what I'm supposed to be doing – I'm always getting things wrong. And I hate having to do things to order. I just want to be able to get up when I please and walk about the fields with a gun, the way I'm used to.'

She felt an unwilling sympathy. 'Poor Teddy! I am sorry for you, but you must understand once for all that I won't marry you. If you dislike the army so much, tell your father—'

'He wouldn't listen,' Scott said bitterly. 'He thinks it's good for people to do what they don't like.'

'Well I don't, and I don't want to marry you, and doing things like this only makes me cross with you.' She glanced over her shoulder nervously. 'Now for God's sake, go, before someone comes! Go on, now, back to barracks, and pray they won't have missed you. Go down the stairs and out of the door in the normal way, and try not to look guilty or you'll draw attention to yourself.'

'But can't I—?'

'Not another word – go!' She propelled him towards the stairs, and watched, biting her lip, as he trotted down them, with every appearance of having his tail between his legs.

She felt horribly guilty as well as angry with him. She ought to have been harder on him from the beginning, as soon as she realised his feelings towards her had changed. Uncle Frederick had been right: Teddy had taken her complacency for encouragement. It was so unfair that a woman couldn't continue on terms of ordinary friendship with a man she had known all her life! But there was no use in struggling against reality, however unpalatable, and the truth was that Teddy was not as intelligent as she. If he got into trouble over this idiotic scrape, it would be at least partly her fault.

'Something has happened to upset you,' the Count said. She re-entered the ballroom just as the music of the first dance finished, and before she could look around, he was at her side, looking down into her face searchingly. Her pulse quickened at the sense of intimacy she felt with him. Already he knew her so well, that he could tell her mood at one glance.

'Oh – it's nothing,' she said.

'Did that young officer say something he should not?' the Count asked.

She was startled for a moment, and then realised that he meant Jerome.

'No, not at all. He's all politeness.'

'Yes, I know that sort of Englishman, and very wearying they must be to a woman of spirit! I promise you I shall never be *all* politeness to you.'

She laughed, the shadows passing for the moment from her mind. 'Thank you. That would be treating me with true kindness! You can't imagine how tiresome it can be sometimes to be a female. No one takes you at your word, or thinks you can mean what you say, or that you know your own mind.'

'I dare say,' he said, offering her his arm as the floor began to fill for the next dance, 'that in England as in Russia there are a great many women who don't mean what they say, or have any mind of their own to know. It's largely the fault of their education, of course.'

'Is Russia like that too? Here women are supposed to be decorations for a gentleman's drawing-room. They're taught only enough to make them useful in that capacity.'

'Yes, it's the same. The *appearance* of accomplishment is all that's required in most cases. But there is one important difference: in Russia women are equal before the law. Empress Catherine saw to that. And a married woman retains absolute control over her own property, which means that she has much greater freedom than any Englishwoman.'

Fleur was struck with this. 'Yes, it must do! With her own independent income, she might leave a husband who didn't please her.'

He smiled. 'Economics and love are not usually thought to be interdependent subjects.'

'I was talking of matrimony rather than love,' Fleur said unguardedly.

'Are they are not the same thing for you?'

She felt her colour rise. 'I know nothing of either, sir,' she said shortly.

'But your mind jumped straight to divorce! You are thinking too far ahead, Miss Hamilton,' he said gravely. 'One step at a time.'

A retort rose to her lips, and then she saw the laughter in his eyes, and realised he was roasting her. 'You mustn't invite me to expose myself like that. It isn't fair.'

115

The music began. At once she longed to feel his arm round her waist, and for an instant was tempted to tell him so; but no, that would be too unbecomingly *fast*. Yet when he took her hand in his, and passed his other arm around her, she knew with mad certainty that he was thinking the same thing. She looked up into his face, and was lost.

'What is it?' he asked. 'What did that searching look mean?'

Out of the reeling of her senses she plucked an amazingly calm response. 'I was thinking that I can tell at once you will be a good dancer. I've been gripped, and hauled on like a halliard, and stumbled over, by too many tyros, to have the least doubt about it.'

'Now you've put me in a quake. I shall be so afraid of disappointing you, I shall probably trip and bring us both down,' he said without the slightest anxiety.

She had been dancing the waltz since she was sixteen, and had known many young men with whom it was a pleasure to dance; but from the first steps she knew this was a wholly different experience. For a while they did not speak; then he nodded to her approvingly and said, 'Very good! You understand that one cannot converse and dance at the same time, and do justice to both.'

'Not if one dances like this,' she said blissfully. 'It's like flying.'

'Have you ever flown?' he enquired politely.

'In dreams, sometimes.'

He smiled down at her, and she noticed how he looked very much more different when he smiled from when he didn't smile, than anyone else she had ever met. His long mouth curled upwards at the corners in a way which made her feel quite hollow. 'Fly, then,' he said. 'We'll talk when the music stops.'

For her choice, in that case, they would never have spoken again, for she would have liked to go on dancing with him like this for ever. She leaned into the strong circle of his arm, feeling by instinct, or perhaps by a kind of telegraphic communication through his hands and eyes, what he was going to do next. Her feet whirled amongst his, and never touched

116

them, and they swirled tirelessly down the long side of the floor and spun at the corners so fast that the lights and the reflections in the mirrors were a dazzling blur.

I never want to stop, she said inside her mind; and I never want to dance with anyone else; and she saw the reflection of her thoughts in his eyes and wondered if she'd said them aloud. And when the music did stop at last, she felt so disappointed she almost wanted to cry.

'It will begin again soon,' he said, as if answering her. 'Until then, we may talk. You are not breathless?'

'No – though I don't understand why I'm not.'

'Remind me to tell you why one day. In the meantime, tell me who told you my name before we met here.'

'Mr Polotski. He's here for the Exhibition. He's the exhibitor of—'

'Yes, I know who he is. What were you doing riding in the Park with him in a barouche?'

'Is the barouche part important?' she asked demurely.

'It might be,' he said sternly. 'Was it yours or his?'

'It's my aunt's. He's staying at my uncle's house in Hanover Square. My uncle is Sir Frederick Hoare, the MP. He knows Baron Brunnow.'

'And your uncle invited him to stay?'

'Mr Polotski is a very nice man,' Fleur said defensively, responding to the surprise in his voice.

'Yes, Polotski is a good man, but he is a merchant, and the English *noblesse* are usually very stiff about such things.'

Fleur smiled. 'My Uncle Frederick is an unusual man. And he's interested in drains.'

'Drains?'

'Drains and sewers. Pipes of all sort, really. I wonder,' she thought of it suddenly, 'whether it's something to do with the mystery of them – never knowing, quite, where they'll lead you? A sort of longing for adventure?'

'What has that to do with Mr Polotski riding in your aunt's barouche?' he asked dangerously.

'Oh, nothing,' she said hastily, 'only Baron Brunnow asked Uncle Frederick to have Mr Polotski to stay, because Mr

Polotski's interested in the new porcelain water-closets, so he thought they'd get on well together.'

He looked enlightened. 'Yes, Polotski's been commissioned to study them by the Emperor, with a view to installing them in his private palace at Gatchina.'

'You know all about it, then?'

'Part of my purpose here is to report on him to the Emperor.'

She was shocked. 'To spy on him, you mean?'

'If you prefer,' he said indifferently.

'I don't think I like that,' Fleur said uneasily. The new concept placed a distance between them, and she didn't want to feel separate from him.

'It needn't trouble you,' he said. 'I dare say that part of Polotski's orders are to report on me. That's the way things work in Russia.'

'But – all in the cause of water-closets?'

He raised an eyebrow. 'You are unusual for an English gentlewoman, Miss Hamilton. You mention the unmentionable, and at a public ball, and to a complete stranger.'

'Oh, but you're not—' It was out before she could stop herself.

He looked delighted. 'That's better. I'm glad you think so,' he said. 'Tell me about your mother and father. Don't they mind your riding in a carriage with Merchant Polotski?'

'Mama died when I was a little girl,' she said. Suddenly, in the way that hadn't happened now for years, she was back in that dread room, crowded with draperies and false smells, facing the Shape on the white bed. She trembled. The musicians were about to strike up again, and it gave him the excuse to take hold of her hand. His fingers were warm and strong, holding hers steady against his breast. She focused on them. There was a flower in his buttonhole she noticed – not clove pinks this time, but a white rosebud, beginning to open a little in the heat of the ballroom. Its pale lips were just parted, revealing its creamy, perfumed heart. It was a pasquali, and the scent was cool and clear; the image of her mother's room receded before it.

'It's over now,' he said. She looked up at him. He regarded her gravely, steadily. 'What about your papa?'

'Papa doesn't care what I do,' she said. It sounded rather harsh, and she elaborated. 'He doesn't mind about that sort of thing anyway. He doesn't mind who people are, only what they do. He's travelled a great deal, you see, and to some very uncivilised places, which makes a difference.'

'Of course it does.' The music began, his arm was round her waist again. 'Now we must dance. No more talking.'

Fleur's mind was whirling almost as much as her body during the second waltz. How had he known she needed comforting? How could she feel so close to him? What would happen next? But when the music ended there was no time for more conversation. Before she could draw breath, he was leaving her.

'I have to dance with Lady Pennington,' he said. The evening was almost over. There would only be another two or three dances, and it would look too particular if she were to dance with him again so soon. Seeming to read the question in her eyes, he lifted her fingers to his lips and imprinted a brief, hard kiss on them. 'Bless you! Don't be afraid – we will meet again.'

'But when—?' she began, hardly knowing what it would be proper to ask.

'You must trust me,' he said abruptly. 'What is your father's name?'

'Sir Ranulph Hamilton,' she said, obedient but bewildered.

It seemed to afford him some satisfaction. 'Ah, very good,' he said, and then he was gone.

There were so many questions left unanswered. Well for him, she thought a little resentfully as she rode home in the closed coach with her aunt and uncle, with her feet hot from dancing and her ribs aching from the tightness of her stays, to say they would meet again and she must trust him! Why was it always the man's part to be active and arrange things, while the woman could do nothing but wait passively for her fate? *He* wouldn't care for it, if he knew there was nothing he could do to determine matters one way or the other. He might at least have dropped a hint about his intentions.

Where could they meet? In the Park? But she had been riding there for two weeks without seeing him. Perhaps, she thought with sudden anguish, he hadn't meant anything by those parting words. Perhaps she had read too much into the whole incident. She was overwrought, her imagination overheated. The man who had rescued her in the Park had danced with her, that was all. What could be more natural, and why should anything more follow?

She remembered that last kiss on her imprisoned fingers, heard him again saying 'Bless you! We will meet again.' So many things he had said! She knew she would go over and over them, trying this meaning and that against them for fit, until they ceased to have any meaning at all. But she *hadn't* imagined it all! He said he had searched for her – she hadn't imagined that; and he said she was like a wild rose. 'Tell me your other name, so that I don't lose you again.' Oh, they must meet again – they *must*!

Her uncle's voice came out of the darkness beside her. 'What a beautiful night! So warm and tranquil. I think this is going to be the best summer we've had for years.'

Aunt Venus replied with some commonplace, but Fleur's thoughts had taken another direction. The summer! He was here for some purpose, as yet unknown to her, but certainly associated with the Exhibition. In October the Exhibition would close and all the foreign visitors would disperse, back to their homelands. In October, or perhaps before, he would go back to Russia. A few months, at the benevolent most, was all she had.

'You shivered – are you cold, Flor, my dear?' said Uncle Frederick. 'Here, sit closer, and I'll put my arm round you. There's not much in these flimsy things you wear to keep out the night air, even on a night as balmy as this.'

It was only an Uncle Frederick arm, but it was comforting. Relaxing against his warm bulk, her chest aching and her feet scorching, Fleur began to yawn.

'Now, here's a charming sight,' said Mr Polotski, rising from his seat at the breakfast-table. 'I did not expect to see you this morning, mademoiselle. Not in bed until four, and up again at seven?'

Fleur sat down and reached for the coffee pot. 'I woke up and couldn't go back to sleep. How did you know what time we got home, sir?'

'I heard the carriage pull up. My room is at the front, you know. And the church clock struck just afterwards.' She covered a yawn, and he studied her pale face and over-bright eyes. 'How was your grand ball? Did you have good dancing?'

'Yes, very agreeable,' she said. 'And you'll never guess who was there.'

'Count Kirov,' he said genially.

She looked at him suspiciously. 'How did you know that?'

'As a matter of fact, my man Stefan heard it from your aunt's coachman, who heard it from one of the porters at the great house, who heard it from one of the lady's maids who was watching the dancing.' She was looking confused, and he added, 'But I would have guessed it anyway. I knew that the Ambassador was to be there with a large party, and I would have been surprised if it did not include Count Kirov.'

'Oh, I see.'

'And if he was there, I should have been surprised if you had not spoken with him.' There was the faintest of question marks at the end of his sentence. Fleur, frowning a little, did not seem to have heard it, but his continuing silence prompted her in the end to speak.

'We danced together,' she said at last. 'But there wasn't really enough time to talk properly.'

'You didn't talk while you danced?'

'No.' She looked a little self-conscious. 'He said – he said that one could not dance and talk at the same time and do justice to both.'

'Yes, he is right,' Polotski said. His lips smiled politely, but his eyes were grave. 'It was – an elegant remark, as one would expect from him.'

'He's a strange man, isn't he?' Fleur said lightly.

'I think most women find him an attractive man,' Polotski said, watching her from under his eyelids as he carefully removed the backbone from a kipper.

'Yes,' she said very quietly, almost to herself. Though her face was pale from lack of sleep, there was a bright spot of colour on each cheekbone. 'I suppose they would.' She thought a moment, and then seemed to make up her mind to something. 'We had so little time to talk, I didn't even find out what he is doing in London. He seemed to know all about you, sir. I wondered perhaps if you knew all about him, too? I suppose he's here for the Exhibition?'

'Yes, I suppose so,' Polotski said. He laid the delicate fire-ladder of bone to the side of his plate, and if he sighed, only the kipper heard it. 'It is not a secret that Count Kirov is one of the Emperor's personal aides-de-camp. His Majesty has many such, all gentlemen from noble families, who report directly to him. They perform special tasks for him – usually investigating delicate situations, or gathering information, or doing detailed studies of new processes or ideas.'

Fleur looked at him keenly. Gathering information? Was that the loathsome 'spying' he had not denied? She didn't want it to be that. 'Is that what he's doing here? In London? Gathering information?'

'Officially he is one of the team of observers for the Exhibition. That is the capacity in which I know of him, through Commissioner Khamensky—'

'Officially? You mean he has some other purpose? A secret mission—'

'If it were secret, mademoiselle, I wouldn't know about it, would I?' Polotski smiled at her.

She blushed. 'I'm sorry. It's just that—' She had no idea what it was 'just', and stopped, staring down at her coffee cup.

'I think perhaps I should tell you something about Count Kirov,' Polotski said. She looked up eagerly. 'But I must warn you,' he went on hurriedly, 'that in Petersburg I do not know him socially. We move in different circles. He comes from an old and noble family: I am a jewelsmith of humble origin. Not so very far back, there were serfs in my family. Well, I'm very rich now, and wealth counts for a great deal, but I'm what you might call *parvenu*.'

'I shouldn't dream of it, sir,' Fleur said with a smile, and he nodded to her, glad she had recovered a little of her poise.

'I wouldn't mind if you did. I believe in calling a thing by its name. What I'm trying to say is that Count Kirov and I don't dine with each other or go to the same parties. What I know of him I know at second hand – just what's common knowledge, in fact.'

'I understand.'

'Well, now, the story I want to tell you is that the Count was betrothed more or less from the cradle to his cousin. She was quite an heiress, apparently, which I suppose was why it had been arranged, and everybody, including the Count, seemed to be quite happy with the idea. And then suddenly, when he was about – oh, twenty, I suppose – at any rate, on the very brink of being married to this cousin, he suddenly fell in love with someone else.'

Fleur had become very still. Her hands were resting to either side of her cup, and she watched them as if they might do something unexpected. Polotski, eyeing her sympathetically, continued with the story.

'She was young and very beautiful, but a nobody. Worst of all, she had no fortune at all, which mattered to the Kirovs because they'd fallen on hard times – though that's another story. But Kirov was made for her, and he wouldn't listen to anyone. He married her.'

'What did his parents say?' Fleur asked in a colourless voice.

'His father was dead by then, so Kirov was head of the family, which meant he could do as he liked. But it broke his mother's heart. She took against the girl very strongly. I don't know all the details of it. All I know is that there was a family rift, which was very bad for Kirov, because he was devoted to his mother. And before there could be a reconciliation, his mother died.'

The fingers of the left hand closed up.

'That was bad enough. As I said, he adored his mother. But then within a year, his wife died too.'

123

Fleur looked up. Her eyes, Polotski thought, were the bluest thing he had ever seen. 'He became a recluse,' she said, remembering Jerome's words. It was not addressed to Polotski, but he answered it.

'Not exactly. He became a little withdrawn and gloomy, which was only to be expected. I've heard people say that his temper grew savage, but I don't believe that. He has always seemed perfectly pleasant-tempered to me; but he's very clever, and he has a way of saying outrageous things, laughing at people to himself, you know, which of course people don't like. He doesn't suffer fools gladly, but you can't expect the fools to enjoy that.'

'No,' Fleur said. Her left hand clenched more tightly, pressing the nails into the palm. 'I suppose he married again?'

'No,' Polotski said, and it was with obvious regret. 'He never married again. They say he buried his heart with his wife. I don't know about that. He's certainly very attractive to ladies, and from all I've seen and heard, he enjoys their company.'

'He dances very well,' Fleur said softly.

Polotski fixed her with an admonitory eye. 'The thing that has struck me, mademoiselle, is that, having broken his heart over his first wife, he now doesn't seem to have any heart at all. As I said, he's very attractive to the ladies, but he doesn't seem to mind how many of them run after him, or break their hearts over him, or make fools of themselves. He takes no pains to warn them off. He's not – *careful* enough.'

'Surely,' Fleur said indignantly, 'it's for the ladies themselves—'

'There's such a thing as leading a person on,' Polotski said neutrally. 'He has a very charming way with him – so I've heard.'

'Yes,' she said. She uncurled the fingers of her left hand. There were four little red ovals in the palm where the nails had pressed. 'Was it a very long time ago – that his wife died, I mean?'

'About ten, eleven years ago, I think.'

'That is a long time,' she said. Time heals, she thought.

124

Even a salted field becomes fertile again in time, and ready for the right seed to drop into it. He doesn't suffer fools gladly, and the fools don't like it. '*Caveat emptor*,' she said, smiling to herself.

'I beg your pardon?'

'Oh, nothing,' she said, looking up at him cheerfully. 'May I pour you some more coffee, Mr Polotski?'

Chapter Seven

Sir Ranulph looked in at the door to the morning-room. 'I'm going home. Is there anything you want me to bring back for you?'

Fleur looked up. 'No thank you, Papa. I don't think so. Oh, but you might remind Mrs Petty about the gooseberries. She hates them so, I'm sure she forgets them deliberately, but if they're not picked soon they won't be fit for jam. Tell her she might pay the little Black children twopence to pick them for her. That will kill two birds with one stone. And she can give them something to eat in the kitchen before she sends them home.'

Sir Ranulph was looking more and more restless during this speech, and broke in at last, saying, 'Lord, Flo, you can write her a letter, can't you? I can't be remembering all your jams and twopences and domestic nonsense! I just thought you might want something brought back for tomorrow.'

'For tomorrow?'

'Your Aunt Ercy's picnic in Richmond Park. She's got up quite a party for it. Have you something nice to wear?'

Fleur regarded him with surprise. He didn't usually enquire about her wardrobe. 'I was going to wear my lavender-blue muslin,' she said, mystified.

He grinned a little self-consciously. 'Oh, didn't I mention? I told your aunt I thought you were looking a bit peaked from missing your long rides, so I said you and I would go on horseback, so that you could have a proper gallop.'

'How very kind, Papa. I should like it of anything.'

'Aye, I thought you might,' Ranulph said, looking pleased with himself. 'So now, have you a smart habit to wear, and all the etceteras?'

'Yes, thank you – but you might in that case bring my tall hat with the long veil. It's in a box in my wardrobe – Sally will know which one. It's a better fit than the one I have here.'

'Very well,' he nodded, and went as suddenly as he had appeared, leaving Fleur to puzzle it out.

The visiting hour brought Aunt Ercy, and enlightenment. After a quarter of an hour of commonplaces, which she felt a necessary preliminary at any visit, she said, 'Fleur, my love, such an exciting day we have planned for tomorrow! As we are to go to Richmond, and as it is not permitted to ride *ventre-à-terre* in the Row, Markby has fixed it with your papa that the young gentlemen and ladies who care to shall go on horseback. I hope you are pleased?'

'Yes, very, Aunt. Papa did mention it to me earlier. He said he'd told you I was looking peaked for want of exercise.'

Ercy looked indignant. 'No, it was I who said that to him!'

'Of course it was,' Venus said ironically. 'How could you be so simple, Fleur? When did your father ever notice the state of your health?'

'At least,' Ercy went on doubtfully, 'I don't think I said that you looked peaked, exactly, because to be sure, I haven't seen you since Tuesday. But I did say that I thought you would like to have a gallop. And Richard is to come, too – won't that be nice? And some of his friends from the 11th, Markby knows which ones. And who do you think he has invited for you?'

Fleur pretended to think. 'Mr Polotski,' she said at last.

Venus drew in a breath, and Ercy said innocently, 'Oh no, my dear, he is far too old, and married besides. But he will be there of course, in Vee's barouche, because Frederick can't come until later, because of a debate in the House.'

Fleur turned a brimming look on her senior aunt, who scowled and said, 'If you say one word, miss, I shall leave the room!'

'I have nothing to say to it, Aunt,' Fleur replied. 'You know I like him exceedingly.'

'I wasn't sure if it was quite proper,' Ercy twittered on, 'because it's so difficult to discover with foreigners quite where they stand, and though he's very rich, he's only a merchant, but Markby says he's a representative of his country, of sorts, which I suppose makes a difference. I hope everyone else understands that and doesn't take it amiss.'

'I'm sure you are doing just as you ought in asking him,' Fleur said gravely. 'Apart from anything else, he is my aunt's house guest. That must be enough for anyone.'

'Oh yes, to be *sure!*' Ercy looked pleased with the thought. 'And they will know when they see him in your barouche, Vee, that he is invited for your sake. But I didn't tell you, my dear, who Markby asked for you.'

'There's no need to invite anyone for me,' Fleur began, feeling instantly scratchy, and then stopped with the sudden and insane thought that it might be Kirov.

'No, dear, but it makes it more comfortable when we come to eat if you've someone to pass things and see to your glass. It's someone you danced with at Hardiway House, and I told Markby I was sure you were enjoying his company – you were talking so easily with him.'

'Who is it, Aunt?' Fleur said, and though she tried to sound natural, she saw Venus flick a questioning glance at her.

'Captain Jerome. I hope you're pleased? Such a nice young man, and quite a favourite of the Duke's, so he's sure to go far. And did you know, my dear, that he's a sort of cousin of yours? Oh, not close enough to worry about, as I told your papa – but his mother was a Ramsay, and cousin to your grandmother on your father's side.'

So that was what Papa was so up-in-the-air about – Aunt Ercy's plans to marry her off to Jerome, which would free Ranulph from the fear of Aunt Venus's scolding.

The complications of who was related to whom was a subject of perennial interest to Ercy, ever since she discovered five years ago that her husband had missed succeeding to an ancient earldom by the narrow margin of a bend sinister in the

127

eighteenth century – which *anybody*, as she had said at the time, meaning the Queen, might have set aside, considering that the parents married only six weeks after the unfortunate infant's premature appearance.

'I'm glad you told me, Aunt,' Fleur said now mischievously. 'The ties of blood are so important, and now I know Captain Jerome and I are related, I shall feel able to look upon him quite as a brother.'

'Yes, dear,' Aunt Ercy said, not listening to a word, 'and I must tell you: it's a remarkable coincidence, but another of our guests is a sort of cousin of *mine* – or, well, of Markby's, which is the same thing to all intents. It was the Prince who pointed it out – or was it Ranulph? I can't quite remember, for they all met together in the Adelphi Rooms – but it doesn't matter which. The point is that his mother was the daughter of Admiral Peters, who married a Miss Strickland whose mother was a Talbot, and the Talbots and Markbys have been marrying each other for ever! So he and Markby are certainly related, though we couldn't decide quite in what degree. But it's certainly close enough for them to call each other cousin, which they did, and very pretty it was too, as the Prince remarked. He said it was just the sort of thing he had hoped for when he set up the Exhibition in the first place.'

Venus had given up long ago and was reading the newspaper with close interest, but this escape was not open to Fleur, who had to make at least an effort to understand.

'*What* was it that the Prince thought pretty, Aunt?' she asked, starting at the nearest end first, in the hope that a tug on it would untangle rather than tighten the knot.

'I told you, dear, the friendship between them, and calling each other cousin. It was symbolic, he said, of the greater friendship between our countries, which meant there would be no more war. As he put it, rivalry between nations would be confined to the useful and productive rivalry of industry and commerce, rather than the destructive rivalry of arms.'

Venus rattled the newspaper belligerently and Fleur, beginning to feel weak, made one last effort to find solid ground. 'I see, Aunt. He's a manufacturer, then, I take it?'

'Who, dear?'

'This new cousin of Uncle Markby's.'

'Markby doesn't have cousins who are manufacturers! Really, Fleur dear, I wish you would attend. Whatever are you thinking of?'

'I'm sorry, I thought you said—'

'I said nothing of the sort! I said his great-grandmother was a Talbot.'

'I'm sorry. I didn't understand where the friendship between nations came into it.'

'Well, because he's a Russian, of course! Really, you are very dull today,' Aunt Ercy said, growing quite animated in the cause of genealogy.

We shall meet again. You must trust me. Everything fell into place with the beautiful certainty of a Mozart symphony, and Fleur found herself feeling astonishingly calm and peaceful, and in perfect charity with her chatty aunt and sociable, suggestible Uncle Markby.

'And Count Kirov will be coming to the picnic tomorrow?' she said happily.

'So I said at the very beginning,' Aunt Ercy pointed out. 'Though I don't suppose I shall have much benefit from his company. Your papa will certainly buttonhole him, and they'll talk all afternoon about their silly flowers.'

Before Fleur could follow up this intriguing suggestion, Dickens entered and announced Mrs Herbert, paying a formal call on Aunt Venus. Other visitors followed in due course, and the subject was not revived before Aunt Ercy took herself off to leave cards on her own list of acquaintances.

Not entirely to anyone's surprise, Sir Ranulph didn't return from Chiswick that evening.

'Once he has his head bent over his microscope, all vestiges of civility leave him,' Aunt Venus said sourly at breakfast the next morning. 'Well, he must make his own arrangements.' But she left a note for Frederick that if Ranulph had arrived by the time he got back from the House, he should bring him down with him.

Fleur, in the wrong hat, meekly took the pull-down seat in the barouche opposite her aunt and Mr Polotski. Buckley had taken Oberon down early in the morning to the Roehampton Gate, where everyone was to meet, so that he would be rested when she arrived.

'Though the likelihood of everyone's being there on time is remote,' Venus commented as they set off. 'That's the trouble with schemes of this sort. Of course Ercy has been my sister for too long not to be punctual, but if she's invited the fashionable crowd . . .'

The plan was to meet at the gate at twelve, for the carriages to promenade along the carriage-drive while the riders had their gallop, and for everyone to meet up again at the Dew Pond by Sheen Common for the picnic at two o'clock. The flaw in the plan was that since Richmond Park was about ten miles from London, everyone would have to leave home at about ten o'clock, an hour of the day some members of fashionable society hadn't witnessed since they left the schoolroom.

When the barouche came in sight of the gate, however, there was already quite a crowd gathered, of grooms holding riding-horses, of mounted gentlemen, some of them in uniform, and a cluster of carriages filled with smart tall hats and the most killing bonnets, all bobbing like flowers cast on a gentle swell as the occupants chatted eagerly to each other.

For Fleur, however, there was only one horseman. Under the shade of a chestnut tree, festive with its blossom-candles, was Count Kirov. He was in civilian dress, and mounted on a very handsome flea-bitten grey which he must have borrowed for the day, for it was certainly no job-hack. His eyes found hers as soon as she came within sight, and as the barouche drew up his lips curled upwards into that particular smile that made her feel as weightless as a soap-bubble, as he touched his whip-stock to his hat in a private gesture of greeting and complicity.

The next half-hour was a confusion of chatter and greetings and arrivals and excuses, and Fleur's attention was never hers to give to that figure under the gold-green shade of the chestnut, himself a centre of polite attentions. Uncle Markby was good-natured and vague, asking after her father and instantly forgetting he had asked; Aunt Ercy was assiduous in her efforts to surround Fleur with all that was handsome and eligible in the male line, while ensuring that the other young females were not neglected, and that everyone knew the riding party must *stay together at all costs*.

At last Venus grew restless and intervened, barking out a few simple orders which penetrated to the brains of the military personnel, and got them moving. Buckley led Oberon to the mounting-stone by the gate, tightened the girths, and nodded to Fleur. Her good bay horse greeted her with a whicker, and an inquisitive nose and velvet lips came round to investigate her gloved hands for the titbit he knew must be there. She mounted, settled her skirts, took up the reins, and joined the rest of the riding party as it moved forward through the gate.

She looked round for Kirov, but found Jerome manoeuvring his chestnut into place at her side.

'Your brother hasn't arrived yet, Miss Hamilton,' he said pleasantly. 'I was rather afraid noon might prove too early for the 11th!'

'But Richard never got up before noon when he was a civilian – except on hunting days,' Fleur said. 'You're evidently more disciplined at Headquarters.'

'We have to be. I dare say you've never seen the Duke in a rage, ma'am, and I hope you never do, but it's a thing that leaves men shivering and strangely shrunken.'

'I'm sure you've never been the cause of it, Captain Jerome. You're far too orderly and virtuous an officer.'

He smiled ruefully. 'Is that how you see me? It doesn't sound very exciting.'

'No, did you want to be exciting? Well, I'm afraid my Aunt Markby has done you up: she told me yesterday she's discovered you and I are cousins, which licenses me to look on you as a brother; and brothers are never exciting, you know.'

He gave her a strangely searching look. 'I wish I might be as useful to you as a brother. Brothers may give advice that strangers dare not offer.'

'Do you think I need some? No, don't answer that. I have to tell you, sir, that on the subject of advice I'm very unsisterly, even to Richard. Ah, there's Miss Cavendish. Excuse me, but I must speak to her: I haven't seen her since she was laid up with an influenza . . .'

Inside the gate, the carriages turned to the right onto the drive, and the horsemen spread out. There were four other ladies on horseback, and about a dozen gentlemen, but it was soon evident that most of the riders wanted to stay with the carriages, and continue the conversations they had begun. So much, Fleur thought, for her gallop; without her father's single-minded selfishness for support, it was impossible for her to break away from the group.

Almost immediately upon the thought, Count Kirov rode up on the other side of her from Miss Cavendish, and said in a low voice, 'There are compensations, however. In such a crowd, we may speak without being heard, and with perfect propriety.'

She turned her head, and was silent a moment, trying to order her unruly senses. Why does he affect me so profoundly? a distant part of her mind wondered.

'What is it?' he asked. 'I hope you were not surprised to see me?'

She laughed, at once feeling more natural. 'No, not at all. I guessed this was all your idea.'

'I told you that we'd meet again, and I always do what I promise. Don't you know that you can trust me?'

For her composure's sake, she could only take that in its literal sense. 'I don't think the question ever occurred to me. But I am amazed at your administrative skill. To involve all these people in your scheme without their knowledge argues abilities out of the ordinary!'

His eyes gleamed. 'I've been used to command all my life,' he said. 'But unlike the man in the Bible who simply says "Do this" and it is done, I've had to deal with the most stubborn and ungovernable people in the world. Your true Russian has an incurable dislike of discipline.'

'You find the English more biddable?'

'Infinitely. I told your father that you would like a gallop, and he told your uncle, who told your aunt.'

'But how did you tell my father? And how in the world did you persuade him I was looking peaked?'

He looked her over briefly in a way that brought the colour to her cheeks. 'If I had done so, it would have been an outrageous lie. But in fact I didn't – I allowed him to tell me so. I merely complained that it was not possible to ride properly in the Park, observed that anyone used to the freedom of the country must pine for a gallop, wondered how ladies in particular, who had so little other exercise, could bear it, and asked what could be done about it.'

'Was that all? Simplicity itself! I can't tell you how astonished I was when Papa expressed concern for my health and enquired solicitously about my hats.'

'It's a very charming one,' Kirov said, glancing at her head.

'Ah, but it's the wrong one – it will fall off at the gallop. Papa forgot to bring me the one I wanted.'

He was suddenly grave. 'Yes, I've known him quite long enough to be aware of how he neglects you. How you must miss your mother! I saw your distress at the ball when you mentioned her,' he went on in a low voice, 'and I understand exactly how you feel. I know what it is to lose the mother you adore.'

Fleur looked at him rather blankly. She hadn't loved her mother – she had really never *known* her mother – and having never looked to either parent for love or affection, she hardly knew how to respond to him.

In the end she said merely, 'But I don't suppose I shall feel the lack of my other hat after all – it doesn't look as though we shall have a gallop today.'

He accepted the apparent rebuff cheerfully. 'Don't worry – I'll arrange that, too, by and by.'

'But now you must satisfy my curiosity,' said Fleur. 'How did you manage to scrape acquaintance with my father so quickly?'

'It was not a scrape, I assure you. I've known your father a long time by reputation. Yes, really! Don't look so surprised. Don't you know he's a very eminent man in his field?'

'Well, yes, I suppose so, though it's always hard to think of one's parent in that light. But I had no idea his fame had spread to Russia.'

'Science knows no barriers,' he smiled. 'It happens that my own father was a keen horticulturalist, though the merest amateur. When he retired from the diplomatic service, he dedicated himself to his hobby. He vastly extended the greenhouses at Schwartzenturm – our estate near St Petersburg – and for a while even tried to grow tropical plants under a controlled environment. That was when he grew interested in orchids. I think he had every book and article your father ever wrote in his library.'

'And that was enough to ensnare Papa?' To do him justice, he was no Lion.

Kirov shrugged. 'I allowed him to think I shared my father's interests perhaps to a greater degree than is strictly the case.'

'Unscrupulous! But how did you get to *meet* Papa in the first place?'

'What could be easier? Khamensky is our Commissioner to the Exhibition: he had the Prince invite me to a meeting of the Royal Society, and the Prince introduced me to Lord Markby. I brought the conversation round to my father's hobby, and Markby at once seized on the happy coincidence, and introduced me to his brother-in-law.'

Fleur was much amused. 'Is this a talent which is peculiarly Russian, or is it yours alone?'

'A little of both, I suppose. In Russia if you want to get something done, you have to find your way through a maze of procedure, or discover short cuts of your own. I prefer the latter method.'

'I'm not sure that you're a very safe person to know,' she said.

'Is your dearest wish, then, to be safe, Miss Hamilton?' he enquired, looking at her intently. Even if she had known how to reply to a question so fraught with possible hazards, she couldn't have spoken just then. After a moment, he saved her the trouble. 'I think we should have our gallop now, don't you think, before everyone becomes too indolent.'

'But how—?'

'Never ask me how! Just trust me, and enjoy yourself!'

It was no use, she discovered, trying to observe his methods. Within a remarkably short time, and without her having been able to see at all how he did it, he had detached the more adventurous half-dozen – including, she noted with amusement, Miss Cavendish, for propriety's sake – from the carriage party; turned Aunt Ercy's fears inside out so that she was positively urging them to take to the open spaces; and started the whole group of them across the meadow at a genteel canter.

The really clever part, she thought, settling into Oberon's comfortable stride, was that he didn't appear to be the instigator – indeed, at the present moment, he was in the centre of the group, at Miss Cavendish's side, giving all the appearance of being carried along by the will of the majority. The grey moved well, and he handled it quietly and confidently as if he had been riding it all his life. He was, she was glad to note, a superb rider.

'It's interesting to see him in action, isn't it?'

She found Jerome beside her again, and inspecting his question, decided it was too perilous to answer. Instead she lifted her eyebrows and made a neutrally enquiring noise.

'The Count,' he elucidated. 'I'd heard that he was a superb manipulator of situations, but it's educational to watch him at close quarters.'

'I don't understand you,' she said, feeling it was the safest answer, and, to deflect him, 'He rides very well.'

'Yes, and on de Burgh's grey – not the easiest horse to handle.'

'I knew it wasn't a hireling. Who's de Burgh?'

'Lord Cardigan's bosom friend. Something of a man about town. Known around the gambling-clubs and racecourses as The Squire of Hell.'

Fleur glanced at his frowning profile. 'You don't approve.'

'De Burgh don't usually lend out his horses.'

135

Fleur considered this oblique criticism. 'How does he come to know him?'

Jerome looked at her now. 'Count Kirov seems to know everyone,' he said shortly. He checked his gelding's stride and went on, 'Only a few days ago you said you had only a nodding acquaintance with him, but now he seems to be on terms of considerable intimacy with Lady Markby.'

Fleur coloured. 'And my Aunt Venus is sharing a carriage with Mr Polotski, and my Uncle Frederick dines with Baron Brunnow. Dear me, I must remind my family to ask your permission before they befriend anyone of Russian extraction!'

Jerome bit his lip. 'I beg your pardon,' he said quietly. 'I was impertinent.' Fleur did not argue with this. After a moment he went on, much more hesitantly. 'I wished only, in my concern for your comfort, to put you a little on your guard. In his own country, Kirov has something of a reputation—'

'You may be concerned about yourself. Count Kirov is a friend of my father's,' she said brittly, and put her heel to Oberon's side. 'Ah, good, we're going to gallop at last!'

Oberon was only too glad to go, and leapt forward with an eager snort. Before he had gone four paces his excitement had infected the other horses, and in a moment they were all streaming away across the open field. Fleur took a moment to glance at Miss Cavendish to see that she was comfortable, and then gave Oberon his head.

The open space and the sound of drumming hooves spurred the horses on, and they began to race each other. Lord James Paget gave the view halloo, and Mr Chigwell of the Bank of England, and Messrs Roding and Newbury of the 17th Lancers took up the cry, giving tongue excitedly like hounds.

'Come on, Miss Hamilton!' Paget cried, looking across at her with a grin. 'Show 'em what you can do! In at the kill, eh? Pride of the Quorn!'

Captain Jerome, she knew, would be leg-shackled by his better manners, which would make it impossible for him to leave Miss Cavendish, whose sedate mare hadn't the pace to obey the 'gone-away'. With a private grin of satisfaction, she leaned forward and whispered to Oberon, who accelerated like a steam train, and carried her past the gentlemen to the front of the group. He was a big horse, and fast, and carrying less weight than the others, and out in front he settled down to a ground-eating pace they would hardly better.

The intoxication of speed drove everything else from her mind for the moment. The brown ears were pricked before her, the green earth rushed by in a blur beneath her; her lips parted to drink in the soft air as it whipped past her face, and the thrilling thunder of shod hooves on turf pounded in her blood. To gallop a horse was the most exciting thing she knew. All physical bonds seemed to be loosened: weeks of drawing-rooms and dining-rooms and the hampering of dozens of petticoats, relieved only by sedate canters in the Park, were wiped away. She felt that she might fly; and was too happy and excited even to notice, much less care, when her hat was whipped off and went tumbling away over the grass.

The trees of one of the copses were up ahead, and Oberon was turning slightly to run parallel with its margin. His ears went back as another horse's thunder impinged on him, and a moving shape called Fleur's eye. It was him, of course, coming up beside her on the flea-bitten grey. It was fast, fast! Even pacing Oberon, it was going well within itself, obviously with speed in hand. Oberon accelerated for a few paces, but his first enthusiasm was blunted, and he was beginning to blow. As the grey stayed level, he slowed, and then dropped back to a canter.

Kirov met her eyes and smiled approvingly. 'He goes well, your good bay! Don't overtire him – we shall want another gallop later.'

She let Oberon come down to a trot and then a walk, and gave him a long rein. He snorted, sneezed a couple of times, and then stretched out his neck comfortably. She glanced back, and saw the others, still cantering, coming up behind; and put her hand up to her head, suddenly aware that it was bare.

'Don't worry, I saw where it went. We shall go back and fetch it later,' he said.

Paget was the first to reach them. 'I say, Miss Hamilton, you set a scorching pace, all right!'

'Oberon was longing for a run,' she said.

He patted his horse's neck. 'My poor old Samson's getting rather past it now,' he said ruefully, 'but you know how it is. He's an old friend, and I get more pleasure riding him than my young horse; and he breaks his heart if he sees me go out and leave him behind in the stable. But I say, sir,' to Kirov, 'your grey's a goer! You might have shown heels to all of us if you'd let him out.'

'No, no,' Kirov said gravely, 'you must not suggest to Miss Hamilton that she didn't win fairly.'

'Oh of course,' Paget said hastily. 'Miss Hamilton always beats. She floored me when I first saw her with one dart from her eyes!'

'In this case,' Fleur said firmly, 'I didn't win because I wasn't racing. I was simply enjoying the gallop, and perfectly unaware of your presence.'

'Oh cruel! You see, sir,' Paget appealed laughingly to Kirov, 'how she tramples on the fallen! She knows I die to serve her!'

'Beauty is cruel,' Kirov said gravely. 'Every poet since the beginning of time has remarked it.'

The others had caught up, and cheerful chatter was exchanged, but Fleur did not immediately attend. What had struck her, and was puzzling her, was the way in which Paget addressed the Count, as if he were of an older generation than themselves, and a mere observer of the frolicking of the young things he had agreed to chaperone.

Sir Frederick arrived at the Dew Pond just as they were finding places to sit for their picnic, which the servants had laid out in the shade of the silver birches. He came driving himself in his two-horse phaeton, and Sir Ranulph was not with him.

'There was no sign of him when I left. I suppose he's wandered off to Kew and forgotten us all,' he said.

'Or Chiswick House, or Sion, or Timbuktu,' said Venus, but without great heat. Everyone was too accustomed to Sir Ranulph's ways to find it surprising, but Fleur saw the Count glance at her with a sympathy she had no need of.

Taking a seat by his wife's side, Sir Frederick beckoned Fleur over, making room for her on the spread blanket, and said, 'I'm afraid I've got something rather unpleasant to tell you. Something I heard today in the lobby.'

'Yes, Uncle?'

'It's about young Theodore Scott.' Fleur's heart sank. 'I bumped into Lord Raglan, and he told me that there's quite a scandal brewing down at Woolwich.'

'Oh dear! What's he done?'

'I'm afraid the young idiot's got himself into serious trouble.' He looked at his niece keenly. 'I'm afraid you won't like this, Flo. He's been going absent from his duties without leave. On the night of the Alderneys' ball, he was supposed to be duty officer, but when the colonel decided to turn out the guard, just for practice, Scott was nowhere to be found.' Fleur said nothing, but her colour was enough to tell Frederick the worst. 'Do you know something about it, love?'

'I saw him at the ball,' she said unwillingly. 'He'd climbed in over the wall. I told him to go back at once. I hoped he might not be missed.'

'Vain hope, I'm afraid. What the deuce did the young fool do it for?'

She met his eyes reluctantly. 'He wanted to dance with me. He thought I'd admire his spirit.'

'Oh Lord! I was afraid of something like that.'

'Yes, I know. You warned me about it. But I thought—'

'Well, yes, even I didn't think it would go as far as this. You see, the ball wasn't the first time. He's been doing it consistently, ever since you came to London.'

'All those times—?'

'Yes, I'm afraid so. Oh, don't worry, he hasn't mentioned your name – he's a gentleman. He's refused to give any reason why he went missing.'

'I wouldn't care if he did,' she began hotly, but Frederick stopped her with a look.

'You would care. The point is, that if he'd been in the Hussars, or one of the fashionable regiments, it might all be looked on as a lark. He'd have been confined to barracks or given extra duties or something of the sort, and the fact that he'd done it for love would rather increase his credit than otherwise. But the Engineers aren't like the rest of the army. It's caused the deuce of a scandal down there.'

Venus broke in. 'There, I knew how it would be! I told you, Fleur, not to waste your time with him, and your uncle warned you, but you wouldn't listen!'

'It's not my fault that Teddy's a fool!'

'Don't be impertinent, miss! If you think it will make you a more attractive *partie* to be involved in a ridiculous scandal like this, you know nothing about society.'

'Why should I be involved? Teddy would never bring me into it.'

'The thing is, love, that the scandal may become public,' Frederick said. 'Raglan was very grave about it all: he's afraid there may be a court martial.'

Fleur went very white.

'If there is, it will be reported in the newspapers, and the fact that he doesn't mention your name won't prevent people from putting two and two together. You were seen often enough in his company. It's the sort of story the newspapers love.'

'If – if it does go to court martial, what will happen to him?'

Frederick shrugged. 'He'll be cashiered. I don't think there can be any doubt about it. If it was just the one occasion – but a persistent offence like that – No, he'll be out on his ear. The Engineers are a stiff-necked lot. They don't like to be made fools of.'

She was thinking. 'Uncle, you could go to the Duke! He's such a particular friend, I'm sure he would do something for you – intervene, have Teddy punished privately, perhaps. He's such a good friend, he couldn't refuse you, and if *he* said it must be so, it would be done.'

Frederick almost laughed. 'Fleur, my love, the Duke of Wellington, interfere in a matter of discipline? Never in a thousand years! You don't know what you're talking about!'

'But surely, Uncle—'

'Listen to me: what the Duke cares most about in life is the discipline, efficiency and reputation of the British army, and every other consideration is subordinated to that. He's said time and time again that a commander must train himself to be indifferent to the fate of individuals, to ignore their feelings for the greater good of the army. He wouldn't intervene to save his own son, if he were guilty – and if he were innocent, he might still sacrifice him in a good cause. No, love, he won't help us.'

'But there must be something that can be done!'

'I wish there were. If it had been one of the other regiments – but the Engineers! I've no influence there. I'm afraid young Scott must take his chances.'

'That's all very well, Frederick, but what about Fleur? What about us? Are we to take our chances too?' Venus said indignantly.

'Face it out, that's my advice,' Frederick said. 'It will be unpleasant, but these things pass. As soon as there's a new scandal, it will all be forgotten.' Venus snorted, and he went on, 'You might go out of London. In fact, if it does go up for court martial, I think you'd better, while the trial's on, and until things quieten down. You might take Fleur on a little trip abroad, Vee. You'd like that.'

'When would the trial be likely to take place?' Fleur asked in a small voice.

'If the papers go up in the next day or two, it would probably be about the middle of June. It usually takes three or four weeks to set it up.'

The middle of June! 'Oh no,' she cried, 'I don't want to leave London. Not now, not when—' She swallowed. 'Not while the Exhibition's going on.'

'Lord, Flo!' Frederick said impatiently, 'you've seen the Exhibition. Try to keep a sense of proportion.'

'It was the Exhibition that caused all this,' Venus mourned. 'I knew from the beginning it was a bad idea, and now you see I was right!'

Fleur did her best to put it from her mind for the moment, and present a social face to the party, but it was difficult. She felt, as she had known she would, guilty; and angry that she

141

should be made to feel guilty. The stupidity, the unnecessary extravagance of Teddy's actions! There was nothing more exasperating, she discovered, than to be the object of an unwanted devotion. When someone you didn't care for bent his neck to you, all you wanted to do was set your heel on it. Their hopeless passion did not arouse your compassion, but a sort of irritated vindictiveness which was degrading to both of you.

She was brooding on these thoughts over an untouched slice of pie, when the Count sat down beside her and said quietly, 'What is it? What's happened?'

She looked up blankly, coming back from her thoughts.

'I saw your uncle speaking to you very seriously. Are you in some trouble?'

She sighed. 'Yes, I'm afraid so.'

'Let me help you,' he said simply.

She looked into his face, and felt a glad and warming sense of comfort and trust, as though, a tired child lost in a crowd, she had suddenly found again the beloved parent who cared for her. But she said, 'I don't think anyone can help in this case.'

'Tell me,' he said, and when she hesitated, he smiled and said, 'You've already seen what miracles I can achieve, in the most adverse of circumstances. Didn't I tell you you may trust me?'

'I think perhaps this may defeat even your powers,' she said with a faint smile. 'Can you take on the whole of the British army, and the Duke of Wellington besides?'

'If *you* ask it of me, I will. But perhaps it may not be necessary. There's usually a way round every bog and thicket. Only tell me what's wrong.'

Feeling, absurdly, already comforted, Fleur told him.

Chapter Eight

That evening they had no engagement. Lord and Lady Markby dined at Hanover Square, and after dinner they, Venus and Polotski made up a table for whist.

Sir Ranulph was already returned when they arrived back from Richmond, unrepentant about missing the picnic, which he had entirely forgotten once he had got back to Chiswick. It was only when the housekeeper came to ask him if he would be requiring dinner that he remembered Fleur was not at Grove Park, and not caring to eat and spend an evening alone, he clapped on his hat and rode back to London.

After dinner, when the whist players had withdrawn to the far end of the long double drawing-room, he reached for the newspapers, and then changed his mind and challenged Frederick to a game of chess. Frederick had been intending merely to sit and chat with Fleur, whom he thought was feeling rather low – and no wonder! – but when he hesitated and glanced towards her enquiringly, she shook her head.

'Don't refuse on my account, Uncle. I'm too dull and sleepy to need company.'

'Play to us,' Ranulph suggested. 'Something quiet and soothing.'

'Yes, do, love, if it's not too much trouble,' Frederick agreed. 'You know you always find music comforting.'

Fleur allowed him to open the piano, light the candles, put out her music for her, and go on thinking that she needed consolation. She did want to be left alone, but not to brood: she wanted to think over the things that had happened that day, and all the things that had been said. Spreading her skirts she sat at the piano, glanced at the music, and began to play a Bach prelude she knew by heart. Her fingers pressed the satisfyingly mathematical music out of the keys, and as she gazed unseeingly at the blurred haloes of the candles, her mind got up and slipped easily away from the quiet room.

After she had told Kirov about Teddy Scott's plight, he had excused himself to her, saying, 'I mustn't remain by your side all the time, much as I wish it, or I'll be making you conspicuous. But we shall talk more later, when we go back to find your hat.'

'My hat! Yes, I'd forgotten about it.'

'Forget it again,' he said. 'I'll remind you at the right moment.'

Richard and his companion Hussars arrived while they were still eating and joined the party, reviving the gaiety, particularly amongst the young ladies, who straightened their backs and lowered their eyelids and smiled their sweetest smiles for those irresistible uniforms.

Fleur was rather apprehensive on seeing her brother approach her, big with news, thinking he must have heard about Teddy, and afraid she would have to go over it all again with him. But it turned out to be horses he had on his mind.

'I say, Flo, d'you know what?' he cried, flinging himself down beside her, and forgetting, in his excitement, to look bored and languid. 'That chap Kirov is a great Go, ain't he?'

'Oh certainly,' she agreed innocently. 'A regular plunger, I imagine.'

'No, but really, don't you know what horse that is he's riding? That's de Burgh's grey! And de Burgh, let me tell you—'

'Is The Squire of Hell – yes, I know.'

'Who told you that?'

'Captain Jerome. He doesn't think Mr de Burgh is nice to know.'

'Well, true enough, Hubert de Burgh is a bit of a Tough, but he's our Guv'nor's bosom-bow, and by Jove, he knows horses! They both do. Lord Cardigan's a rattlin' rider, hunts six days, goes over everything straight as a bird! But the point is, neither of 'em would dream of lending a horse to anyone but each other. So this Kirov must be a great gun, besides being a famous hard rider, because that grey's the deuce of a handful let me tell you!'

'It seems a very quiet, easy ride,' Fleur remarked, and Richard flushed with excitement.

'That's exactly the point – and don't gammon me that you don't know it! I'm going to go and pay my respects to him: after all, he's a friend of my colonel's.'

'Now, Dick, don't make a nuisance of yourself,' Fleur said hastily.

'I'm not,' he said crossly. 'I'm doing what's proper. You don't understand etiquette – females never do. But I wish Pa was here – I bet he'd like to know Kirov.'

'You're after the party – they're already great friends. Count Kirov knows a great deal about horticulture.'

That gave Richard pause. 'You can't mean it? Not a great gun like him, interested in flowers?'

'His father was a noted amateur in his own country.'

'I expect that's it, then,' Richard decided happily. 'After all, if anyone asked me about flowers, I'd probably know a good deal, just from hearing Pa talk. You pick it up, don't you, without meaning to?'

He hurried off. Fleur watched apprehensively, but Kirov seemed to accept his attentions equably, and from Richard's excited blushes and eager expression, the Count seemed to be living up to his expectations.

A little later Richard came back to say importantly, 'I've fixed it up with Kirov, Flo, for us all to go back and find your hat. We'll set off before the rest, because it will probably take us a while to find it. It seems only you and Kirov have an idea where you lost it, but he insists I come along to play propriety, since Pa ain't here. He thinks just as he ought, don't he? So I've asked Brooke to ride with us too – four pairs of eyes being better than three!'

'That's very kind of you, Dick,' she said gravely. A picture formed itself in her mind of Richard and his friend Brooke beating the bushes assiduously after the missing hat, while she and Kirov rode along behind, enjoying their conversation in privacy and perfect propriety.

Reality turned out to resemble her imaginings closely. 'I'm beginning to think you're a very unscrupulous person,' she said as they rode along side by side, some ten yards or so behind the gallant Hussars. 'When it comes to securing your own ends—'

'Not unscrupulous – just thorough,' he said easily.

'So thorough you even convinced my Aunt Markby that you were related in order to get invited on this picnic!'

'Not at all,' he said seriously. 'It was she who told me we were related. I simply told her who my mother was, and she did the rest for herself.'

'Yes, I rather imagine Aunt Ercy could find she was related to the Sultan of Turkey if she dug deep enough. It was true, then, about your mother?'

'Of course. She was the daughter of Admiral Peters, and her mother's name was Strickland, which seemed to afford your aunt great satisfaction! She was a very remarkable woman, my mother, and very brave. Before I was born, during Napoleon's invasion of Russia, she went to war with my father and rode everywhere at his side. She always said she could face any hardship or danger as long as she could be with him.'

'Why did she go to Russia? It seems a long way from home for the daughter of an English admiral.'

'He died when she was a very young woman, and she was forced to become a governess, having no other means of supporting herself. She worked for a diplomatic family, who were in Paris during the Peace of Amiens, and when the Peace ended suddenly, they fled back to England, leaving her behind.'

'Good God! How despicable!'

'Yes, and she was in great danger – Napoleon imprisoned several thousand English people who didn't leave the country in time. But fortunately my father was in Paris. He'd met her through her employers, and fallen in love with her, and when he discovered her plight, he rescued her and took her back to Petersburg with him.'

'And married her? What a wonderful story!'

'It wasn't quite as simple as that. He was already married at the time. They were kept apart for many years, and my mother married someone else. But yes, eventually his wife

146

and her husband died, and they were able to marry each other at last. And then Napoleon was defeated, and I was born. Those events are probably not as casually distant from each other as they may seem,' he smiled.

'She must have loved your father very much.'

'Yes. When he died, she died a little too.'

She looked sideways at him. He was riding the big grey on what appeared to be an easy rein, relaxed in the saddle, but with the very upright posture of the cavalryman. He was a natural rider, graceful, but giving the impression of great strength: his hands, quiet on the reins, and his strong wrists were a spring which kept the horse's great surging power delicately buoyed against the hard restraining muscle of his back and thighs.

All this he did so naturally that his mind was free to range as it would, and at the moment, she could see, he was far away. The hard lines of his mouth had softened, his eyes were distant, and his face looked younger as he contemplated some far-off and beloved object with affection and sadness.

'What was she like?' she asked.

He didn't answer for a moment. Then, without looking at her, he smiled and said, 'Like you,' surprising her. She made a sound of enquiry, and he went on, 'Oh, not in looks, but in her manner; and she spoke like you. She had an excellent mind, and a better education even than my father's. She and I used to converse by the hour. I never tired of talking to her.'

'That explains why you speak to me as you do. Men don't usually speak to women like that, as if they were people too. Not even my brother or my father—'

'No, I know,' he said, as though it were something he knew by experience, at first hand. 'She taught me what true communion is, and it's always rare. She shaped my mind, guided my thoughts. I miss her,' he said quietly. 'She died – oh, twelve years ago, but still sometimes when I go into certain rooms, particularly at sunset, I expect to see her there. And still I can hear her voice . . . It was she who taught me to see Russia. The outsider always sees more clearly.'

'Were you her only child?' she asked – a little dishonestly, since she knew he had a brother.

'No,' he said, 'but I was her first.' Abruptly his eyes changed focus. He looked at her almost appraisingly, and the lines beside his mouth hardened again. 'I have a younger brother Petya – a much younger brother! He's twenty-eight, and the darling of the Guards' mess. I've had to be a father to him since *my* father died, and a more arduous task you can hardly imagine.'

'Perhaps your father's death affected him very deeply,' Fleur hazarded, and he gave her a rather hard smile.

'No, you miss your guess. Petya was only six, and I doubt whether he remembers much about it. It was I—' he stopped.

'I'm sorry,' she said at once. 'You don't want to remember it.'

'No, I don't want to, but I do. Don't be sorry – I'm glad to talk about it to *you*. It all began with that hideous business with the Decembrists. Do you know about it?'

'A little,' she was glad to be able to say.

'It was all so futile, and so frightening. There'd been other rebellions, many of them, in our history; but they were all palace revolutions, one faction of courtiers against another, struggling for position or privilege. Usually they aimed to substitute one Tsar for another. But this was different.'

He paused for such a long time that she thought he wasn't going to go on. The golden afternoon was very still. The breeze had dropped, and even the birds were silent in the full-leafed trees. The only movement came from the two Hussars who, ranging ahead like dogs, drew farther off all the time, beating back and forth across the line and calling to each other, soft cries as harmless and golden as the afternoon. The only other sound was the creaking of the saddles as the horses brushed through the long grass, pacing each other, their heads nodding peacefully. They swished their tails in unison, brushing the fat grass pollen from their summer-round flanks; their muzzles were mealy with it.

He said, 'This was different. For the first time a group of idealistic young men got together to try to change things for the public good. They didn't want a change of Tsar – they wanted no Tsar at all, or at least a constitutional monarchy, as you have here, with accountable government, freedom for the serfs, and a general franchise. Laudable aims, you might say. Most of them were good men – young and foolish, perhaps, but good at heart. My brother Sashka was one of them.'

'Your brother?'

'My half-brother, my father's son by his previous wife. Sashka was my hero, even though he was my parents' favourite, which ought to have made me hate him. Yes, my mother's favourite too, but I even forgave him that. He was a godlike young man, tall and beautiful, with golden hair and golden eyes and the disposition of a young god. I never knew him to frown or say a cross word. The servants adored him. He had more friends than he could have kissed in a day, one after the other. He was an officer in the Semyonovksy Guard – one of the crack regiments. When it came out that he was a conspirator, something in my father sickened and began to die.'

'It failed, of course – the rebellion?' she prompted gently. She felt from him that he wanted to tell the story now, that he could part with some of the bitterness by telling it to her.

'It never really began.' His eyes had gone away again; now they seemed to reflect a cold place, far from the summer meadow before them. 'It was the most fantastic scene: the Senate Square, with the Admiralty on one side and the Senate building on the other; on the south side the cathedral, St Isaac's, all scaffolding, still only half built; the fourth side open to the River Neva, frozen solid, and the smudge of buildings against the sky on the far bank. It was a bitterly cold December day. The sky was a dirty yellow-grey, like trampled snow. It never really got light. The days are very short and dark in Petersburg in December.

'And there were three thousand rebel soldiers, in their greatcoats and caps, lined up with their backs to the Admiralty, waiting for orders. They stamped their feet and grinned at each other and fiddled with their muskets, half excited, half afraid. There was a crowd of civilians, too, behind them, egging them on: they gave them hunks of bread and sausage to keep them going, and passed flasks of vodka back and forth along the line.

'And on the other side of the Square the loyal troops were lined up, with Emperor Nicholas on his horse in the middle of them. He'd only been sworn in that day. It was the first day of his reign, and there he was facing a rebellion.'

'What did he do?'

'He didn't want to shoot them. Any other Tsar would have opened fire and been done with it. He had nine thousand men, plus artillery, on his side. But he didn't want the first day of his reign to be marred by bloodshed. So he sat there on his horse, and willed them to go away. All day long they faced each other across the Square. It was like a dream, one of those strange, frozen dreams, where some danger's coming at you, and you find you can't run or cry out.'

'Didn't he try to talk to the rebels?'

'Oh yes, he sent envoys to reason with them. First he sent old General Miloradovich, the hero of 1812, because everyone liked him, and he had a reputation for fairness and decency. He addressed the rebels, but they wouldn't listen, told him to go back; and when he did turn his horse to go away, they shot him in the back.'

'Oh, mercy!' she cried in distress.

'Each envoy he sent they shot at. Some were killed, others escaped. And still Nicholas sat there, waiting. But when it started to get dark, and the rebels began to fire off their muskets – not very purposefully, it's true – the Emperor knew he had to do something. In the dark, anything might happen. So he had the artillery load their pieces with case-shot, and gave the order to fire. Thousands were killed; others ran, and were hunted down through the night by the cavalry. They knocked holes in the ice on the Neva, and shoved the bodies through. And they arrested the conspirators and shut them up in the Peter and Paul Fortress to face trial.'

'And your brother—'

'Yes, Sashka was amongst them. Papa was like a man in a trance. He walked about our house, his face white, his eyes – I can still see his eyes! He couldn't believe it of Sashka – such a thing had never happened in our family. He begged the Emperor permission to interview his son to get at the truth – and the truth was what broke his heart.' He shook his head, as if with disbelief. It was all so long ago, yet she saw it was as fresh to him as yesterday.

'The soldiers, you see, the common soldiers, didn't want a republic or a constitutional monarchy. They couldn't have understood it and wouldn't have trusted it. They understood about Tsars. As far as they were concerned there were good Tsars and bad ones, and the good ones were the ones who gave them more pay and fewer lashes.

'So the conspirators told them that Nicholas was a usurper, that his brother Constantine was the true Tsar, and that the purpose of the rebellion was to remove Nicholas and place Constantine on the throne. When Constantine was Tsar, they said, all the troops would get a rise in pay and better conditions. Oh, I expect they promised all sorts of things! But that was what Papa couldn't forgive, you see, that they had lied to the soldiers. When he came home from the Fortress, he looked old, so old, and his face was grey. My mother ran to him, cried out his name, took hold of his hand, but he didn't look at her. I don't even know if he knew she was there. He looked at me – I was so frightened! – and said, "He lied to them. He lied to the men. He let them go to their death for a lie." '

There was a distant halloo from Richard and Brooke. Fleur saw them waving, small figures in a distant landscape, nothing to do with her. She was with Kirov in another place.

'Mama wanted my father to plead with the Emperor for clemency. She was distraught – she didn't care whether Sashka was guilty or not, she only wanted him to live. But Papa wouldn't do it, not for a son who had betrayed both the Emperor and the men in his command. He shut his heart to Sashka, and to my mother's tears. But I understood. I grieved bitterly for Sashka, but I understood.'

'What happened to him?'

'He wasn't executed. The Emperor seemed more shocked than angry. He seemed not to be able to believe these young men – the gilded favourites, who owed everything to the throne – had betrayed him. Only five of the ringleaders were hanged in the end, and the rest – two hundred or so – were exiled. Sashka was one of those. He was in the first convoy. We watched from the window of our house, Mama and I, as they marched down the Nevsky Prospekt on the beginning of that long, long journey to Siberia. He looked up as he went by, but I don't think he could have seen us. That's the last sight I ever had of him, huddled in his greatcoat and cap, turning his white face towards us as they marched him away.'

'Did you ever hear from him again?'

'They weren't allowed to write, of course. The next thing we heard was a year later, simply that he was dead. We never knew how, or why, but I think he just pined away. He'd always been like the golden sun at the centre of his own universe. He wasn't one who could have lived with disgrace, and without love. The day after we heard of his death, Papa had a stroke.' His face quivered and he bit his lip. 'He didn't die straight away. He lived on for two years before the second one finished him. Ah, that was cruel! That was the cruellest thing!'

'I'm so sorry,' Fleur said helplessly. She longed to offer him solace, but what could she possibly say or do in the face of such memories? But he looked at her and a faint smile came to the greyness of his eyes, and when she impulsively put out her hand, he took it, folding his fingers around hers as though he were accepting a gift.

'Halloo, Fleur! I say sir! Didn't you hear us yelling? We've found it! Oh do come on!'

Richard's healthy young voice shattered the intangible bubble that had built up around them. Oberon flinched, rudely wakened from a half-doze. Fleur withdrew her hand a little self-consciously, and Kirov, checking the grey, who had begun to fidget, resumed with instant fluidity his public face. He pushed forward, calling out calmly, 'Are you sure it's the right one?'

'Well, sir, I don't suppose there are that many lost hats in just this place,' Richard replied, ludicrously serious.

'He's roasting you, Dick!' Fleur called, sending Oberon into a trot. Bay and grey napped at each other, Kirov met her eyes with a smile of complicity, and then they both began to laugh as they spurred forward and cantered down to meet the young men.

The Bach prelude came to an end, and silence fell on the room. Under a yellow flower of gaslight at the far end, seen through the dividing arch, the whist players were talking softly as they marked their scores and waited for the cards to be shuffled and dealt again.

In the centre of the room, the chess-table was set up before the fire, for the house was cold at night, even in May. Her uncle and her father, both tall, lean men, were bowed a little over the board like two brooding storks, mirror images of each other. Each had one elbow on one knee, head propped in hand, while the other hand rested lightly on the edge of the board. There had been no sound or movement from either of them for some time. She had no idea whose move was waited for. Perhaps they hadn't either.

The fire flickered above its red heart, little blue-green flames running and popping over the surface of a large coal. A servant must have come in and made it up without anyone's noticing. On the mantelshelf above it a French bracket clock ticked with a light, swift, somehow feminine sound; while the longcase clock in the corner added its soft, heavy, leisured clunks from the shadows, dropping them like stones into the deep pool of time.

Outside in the street, the evening traffic was muted by the heavy velvet curtains into a steady grumble below the level of attention. She imagined the gaslit streets stretching away on all sides of her, interspersed by the dark patches of garden, where night had turned green to black and the great trees lived out their mysterious lives, whispering only to the wind what they saw and knew. Above the gaslight there were roofs, the slates electric blue and glistening in the moonlight, laid out street by street like playing cards across the vast stretch of London.

And somewhere out there, under one of those roofs, beside

153

one of the fires, *he* was. She still didn't know where he was staying. She wished she knew his direction, so that she could imagine it, imagine the street, the house. She thought of herself as a spirit, rising on a breath out of her body, rising through the ceiling, through the roof, out into the dark, moon-lit air, to hang unseen above the city, turning slowly on the air, looking for him. She would feel his mind reaching out for hers, and would turn towards it gladly . . . He was thinking about her, she was sure of it. She felt already so connected to him. All that he had told her that day was a gift of himself to her, to make those invisible ties stronger.

'She taught me what true communion is, and it's always rare.' They didn't understand, Jerome, even Polotski, when they tried to warn her away from him. They didn't understand with their small, conventional minds, that this was something quite, quite different.

A rustle of movement, and a quiet click, followed by the sound of her father chuckling: she came back down into the room with a bump.

'Oh, I didn't see that coming! That's very neat!' her father cried, sitting back from the board and contemplating the move Uncle Frederick had presented him with.

'You weren't concentrating. You knew that rook was covered!' Frederick turned round, still smiling, and looked towards Fleur. 'In a dream, Flo? Have you had enough, or would you like to play me some more?'

'If you wish. I'm not tired.'

'What about that pretty piece you used to play. Mozart, wasn't it?'

'Beethoven.' And she flexed her fingers and plunged into the rippling sonata, and the candlelight stirred and glittered on her hanging ringlets as they quivered to the vibration of her movements.

Dickens opened the door to Fleur, and glanced past her down the steps. 'Oh, miss, there's a visitor, asking for the master. I said we were expecting him back any moment, and he said he'd wait.'

'Sir Frederick's gone on to Old Palace Yard,' Fleur said, drawing off her gloves. 'Who is it?'

'Count Kirov, miss. Should you like to see him? He's in the library, miss.'

'Yes, Dickens. Show him up to the drawing-room, if you please. I'll just go and take off my hat.' And blessing her luck, she ran up the stairs.

A little later Kirov rose with a glad and questioning smile as Dickens opened the drawing-room door for her.

'It's good of you to see me, ma'am. I hope I'm not disturbing you?'

'Not at all,' Fleur said. 'My uncle was intending to come back here but a message came asking him to call on Lord Granville, so he left me at the door.'

Dickens closed the door behind him, and Kirov crossed the room swiftly to kiss her hand and say, 'I am glad of the chance to speak to you alone! How well you look!'

'Thank you. I think the day in Richmond set me up. It was almost like being in the country.'

'You've been to the Exhibition this morning?'

'Yes, to the Moving Machinery Court again. There's always more to see, no matter how many times you visit! We were looking at the small machines today. In some ways, they're even more fascinating than the big ones. There's a very ingenious one for making cigarettes and wrapping them up in paper, and another that makes soda-water out of plain water and gas . . . The great steam-engines are thrilling, of course, but there's something so fascinating about such a finicking process being performed by a machine!'

'Yes, I know what you mean,' he said. 'Sadly, in my country we're only just beginning to make use of the most basic machines. I'm afraid it will be a long time before we reach the refinements of machine-made cigarettes and Seltzer!'

'But there's nothing to stop you having them, surely? With such a big country, you must have enough iron and coal, and more than enough labour?'

'Ah, if only it were that easy! I'll explain it to you one day, when we have enough time.'

'Yes, of course you didn't come here to discuss machinery with me,' she said with a faint smile. 'Can I give my uncle a message?'

'I have something to tell him, but I am happy to have the chance to tell you privately first, since it concerns you most.' She sat down on the sofa and invited him with a gesture to sit beside her. 'It's about your friend Mr Scott.'

'Oh!' Fleur coloured a little. 'Have you heard something new? Uncle Frederick was asking yesterday whether the papers had gone up to the Board, but he couldn't find out anything.'

'There's to be no court martial,' he said.

'Oh, I am so glad!' Impulsively she took his hand. 'Thank you for coming to tell me! Where did you hear it? Is it certain?'

'Yes, quite certain,' he said, not finding it necessary to release her hand. 'The matter has been adjusted privately between the Colonel of the regiment, Lord Raglan, and the young man's father.'

'Oh Lord, his father! I suppose he's very angry?'

'I couldn't say, not having met the gentleman. But it's been arranged that, for the better good of the whole regiment, there will be no charges against Mr Scott, provided he leaves the Engineers at once, of his own will.'

'Oh poor Teddy! To go home in disgrace! He was never his father's favourite – brought up in the shadow of his elder brother, you know. Harry was always being held up to him as an example of perfection. It's enough to sour any constitution!'

Kirov smiled. 'I imagine so.'

'But at least there'll be no public disgrace, which is everything! Where did you hear it?'

'From Mr Brunel. And Mr Scott won't be languishing at home under a cloud: Brunel thinks he has rather a talent for bridges, which would be better employed in a civilian rather than a military environment.'

'Mr Brunel intervened on his behalf?' Fleur asked in astonishment.

'That's what persuaded the Colonel eventually not to make charges – he didn't want to jeopardise the young man's new career at the outset. Brunel is to take him on as an assistant engineer in the Great Western Railway Company. I think it will suit him very well.'

'Oh yes! Of anything! And it will mean he's away from home most of the time—'

'And away from London. You won't be plagued by him any more.'

She stared at him, thinking it through, and he watched her, plainly amused at her visible thought processes. 'Just a minute – how did Mr Brunel know Teddy had a talent for bridges? And how did he know he was in trouble? And why should he stir himself to interfere on Teddy's behalf?'

'I can't imagine. Perhaps he's a philanthropist.'

'You've had something to do with this,' she said. 'No, I correct myself – you have arranged the whole thing! Somehow you brought them all together and persuaded them to do exactly what you wanted, didn't you?'

'Do you want me to lie to you? Will the truth embarrass you? Very well – I did it,' he confessed, and struck himself on the breast, bowing his head in mock contrition.

'Good heavens! How very, very kind! But – why? Why should you go to so much trouble for a young man you don't even know?'

He shook his head at her, as if amazed by her stupidity. 'Why, indeed? You wish to pretend it was not your specific request? You asked me to take on Lord Wellington and the British army – but in the end, you see, it wasn't necessary.'

Her thoughts were in a whirl. He had done it for her, because she had been upset by Teddy's plight, because she was facing an unpleasant scandal. He had wished to save her unhappiness and embarrassment. Perhaps also, so that she didn't need to go out of London? And even, perhaps, to remove Teddy from her court. Kind, so kind! But was it more than that?

'I don't know what to say,' she began, and was interrupted by the door opening. She snatched her hand back from his, and looked round to see Aunt Venus stepping across the threshold.

'Ah, Count Kirov! How very nice of you to call,' she said, advancing with her hand extended.

Kirov rose. '*A votre service, madame*,' he said, bowing over the hand. He always spoke French to Venus, a circumstance which had won her favour early on. She liked to think of herself as wholly French, and was delighted to believe that she had so impressed the Count that way, he had never attempted to address her in any other tongue.

'I'm sorry my husband and I were out when you arrived, but I trust my niece has kept you entertained. But Fleur, what were you thinking of, not to offer his excellency a glass of sherry? Ring the bell for Dickens. And, Count, you must do me the favour of coming to dinner today, if you are not already taken.'

'Thank you, madame, I am at liberty.'

'Good, then please consider yourself engaged. We have a small party of guests tonight, whom I think you will find very interesting. It is in the way of a *talking* dinner, you understand . . . There' s no need to keep you any longer, my love,' she said to Fleur, who had no choice then but to take her leave.

She was rather quiet during dinner. The company was mostly of the older generation. That would not normally have prevented her from joining in the conversation with interest, but on this particular evening she was content merely to listen, the better to observe the Count, who was sitting three places down and on the opposite side from her.

He was involved in a four-way discussion with Sir Frederick, Mr Herbert and Mr Polotski about public health, a topic which effectively silenced the women in between them and condemned them to listen to what Aunt Venus believed should never be talked about at all, leave alone at table. Fleur felt excused, particularly in view of her interest in the subject, in keeping her head turned that way as if she were following the conversation, though in reality she didn't hear a great deal of what was said. Without appearing to do so, she was able to study the Count during most of the meal.

He was looking particularly distinguished, she thought, in evening dress. The stark black and white suited him, made him look more handsome than ever, with the single ribbon and medal of some Russian order gleaming discreetly at his neck, and the huge emerald at his signet ring flashing whenever he moved his left hand. She watched his profile as he listened, smiled when he smiled, followed the movement of his lips when he spoke. She knew that he was aware she was watching him, for whenever his head turned her way for any reason, his eyes would seek hers briefly.

As there was formal company, Fleur and her aunt were obliged to retire to the drawing-room with the other females, leaving the men to smoke their cigars and drink their brandy. It was a custom Venus detested, and Uncle Frederick could be relied on to allow the ritual to go on for no more than half an hour before bringing the men through to join the ladies. Still, it meant a separation, and when the men did come through, Fleur knew her part would be to entertain the younger set. She would be unlikely to be able to talk to Kirov. He would be occupied with the senior members of the party that evening.

While her aunt settled herself with the older ladies, Fleur accompanied the younger ones upstairs where they adjusted their toilettes and chatted lightly amongst themselves. Fleur listened to them without hearing them. She felt as though there were a barrier between her and the rest of the world, transparent but impenetrable. Nothing was real but that tall man with the glowing eyes, whose soul spoke to hers without needing words. When it was time to go downstairs again, Fleur shepherded the young ladies out of the retiring-room, but then lingered for a few minutes alone, daydreaming, savouring the anticipation of seeing him again. She wanted him to be already in the room when she came down, so that she could see his eyes turn towards her as she entered.

She lingered so long that the tea and coffee trays had been brought in already, and she entered the long drawing-room to find everyone crowding round the table or standing in small groups with their cups, talking. There was a wall of sound, and everyone was so preoccupied that she entered unseen and

159

was able to stand just inside the door observing, herself unobserved.

She couldn't see Kirov. The door through which she had entered was in the shorter section of the double room, next to the archway. The rest of the dividing wall obscured much of the other part of the room from her view. Gradually she became aware of a conversation going on just to the other side of the arch, between two people unseen to her. As she began to distinguish the words, she recognised the voices and almost immediately the import.

'It's a delicate situation,' Captain Jerome was saying.

'Too delicate for me, old chap,' protestingly, from Lord James Paget. 'Not in my line at all.'

'But you've known her so much longer than me. As an old friend, couldn't you—'

'Certainly not! It would be the greatest impertinence!'

'From me, perhaps,' Jerome said persuasively, 'but from you – or perhaps you could speak to her, in a kindly way—'

'You don't know her,' Paget said hastily. 'And besides, I'm not convinced there's anything to say. In fact, you know, I think you've mistaken the whole thing. Sure of it! Good God, man, he ain't one of us, you know!'

'That's precisely the point: he doesn't understand our ways. I've seen the way he looks at her; and he seeks her out in a very obvious manner. There will be talk – undesirable talk.'

'Oh nonsense! You've imagined the whole thing! He has a fatherly interest in her, that's all. After all, he is a friend of her pater's. Nobody's going to think anything other than that, I assure you . . .'

'Ah, there you are!'

Fleur whipped round, her face as instantly scarlet as if she had been dipped into hot water. The Count had come in at the door behind her, silently.

'I'm sorry, did I startle you?' he said, surveying her brilliant cheeks.

'I wasn't expecting you to be there,' she managed to say. 'I thought you were in the other end of the room.'

'I was. But when I realised you were not in the room, I

slipped out of the other door in the hope of encountering you. I wanted to ask you to forgive me for neglecting you this evening.'

'I see that you have no choice,' she said awkwardly.

'No,' he said with a mock-rueful smile. 'Your uncle provides me well with company and conversation! That's the devil of all our polite meetings – I never have enough time to talk to you properly, undisturbed. I've been thinking: perhaps we could ride together in the Park. Can you come alone? Is it permitted?'

She looked surprised. 'We'd hardly be undisturbed. Between us we probably know everyone in London. We'd be obliged to greet someone every five yards.'

'Not if we meet very early. I'm accustomed to taking my ride before anyone's about. I usually exercise at around eight o'clock in the morning.'

'Ah, so that's why—' She stopped herself.

He smiled. 'I like the way your unruly tongue betrays you. So you looked for me in the Park, did you? Well, now you know. Will you come tomorrow?'

She hesitated. 'I – I'm not sure. It may not be in my power—'

He lifted his hand slightly. 'I understand. Don't worry, I shan't ask you to commit yourself to it. I shall be there anyway, at the Stanhope Gate at eight o'clock. If you can come, well and good. And now I must go before I'm searched for. I'm absent without leave, you know!'

He was turning away when something seemed to strike him, and he turned back, searching her face keenly. 'You seem a little subdued. Is anything wrong?'

Eavesdroppers proverbially hear what they don't like, she thought; and decided instantly that here was one thing she would not share with him. Jerome's suspicion and Paget's lack of it were equally insulting, beneath his notice and therefore beneath hers. He had rescued her from the importunity of one unwanted admirer, but she wouldn't like to ask him to make a habit of it.

'No, nothing at all,' she said lightly.

Chapter Nine

She slept fitfully, with convoluted dreams, and woke every quarter-hour thinking she had overslept. When the clock of St George's struck seven, she rose with something like relief and went to pull her bedroom curtains and look out.

It was a perfect morning, clear and dewy, the sky high and pale with the promise of heat. She pushed the window all the way up, and leaned out, resting her hands on the cold stone sill. The air was mild, almost warm, carrying rising birdsong and the distant sound of early traffic in Oxford Street. At the corner of Harwood Place a very dirty boy was half-heartedly sweeping the crossing, pausing frequently to lean on his broom and blink in the patch of sunlight he had found. An elderly lady's maid with a sour expression issued from the door of Lady Melrose's house, leading her ladyship's two greyhounds on a leash. They stepped delicately on pointed toes like dancers, but she held the leash with the tips of her fingers, as though she feared contamination.

Immediately below her, Fleur could see the truncated figure of Philip, the youngest footman, polishing the brass furniture of the front door. His elbow jerked in and out with the violence of his rubbing, and he was singing to his own rhythm one phrase of a popular song, repeated over and over:

> *She's my dove, my little skylark, and my*
> *Touree-ay, she's my touree-ouree-ay.*

She smiled to herself and pulled her head in, singing the absurd words under her breath. *He's my touree-ouree-ay* . . . It was a perfect day for getting up early. The morning was an exquisite water-colour in a golden frame, and she wanted to be

162

out in it, and ride before the rest of the world rubbed the gilt off, and smeared the delicious colours. Nothing could be more natural; and if she should happen to meet an acquaintance in the Park, so much the better!

She dressed herself in her dark blue riding-habit, and ran downstairs. The house was quiet, and she encountered no servant until she reached the front hall. There the youngest footman stared at her in astonishment, and immediately began to look round nervously for someone senior to tell him what to do about her.

'Close your mouth, Philip,' Fleur said kindly, 'and put down your polishing cloth. I want you to run round to the stables, and ask whoever is there to saddle my horse and bring him round to the front door immediately. Do you understand?'

'Yes, miss,' Philip said, with the gravest doubt apparent in his voice. It was something he'd never been asked to do before, and he had all a servant's dislike of the unfamiliar task and the hidden pitfall.

'Quickly then,' said Fleur 'Don't stand there like a stock.' He scuttled, with a curiously hunched motion indicative of his inner conflict between the desire to obey and the fear of offending domestic etiquette.

It seemed an age before the clopping of hooves sounded in the street outside, and Fleur hurried to the door, only to find Buckley standing at the foot of the steps, dressed to ride and holding two horses. His expression, she saw at once, was both determined and suspicious.

'Thank you, Buckley,' she said firmly, 'but I shan't need you.'

'Beg your pardon, Miss Flora,' Buckley said, without flinching, 'but if you're going riding in the Park I'd better come with you. We don't want no more trouble like last time.'

That was the worst of these old family retainers, she thought savagely: they always took advantage. 'I don't want you, Buckley,' she said, 'and that's final.'

'No, it's not, miss,' he said infuriatingly. 'Her ladyship wouldn't like it, as well you know. And whatever are you going out at this hour for? No one else in the house is up. You're up to some mischief, I'll be bound!'

To her own annoyance, she felt herself blushing. 'I'm going to ride in the Park, while it's quiet, and before it gets too hot. I see nothing strange in that – and it's none of your business anyway. Good God, I'm not a child!'

'No, miss, you're a young lady, which is just the point,' Buckley retorted. 'Young ladies can't be too careful.' He noted the set of her jaw and went on, 'Come on now, Miss Flora, you know I'm right. I'm not going to let you ride alone in no Park, and that's final. It's not safe and it's not proper!'

She felt her temper rising. 'I'm not going to ride alone,' she began, and Buckley gave her a triumphant smile.

'Well, miss, all the more reason, then!' he said, and added wheedlingly, 'Don't you worry, I'll ride along behind as quiet as a mouse, and you'll never even know I'm there. I've took care of you ever since I put you on your first pony. You can trust old Buckley, can't you?'

'Oh, very well,' Fleur grumbled, knowing she would never shift him, 'come if you must.' She met his eyes defiantly as he helped her to mount; and as he settled her skirts for her, he gave her the ghost of a conspiratorial wink, which she ignored loftily. As soon as he let go of her rein she touched her heel to Oberon's side and rode away, leaving him to catch up as he may. It was a very small satisfaction.

But as soon as she rode through Stanhope Gate and saw the Count under the trees a little way off, her heart lifted so that she forgot her annoyance with Buckley. In any case, she thought, noting the mounted attendant with him, he has quite a different attitude to servants from us. He ignores them a great deal more, and would probably expect me to be followed by a groom, if he thought about it at all.

'There you are!' he said gladly as she rode towards him. 'I didn't know if you would come.'

'Isn't it a beautiful morning?'

'Perfect. I hope you aren't too tired, getting up so early?'

'Not in the least,' she said. 'At home – in the country – I'm always up early.'

'At home – in the country – I don't suppose you go to bed so late,' he mocked her. He turned his horse and they began to walk them along the tan.

'You have a different mount today,' she remarked.

'A hireling. De Burgh wouldn't lend his grey devil for everyday purposes. Besides, I'm happy to have an easy ride this morning, so that I can give you my full attention.'

It was things like that that made her heart bound so unguardedly. She lowered her eyes, seeing from under the lashes that he was watching her confusion.

'The blush is very becoming,' he said. 'Such a natural colour. I'm so glad you haven't learnt all the feminine wiles – or at least, if you've learnt them, you don't play them off on me. It's tedious always to get the same, conventional reaction when I say something unconventional.'

That made her laugh. 'I assure you I know everything a well-brought-up young woman ought to know about correct behaviour.'

'But you don't care to put it into practice. Well, neither do I. There's so much falseness in polite society. It's particularly tiresome that young women should be taught to languish and giggle and swoon. Far better that they should be given a sound education and taught to converse rationally.'

'Far better,' she agreed, 'but until other men think as you do, the poor creatures would have no one to converse rationally *with*. All the men who've dangled after me for the last six years have been determined to think me a fool. They're quite taken aback when they discover I have any wits at all. They really don't like it, you know. They'd much sooner talk baby-talk to me, and pay me idiotic compliments.'

'My poor girl, you must have been so bored!'

'Well I was, but I suppose it's the same wherever one goes. It's a woman's lot to be bored.'

'A man's, too. To find agreeable company of either sex is almost impossible in Petersburg. If anyone ever has the misfortune to learn anything at school or college, they make very sure to forget it before they go into society.'

'Then Russia is just like England after all,' she said, thinking of Richard, and Teddy Scott, and Lord James Paget. Jerome seemed different, capable of intelligent conversation – but then she didn't like Jerome, she remembered hastily.

'No,' he said. 'Russia is very different from England. More different than I think you can imagine.'

'Different in what way?'

He thought for a moment. 'I suppose, most of all, in size. When I first came to England I felt so cramped, as though the sky were coming down on me, and the trees and houses crowding in to crush me.'

'Oh dear, how disagreeable.'

'That was only at first.' He glanced around him, thinking. 'When I was a child, about six years old, my father gave me a puppet theatre for my birthday. It had a little stage behind looped curtains, and you worked the puppets through the top. Rose and I used to do plays for the servants. It had scenes you could let down: gardens and temples and forests, everything, all in miniature – perfect in detail, and painted in bright, clear colours like jewels, and so tiny! But when you crouched down and put your face up close and looked in through the curtains, there was a sort of magic – the little scenes became real, and you could almost think you might step into them.' He smiled. 'England seems like that to me; but here, the magic really happens.'

She was charmed. 'How well you describe things! I can see exactly what you mean.'

'I can't take all the credit for it. My mother told me long before I ever came here how I would find it. My father, too. He came here in his youth, and his father before him, on the Emperor's business.'

'Is that what you're here on – the Emperor's business?' She had meant to ask who Rose was, but the new tack was more interesting.

'All Russian business is the Emperor's business,' he said gravely.

'Don't tease,' she said. 'You know what I mean. Mr Polotski said you are one of the Tsar's special aides-de-camp.'

'What is there in that to surprise you?'

'I beg your pardon. I didn't mean to sound surprised. It's just that – well, what I mean is, after your brother's trouble—'

'You thought the family would be in disgrace.'

'Everyone says that your Tsar is harsh and vindictive, so I thought—'

'Oh no. He isn't like that at all.' She waited, and he went on, 'Yes, it's true that for a while we were under a cloud. It was a shocking thing for the Emperor, to be so betrayed, and by members of the noblest families. Some of the conspirators had been cadets with him: he'd known them all their lives. For a long time he didn't know whom he could trust, and it made him nervous and suspicious.'

'And did he trust you?'

'Not at first. We lost some of our privileges; and then when Papa died, all his pensions died with him, so we were – not exactly poor, but less well off for a time. But the Emperor was never vindictive. He refused ever to reinstate those he'd found guilty, but he didn't persecute their families, as others in his position would have. In many cases he provided for their wives and children; in most he allowed their estates to be inherited. And he never blamed me or Petya for Sashka's fault.'

'Then he isn't the cold, cruel tyrant we're told he is?'

'I've had nothing but kindness from him. He's proud, and jealous of his position, and a stern disciplinarian: his public face is perhaps cold. But cruel? No, never.'

'And tyrant?'

'He is the Emperor,' Kirov said simply. 'He expects his commands to be obeyed without question. He's always had a love of order and symmetry – I suppose it comes from his military background. He believes perfect discipline will give rise to perfect order, and that's what he wants for our country.'

'An army – with himself giving the commands,' she said. It sounded abominable to a freeborn Englishwoman.

Kirov frowned. 'He doesn't give his commands arbitrarily. He wants what's best for Russia and for the people, and as he was chosen by God to be the father of his country, it's obvious that he and he alone knows what's best. Unfortunately, knowing what's best and achieving it are different matters.'

'But why? Surely his orders must be obeyed?'

'Yes, of course, and if he could be everywhere at once, everything in Russia would be done as he wants it. In Petersburg, for instance, where his influence is direct, there's very little corruption in the bureaucracy. But outside Petersburg—' He shrugged.

'Can't the law punish it?'

'There speaks England! Listen, I will tell you: Russia is a vast country, thousands of miles across. There are no railways – well, only one, from Petersburg to Moscow, and that's only just being finished. There are no hard-surfaced roads like yours, no canals. No mail coaches, no telegraph. It takes months for a message to travel from the outlying regions to Petersburg. So the regional governers rule like petty princes. Within their territory, their power is almost absolute.'

'Why almost?'

'Because the real absolute power lies with the Emperor: he can overturn any local decision if he wishes. So it often happens that difficult decisions simply aren't taken. From the lowest level onwards, they're referred to the next in seniority up the line – and if he doesn't care to risk making the wrong decision either, the problem may eventually go all the way to the Emperor himself. But he already has far more work than he can possibly get through, so an answer, if it's forthcoming at all, may not reach the questioner for years.'

'But how wasteful!'

'Yes, and as you can imagine, it opens the field to all sorts of corruption.'

She frowned. 'I'm afraid I'm not very good at imagining corruption.'

'I expect you haven't had much experience of it in your well-regulated life,' he agreed. 'I'll give you an example. Say at the lowest level a man has a request or complaint. He has to bring it to the attention of the local petty official – we'll call him

Giorgy. Now, Giorgy reports to his superior, whom we'll call Ivan. But Giorgy has dozens of such requests every day, and even if he hasn't been instructed specifically by Ivan not to bother him – which is often the case – he must still choose which of the many to refer and which to reject. Unless he's an exceptionally honest man, the temptation to profit himself by the selection will be too great.'

'Yes, I see that. But surely some Giorgys must be honest?'

'Certainly – at least to begin with. But if Giorgy is entirely honest, the likelihood is that Ivan is not. And if both Giorgy and Ivan are entirely honest, there may be another twenty officials to pass through before a decision is made, and what are the chances that they're all honest?'

Fleur looked as though she would argue the case for total universal probity, but then changed her mind. 'Giorgy needn't let others corrupt him, however. He might stay honest himself, and mind his own soul.'

'He might,' Kirov agreed. 'But if he annoys his less scrupulous superiors, he will lose his job. And if in his honesty he stands in the way of some man below him, that man will probably inform dishonestly against him, or bribe someone else to do so, and have him removed in favour of someone more amenable.'

'Oh surely not—!'

'And at the very least, our honest Giorgy will see those who do not struggle against corruption profit and prosper where he remains poor; and after a while he will cease to try to swim against the stream.'

She was shocked. 'It all sounds so horrible!'

He smiled suddenly. 'It isn't as bad as you might think. There's plenty of petty tyranny, but your average Russian is incapable of sustained oppression: he soon gets bored and lets things slip. Fundamentally he's both lazy and good-natured, you see. To be truly tyrannical would involve a great deal of effort, and there are better things to do with one's time. Of course, by the same token, he's incapable of sustained good, when it requires effort and self-sacrifice.'

'How can you say such things of your fellow countrymen?'

'You forget I'm half English. My mother taught me to see things with the eye of the outsider. And as she used to say, the saving grace of Russia is that even the corruption is inefficient!'

'All the same,' Fleur insisted, 'the Emperor ought to be able to do something about it, if he has absolute power.'

'In theory he has, but in some ways it's only an illusion.'

'What can you mean?'

'My mother explained that to me, too. The Russian character, she said, is a contradiction. Russians are deeply anarchical: they dislike rules, they resent being told what to do. Yet they love the idea of authority, its magic, its mystique. God is the ultimate authority, and they worship Him, but of course He doesn't interfere too much in their everyday lives. The Tsar is the symbol of absolute earthly power, and as such he's almost worshipped, too. The peasants call him their Little Father: he's the source from which all blessings flow, all plenty, all privilege – but he's far away in St Petersburg. For day-to-day matters, there's the local government official. They don't have to worship him, and his rules may be evaded, or ignored, or he may be bribed or bought off, or blackmailed into compliance. It's a game, you see, and one they've a good chance of winning.'

She regarded this apparent chaos with the horror of one brought up in the tradition of centuries of orderly government. 'But don't you hate it? Don't you – and people like you – long to change it?'

He shrugged. 'The system exists; it's stable. If you alter one part of it, the whole will collapse. None of us has the power to change it – only the Emperor has that. But the Emperor most of all can't make changes, because the resultant landslide would sweep him away too. It is like a Sisyphean boulder, poised halfway up a mountain slope: the only reasonable option is to strive to hold it in place.'

'It must be frustrating for the Tsar, if he really does care about your country.'

'Yes, it's hard for him. He has nerves, you see. It's all wrong for a man in his position to have nerves, don't you think? If he were really cold and cruel, he might rule more easily. As it is, it gives him great pain.'

Fleur couldn't help wondering how far his view of the Tsar was influenced by personal gratitude, but pushed the thought aside as unworthy prejudice. 'He's lucky to have you to defend him,' she said.

Kirov smiled. 'He doesn't need me to defend him! He's the Emperor – I serve him.'

'Ah yes, and you still haven't told me what your special task is here. I hope it isn't only to spy on poor Mr Polotski.'

'Don't worry, I shall have nothing but good to say of your friend. No, my commission is to observe all I can of government administration, particularly local government, to see if there is anything His Majesty might adopt to improve matters in our country. You manage things very differently here, with your squires and magistrates.'

Fleur's brow cleared. 'Oh I see! In that case, Uncle Frederick ought to be able to help you: he knows a great deal about such things. And Mr Scott – Teddy's father – was a Justice of the Peace for many years.'

'Yes, so I've already discovered,' Kirov said. 'In fact, Mr Scott has asked me to dine with him and his family next week to discuss the subject.'

She laughed. 'You're always ahead of me! You don't need my help, I can see.'

'No – but your company is another matter,' he said. 'Shall we canter a little? Decorously, of course – I haven't forgotten the rules!'

During the first interval of the opera, Captain Jerome came to the Hoares' box, appearing almost at the instant the curtain fell and thus considerably outdistancing his rivals.

'May I beg your niece to take a turn with me along the loggia, ma'am?' he addressed Aunt Venus. 'It will be a long evening, and a change of position is most refreshing.'

'Do you suppose I'm in danger of falling asleep?' Fleur asked, raising her brows, but her aunt approved of Jerome, and felt his initiative in arriving first should be rewarded.

'Yes, do go, my love. You will be sitting all evening,' she said.

Fleur accepted with reasonable grace. She was not averse to stretching her legs, and as the loggia ran right round the theatre at dress level, they would pass all the places it was most likely she would encounter Kirov. She had not been able to spot him before the lights went down.

The loggia was decorated with a heavy red-and-gold striped paper, with handsome gilt-framed mirrors at regular intervals, and between them shallow alcoves containing velvet-upholstered seats just wide enough for two. There was a thick red carpet underfoot, and gas chandeliers overhead lit it luxuriously. It was the favoured place to stroll and be seen, to nod to one's acquaintance and compare toilettes and coiffures.

Jerome seemed to have something on his mind. After exchanging a few polite phrases about the opera, he lapsed into a troubled silence, but Fleur hardly noticed it, her thoughts very much elsewhere.

After that first early-morning ride with Kirov, they had met at the same time most mornings. In the course of their rides he had told her a great deal about Russia. She had become so fascinated with the subject that she had even drawn books on it from the circulating library, and was halfway through J.B. Kohl's recent *mémoire* at the moment. As she had been reading it just before the dressing-bell this evening, her mind was full of questions she wanted to ask the Count.

Their meetings had been delightful to her. Never before had she enjoyed such complete mental communion with another person; never before had she been less lonely. Their conversation was not confined to Russia, of course – that was the joy of it. They talked about anything and everything, and she felt an exhilarating sense of freedom in the knowledge that there was no topic she might not broach with him.

When they had parted at the Stanhope Gate this morning she had forgotten to ask him if he would be at the opera, but as it was a gala performance she assumed he must be. Her eyes were busy scanning the faces in the crowd when Jerome finally brought himself to the sticking point.

'Your father is away from London, I believe?'

'Yes,' Fleur said, without looking at him. 'He's gone up to Edinburgh to address a meeting at the Botanical Institute.'

'Will he be away long?'

'I've no idea. Several days, I expect. One never knows with papa,' she said indifferently. 'He moves in a world all his own.'

'Yes, I've heard that said,' Jerome said gravely. 'I suppose even when he's at home, his mind is a great deal occupied?'

Now Fleur looked at him, some warning beginning to stir in her mind. 'I had no idea you'd such a personal interest in my father,' she said.

'Not in your father, Miss Hamilton, but in you,' Jerome said awkwardly. 'In your welfare and comfort.'

For a surprised moment she thought he was going to make her an offer. But his expression was not lover-like: it was almost grim. She began to guess what was coming. 'Thank you, but I'm very well and comfortable,' she said quellingly.

Jerome persisted. 'I thought you were looking a little tired, ma'am. I was afraid you might be finding your early-morning rides too much for you, with all your evening engagements.'

'Sir, you are impertinent,' Fleur said, so astonished at his directness she hardly had room for anger.

'I beg your pardon – I don't mean to be! But I know you've been meeting Count Kirov in the Park, alone, and I wondered what your father would feel about it—'

'It's none of your business!' she said vigorously. 'Have you taken leave of your senses?'

Jerome bit his lip. 'I do know very well that it's not my business, and it's made it all the more difficult for me to address you on the subject. But your meeting him in that way presents such an odd appearance that I thought—'

'You'd better not tell me what you thought,' Fleur flashed at him, 'if it's of a piece with the rest of your insufferable impertinence!' She withdrew her hand, preparing to leave him. Having failed to persuade Paget to interfere, then, he'd decided to do it himself! How dared he! She wished she might tell him she had overheard his words to Paget, but she couldn't so expose herself.

'Please, Miss Hamilton, believe me that I've no wish to be impertinent,' he said in a low voice, and with such sincerity that she paused despite herself, allowing him to go on. 'But I've known Count Kirov for some time, and I've seen him in his own environment, in Russia. I know things about him that you don't, and I'm afraid he may have taken you in.'

'I am not a child, or a green girl, Captain Jerome!'

'I know that, ma'am. I'm a great admirer of yours. I know very well you have as keen an intellect as any man. But Kirov has no good reputation in St Petersburg where women are concerned. I know how charming he can be, and how he can appear to mean more than he does by what he says. I beg you will just allow me to ask you one question: has he offered for you?'

'No, I will not allow it,' she retorted. 'You will return me to my aunt's box, if you please.'

He turned with her, regarding her furious profile with an anxiety she didn't at all like. 'He hasn't, then. I was afraid of it.'

She whipped round on him. 'We meet in the Park, sir – not that it's any concern of yours – in order to converse, that's all!'

'But why, then, must it be in the Park, and in that way?'

'Because it's impossible to have a private conversation of any length at a public function.'

Jerome continued to look grave. 'I don't wish to upset you any further, ma'am. I would only ask you to ask yourself why he's involved you in such an appearance of clandestine behaviour. If he felt that to converse with you in that particular way were entirely acceptable, would he not be happy to do so in your aunt's house, or at any public gathering?'

Fleur stopped and turned to face him, searching his expression for his meaning. 'How do you know about it?' she asked abruptly. 'I've never seen you in the Park at that hour.'

'Grooms usually exercise their masters' horses early in the day,' he said. 'It will be common knowledge soon enough.'

She was thinking rapidly, her anger with him subordinated to the unwelcome question he had planted in her mind. 'Our conversations are entirely innocent – such as anyone might overhear.'

'Then why,' he asked, still more gently, 'does he make so sure no one does overhear them?'

'Because—' She stopped. Because if he were seen deep in private conversation with her at every social function; if when he called at Hanover Square she was seen to be the object of his visit; there would soon be a general expectation that he meant to ask her to marry him. That was the truth, wasn't it? She writhed away from the question, but her basic honesty held her to the point. He was taking care, wasn't he, not to raise those expectations?

But, her heart told her, he had not been careful. He *had* raised them – not in the general public, but in her. She hadn't been thinking specifically in those terms, but the conventions of her upbringing had been working away in the back of her mind all this time. She'd been assuming, unconsciously and without words, that he would not talk to her so freely, would not enjoy her company so intensely, if he were not in love with her.

Suddenly Kirov's face came before her in memory, and she suffered a revulsion against Jerome's handsome, young, very English one. He knew nothing of the matter. He didn't know Kirov at all – not as a woman could know him, not as *she* knew him. Had Kirov not told her himself how the conventional young women of Petersburg society bored and sickened him with their incomprehension and insincerity? What was between Kirov and her was different from any other relationship, and could not be judged by other standards. Jerome might mean well, but he was simply not capable of understanding. And he was certainly unforgivably impertinent.

'I refuse to discuss it with you any further,' she said. 'I understand the situation far better than you, and I assure you I'm well able to take care of myself. And now, if you please, we'll return to my aunt.'

Jerome could only do as she asked, but he didn't look as though she had allayed his fears.

*

Fleur's mind wandered rather far from the opera during the second act, and during the second interval she was grateful for the appearance of Lord James Paget, who brought her an ice-cream and a long and involved story about the genealogy of a horse he'd just purchased, to which she could seem to listen without having to concentrate. She liked Paget, not least because she knew he would entirely have forgotten what Jerome had said to him about herself and Kirov.

Kirov finally appeared just before the third act. She saw him coming into a box on the other side of the auditorium, in the company of Baron Brunnow and Monsieur Labouchère and their wives. He was helping Madame Brunnow into her seat, bowing solicitously over her, and Madame turned her head and smiled up at him as though he had said something particularly fascinating. The diamonds on her bosom flashed like lighthouse beams as she laughed.

Fleur sat up very straight, her cheeks warm, her hands gripped together in her lap, willing him to see her. He straightened at last, looking around him almost lazily. The lights flickered and began to dim. He stepped to the side of the box to pull out his own chair, and as he stooped to it, he looked straight across at her, smiled, and bowed his head.

Immediately she was flooded with relief. He had known she was there; he had looked for her. He had obviously been delayed by business from coming early enough to speak to her: the Russian Ambassador and the President of the Board of Trade between them might well keep him from his pleasures! His time, indeed, must be very much occupied, and the fact that he spared so much of it for her must mean that she was very important to him.

Perhaps when they met in the Park tomorrow, she would ask him – but no, of course she wouldn't! There was nothing she could possibly ask him about his behaviour or his intentions. In any case, she trusted him. He had said to her in the very beginning, *trust me*, and she did. With her honour and her heart, as with her life.

*

'I'm sorry I couldn't get to speak to you last night,' Kirov said, checking his hack from snapping at Oberon's inquisitive muzzle. 'I had hoped to give myself the pleasure of calling at your aunt's box in the interval, but we lingered so long over dinner there was some doubt that we would go on at all. It was only at Madame's insistence that we did – the Baron thinks everything inferior to the Russian opera.'

'She seemed to be finding you very amusing,' Fleur said.

'She laughs easily,' Kirov said dismissively. 'But I'm so glad you understood my signal and came to ride with me this morning, my dear friend, because tomorrow I must go away—'

'Away?'

'Don't look so tragic. It's only for a short time. I've been invited by Lord Cardigan to spend a few days at Deene Park, and then Lord Granville's arranged for me to visit some factories in Birmingham and Manchester. I shall acquire a good deal of useful information, I think. His Majesty is very interested in factories – particularly in the condition of factory workers. He believes they're worse treated than our most miserable peasants.'

'But at least they are free,' Fleur pointed out, feeling her patriotism rise at the implied criticism. 'Unlike your serfs.'

'That's the point, of course – only a madman would treat his belongings so badly as to damage them.'

'Belongings? But how can you bear to think of another human being as a possession? Don't you loathe the whole concept of slavery?'

'I would like to see serfdom abolished,' he said easily, puncturing her indignation. 'Every man of sensitivity does. Ngorny here,' he gestured over his shoulder towards his manservant, riding well to the rear beside Buckland, 'is a free man – that's why he serves me so well. One is never well served by slaves: they have no incentive to be industrious. If you ask a serf for a glass of water, he'll pass on the order to someone else, and so on and so on until it reaches someone too lowly to refuse it. By the time the water comes back to you, you'll either have stopped being thirsty, or you'll have been reduced to drinking out of the flower vases.'

Fleur smiled, though the idea of slavery made her, like any English person, feel uneasy; and though he had told her on other occasions that serfdom was not the same as slavery, she couldn't see that there was any significant difference.

She was about to ask him more about his proposed visit to Manchester when they were interrupted. She had grown so used to their rides being unobserved by any but grooms, that she looked quite blank when she saw a gentleman riding towards her calling her name. Then she recognised Teddy Scott, and at the same instant heard Kirov draw in his breath and mutter something that sounded reprehensibly like *Au diable*!

They drew rein, and Scott rode up to them. 'Hullo, Fleur! What a surprise meeting you here,' he said unnaturally. 'It's been such an age since we met! How are you? You're looking wonderfully well, as always.'

'Hullo, Teddy,' Fleur said, without marked enthusiasm. She didn't want to be disturbed at the moment; and she hadn't entirely forgiven him for almost plunging her into scandal. She was surprised, too, at his failure to greet the Count, considering he had been a dinner guest at Elmwood – quite leaving aside the little matter of having saved Teddy's bacon. 'You know Count Kirov, of course,' she said pointedly.

He favoured Kirov with a slight, stiff bow. 'How do you do, sir?' he said, without looking at him. Fleur stared in astonishment, though Kirov seemed more amused than annoyed, but before she could remonstrate, Scott went on clumsily, 'Now I'm here, I can escort you home, Fleur. There's no need to bother Monsieur Kirov any further.'

'What on earth are you talking about, Teddy?' Fleur said, still not understanding. 'I'm not ready to go home. What are you doing here, anyway?'

Scott was vexed. He had forgotten Fleur's disastrous habit of saying whatever jumped into her mind, without thinking about the appearance of things. He gave her a rather glassy smile.

'Well, never mind that for now,' he said pointedly. 'It's just as well I did happen to come along, isn't it? It seems I must make a habit of rescuing you in this Park.'

'I don't need rescuing, thank you,' Fleur said in astonishment, and then frowned, puzzling it out. 'Did you come here deliberately to meet me? How did you know I was here?'

'Oh Lord, Fleur, everyone knows it – or at least,' he corrected himself hastily, 'several people do. I thought it would be best if I – I mean, I am an old friend, after all. You couldn't object – no one could object—'

'Just a minute,' Fleur said fatally, 'did Jerome send you? Good God, is there no one with whom he won't discuss my affairs!'

'Of course not,' Scott said, flushing. 'He just happened to mention that if I came along here at this time, I might possibly find you. And if I did – at any rate,' he changed what he was about to say hastily, 'I can ride back with you, at all events: that's all that matters.'

'No it isn't! I don't want to ride with you, and indeed I shan't ride with you. You're being impertinent, and a bore, and you will oblige me by going away this instant!'

'Now look here, Fleur—'

'No, you look here! Who on earth do you think you are, Teddy Scott? If there's any rescuing to be done, Count Kirov can do it without help from you.'

'For God's sake,' the goaded Scott blurted out, 'it's him I've come to rescue you from!'

There was a moment of ghastly silence. Fleur stared at him, and then looked at Kirov, wondering if he were going to intervene, and why he hadn't done so before. At this last ridiculous statement, she had been torn between anger and laughter, but when she glanced at Kirov's face, expecting him to be either amused at Teddy's nonsense, or scornful of his impertinence, she saw that he was looking grave and thoughtful. It gave her pause; and in the pause, her anger won over all the other emotions.

'Why does everybody in London think they have the right to order my life for me?' she cried wrathfully. 'Am I a child? Am I an imbecile? And you, of all people – how dare you

179

suggest such a thing? You've every cause to know of Count Kirov's goodness and generosity, after all the trouble he went to, to get you off. You'd have been court-martialled and cashiered if it hadn't been for him!'

In the background of her anger she heard Kirov sigh 'Ah, no!' but she was too roused to heed him now.

'I'm disgusted with you!' she went on scaldingly. 'You ought to be grateful to him, not making ridiculous accusations, without the slightest cause! You seem to forget you're beholden to him!'

'I don't forget it!' Scott flared, angry in his turn. He turned towards Kirov. 'I'd be grateful to you for what you did, sir, if I thought you'd done it for me, or even out of the goodness of your heart! But I know you only did it to ingratiate youself with Fleur, and blind her to your plan. And you—' turning back to her, 'just can't see it! You can't see what he's doing, how he's compromising you! If this goes on, you'll have no reputation left!'

Now Fleur did laugh, but it was hard, angry laughter. 'You're a fool, Mr Scott! Compromising me indeed! Riding in the Park, in full daylight, with two servants in attendance? How was it, I wonder, that when I rode here in your company, I was not ruined for ever?'

Scott was caught wrong-footed. He looked wildly from one to the other. 'That was different,' he cried at last. 'You know it was.' He turned to Kirov. '*You* know it, anyway!'

Kirov was still looking grave, but he shook his head at that, and said, 'No. I must say, I don't see that it is different at all.'

'Because I've known her all my life! Because I love her! All the world knows that. My intentions are honourable. But you – do you mean to marry her?' Kirov stared at him without answering. 'Well, do you? Because I do!'

Fleur pre-empted Kirov's response. 'Oh do you, indeed? You *mean* to marry me, do you?'

'I'm sorry, Fleur. I didn't mean it like that. You know what I meant.'

'And I'll tell you without disguise what I mean: that I don't want to marry you, that I never will marry you; and that if you don't go away this instant and stop making a spectacle of yourself, I shall never speak to you again! Come, Count, shall we ride on?'

She sent Oberon forward, with such determination that Scott could find no further words to prevent her; and dismissed like a troublesome dog, he could only watch crestfallen and anxious as she and Kirov trotted their horses away down the tan. The two servants followed: Buckley gave Scott a hard and meaningful look as he passed, but Ngorny glanced neither to left nor right. Scott watched miserably until they were out of sight, and then turned his horse homewards, feeling foolish, angry, worried, and above all, as sore inside as if something had been ripped out of him.

When they had trotted far enough and hard enough for the steam to have escaped a little, Fleur slowed Oberon to a walk, sighed, and then gave a rueful laugh. 'Of all the stupid, impertinent, ridiculous things—! I would apologise for that idiotic boy, except that it would do him too much honour.'

'The pains of unrequited love are fierce,' Kirov said. 'I respect his motives, even if I abhor his manners.'

'I hope you don't think,' Fleur said suddenly, distrusting his calmness, 'that I led him on in any way? I've always made my feelings known quite clearly to him, without disguise.'

'Oh yes, I'm sure you did,' Kirov said. He turned his head and surveyed her face with an intensity that made her feel breathless. 'Knowing you as well as it is my inestimable privilege to know you, I'm sure you've always let him know exactly how you felt.'

BOOK TWO

Siberian Orchid

Chapter Ten

The wind had been blowing briskly from the west, with just a touch of north in it, enough to make the weather as raw as you would expect it in April in the Baltic Sea. The ship, the *City of Newcastle*, had made a quick passage since calling in at Danzig, but the passengers had seen little of one another. Until she'd made her northing past the mouth of the Gulf of Riga, and rounded Dago Island, the *City of Newcastle* would have to sail close-hauled; and, as the experienced sailors amongst the passengers assured the tyros, sailing close-hauled is death to shipboard society.

Once they'd entered the Straits of Helsingfors, these same experts explained, the westerly wind would be fair for St Petersburg, and then they'd see how different things could be. Since most of the tyros were at that moment wishing they were dead, they had little interest in dining and dancing, and the thought of running free did not inspire them with delight.

But the elements had a mind of their own, and just as the ship might be expected to draw full advantage from the wind being from the west, it moderated and swung right around to blow gently but persistently from the east, dead foul for St Petersburg. The *City of Newcastle* hove-to – to the relief of many – and at length the captain announced that they would put into Reval until the wind veered southerly enough for them to continue.

Fleur was standing with her father on the section of the foredeck reserved for passengers when her brother brought the news. With the change of wind, the skies had cleared, and though it was still cold, a pale sun was shining from a sky of the most heavenly deep blue. Passengers who had not been above-decks since Danzig were creeping out, pale and uncertain, to snuff the air.

Fleur had not been troubled by the rough passage. Years of

being jolted about in carriages over unmade roads had obviously inured her, and visiting the homes of the poor and sick had given her a resistance to unpleasant smells which proved very useful in the bilge-scented confines of a wooden ship. In fact the only occasion she had ever been travel-sick was the first time she went on a railway train: the unaccustomed smoothness of the ride had nauseated her.

While confined to her cabin, she had spent her time reading, writing her diary, and daydreaming; but though she had kept herself occupied, she was very glad to be out in the fresh air again, with the prospect of company and diversion.

Now there was a grinding and shuddering noise which shook the timbers under their feet, and the gulls which had been sitting on the water, bobbing gently and eyeing the ship with interest, flew up, yarking in alarm. The great paddle wheels on either side of the ship began to turn, digging into the blue-black water and shovelling it out white and glittering as they began to pick up way. Turning to look aft, Fleur saw the plume of grey smoke rising almost vertically from the black smokestack, wavering only a little before it dispersed on the gentle air.

She leaned over the taffrail again to watch the paddles, marvelling at their size and power.

'If the wind is against us,' she asked idly, 'why don't we use the steam-power to get us up the Gulf?'

'It's not meant for that,' Richard said. 'It's only meant for getting the ship in and out of harbour. We wouldn't be carrying enough coal, anyway. Frankly, I doubt whether ships will ever be able to carry enough fuel to make complete journeys under steam power. It's not practical.' He looked at the black smoking stack with distaste. 'Horrible dirty things, steam-engines. They ought to keep them in factories, where they belong.'

'Oh Dick,' Fleur laughed, 'you're always against everything, until it turns out to be to your advantage. Look how you complained about steam railway trains—'

'Yes, and so I do – spoiling the hunting and frightening the horses! Some of the best runs have been ruined, with

186

dashed great iron roads right across the middle of them!'

'Yes, but then when Stegghampton invited you to Gretton for the hunting, you were very glad to take your hunters up by the railway, to save them the long journey by road.'

'That's a different matter,' Richard said hotly, and searched visibly for a difference. 'There's the danger of fire, for one thing. It'd be madness to have a great burning furnace in a wooden ship—'

Sir Ranulph, who was staring at the distant smudge of land and had not appeared to be listening, snorted at that. 'Stuff! You don't know what you're talking about, my boy. Why, in the future – and not very far ahead, either – ships will be made of iron, and driven entirely by steam power. Sailing in wooden ships like this will be a thing of the past.'

'Well I hope I'm not around to see it,' Richard said, offended, and pointedly moved a few steps further along the rail.

'Papa, you're roasting me! Ships made all of iron? They'd sink, for sure,' Fleur protested.

But Sir Ranulph's attention had departed again: staring out to sea, he smiled vaguely but didn't answer her. However, a gentleman standing to her other side lifted his hat politely and said, 'It's quite true, mademoiselle! An iron ship is no more likely to sink than a wooden one.'

She turned to look at him cautiously. He was a very average young man, perhaps a few years older than her, not particularly tall, not particularly handsome. He had an ordinary face, which for a moment seemed fleetingly familiar to her, and ordinary brown hair. He was dressed in a caped greatcoat of good material and cut, made peculiar only by the fact of having a fur collar. Still, a fur collar was allowable, given that they were in the Baltic; and a quick glance downwards established that his boots were all one could wish of a gentleman.

'But wood floats, sir, and iron does not,' she observed.

'True; but a ship floats not by virtue of what it's made of, but because of its shape.'

He smiled winningly, removing his hat and turning it upside down.

'It is the air *inside* the ship, you see, which makes it float,' he said, waggling his fingers about inside it. 'If I were to set this on the water, like this, it would float along quite merrily; but if I tilt it and it fills with water—' He made a throwaway gesture. '*Voila*! Another expensive visit to my hatter becomes necessary!'

'Yes, I see,' she said. 'And the principle is the same for every material?'

'Certainly. As long as the shape is right—' He gave a very Baltic sort of shrug.

'Thank you for explaining it,' she said with satisfaction. 'I do like to understand things properly.'

'And now I'm afraid you will never wish to speak to me again.'

She was startled. 'Why?'

'Because it may be useful to have a knowledge of engineering, but it's not *gentlemanly*. I should never have exposed myself,' he said, with such a ludicrous expression of remorse that she couldn't help smiling.

'You mustn't say so, not when I've just displayed a very unladylike desire for the same knowledge!'

'Ah, then our gentility must perish together! That's just as well, since we are heading for Reval, where experience leads me to believe it's impossible to be genteel for very long. A wonderful English word, "genteel", don't you think? Such a stinging condemnation, under the guise of a compliment! English is a pleasant language – it is possible to be more rude without appearing to than in any other tongue I know.'

Fleur laughed. 'Yes, you're quite right. My aunt is masterly at it, though she counts herself English only by adoption. But I've noticed that whenever she wants to be particularly cutting, she never uses French.'

'Of course not. French is merely the language of food and of protocol,' he said innocently.

'It's usually said to be the language of love,' Fleur reminded him.

He shook his head. 'A grave mistake. One might be a cook or a diplomat in French, but not a lover, never a lover.'

'Why so, sir?'

'Because, mademoiselle, the language of love must be direct and sincere, and it's impossible to be either in really good French. That's why it suits cooks and diplomats – they both have to lie for their professions.'

'I think you are very dangerous to know,' Fleur laughed. 'If I talk to you much longer, I shall have no convictions left!'

He smiled and raised his hat. 'Then I'll take my leave for the present, mademoiselle, secure in the knowledge that on such a small ship we shall certainly meet again.'

She bowed her head, indicating no great objection to the idea. He had a pleasant, gentlemanly air, and she had enjoyed his nonsense.

'Indeed,' he went on, 'if I don't mistake, we'll all be asked to dine at the Governor's house tonight. He's obsessively sociable, and he has a noted cook – noted for Estonia, that is. If we meet under his roof, you will hardly be able to refuse the acquaintance.'

'You forget one thing, sir,' she said gravely. 'We haven't been introduced, so we can't be said to be acquainted.'

'Oh, I'll soon remedy that! On shipboard, you know, it's quite the thing to introduce onself.'

He swept his hat across his stomach in a parody of a court bow, and, straightening up, twisted his flexible features into the down-the-nose expression of a Grand Vizier of great dignity.

'Peter Nikolayevitch Kirov begs to take his leave of you, mademoiselle. *A la prochaine!*'

For a few moments after he'd gone, she wondered whether she'd misheard him, or imagined the whole thing. But no, he had said what he said; and she remembered also that faint, fleeting familiarity of his face. He didn't look much like his brother. There was just a slight family resemblance, perhaps, in the cast of features, but where Kirov senior was tall, strikingly handsome, distinguished-looking, his cadet was merely pleasantly nondescript.

She had no leisure just then to think about the extraordinary coincidence of meeting him, for Richard was wanting her attention. Then there was all the excitement of coming into port: the pilot coming on board, manoeuvring up to the dock and tying up, all the sights and smells of the harbourside, and then a stream of health and customs officials passing up and down the gangplank and getting in each other's way.

She had to give at least an appearance of interest in what was going on; but at last she was able to claim with some truth that the noise and bustle and the brightness of the sunlight on the water had given her a headache, and she was able to escape below to her cabin.

Kirov! The mere mention of the name had stirred up all the feelings she had thought were safely buried. For more than a year she had not consciously thought about him, had considered herself cured of the sickness; but this chance meeting with his brother showed that under the veneer of normality she presented to the world, nothing had really changed.

A turmoil of pain and confusion overwhelmed her. Alone in her cabin, she sat down on the edge of her cot, and the cheerful noise of the harbourside faded from her consciousness as she thought back to that time, almost two years ago, when she had last seen him.

After their ride in the Park, she had not seen Kirov again before his departure for the north of England. There had followed two weeks which she remembered as grey and featureless. London seemed unbearably dull without him: too crowded, too noisy, too dirty, too hot. The parties, dances and dinners she went to were flat, the people boring, their conversation tedious.

When would he return? was the question she teased herself with endlessly and pointlessly; and how soon would he declare himself? That he must do so seemed certain. She was sure he must have understood Teddy Scott's outburst, and would be anxious to save her further possible embarrassment. It was simply the worst of bad luck that he'd been forced to leave London at that moment, with their affairs unresolved. And of course he was too much a gentleman to dream of writing to her. But as soon as he returned, he would call at Hanover Square, and everything would be made right.

Staring sightlessly at her cabin wall, her fingers clenched together in her lap, she remembered again the horror of that first meeting with him after his return. The first she knew of his being back was his card on the hall table when she and her aunt returned from a drive one morning. She felt a huge disappointment, and inwardly cursed their bad luck in having missed each other. But he would certainly call again later, she thought – and spent an interminable day straining her ears after every sound in the street outside, and starting at every knock on the door below.

He didn't come, and as their evening engagement was with family friends, she knew she wouldn't see him there. But he must call the next morning. She went to bed full of hope and anticipation, slept badly, woke far too early, dressed with special care. Refusing all invitations to stir out of the house, she spent a second long day waiting, her nerves stretched to the limits of their endurance, her thoughts puzzled and disturbed, her heart alternately trusting and misgiving. *Surely he must come! Why didn't he come?*

She didn't see him at the ball at Grosvenor House that evening, and assumed that he was not there. Some business had detained him, perhaps. Yes, happy thought! That must be it. He had been so busy since his return to London that, however much he longed to, he simply couldn't find the time to come to her. Neither Brunnow nor Khamensky was at the ball either. They were probably all burning the midnight oil together on Imperial business.

The next morning hope rose again, bruised but unrepentant. But her plan to stay at home and wait for his call was thwarted by Uncle Frederick, who invited her to go with him to the Exhibition, and in a perfectly pleasant way would not accept a refusal.

Fleur was forced to go, doing her best to cheer herself with the thought that he might be at the Exhibition too; and that if he did call at the house and find her out, he would surely, *surely* leave a message of some kind to say when he would call again.

But it was at the Exhibition that she saw him. Her throat tightened as she remembered that chance meeting: his surprise on seeing them, his tell-tale, momentary hesitation before turning aside to give them the encounter; his perfect, cool, undifferentiated politeness. He spoke to her and to her uncle as to any common acquaintance, answered her eager questions about his northern tour briefly and formally, returned her puzzled, questioning looks with a blandness that defied penetration. And then, without her knowing how he had done it, he had bowed and taken his leave – without any hint as to when she would see him again.

Like an automaton she had walked on with her uncle, her mind crying questions that no one could answer. She *couldn't* leave it like that! With shame she remembered her pitiful subterfuge, how she had tugged her hand away from her uncle's arm and babbled something about having dropped her handkerchief, how she had scurried away from him, pushing through the crowds like any idiotic, love-stricken schoolgirl in pursuit of Kirov.

She caught up with him, touched his arm. He stopped and turned, she looked up into his face – oh, a marble face, stern, closed to her! Why had she not let it be, gone away then in silence, kept her pride? But she hadn't been able to believe that he could change so completely. *What's happened? Why have you gone away from me?* she wanted to ask, but she could not quite do it. Instead, falteringly, she had asked him – the mortification of it! – if they would meet as usual in the Park the next morning. She added – how could she bear to remember? – that they had a great need to talk.

And he looked at her gravely and said nothing. For a long moment, he said nothing at all; and then he thanked her for her kind invitation, which he feared he must refuse, as he was too occupied with Embassy business. Then he bowed with perfect politeness and went away, leaving her scarlet-faced and quivering as though he had struck her. Scalding tears of shame and pain welled up in her, and she needed all her strength to fight them back, for she couldn't weep in public.

She had to return to her uncle and somehow pretend that nothing was wrong.

Bad as that had been, there had been worse to come. There followed two weeks in which, as if by the design of a malignant fate, they encountered each other every day at public functions. He treated her each time they met with the same formal courtesy he used towards everyone else, but which to her, from him, was like a blow. Every social event was a nightmare, to be lived through somehow, until she could retire at last at the end of each long day to her chamber, exhausted with emotion, there to cry bitter tears of humiliation and self-reproach.

She began to look so drawn that even Venus noticed it, and said that the Season was proving too much for her.

'You seem quite pulled, my love. I think we had better go out of London as soon as possible. It's always intolerable in the summer, and this year, with the Exhibition . . . As soon as the House goes into recess, we'll go into the country.'

But when it came to it, she asked to go home. She wanted only to be left alone, to be allowed to hide herself away until she had discovered some way to live with what had happened, and worked out some plan for facing the world again.

For there had been one more meeting with him; her last – the last time she had ever seen him. It was at a public ball, given for the benefit of a hospital which was in Sir Frederick's patronage. Fleur's ballgown had suffered some slight damage from a clumsy partner, who, attempting to hold her too closely in the waltz, had tangled his feet with her skirt and torn the silk edging from the lowest flounce of the rose-pink gauze.

Too weary with unhappiness to mind very much, she accepted the young man's apologies absently, and was almost glad of the excuse to retire to the ladies' room. There the attendant maid examined the damage with a shake of the head.

'It's not such a big tear, miss, but this net's so delicate. I'll have to fold it under before I sew the ribbon back on, or it'll fray. It'll never be the same again. What a shame! Such a lovely gown as it is, and such a pretty colour . . .'

The unimportant small mishap for some reason undid her. Staring down at her spoiled finery, she felt the tears begin to seep from under her eyelids, and was helpless to prevent them.

The maid was distressed. 'Oh, don't take on so, miss! I dare say it won't show so much, not right down at the hem. There, there, don't cry any more!'

The good woman had sewn her skirt, bathed her temples in lavender-water, patted fresh powder on her shoulders, and offered all sorts of comfort, for the wrong hurt. Fleur composed herself at last, managing to push down the lump of misery into its accustomed place, and left her, walking slowly towards the ballroom and the sound of music. The corridor was empty; and then a door to an ante-room opened, and Kirov stepped out into her path.

They were no more than two feet apart; they could not possibly avoid the encounter. She stopped dead, her self-possession gone, able to do nothing but stare at him dumbly, aware that her feelings must be showing in her face but helpless to hide them.

'Miss Hamilton,' he said, beginning a formal bow; and then he stopped, straightened, and stood looking at her almost blankly, as though he, too, had no idea how anything more was to be said or done. He was, she saw, for once not completely in control, and his uncertainty undid what little progress she had made towards shutting him out. Everything in her yearned towards him again, her idiot heart still not having learned its lesson.

He was surveying her face. 'Are you ill?' he asked suddenly. 'You look so thin and pale.'

'No, I'm—' she began, and then knew that if she spoke, she would cry. She stopped and shook her head, lowering her eyes from that too-vivid face, struggling for composure.

He stood there, seeming uncertain what to do. He seemed to want to talk to her, without knowing what to say. At last he said, 'I shall be leaving London soon. Next week I return to St Petersburg.'

The words fell like the deathly sound of the first clod of

earth striking a coffin. She looked up, suddenly dry-eyed, the tears driven back to their source by the finality of it. 'Your task here is finished?' she asked.

'I've been recalled.' He paused. 'The Emperor doesn't like any of us to be away for long. I don't suppose—' He stopped again. 'I don't suppose I shall be able to return.'

She nodded. 'Then, I wish you a pleasant journey,' she said, and held out her hand. She was astonished at the calmness of her voice. Her hand, she observed, was a triumph of steadiness. Who was it who was doing this? Surely not her.

'Yes,' he said, but he didn't move to take it. For a long moment he looked at her with that same blank stare, almost like someone who has suffered a severe shock. She had once seen a child, knocked down by a cart in a lane, look like that. Then he seemed to make up his mind. He appeared to shake some thought away, and resumed his formal, polite expression.

'Yes. Thank you,' he said. He took her hand, bowed over it, released it, and turned away.

And that, Fleur thought, is that. The calmness was using up all her strength, and she thought she must soon get away somewhere to be alone, or she might actually fall down. She tried to gather herself to go, but found she couldn't move, not while he was still in sight, walking away from her down the corridor.

And then he turned. At the end of the passage, as he was about to turn the corner and out of sight, he looked back at her, one long, burning look, his beautiful golden eyes full of such misery that her own unhappiness seemed to her in that instant, by comparison, but a fleeting ache. And then he was gone, out of sight, and out of her life for ever.

The next day she went home to Chiswick in a state of collapse. She remained there for the rest of the summer, scarcely stirring out of the house, and then only to walk about the garden, or sit in a sunny spot, like an invalid.

It had been like an illness – the first fever of grief, then the lethargy, and then the long, slow process of recuperation. Little by little she rebuilt her routines, took up her old occupations, resuming her reading, her writing, her sewing, her walks, her rides, her charitable concerns.

The odd thing was that no one seemed to notice what had happened to her. She was thought to have returned to the country because the mad whirligig of social life had overtired her; and out of sight seemed to be out of mind. Uncle Frederick rode out one day to see how she was going on, and there were other formal calls from acquaintances and neighbours, but all seemed to think she was looking much better, and observed comfortably that the country obviously suited her best.

Aunt Venus wrote her usual letters full of news and names, Aunt Ercy sent pressed flowers and a recipe for a tonic drink which the dear Prince had recommended. Richard scrawled two notes about field days and parades, complained about the insufficiency of his allowance and wondered that she didn't come back to Town now she was rested. Her father appeared at the house from time to time in the course of his wanderings, and greeted her vaguely or energetically, according to his mood, without seeming to wonder why she was there as opposed to anywhere else.

Only Buckley seemed to understand. When she confined herself to the house, he called daily with spurious questions about the horses in order to look her over keenly to see whether she was still off her feed. When she graduated to the garden, he often turned up with titbits of village news. He brought her gifts: a particularly beautiful brown egg he thought she might fancy for her luncheon, or some mushrooms he had picked in the paddock, which he knew she was especially partial to, or a handsome trout he'd tickled out of Mr Scott's brook – but not to tell anyone, Miss Flora, or they'd take him up for poaching – she knew what Mr Scott was like about his game rights!

His unobtrusive sympathy was balm to her aching heart, and gradually the healing process took over, and she learned to live with herself again, and then, slowly, with the world. And then at last she was able to think about what had happened and, as she thought, put it to rest.

She thought she understood. He *had* cared for her; she was sure of that; but as a friend; and not understanding their social customs, he had overstepped the invisible boundaries, and unwittingly given rise to false expectations. When he discovered, through Teddy Scott's clumsy intervention, what his intimacy had brought people to suppose, he had done his best to repair the situation by withdrawing from her, and treating her thereafter with that wounding formal politeness.

He had never meant to marry her, never meant her to love him. That was her mistake. And his rough remedy had worked, as far as she knew. Her reputation was unsullied, her shameful secret safe.

Of that last, agonised look he gave her, she didn't know what to think. Well, he was a man of mature years, who had suffered much in his life. She could have no idea what secret troubles he carried with him. Or perhaps it was merely a look of remorse for the suffering he must have known he had caused her. On the whole, she thought that was the most likely explanation. So she drew the line under the account, and closed the book, and refused to allow herself to think of him any more.

By the following spring she was ready to resume a normal social life. When Aunt Venus wrote deploring her eremitical life, and invited her to London for the Season, she accepted with at least an appearance of gaiety. Lord James Paget duly presented himself, and she accepted his escort to a number of social events. She liked him – he was pleasant company, and very faithful in his attentions – so she was kind to him, and he blossomed with new hope.

She began to think that she might marry him. He would make a safe, undemanding husband. His property and title were good, he would be kind to her, and he liked horses. She thought she might get along with him very well; and marriage with him would make sure that no one ever suspected her of nursing a broken heart. That would have been the worst thing. She had offered all the love stored up through a lonely childhood and solitary adolescence to the wrong person, and had been rejected. Like the greenest of innocents, she had

197

exposed her tenderest feelings for all the world to see, and to the pain of trampled love was added the bitterness of wounded pride and damaged self-esteem. She had made a fool of herself, and it would be long before she could forgive herself her folly.

So she allowed Paget to escort her, and as they began to be seen together, there was a wakening of supposition about them, which she took no great pains to suppress. When she parted with him to come on this trip, it was with the unspoken understanding that when she returned in the autumn, she would probably allow him to propose to her. Since then, without consciously thinking about it, she had accepted that he was there in the background as something she would be going back to, and the idea was neither exciting nor dismaying, but comfortable. Comfort was all she now aspired to.

Of course, she had known that there was a possibility she might meet Kirov in St Petersburg, but it was a remote possibility. The Polotskis did not move in the same circles; and if they passed in the street, there would be no necessity for more than the bow of common politeness. And of course, he might not even be in St Petersburg – as special aide to the Tsar, he was just as likely to be away somewhere on a special mission.

It simply would not have been possible for her to anticipate that before she even got to Russia, she would have fallen into conversation with his younger brother. If she had been an Unbeliever, this alone would have made her believe in God – but in a God with a distinctly mischievous sense of humour.

The Governor's house was a strange-looking edifice of red brick and grey stone, buried in a surprisingly burgeoning garden, considering the latitude. Architecturally it aimed at catholicism rather than distinction. If it was true that imitation was the sincerest form of flattery, the architect had plainly set out to compliment the Turks, the Poles and the French as well as Palladio and the Ancient Greeks.

Inside, however, all was light, warmth and comfort, and the tall, villainous-looking but extremely kind Governor and his rather dumpy wife – who looked as though she would be more at home in a peasant scarf than a tiara – welcomed the travellers as though they had just stepped out of a cramped and chilly stage-coach after a long journey, offered all manner of warming drinks, and urged them to move closer to the fire.

The Governor and his wife spoke neither French nor English, and as Fleur spoke no German, her duty to her host and hostess was soon done. Her father, who spoke most languages, talked to the Governor about his garden, and Richard drifted over to join another young blade with whom he had tentatively been making friends that afternoon on board the ship. Fleur stood warming her hands at the fire, and watching the grouping and regrouping of the company without feeling the need to join in.

A few minutes later, however, the younger Kirov arrived, and having greeted their excellencies, headed straight for Fleur like one claiming an old friend.

'You see, I was right, wasn't I? I knew it would be dinner at least, and if the Governor could be sure of the wind staying foul, there'd be a ball tomorrow, too.'

'He seems a very kind man, despite his appearance,' Fleur said.

'Oh, he simply loves company. Our ship's misfortune is nuts for him.'

'Nuts for him? How very colloquial! You speak English better – you speak it very well,' she caught herself up hastily.

'I've had many English friends – mostly soldiers, so you must forgive a certain coarseness. I'm a cavalryman, you know, and we can always spot each other, wherever we are. That young man over there, for instance – he's a Hussar if ever I saw one! He looks, as you English say, a regular plunger!'

'Thank you. He's my brother.'

'No, is he? And tell me, is his name Smith – John Smith?'

'Of course not. It's Richard Hamilton.'

Count Peter grinned impishly. 'There now, Miss Hamilton, that saves you the impropriety of having to tell me your name. Didn't I do it nicely?'

'A transparent device. I knew exactly what you were up to.'

'Then it was very good-natured of you to go along with the

plot! It just shows, doesn't it? A lot of Russians say that the English are stiff, but here you are, a nice Hussar's nice sister . . . Nice is a good word, isn't it?'

'Very nice,' she agreed. 'The name Hamilton doesn't mean anything to you, I gather?'

He wrinkled his brow. 'Should it?'

'No, not at all,' she said. He hadn't mentioned her, then. She didn't know whether to be glad or sorry.

He seemed about to pursue the thread, but was distracted by the opening of the double doors at the end of the saloon. 'Ah, good, here come the *zakuski*,' he said, rubbing his hands with anticipation. 'I'm as hungry as a Polish horse! Now, Miss Hamilton, if you've never had it before, you must allow me to introduce you to caviare.'

He offered his arm and led her towards the long table which had just been wheeled in, and which was covered with foods of all kinds, some being kept warm in chafing dishes, some cold. The rest of the company was crowding in eagerly, causing a certain amount of jostling.

'Of course, some of these poor creatures haven't eaten for days,' Count Peter murmured. 'Hold tightly to my arm, Miss Hamilton. This is a struggle for survival. Give no quarter.'

The caviare was an unpleasant-looking grey mess, but she allowed him to provide her with a portion, and some kind of local muffin, toasted, to eat it with.

'And to go with it you must have vodka,' he decreed, gesturing to the footman. The bottle was being kept cold in a bucket of ice, and Fleur looked doubtful when she was given her small glass.

'In England ladies do not drink spirits,' she said.

'Then let us thank God we're not in England,' he said simply. 'You can't eat caviare without vodka, that's the law. Your health, Miss Hamilton!'

She sipped – and choked, to his undisguised amusement, which set her on her mettle. She tasted the caviare and thought it mildly unpleasant, but would not be beaten, sipped again, tasted again, and by the third attempt was beginning to see the point. Eaten with the buttery, floury muffin, the saltiness of the caviare became piquant rather than overpowering, and the fiery tang of the spirit readied the palate for another attack.

He watched her with open amusement, and when she had finished he cried, 'Bravo England! That's the spirit that held out against Napoleon! You were determined not to be beaten, weren't you?'

'Not at all. I enjoyed it very much,' she said with dignity.

'Have some more,' he suggested slyly.

'No thank you! I'd like to try something else now.'

He selected for her some cold buttered eggs sprinkled with paprika, small pastry cases filled with smoked chicken and peas, and mushrooms stuffed with minced meats. He replaced the vodka with a glass of champagne. 'Russian champagne: much better than the French.' He served himself, and then guided her to a quiet corner, out of the press. 'And now, Miss Hamilton, if you are comfortable, *votre histoire*, if you please! I like to be entertained while I eat. Tell me everything about yourself.'

'Where shall I begin?'

'It doesn't matter. We'll know everything about each other sooner or later. Begin by telling me why you are going to St Petersburg.'

'My father is a botanist who specialises in the study of orchids. Most orchids grow in temperate climates, but there are stories about a variety that grows in Siberia, north of the Arctic Circle. My father is to make an expedition in search of this Siberian orchid, and when he finds it and brings it back, it will be named after him, which will make him very happy.'

Count Peter frowned. 'Hamilton, Hamilton – wait a minute, is your father Sir Ranulph Hamilton?'

'Yes. You have heard of him then?'

'I should think I have! My father had all his books at home. And my brother met him when he was in London two years ago. But this is splendid! Dear Miss Hamilton, that means we are almost family! No wonder you thought the name ought to mean something to me.'

'I thought that your brother might have mentioned – mentioned my father.'

'Did you meet Sergei too? A dull dog, isn't he?' Count Peter said casually. Fleur blinked at the description, but said nothing. 'Why,' he went on, 'if I'd met a golden goddess like you, I'd have talked about you for ever! But tell me, what are you going to do while your father goes orchid-hunting? You can't mean to go to Siberia with him, I hope? It's a most uncivilised place.'

'I shall be staying with the Polotskis. They've invited my brother and me to stay for as long as we like. Papa will collect us on his way back.'

'The Polotskis? Do I know them?'

'Mr Polotski discovered the Polotski Emerald.'

'Oh, that Polotski!' He looked enlightened, and then puzzled. 'I shouldn't have thought they were of your sort.'

Fleur grew defensive. 'I like Mr Polotski very much. He stayed at my aunt's house in London, and we became great friends. He promised me then that I should visit him, so that I could see something of Russia, and I'm very grateful to him for asking me.'

Count Peter hastened to soothe her ruffled feathers. 'Oh, he's a very good sort of man, I'm sure. I only thought – however, I'm sure they'll make you comfortable. We aren't acquainted, but I've seen him around the Court once or twice. Or at least, I think he's the man I'm thinking of. What a thing, though, to find that great emerald, sitting there in a river, waiting for him to come along! And then just to give it away to the Emperor!'

'It was too big for him to sell,' Fleur said. 'No one could have afforded to buy it.'

'Not in one piece, but if he'd broken it up he could have sold it and made his fortune.'

Fleur looked shocked. 'He couldn't have done that! It would have destroyed its value.'

'Not it! It had no value as it was, only as a gift to sweeten the Emperor. And then His Majesty went and gave it away to your Queen, so poor old Polotski will soon be forgotten.

He'd have done better to make his money while he could.'

Fleur said nothing, reflecting on how different Count Peter was from his brother.

'Well, Miss Hamilton,' he went on, 'I hope you will allow me to call on you in Petersburg, now that we know we're practically cousins! Will you be staying long?'

'Papa intends to be away for six months. I expect him to collect me to go home in October.'

'Oh, then there's plenty of time. You must come out to our *dacha* one day – it isn't far from Petersburg. It's the strangest place you ever saw—'

'Stranger than this house?'

He grinned. 'Built by the same architect, I should say. And how is it that your brother can be away from his regiment for so long?'

'He's in the throes of a promotion. He's a cornet in the 11th Hussars, and there's a captaincy which will become vacant in six months' time. But by our laws he can't be a captain until he's been a lieutenant. So Papa bought him a lieutenancy in another regiment, and Richard transferred, served one day to get his qualification, and then went onto half-pay. He'll stay on half-pay until his captaincy comes up, then transfer back into his own regiment and onto the active service list again.'

Count Peter listened with close attention to all this. 'What an excellent system! I must say you English have everything worked out so comfortably! It's much harder to get on in our country. I must get to know your brother better. Do you think he'd like to be invited to our mess?'

Fleur warmed to him. 'I'm sure he'd like it above anything,' she said.

'Then I'll do it. He looks a jolly sort of fellow, and I'd like to make him comfortable. Our mess is the best in Petersburg. Do you like the ballet?'

'Yes, very much.'

'Then perhaps you'll let me take you one day. Oh, and your brother, of course!'

She laughed at the thought of Richard at the ballet. 'Richard would sooner spend an evening being roasted on a spit than watch the ballet.'

He grinned. 'Strange how sibling blood can produce such differences! Take my brother, for instance. I shouldn't want to inflict him on you for an evening. He's such a cold fish! Do you know, he can be with a woman for half an hour together, without making her laugh.'

She smiled, rather reluctantly, and said, 'Our meetings in London were of the formal sort. I didn't know him very well.'

'The best way, I assure you! Well, this is very satisfactory. One way or another, we're sure of meeting again and again in Petersburg. How glad I am the wind changed! It will make all the difference to the summer.'

Fleur thought that he little knew how right he was. What hope now of avoiding all contact with Kirov senior? And then she thought, if I had really wanted to avoid him, would I not have discouraged his brother's friendliness? Have I not brought this on myself?

Yes, of course. Underneath it all, she wanted to see him again, tell herself what she might about indifference and pride. And that was a lowering thought.

Chapter Eleven

The wind veered southerly during the night, and the Governor of Reval was deprived of further society. The *City of Newcastle* got up steam and went out of harbour at first light, and once clear of the cape shook out her courses and sailed close-hauled up to St Petersburg.

Fleur's first impression of the great port of St Petersburg was one of chaotic busyness. The approach was through the Gulf of Kronstadt, divided in the middle by the island on which the low, grey bulk of the fortress guarded the channels to either side. The ramparts bristled with guns, with the blue and white Imperial flag fluttering above. A cluster of spars marked the position of the dockyard, and a number of warships – rather antiquated and shabby to Fleur's eyes – rode at anchor under the shelter of those grinning muzzles.

Both channels were crowded with ships showing the flags of all nations: merchant ships, cargo boats, and coasters being guided through the treacherous sandbanks by fussy little black tugs; fishing vessels of all sizes, luggers, pinnaces, pleasure launches; and customs cutters darting amongst them like anxious sheepdogs. The vessels crowded into the harbour, competing for space to tie up and unload. Some had had to anchor to wait their turn, and around each of them the water was covered with a bobbing mass of shoreboats and bumboats, looking like the cloud of little black summer flies that descends on a sweating horse.

'It's always like this when the ice first melts every spring,' Count Peter said. He had stationed himself at her elbow and was looking on the scene with satisfaction. 'How good it is to be back home! Russia is the most wonderful place on earth, and Petersburg's the most beautiful city. You'll see.'

Fleur liked him for his simple enthusiasm and was quite prepared to believe him. Her first glimpses were not disappointing: she had travelled all this way for novelty, and the quayside was crowded with strange-looking people. Peasants with bushy beards, wearing dirty sheepskin coats, baggy trousers and boots, were unloading crates and bales of cargo from the ships, shouting at each other and flinging their burdens about with a light-hearted ease that promised many breakages. There were merchants in long-skirted kaftans, whose beards flowed to their waists, elaborately curled. They were examining goods and arguing with pursers and customsmen, uniformed officials who looked either harassed or unapproachable, and whose beards were short and neat. And here and there were various military men, with cavalry moustaches and luxuriant side-whiskers. There was hardly a clean-shaven face to be seen. Fleur began to understand her aunt's prejudice.

Everyone shouted, and everyone gesticulated vigorously as they shouted; but it all seemed very good-natured, and there was as much laughter as cursing, even when there were mishaps. She saw a fine bull being unloaded from an English ship, bellowing mournfully as it was swung in a canvas sling high above the teeming quayside. As soon as its feet touched the earth it lashed out with a hind leg, and managed to send a man flying, which brought forth gales of laughter, even from the victim. The bull didn't like the laughter, and bellowed the louder, swinging its wicked head at everyone who came near.

'He looks a lively one,' Count Peter said. 'He'll put spirit into somebody's herd.'

'Are you interested in selective breeding?' Fleur asked unwarily.

'It's the only kind I care for,' he said seriously, putting her to the blush; then, kindly looking about for something to divert her, 'Look, over there, Miss Hamilton – there's a real Petersburg sight for you.'

A group of single-horse vehicles was drawn up at the end of the quay, each attended by a bearded, sheepskin-clad man. They sat on the drivers' seats, or on the ground smoking or eating, or lounged together talking animatedly, casting sharp glances around them all the while, to make sure they weren't missing anything. They reminded Fleur of starlings.

'They look like hackney-drivers,' she said.

'Very sharp of you! *Izvozchiks* in Russian. We have more cabs than in any city on earth, because it's impossible to walk here. In spring and autumn the streets are bogs, in summer there's terrible dust, and in winter deep snow. We'd be lost without them.'

'They seem cheerful sorts.'

'Oh, they're tremendous fun – full of stories and jokes, despite their hard life. They're nomads, you see, living with their carts day and night. They sleep in them or under them, and wandering tradesmen sell them tea and bread and *kvass* – that's a kind of liquor – and hay for their horses. They're the best drivers in the world, too.'

'Oh really?'

'Yes, really! Don't look so sceptical. They fly along at a tremendous speed, talking to their horses all the time. They never use the whip. It's a kind of running conversation – "Come my brother, my friend, my little white pigeon," they croon to him. "Look where you're going, my darling. Mind out for that stone. Faster, my sweetheart, faster!" Oh, they're wonderful fellows! Many's a bottle I've shared with an *izvozchik* late at night on my way home from some party – and many's a time I've been carried up to my bed by one of them, too!'

She shook her head. 'Reprehensible! I'm afraid you've been very badly brought up.'

'You shouldn't say so. I had an English nurse.'

'I don't believe you.'

'It's true. English nurses are highly prized in Petersburg, you know. My dear old Nanushka! She died a few years ago. How I cried!'

With an English mother and an English nurse, Fleur thought, it was no wonder he spoke the language so fluently – more so even than his brother. She looked across to the clustering skyline of the city of St Petersburg. *His* city – he was there somewhere, perhaps, going about his business, unaware that she was so near. And when he became aware of her arrival, what would he think, what would he do? If they met, how would he behave? It would be better all round if it turned out that he was away somewhere, but she couldn't help hoping that—

She heard her name being called, and realised guiltily that she had been trapped into thinking about him again. She turned. Richard was hurrying towards them, clutching his hat as he edged through the crowd.

'I say, Flo, there you are! Come on, Papa's waiting for us. There's a servant here to take us to the customs house. How d'ye do, Kirov!'

'Hullo, Hamilton. Are you going, then? I shall call on you in the next day or two, and take you to the mess and introduce you to everyone, as I promised.'

Richard looked pleased. 'Very good of you,' he said, offering Fleur a perfunctory arm. 'I'm looking forward to it. Come on, Flo. I say, Kirov, do you know my direction in St Petersburg? I'm dashed if I do!'

'Don't worry, I shall find you out. I shall come and poke you out of your burrow all right, wherever it is. Miss Hamilton – your servant, ma'am!'

He bowed low, but fixed her with an amused and mocking eye. She returned a grave curtsey, and allowed Richard to drag her away, reflecting that Count Peter had something of what seemed to be a family ability to manipulate situations. His engagement to call on Richard, she felt sure, was at least partly a subterfuge to call on her, and she didn't know whether to be pleased or sorry about it.

Their passage through the customs house was slow, because of the extent of Sir Ranulph's expedition equipment, and particularly the vast quantity of books he had brought with him. The officials seemed puzzled rather than suspicious, but were still arguing amongst themselves when rescue arrived in the unlikely shape of Mr Polotski.

He came striding in, rolling a little on his springy toes, fair and circular and handsome as Fleur remembered him, and looking, in his fur greatcoat, like a blonde and genial bear. He greeted everyone cordially, took in the situation, and then launched at the officials a tirade which made them shrink and cower. Within minutes, it seemed, all the boxes had been repacked and roped, and the Hamiltons were being led out into the thin April sunshine, and freedom.

'I'm so sorry you should have been held up like that,' Polotski said as he conducted them to his carriage. 'Those men are good enough fellows, but they're like mules, they need a beating every now and then to get them along. I meant to be here to meet you, but I was held up on the way. However, my servant found you all right, didn't he? Here we are, here we are, this is my carriage. Don't worry about your luggage – my men will see to all that.'

The large open landau was lacquered a glossy black, with a team of four perfect white horses harnessed up to it. Inside the upholstery was pale blue velvet trimmed with gold fringe, and the coachman and footman were dressed in livery to match. Fleur blinked a little at the ostentation, and wondered whether everything was going to be like that. Polotski saw them in and then climbed up himself, and the footman arranged two great fur rugs over their knees and tucked them in.

'It's still a little chilly,' said Polotski, 'but I thought you'd enjoy the open carriage for your first view of the city. You see so much more . . . Are you quite comfortable? My dear wife wanted to come and meet you, but I absolutely forbade it. I hope you will forgive me, but she really isn't strong, and I didn't know how long we might have to wait. My poor Sophie, she hasn't been at all well lately . . .'

The carriage moved away from the customs house and the driver put the horses into a smart trot. Soon they had their first view of the wonderful city, and it was impossible even for Sir Ranulph not to marvel at its broad streets and great open spaces. The immense houses were painted in the most wonderful colours – primrose and robin's-egg blue, leaf-green, rose-pink, sky and terracotta. The city was divided and subdivided by a network of canals, sparkling in the oblique sunlight between handsome granite quays, and spanned here and there by delicate, arched wooden bridges. There were tree-lined boulevards and glimpses of gardens, statues and fountains, and an astonishing multitude of churches, whose gilded and enamelled domes glinted like jewels, each one crowned with a glorious golden cross reaching into the pale sky.

They stared and wondered, and kind Polotski kept up a running commentary on the places they passed, punctuated by more domestic information.

'The Trotsky Bridge; and this is one of the principal market-places. Of course, everything's rather quiet at the moment, because we're still in Lent. But only a few more days, and then it'll be Easter, and all the fun will start again. Lyudmilla, my little girl, wanted to come and meet you too, but I told her to stay at home with her mother. I didn't want her to tire you with her chatter before you'd got your bearings. She's so excited about your visit . . . Ah, this is the Nevsky Prospekt, our main shopping street. Like your Regent Street, perhaps, only a little bigger . . . The Holy Mother of Kazan Cathedral, over there. We go to St Anne's mostly, because it's nearer, except if there's some special festival . . .

'We didn't know exactly when you'd be arriving. Sophie and Milochka – that's what we call Lyudmilla – have done the flowers in your rooms five times in the past week. I hope you'll be comfortable. If there's anything you want, you must ask . . . The river is the Neva, of course. It's everything to us, the source of life, as they say the Nile is to the Egyptians . . . Sophie's picked out servants to take care of you, since you didn't bring your own, but if you don't like them, you must say so at once, and we'll change them . . . This is called the English Quay – oh, and there's the house of our old friend, Count Kirov—'

Fleur was startled into comment. 'What, all that?'

'Yes, that's the Kirov Palace. Rastrelli designed it – I believe it's much admired; and I understand the gardens are beautiful. I've never been inside it, of course. And the one with the spire, there, is the Admiralty . . .'

Fleur had ceased to listen. She stared at the vast expanse of the façade of the Kirov Palace, painted pale blue, with the pillars and porticoes a contrasting white, like the mock pediments over each of the innumerable windows. It was no use to tell herself that space here was no object, and that all buildings were bigger. She remembered Kirov telling her how he had watched his brother march away from 'the window of our house', and the picture his words had formed in her head simply would not be reconciled with the gigantic nobleman's residence before her.

How more than foolish she had been to suppose that she, Miss Fleur Hamilton of Grove Park, Chiswick, could be the object of a man who owned such a palace – and presumably another like it in the country – and who knew what else? Count Kirov, to think of marrying her? It was a joke – a bad joke! She felt humbled by a new realisation of her folly; and the contemplation of various old saws about pride and fall prevented her from taking in much more of what Polotski was saying.

At last they turned off the Nevsky Prospekt into a road only slightly less narrow, and then into a more humble street which was only, say, twice as wide as Regent Street. Finally the landau pulled up in front of a big, square, handsome house of red brick edged with white coping stones. White stone steps with a wrought-iron balustrade curved up from either side in a handsome sweep to the front door; to the side of the house was a glimpse of a large courtyard behind which evidently housed stables and coach house. It was not on the same sort of scale as the Kirov Palace, but it was at least four times as big as Grove Park.

More lessons, Fleur thought, about pride and prejudice. Mr Polotski smiled round at his guests with such genuine and unassuming pleasure that she felt ashamed that she had even found it possible to defend him to others of her own social order.

'And here's our little house! I do hope you'll be comfortable here.' The footman opened the carriage door and let down the step, and Polotski bounced nimbly down and turned to offer Fleur his hand. The door of the house opened and four men-servants came out and began to descend in stately order, two to a side. Behind them a female figure appeared in the door-way. Polotski's smile broadened. 'And there's my dear Sophie! How pleased she'll be that you've arrived at last.'

The house servants were still coming down the steps, but now they were brushed aside by a whirlwind followed by two small noisy dogs. It rushed up to the carriage, skirts and curls flying, and flung itself onto Polotski's broad front crying, 'Papa, Papa, you're back! And is this them? Oh, I'm so glad you've come! I thought you'd never get here!'

Polotski hugged her and set her gently aside saying, 'My daughter, Lyudmilla Ivanovna. This is Miss Hamilton. Milochka, don't be so wild, my darling. What will she think of you?'

Milochka turned her radiant smile on Fleur. 'Oh dear! But she's sure to find out about me sooner or later, so perhaps she had better know the worst now. Miss Hamilton, how do you do? I was the despair of my teachers at the Smolny. They said I was an abominable little gypsy. But I do so want you to love me, and so—' She placed the tips of her fingers against her breast, lowered her head, stretched out the other hand in a graceful sweep, and sank to the ground in the beautiful, dedicated curtsey of the prima ballerina.

Polotski's 'little girl', whom Fleur had been expecting to be ten or twelve years old, was a young lady of eighteen or so. Adjusting her ideas rapidly as Milochka rose from the curtsey with perfect control, Fleur said, 'How do you do? How very well you do that! I wish I had half your gracefulness.'

'Oh, we learned the dance at the Smolny – that was my school. It's the best school in Petersburg.' She stopped dead, and stared at Fleur with wide eyes. 'But you're so beautiful! Papa said that you were, but he didn't tell the half of it. You're as beautiful as an angel! Oh, I do hope you will love me!'

'I'm perfectly sure I shall,' Fleur said, amused. 'And you are very pretty too.'

She was indeed – a slender and graceful girl with a blooming face, soft fawn hair and wide brown eyes, a straight little nose, a neat, pointed chin, and the innocent and exuberant charm of a fox-kitten. She would be hard to resist, Fleur thought; and as Richard descended from the landau and came forward to be introduced in his turn, it was plain that he didn't even try. His plunger's self-possession fled as she turned that innocent rose of a face up to him. He blushed, stammered, and bowed over her hand in a dumb admiration that made him seem no more than eighteen himself.

Sir Ranulph's politeness was purely formal: he was much more interested in the cart loaded with his equipment which had just caught up and was turning into the stableyard behind the house. He could not, however, in decency run off after it, for the lady of the house had now descended the stairs, and was coming across to them with her hands extended in a warm and motherly welcome. She was a small woman, rather pale and careworn, but with the soft autumn of what must have been a great beauty still lighting her face.

'Oh you poor dears, what a long journey you've had! You must long to take off your things and rest. And tea, you must want tea! Vanya, dear, we mustn't keep them standing out here in the cold.'

'No, love, of course not. Miss Hamilton, my dear wife

Sophie. Sir Ranulph Hamilton, and Mr Hamilton. There, have I the forms right? Good, then let's go in! I think it's going to rain any moment. Oh, Sir Ranulph, don't be afraid for your baggage, I promise nothing will be broken. I've told my very best man to take personal charge of it all. Yes, here comes the rain, I knew it. Milochka, love, lead the way – quickly now!'

Fleur found herself feeling at home in a surprisingly short time, considering how many things were different about her surroundings; but of course it was because the Polotskis were so very welcoming. Mr Polotski was the same genial, amusing man she had grown fond of in London; Madame was gentle and kind, and if at times she was rather preoccupied, there was always Milochka to chatter and exhort and entertain. She had taken the greatest fancy to Fleur, and admired everything about her with an openness which would have been embarrassing if it had not been so obviously sincere and unstudied.

There was much to get used to about the house. For one thing, all the rooms, which were very large, led into one another around a central staircase hall, the 'inner' rooms being separated from each other by sliding doors. In each room a great Dutch stove stood glowing, fed by birch logs, and with the double windows keeping out every vestige of cold air, the climate inside the house was, Fleur thought, almost Italian.

As Polotski had told her in London, the women wore light dresses all year round, so when they went out they had to put on a great deal of outer clothing. This was all kept in the vestibule inside the front door, and a servant sat there all day, whose sole duty was to help the family and guests on and off with their outer garments. Madame Polotski considered Fleur's capes and cloaks quite inadequate, and with a motherly shake of the head and click of the tongue, provided her with a felted-wool underjacket, a quilted, sleeveless waistcoat for especially cold days, a heavy wool greatcoat, and a fur coat in case it snowed again.

'Which it might very well do, my dear, for it's only just May, after all.'

Fleur's room seemed huge to her, a vast expanse of polished

wood-block floor and pale blue and white carpet, below a ceiling twelve feet high. It was crammed with furniture of varying styles, some modern, some old, much of it obviously spoils of the French Revolution. And there were Italian marbles, Dutch ceramics, Turkish metalware, a vast English sofa upholstered in blue plush velvet – the spoils of a lifetime of travel, but assembled, she was afraid, without discrimination.

It was arranged, like all the rooms, as a sitting-room, with the bedroom appurtenances hidden behind tall Chinese screens. Fleur found it rather odd that there were no separate bedrooms, but was assured that this was the normal way in Petersburg.

As well as the vases of flowers, leaves and berries which Milochka arranged painstakingly for her every day, there were two great pots to either side of the window containing growing plants. One was an ordinary English ivy – much prized in Russia – and in the other something called 'Dutch vine', which had glossy, dark green serrated leaves.

Their luxuriant growth had been trained all round the room, winding about pillarets and statues, framing pictures, festooning the door and window frames, and even hanging from the tester of the bed. The idea of such 'living decoration' seemed charming to Fleur; and Madame Polotski told her that in the summer they brought in pots of jasmine, heliotrope and roses too, to add their scent and colour.

A less agreeable innovation was the lack of indoor sanitation. There was no running water – all water was fetched daily from the Neva in great vats – and no water-closets. Fleur had grown used to the comforts of modern life, and found the very idea of chamber-pots disagreeably primitive. There were plenty of servants to attend to the business, and they, of course, made nothing of it, but still it was a long while before she could reconcile herself to the lack of privacy.

There was a huge number of indoor servants. She began to recognise the faces, but there were too many for her to learn their names. Since there were no bells in the house, there were always servants waiting around to be sent on errands, and this, together with the fact that they had to pass through one room to reach another, was another way in which Fleur found her privacy invaded.

Madame Polotski had detailed a young Swiss girl named Catherine – known as 'Kati' – to wait on her, and Fleur grew used to her presence in the room, and indeed at her heels wherever she went; but she would quite often emerge from her screened-off bed to find half a dozen other serfs in the room. They were cheerful, friendly, inquisitive, argumentative sometimes, but never shy or retiring, and the idea that she might wish to be alone never occurred to them.

The first few days passed in a turmoil of new experiences, through which Madame Polotski did her best to steer her guests with kindness and patience. Again and again she apologised for the lack of entertainment, which she assured them would change after Easter; but Fleur, at least, was glad to have only the house and family to get used to for now. Their days were spent mostly in driving about the city seeing the sights, their evenings, after dinner, devoted to reading, conversation and music. Milochka played and sang prettily, but with more show than accuracy. When they had settled down, Fleur promised herself that she would introduce her to the notion of daily practice.

Madame Polotski apologised almost as frequently about the plainness of the food, but Fleur found it wholesome, tasty and satisfying. There were a variety of soups – cabbage, mushroom, beetroot, potato – which were always delicious; vegetable patties, filled with onion, mushroom, or spiced potato; fish grilled over charcoal, served with lemon juice or aromatic vinegars; salmon with green peas, and Volga river trout, a great delicacy. For puddings they had tapioca boiled in red wine, fruit juices thickened into a cream with arrowroot, and dried fruit and store-apples. Fleur was impressed by the strictness with which the Lenten fast was maintained for the whole period, and not just confined to one or two days a week. The Russians, she thought, were much more serious about their religious observances than the English.

For Sir Ranulph the days passed in a frenzy of preparation for his departure for Siberia, which was to take place as soon

215

as he had everything assembled. Polotski abandoned his business to help, and the two of them were absent from morning until night. Richard had therefore to keep company with the females of the house, and it was fortunate in a way, Fleur thought, that he had taken such a fancy to Lyudmilla: otherwise he might soon have grown bored, and in her experience, Richard never made any effort to hide his boredom.

'What a wonderful girl she is!' he raved to Fleur when they found themselves alone together for a moment during the first week of their visit. 'Such a beauty! That complexion, those eyes – and she's so vivacious! Always laughing! She knocks our haughty English beauties into a cocked hat.'

'Yes, she is very sweet,' Fleur agreed, privately amused.

'Sweet?' Richard looked amazed at the inadequacy of the word. 'Why, she's the most wonderful girl I've ever met! She's – she's—'

'Yes, of course she is. But tell me, Dick, how ever do you manage to understand each other? She doesn't speak any English, does she?'

'We talk in French, of course,' Richard said with dignity, avoiding her satirical eye. As far as she knew, he had never spoken a word of French since he left school, and even at school he had avoided it as far as humanly possible. Aunt Ercy, unlike Aunt Venus, was thoroughly Anglicised, so he hadn't even been exposed to it in babyhood, as she had.

'I suppose love will always find a way,' she murmured. 'In any case, you do seem to spend most of your time staring at her like a moonling with your mouth open, so I suppose words aren't strictly necessary.'

Richard didn't like being teased. 'I tell you what, Flo Hamilton – if you don't sweeten your tongue, you'll never get a husband,' he retorted. 'You'll find men don't care to shackle themselves with a shrew.'

Fleur only laughed. 'Don't be cross – I didn't mean it. You're too handsome to look like a moonling. I'm sure she thinks you're completely the thing.'

He was mollified enough to risk confiding in her. 'Oh, never mind that. The thing is, I wonder when you think it'd be a good time to speak to Pa? I mean, he'll be off any day now, and then there's to be no getting at him for six months.'

'Speak to him about what?'

Richard blushed. 'About Milochka, or course! She's the most wonderful girl in the world, and I—'

'Wait, wait, slow down!' Fleur said, holding up her hands. 'You've only known her for three days.'

'What does it matter, when you meet the perfect person?' Richard said earnestly.

'It's customary to get to know someone a little before you talk about marriage.'

'I feel as if I've known her for ever. And I know I shall never feel like this about anyone else.'

Fleur controlled her desire to smile – after all, hadn't she said the same things to herself about Kirov? Naturally she felt her experience was quite different from her little brother's, and that her feelings were serious and valuable while his were mere passing fancy. But of course he would think exactly the same about his own passions; and in view of her record of self-deception it behoved her to be both kind and patient.

'I don't think Papa would see it that way, love,' she said gently. 'Besides, his mind is elsewhere at the moment, and it would only annoy him to be interrupted with what he would see as an unimportant—'

'Unimportant! But she's—'

'An angel, yes, I know, but you know how Papa is. Anyway, why such a hurry? You're here for six months, living in the same house as her. You've all the time in the world.'

He looked gloomy. 'You may think so, but I tell you a beauty like her will soon be snapped up. If I don't get my word in quickly, she'll be betrothed to someone else, and that'll be that.'

There were many things Fleur might have said – that there seemed very little chance either father would agree to such a match even after a long courtship, and none that they would agree on a courtship at all; that the lovely Lyudmilla might have views of her own about marriage which he hadn't investigated; that if he was so sure she would accept someone else within six months he could not believe her to have strong feelings for him.

But she said none of them, of course. Love is blind, she told herself; and as soon as they began to go into society again, Richard would fall violently in love with someone else equally unsuitable, and the lovely Lyudmilla would be forgotten.

'Don't worry,' she said instead. 'Everything will work out for the best. It always does.'

'You would say so,' Richard grumbled. 'You don't know what it's like to be in love.'

Fleur was sitting with Madame Polotski in her own room, doing some essential mending. For once they were alone. Milochka was busy with the eldest daughter's daily task of going through the store-cupboards with Borya, the cook, to see what needed replacing; and Richard, Fleur assumed, would be hanging around somewhere where he hoped he would bump into her by accident. She was afraid that her brother was going to begin to grow bored any day now. Papa had been gone three days; they had been in St Petersburg for over a week, and she doubted that being in love with Milochka would be enough to keep Richard occupied for much longer.

For the moment, however, Fleur put him from her mind, occupying her hands with stitching lace onto a new chemisette which the nimble-fingered Kati had made for her, and her mind with chatting to Madame Polotski. Madame spoke no English, so they conversed always in French, and this, together with her kind, motherly air, gave Fleur a curious feeling of safety, as though she might really confide in her, and be understood, and comforted. She had never had a proper mother of her own, and the daughter-love she had never had the chance to spend seemed to want quite naturally to flow towards this gentle woman with the tired face.

What did daughters talk about with their mothers, she wondered? For that matter, what did husbands and wives talk about, or lovers? She had never had anyone of her own to love, and the realisation made her feel sad and empty, as though she were not a complete person, as though she were

218

only the first outline of a portrait, lightly sketched in, but never finished.

Madame had been telling her about her courtship with Polotski. 'He no sooner saw me than he wanted to marry me – and told me so as well. You might not think so to look at him, but he was a very passionate and impulsive man, and it was love at first sight with him.'

'And was it the same for you?' Fleur asked. The luxury of discussing love with another woman had never come her way before.

Madame oversewed a stitch and cut the thread. 'It was an odd thing,' she said thoughtfully. 'I knew with my mind that I loved him before I really *felt* it to be so. The moment I saw him I knew that we would be important to each other. But as to feeling with the heart all the things one is supposed to feel—' She stopped speaking while she waxed a new thread and threaded her needle. 'Of course, men are much more volatile than women. I think we take our feelings more seriously, and are more careful about them – and indeed, we must be so. We dare not take things lightly, as men sometimes do.'

She glanced at Fleur a moment, and then looked down at her work again. 'I had nothing to fear with Vanya, though. He did everything just as he ought. In Russia, a man who is serious in his courtship goes first to the girl's father, to get his permission to proceed. A good, decent man wouldn't dream of giving people anything to talk about, by singling out a young woman without her father's approval.'

This was too close for Fleur. She wondered whether Polotski had said anything to his wife about Kirov's attentions to her. She would have liked of all things to discuss it with Madame, but knew of no way to introduce the subject. Besides, supposing Madame disapproved? Instead she said, 'He told me that he sang to you to make you fall in love with him.'

Madame's eyes warmed at the memory. 'So he did. He had a very fine voice.'

'He still has. He caused an uproar in London by singing in public, in the Park.'

Madame smiled. 'Did he? That was very improper. I hope

219

you were stern with him. I never could be. Of course, I'd already decided to take him before he sang to me, but I let him think that's what won me. Men are simple creatures, even the best of them. They like things to be tidy and logical. They like reasons for things that have no reasons. Why should I love him rather than anyone else? But I did, and I do. There's no rule about it.'

No, Fleur thought, no rule – except that once you start, you can't leave off. Madame glanced at her again, a casual-seeming glance that took in everything.

'Vanya grew very fond of you in London, you know. He's talked to me a great deal about you.'

Fleur met her eyes steadily. 'I like him very much, too,' she said neutrally.

Madame took a stitch. 'He said he found you wonderfully easy to talk to, as indeed I do, my dear,' she went on, her eyes on her work. 'Almost as if you were Russian yourself. But then he wasn't the only Russian you got to know in London, was he? I believe you met Count Kirov, too.'

'Yes,' Fleur said. For the life of her she could think of nothing more encouraging to say.

'He's a strange man, by all accounts. I've never met him, but of course people of his position in society are talked about. He made an unfortunate marriage, which ended in tragedy, and it spoiled his temper, so they say. Men are not good at bearing disappointment. They tend to take it out on other people, or on themselves. In his case, a little of both, I think.'

Fleur said nothing.

'I felt very sorry for him,' Madame went on unemphatically. 'He and his wife had no children, which I believe was a great sorrow to them. I know how he must have felt. Vanya and I would have liked more children, but it wasn't to be. Of course, we have Milochka, and we both adore her, but we'd have liked a son, too, to carry on the business. Several sons, for preference. And Count Kirov must feel it much more, because he hasn't even a daughter.'

'I wonder he doesn't marry again,' Fleur said, surprising

220

herself at the evenness of her voice. 'But perhaps he loved his first wife too much, and can't forget her?'

'Well of course he's supposed to have buried his heart with her, as the saying is, but I don't believe it.' She looked up. 'In my experience, a man who has loved a woman successfully will find a way to do it again. They get better at it with practice, you see. From what I've heard about Count Kirov, he's never learnt how to love at all. But of course, I've never met him. You must know him better than I do. What would you think about that, my dear? Do you think I'm near the truth?'

The tone and the expression were mild and inviting, and Fleur longed to confide, to pour out everything that had puzzled and hurt her, and perhaps just by talking to understand it. But she had no habit of confidence, and while she was still strugglling to break down the barrier of reserve life had built up in her, they were interrupted. The chamberlain came in to announce a visitor.

'It's Count Kirov, *barina*,' he said impassively, blissfully unaware of the shock he was delivering to at least one of his ladies.

'Count Kirov?' Madame said in plain astonishment. She kept her eyes from Fleur's face, an act of heroism as well as kindness. 'Are you sure, Igor? Calling on me? But I am not in the least acquainted with him.'

'Calling on the *barishnya*, with your permission, *barina*,' Igor said. 'He and another young gentleman.'

Madame looked towards Fleur now, to see whether she would welcome such a visit or not, but there was nothing to be learned from the rigidly cast-down eyes and the flushed cheeks but a natural confusion. Inwardly shrugging, she said, 'Very well, Igor. You had better show them in.'

There was a long and palpitating pause, during which neither could think of anything appropriate to say to the other, before the doors slid back again, and Count Peter was shown in, accompanied by a tall, thin guardsman with huge sidewhiskers and a tremendous beak of a nose.

'Madame Polotski,' Count Peter cried, performing a flourishing bow, 'I beg your pardon for calling on you in this unceremonious way, but I presume on my acquaintance with your honoured guests. Miss Hamilton and her brother and I all met on the boat, and you know how it is with shipboard friendships: they flourish like a vine in a hothouse! By the time we reached port, we counted ourselves old friends – practically cousins, you know!'

Madame, still astonished, said evenly that no excuse was needed, and that she was pleased to receive him.

'He's imposing on you, madame,' Fleur said sternly. 'May I present to you Count Peter Nikolayevitch Kirov, and—?'

'My intimate friend, Prince Maxim Foskine, of our regiment,' Kirov supplied.

'Mesdames, the very greatest pleasure,' Foskine murmured, with a deep bow.

'But why so severe, Miss Hamilton? What have I done? Did I not promise to call? And here I am,' Count Peter said in wounded accents.

'Yes, ten days late! My poor brother has been waiting in vain for you to redeem your promise to take him to your mess. He's been moping about the house, thinking himself forgotten. Is this the action of a friend?'

Peter laughed. 'Oh yes, I assure you! Isn't it, Max?'

'I'm afraid so, madame,' Foskine said sadly. 'The closer a friend is to you, the more he feels he can let you down without explanation, and the more he expects you to forgive him. I assure you that when Peter Nikolayevitch neglects you so badly, it's proof of the firmest friendship.'

'That is the most abominable nonsense,' said Fleur. 'Don't suppose for an instant you can impose on Madame Polotski. She's far too wise in the ways of the world to be taken in. You had much better tell the truth, Count Peter, and throw yourself on her mercy.'

Madame looked at her thoughtfully, and then at Kirov. 'Yes indeed! The truth or nothing, if you please.'

Peter made a comical face and dropped to one knee in front of her, clasping his hands together. 'I am penitent! Dear Madame Polotski, can you look upon my miserable remorse and still find it possible to harden your heart, as the cruel Miss

Hamilton plainly does? You're a mother, with a mother's tenderness! Won't you plead for me? I should have come before, I admit it. What more can I say?'

Madame was smiling now. 'I can't plead for you unless you've a good excuse, you know.'

'I've the best excuse in the world – I forgot! Life is so full, isn't it? And one means to do things, and somehow they don't get done.' He bounced to his feet again, and turned on Fleur, spreading his hands to her. 'You see how disarmingly I tell the truth. I really did mean to call on you at once. Won't you forgive me?'

'It is exactly as I supposed,' Fleur said severely. 'You're an idle, frivolous young man, and not to be depended upon – and since there is obviously no curing you, I forgive you freely.'

'Yes, it's plain you really are an old friend, ma'am,' Foskine said. 'You know Petya so well!'

Peter smiled round them. 'Then since we are all friends, I can get on with issuing the invitation I came charged with. I have come to arrange with your brother to visit our mess, of course, but there's also the matter of the ballet. You did say you would like to go to the ballet?'

Fleur bowed assent.

'There's a performance next week I think you would enjoy,' Peter went on. 'I should be honoured if you, Madame Polotski, and Miss Hamilton, would be my guests. And of course if your good husband and Mr Hamilton should like to—'

The door behind Madame Polotski opened and Milochka came running in with her dogs and Richard close behind her.

'Oh Mama, Stenka said there were visitors—'

It was beautifully done, Fleur thought. Even she wasn't sure if it were entirely unstudied or not. Milochka stopped in apparent confusion, an exquisite vision in dusky pink, ribbons and soft fawn curls, and murmured a breathless apology.

'Yes, love, we have visitors,' Madame said imperturbably. 'This is Count Peter Kirov and Prince Maxim Foskine. Gentlemen, my daughter Lyudmilla Ivanovna. And Mr Hamilton you know, of course?'

Milochka curtseyed with her inimitable grace, and the two visitors bowed low in response. Fleur noted the surprised admiration in Peter's eyes which was his instant and unguarded reaction to the lovely vision; and she saw from Richard's face, in which delight at seeing Kirov again struggled with resentment, that he had noted it too.

The invitation to the guards' mess was repeated to Richard and the arrangement made, and Milochka, naturally, was included in the invitation to the ballet. Milochka was delighted, and displayed a mixture of innocent, almost childlike excitement, and the beginnings of a subtle coquetry, aimed towards Peter Kirov. She obviously found him very attractive, and Fleur felt sorry for Richard, as he struggled to conceal the first pangs of jealousy.

The conversation grew lively, and other plans began to be talked of. It was obvious that the acquaintance was not going to end with a single visit to the ballet.

'Oh, what a summer we shall have!' Count Peter cried out at one point. 'What luck that we met on the boat as we did, or none of this would be happening now! We shall all be meeting again and again, and we'll have the liveliest times, I promise you.'

Fleur glanced from him to Milochka and then to Richard, aware from the corner of her eye that Madame was seeing all she saw, and probably more. 'I haven't a doubt of it,' she said.

Chapter Twelve

Fleur was sitting up in bed writing to Aunt Venus.

'—by lamplight, of course. They have no gaslighting here, not even in the Tsar's palace – another way in which life is, at times, disagreeably primitive. They light the streets with flaring torches, which makes it rather like stepping back in time to a darker age!

'I have now had closer acquaintance with the *izvozchiks* I

mentioned in my last letter: they're an obtrusive part of street-life here, and the subject of much folk lore. The drivers come from many parts, and have their own character: the Germans are said to be reasonable, the Finns gloomy, the Poles reckless – though I can hardly believe any *izvozchik* would really be reckless, for the law is that if horse or carriage should so much as touch the foot of a pedestrian, the poor driver is liable to be flogged and exiled to Siberia, whether the accident is his fault or not.

'Speaking of carriages, I must tell you that I have now seen the Tsar! It was in the Prospekt, when I was driving with Milochka. There was a shout of *Gosudar! Gosudar!* and Milochka pinched my arm and nudged me, saying, "It's the Emperor, Fleurushka!" (As she calls me). He went past in the most humble one-horse carriage, with no guards or outriders, wrapped in a plain cloak as if he were a clerk on his way to the counting-house! I am informed that this is the style of the Tsars since Peter the Great, and it makes them very popular with the common people.

'I thought him very handsome, from the glimpse I had of him; and I hear nothing but good of him, of his honesty and industry and virtue. He interests himself very closely in the cadet schools, often appearing without ceremony to take their drills in person and exhort them to be obedient and diligent.

'It makes it the more surprising that you say everyone at home thinks him violent and bloodthirsty and believes him determined to go to war over the division of Turkey. That is not the mood here, I assure you! Everyone says war is the last thing the Emperor wants, that he is as dedicated to peace as we have all been since the Great Exhibition.

'And the common people don't want war. The peasants hate military service, though it's no longer for life, but only for fifteen years. Even so, when a *mouzhik* is chosen, his village mourns him for dead; and amongst the domestic serfs, being sent for military service is used only as an extreme punishment.

'Oddly enough, I often hear it said that the English are treacherous and bloodthirsty, and that England is longing for a war on any excuse. Of course, I refute *that* at every opportunity! But you'll be glad to know that everyone is united in hating Louis Napoleon!'

She paused to flex her fingers, and referred to her aunt's letter before continuing.

'You ask me about the condition of the serfs, and I can tell you that most people here seem to think it's inevitable they will be freed sooner or later. The Emperor has already had several commissions to enquire into how it can be done, but there always seems to be some complication about compensation, or fear of anarchy, that halts the progress. Most people want serfdom to be abolished, though I fear in many cases this is not from moral or religious scruples, but because it's commonly accepted that paid servants work harder and give better service than serfs.

'Foreign servants are paid very high wages – you would be surprised how high! – and there is a growing trend towards employing former soldiers for wages. Serfs who survive their period of military service are automatically given their freedom, but of course by then they are completely separated from ties of home and family, and have nowhere to go and no means of supporting themselves. They make admirable servants, having learned unquestioning obedience in the army, and being, moreover, extremely hardy; but they are often taken advantage of, and paid very poorly.

'With all the evils of the system, however, I have to say that the serfs don't seem particularly unhappy. They live in Spartan quarters and their food is very simple – black bread or buckwheat porrage, salted cucumbers, cabbage, and occasion ally fish. But there are so many of them, their work is not hard and most of them seem cheerful and not at all cowed. It may be different outside the capital, of course; and no doubt there are masters who are cruel and arbitrary, but – I suppose naturally – I have seen nothing of that.'

She turned the page and began a new subject.

'Our social life is now very full, though much of it I think you would find tedious. The Polotskis have a great many friends, but they are not of your sort, Aunt! They're of the merchant class, solid, respectable, and I have to say, rather dull, but they are kind-hearted and hospitable, and there is not the least pretension about them. Our evenings with them tend to involve a large dinner, followed by conversation, cards or other games (they have a form of whist here called *biritsh*, and they're very fond of riddles and guessing-games and the like) and music; or sometimes an impromptu dance, if there are enough young people present.

'I am much in demand to describe England and the English way of life, and they are charmingly surprised to learn that my routines at Grove Park are not so very different from their own. The aspect that causes most surprise is that I visit the sick and poor and try to help and advise them. They not only think this is very strange of me, but they are surprised the sick and poor allow it! In Russia the *mouzhiks* worship tradition. Everything must be done exactly as it always has been, however foolish or inefficient the system is; and if a master tries to change something, even for the serfs' own good, they grumble and complain; and if he persists, retaliate by destroying his crops or burning down his house.

'But you will be glad to know that our evenings are not all spent amongst the middling sort: we have been into Polite Society a good deal, too, thanks to Count Kirov. No, this is not "our" Count Kirov, but his younger brother Peter whom we met, by strange coincidence, on the ship coming here. He's a very pleasant young man, though I'm afraid he's what you would call "a fribble" – devoted to pleasure and without a serious thought in his head. However, he's been kindness itself to Richard, taking him riding (and supplying him with mounts), hunting, and fishing; making him an honorary member of his mess; and introducing him to just the set of young cavalry plungers he feels most at home with.'

She paused again. Only in Peter's attentions to Lyudmilla could Richard find anything to criticise. Fleur had watched the situation with amusement and bemusement, for Peter's campaign was so subtle that even she didn't know what its object was. He escorted Fleur, Lyudmillá, and Madame Polotski, in all permutations, to all manner of entertainments, ingratiating himself with all of them in different ways, so that it was impossible to tell which of them was acting as chaperone to whom.

Richard was naturally convinced that Peter's object was Milochka, and he resented the Russian's easy charm. But Fleur felt that there was too much lightness in the way he treated Milochka to suggest any serious intention. Most of the time, she was almost sure he meant only to be kind to all of them.

He had absorbed himself effortlessly into the Polotski household, even to the extent of being automatically invited to every family entertainment. It amused Fleur to watch him at these dull soirées, insinuating himself into the good graces of solidly respectable dames who would be horrified if they knew what he had been up to in the small hours of that morning. But like the drawing-room chameleon he was, he seemed just as much at home chatting about minor ailments to a stout elderly merchant's wife in purple satin, as when he lounged in a corner of the Kirovs' box at the theatre and discussed modern drama with a lady-in-waiting to the Empress.

He was plainly a most adaptable man, and if such extreme flexibility suggested a certain lightness of character, it did not make him the less pleasant a companion. Fleur liked him very much, found him entertaining company, and felt at ease with him. She chatted to him, laughed with him, and teased him, and never felt aware of his masculinity, or at least never felt that it was something she needed to take notice of: it was almost as though he were a comfortable female friend. It was quite different from the way she had felt with his brother. There was none of that burning intensity about her friendship with Peter; none of the sense of importance she had had about every moment spent with Kirov.

She resumed.

'Most of the wealthy people will be going out of the city soon, to spend the summer on their country estates, and there's a flurry of last dinners and balls. We have been invited to one at the Kirov Palace, and naturally we are all very excited at the prospect of seeing the inside of it, for it's a noted building and quite one of the "sights" of Petersburg.

'Madame Polotski was doubtful about the propriety of accepting an invitation from a bachelor, but Count Peter assured her that there will be a hostess present – his elder sister Marya Vassiliovna. I was naturally surprised at the sudden revelation that he had a sister, when she had never arisen in conversation with either Kirov brother; but it seems she is a half-sister, the daughter of his mother's first marriage, and very much older than him, so perhaps there is not normally much contact between them.

'The arrival of the gilt-edged cards made me feel absurdly nervous – it will be the grandest thing I have been to since my arrival in Russia. I began worrying whether I should make some dreadful *faux pas* and disgrace myself; but Milochka's old nurse-turned-lady's-maid, Nushka, pointed out that I had been presented to the Queen of England, and that made me feel rather foolish. My maid Kati has made me the loveliest gown. They don't use mantuamakers very much here: it's the established thing for a lady's personal maid to make all her clothes, even down to her corsets and bonnets—'

Reflection had taught Fleur better to understand her unexpected reaction to the idea of going to the Kirov ball. It was not that she feared meeting the elder Count, for Peter had told her, apropos of something else, that he had been in Moscow all winter, and would be going directly to the summer estate near Kirishi without ever coming to Petersburg.

But still she would be going into *his* house, to walk in the rooms where he had grown up and lived with his family and with his wife, and she was afraid of what she might feel. It did serve, however, to put Count Peter into a different perspective: he might be the Russian equivalent of a Bond Street Beau, but he came from one of Petersburg's leading families, the son of a man who had been a favoured minister of the Tsar of All the Russias. His family's wealth was probably, by English standards, unimaginable, and he had been brought up in a palace so large that no one had ever counted the rooms.

As she had underestimated – to her cost – the social position of the elder brother, she was in danger of doing the same with the younger. Not, of course, that there was any question of her falling in love with Peter Nikolayevitch, but—

She heard someone come into the room. The light pattering tread told her who it was even before the scratching at the screen and the urgent whisper: 'Fleurushka! Are you awake?'

She put down her pen. 'Yes – it's all right.'

Milochka appeared, followed by her two dogs. She was in nightgown and wrapper, with a lacy cap over her loose curls, and her feet, as usual, were bare. 'I wanted to talk to you. You aren't sleepy?'

'Not at all. Come up on the bed and put the quilt over your feet. They must be frozen.'

Milochka looked down at the distant appendages as though surprised to see them. 'I forgot my slippers. But they never feel cold.' She climbed up onto the bed all the same, wrapped the quilt around her, and sat hugging her updrawn knees. The dogs sat side by side, sweeping the floor with their tails, gazing up imploringly. They slept on Milochka's bed, but Fleur disliked finding dog hairs on her sheets, and had firmly refused to allow them up.

These night visits had become a regular thing. Two or three times a week Milochka would come pattering in after everyone was in bed, eager to talk – for however much Fleur might value Madame Polotski as a confidante, her daughter was at the age when parents seemed as remote as the ancient Olympian gods, and about as understanding.

She was also at the age when sleep seemed the least appropriate thing to do with the hours between eleven and three, and many was the time Fleur had finally drifted off to sleep to the sound of Milochka's voice chattering about her hopes and concerns, as soothing and unimportant a sound as the flowing of water over stones.

This evening, however, she plainly had something on her mind. After a little preliminary rocking, she said, 'I'm so excited about the ball tomorrow, aren't you? To see the inside of the Kirov Palace! I've driven past it so many times – and they say the gardens are magnificent.'

'You won't see the gardens tomorrow.'

'No, of course not, but once we've been invited the first time, you never know what may happen. There may be all sorts of other invitations.' Fleur looked doubtful, and Milochka said anxiously, 'You are excited about it, aren't you?'

'Of course. I'm looking forward to it very much. Why do you doubt?'

'Oh, I don't know. Because you look strange sometimes when someone mentions Count Kirov; and when the invitations came for the ball you looked as though you didn't like it.'

She had thought she'd outgrown the tendency to start at the name of Kirov. She must be more careful in future. She smiled reassuringly and said, 'I expect I was just wondering what to wear.'

'Oh, heavens, yes! Isn't that always the first thing one thinks whenever an invitation arrives? Only Papa is so good, I knew he'd allow me a new gown! Because after all, for such an occasion, it would be the dowdiest thing to wear something that everyone had already seen. Oh, and I've had the nicest thought about my hair—'

Fleur glanced at her unfinished letter. 'Have you come to talk to me about your toilette, or had you something important to say?'

'Oh, am I chattering again?' Milochka said, unoffended. 'I shan't bore you, then – I just wanted to ask your opinion of Peter Kirov.'

'In what way? He's a very pleasant young man.'

'Of course he is, but what do you think about him as a husband?'

Fleur was startled. 'I haven't thought about him as a husband at all.'

She laughed. 'Oh, not for you! He wouldn't do for you – you're far too beautiful to be wasted on him. And you're too serious – you couldn't marry a chatterer, which he is, isn't he? No, I meant for me. I'm thinking of marrying him.'

'Are you, indeed? And has he said anything to you on the subject? Or don't you consider his opinion matters?'

'Now don't be sharp with me, darling Fleur! Of course he

231

hasn't said anything to me – it wouldn't be proper. I just wonder if he'd be the right person for me.'

'Milochka, I don't think he means anything seriously by his attentions,' Fleur said, somewhat embarrassed to find herself in this position. She thought of her own idiotic ambitions regarding that family, and winced inwardly.

'Oh, not yet of course; but he likes me, and I like him.'

'I don't think the idea of marrying you would cross his mind,' she said with difficulty.

Milochka looked surprised. 'Why not?'

How to put it delicately? 'Because he's from a different sort of world from you. A different order of society.'

Milochka looked puzzled for a moment, and then her brow cleared. 'Oh, you're being English, aren't you? But that doesn't matter – Papa's tremendously rich, and that's what counts in Petersburg. I'm an heiress: I can marry anyone I want. I only wonder whether I'd like him, you see. I sometimes think he's rather silly. What do you think?'

'I think,' Fleur smiled, 'that there are lots of other young men you like just as much. There's no hurry, is there? I should wait until you meet someone you feel very strongly about.'

She thought about it. 'I suppose I might. The trouble is I don't seem to feel strongly about anyone. I feel as if it doesn't really matter who I marry. Don't you sometimes feel like that?'

'I've no intentions of getting married,' Fleur said firmly, 'so the matter doesn't arise.'

'Oh.' She pondered, resting her chin on the point of her knees, the pale brown silk of her hair hanging like a canopy all around her. She only wanted a pair of feathery wings sprouting from the back of her white nightgown, Fleur thought. 'I do like your brother, though, very much. He's so romantic, and of course he looks like darling you! But I suppose he'll be going back to England in the autumn, and I shouldn't like to live there. Papa told me how badly married women are treated in England. I don't wonder you say you don't want to be married: imagine giving up all your money and your rights to your husband!' A happy thought seemed to strike her. 'You ought to marry a Russian man and stay here! Perhaps you might marry Peter Kirov after all. I expect he'll get more serious as he gets older.'

'Only if you can spare him, my love.'

'Now you're laughing at me! Oh well, never mind. I dare say he wouldn't do for either of us.' She yawned. 'I suppose I'd better let you go to sleep. Nushka thinks I'm in bed. She always wants me to go to bed early when there's anything special going to happen. As if you can sleep in advance! And as if it would make any difference if you could!' She unfolded herself with her long-legged, dancer's grace, and then bent forward to offer her face for kissing. It was a charming gesture, with all the unstudied confidence of one whose offer had never been refused.

'Goodnight, Fleurushka. It's going to be a lovely ball – and something exciting's going to happen at it. I can feel it in my bones, as Nushka says!'

The Kirov Palace was lit up like Grosvenor House when the Polotski carriage joined the queue leading up to the main door. There was quite a crowd of onlookers gathered to watch the arrivals, and a small detachment of soldiers was restraining them and making a pathway to the door, like a guest-decoy, drawing them up the steps and into the magnificent entry-hall. There liveried servants were waiting to remove the guests' outer wraps, and a further decoy guided them up the fifteen-foot-wide Grand Staircase to the receiving-line.

In spite of Nushka's common-sense words, and in spite of her complete satisfaction with the gown Kati had made for her – of a pale, creamy yellow shot silk trimmed with the most exquisite lace and thin silk ribbons – Fleur was still nervous. She felt rather light-headed, though of course that might have been because of the heat of the candlelit hall. Under the silk skirt and three linen underskirts, she was wearing a stiff horsehair petticoat. It was abominably hot, and scratched unpleasantly when she sat down, but it was at least less heavy and bulky for dancing than the twenty linen petticoats it would otherwise have taken to hold the skirt out into shape.

Raising her skirt by a fraction of an inch with the tips of her fingers, she began to mount the stairs behind the Polotskis, and in front of Lyudmilla, on Richard's arm. She had to move slowly, and concentrate, for her skirt only just cleared her foot at each step. There was a wall of noise all around her, made up of the presence of several hundred people all conversing at once, and the distant sound of a large orchestra in the ballroom.

Each individual stair had a footman at either end, wearing the Kirov strawberry-red livery, with white breeches and stockings and white gloves. She glanced at them as she mounted step by step, but their faces were expressionless and their eyes fixed on the middle distance. Were they there, she wondered, to leap forward and catch anyone who stumbled, or failed on the long climb? They cut off the view to either side, while the view ahead was closed by the backs of the guests before her. She was hemmed in, sight and sound, urged on from below like an immeasurably privileged climbing-boy in a dazzling chimney.

The top of the staircase at last. Her heart was beating under her ribs like a trapped bird from the tightness of her lacings, and she was glad that there was a moment's pause during which she fought to catch her breath. Then they were moving forward again; she heard the major-domo mangling her name and Richard's in company with the Polotskis'; and they had reached the receiving-line.

There was the hostess: a small woman in a strangely girlish gown of rose-pink; her fair hair gone grey, yet dressed with roses; and the worn and beautiful face of a ravaged child. It was a face at once extraordinary and heartbreaking, a face that made you want to stare and stare; but Fleur had no leisure to do so. There was another call upon her attention even more urgent. For standing beside Marya Vassiliovna was the host: the elder Count Kirov.

Fleur turned her startled eyes up to him, and for a moment everything seemed to fade away – the noise, the lights, the people, all were gone, leaving her alone with him as if on the top of a mountain, with nothing around them but the void of air. They looked into each other's faces, and the two intervening years seemed to fold in on themselves, so that it was as yesterday that she had last stood thus before him.

All that she had suffered, all her struggle and resolution, all the proverbial healing powers of Time, counted for nothing. She looked at him, and loved him. In that single moment of ringing silence, they were alone, and close, and complete, like a perfect circle, and she knew that nothing had changed, and that nothing ever would change.

Then she was back with a jolt in the real world. The wall of sound was apparent again, and in its foreground the Count's familiar voice was saying, 'Miss Hamilton, I'm glad to welcome you to my house. May I have the honour to present to you my sister, Marya Vassiliovna Tchaikovskova? Rose, my dear, this is Miss Fleur Hamilton, of whom I have spoken to you.'

There could not have been more cordiality in his voice. Fleur curtseyed rather blindly, and found her hand in that of 'Rose', who said, 'I am very happy to make your acquaintance, Miss Hamilton. Seryosha has told me so much about you. I hope we will have the opportunity to get to know each other better.'

She spoke in English. Her voice was sweet and musical, and when she smiled, the ruin of her face seemed to be smoothed away, and she looked like a very young woman, or a child on the brink of womanhood. Fleur found it possible to draw in air, though her chest ached as though she had been holding her breath.

'I hope so too, madame,' she said. And then her eyes would not be denied any longer. She turned to Kirov.

He was looking at her, of course, and his beautiful eyes were shining with an expression she remembered from their good times together, before he had grown cold. Why was he being so kind? It gave her such a feeling of closeness, a feeling of intimacy with him which she knew was completely misplaced. It was as if every fibre of her, every nerve-ending, were somehow in tune with him, as if they were parts of the same whole which could never be completely separated. She was having all sorts of feelings towards him which she didn't at all know what to do with, because despite the evidence of her senses, her intellect told her that this was all wrong, that

235

he did not care for her, that she was in grave danger of making the same painful mistakes all over again.

He had her hand now. He lifted it to his lips and touched it lightly, and gave her – oh, such a *kind* look. 'I'm very glad to see you again, my dear friend,' he said. 'We must find time to talk later.'

The pressure of guests behind her eased her naturally from his side, and she moved away without being aware of it, to find herself accosted by Count Peter. The look she directed towards him must have been at least questioning, if not reproachful, for he spread his hands and said, 'I didn't know he'd be here. He arrived from Schwartzenturm this morning, quite unexpectedly. Rose left a letter behind explaining about my ball, and when he got back and found it, he got straight back in his carriage and came here. It's just like him to thrust himself in where he's not wanted!'

His tone was disparaging, and she raised her eyebrows.

'Oh, he'd go to any lengths to spoil things for me, I promise you!' he complained. 'If Rose thought it was all right for me to have a ball, I don't see what call he had to say – oh well.' He shrugged up his shoulders evidently recollecting that this was not the time or place to reveal family hostilities. 'She's wonderful, isn't she, my sister Rose?'

'She seems – very charming.'

'Yes, she's that all right – but wait until you get to know her! Oh, she's looking at me. I'm sorry, I must stay and do the pretty with my brother. But when the ball begins, you will promise to have the first dance with me, won't you?'

Fleur was beginning to recover. 'Yes – very well. If you wish.'

'You might sound a little more enthusiastic,' he said, pretending to be wounded. 'I'm the best dancer in Petersburg, after all.'

Fleur remembered involuntarily the Duchess of Alderney's ball, when she had waltzed with the Count, and silently begged leave to differ, and Peter looked at her oddly for a moment before turning away, almost as if he had heard her thought.

*

Richard caught her up, with Lyudmilla still on his arm. 'I say, Flo, what a surprise seeing Count Kirov here!'

'He greeted you like an old friend, Fleur,' Milochka said, eyeing her thoughtfully. 'Did you see much of him in London?'

'Yes, quite a lot,' Fleur said absently.

'Do you think him a handsome man?' was the next question, but Milochka didn't wait for an answer. 'For myself, I think there's something rather frightening about him. He's so tall and – there's something about his eyes, don't you think? Something strange.'

Fleur shook her head, unable to answer that.

Richard was coursing a line of his own. 'Did I hear Petya ask you to open the ball with him?'

'He asked me for the first dance,' Fleur corrected, 'but it will be for Madame Tchaikovskova to open the ball, surely?'

'Oh, well, whatever the form is, you're spoken for,' Richard said impatiently. 'So will you dance the first with me, then, Milochka?'

'Yes, gladly,' she said.

Gradually the company filtered through into the vast ballroom, which was lit by eight great chandeliers each containing a hundred candles. These were further reflected in the long, gilt-framed mirrors on the walls, and from the glazed doors that led onto the terrace overlooking the famous gardens. They filled the air with a powerful smell of wax, which mingled with the perfumes of the women, the hair-oil of the men, and a whiff – not entirely unpleasant, like a touch of vinegar on an artichoke – of sweat from the servants at the doors.

At one end was a dais, where a large serf orchestra was seated on spindle-legged chairs, their instruments at rest for the moment as they waited for the signal for the ball to be opened. The company milled slowly around the edge of the chalked floor. It was very hot. Already the women's fans were working: the fluttering movement, caught out of the corner of the eye, looked like the flapping of pigeons trying to balance on too thin a branch.

Fleur felt acutely conscious of everything, every smell and

sound, and particularly of her own body: the white tightness of the strings around her waist, the constriction of her corset against her ribs, the blood-heat of her cheeks, the warmth of the air on her lips, the oiled, silken feeling of the two long ringlets of hair which hung, one over each bare shoulder, against her upper breast. At every beat of her heart she could feel her pulse tick in several different places – in her scalp, in her throat, in her stomach, behind one knee.

We must find time to talk later he had said. But what, what, what would he say?

And then both Kirovs were there, Peter arriving at one side of her in the same instant that the Count reached her from the other direction. The brothers stared at each other with the faint, satirical hostility of two cats.

'My dance, I think, Miss Hamilton,' Peter said, almost defiantly, watching his brother's face. 'I've come to claim you.'

He offered his arm and Fleur began to take it, but Kirov shook his head.

'I am to open the ball with Miss Hamilton.'

Peter reddened instantly with the accustomed indignation of the younger brother. 'I asked her first—'

'She is the guest of honour, and I am the host. Even you, Petya, must see that it is for me to open the ball with her.'

'I hadn't – I didn't know I was guest of honour,' Fleur said a little blankly. From Peter's expression, she thought that probably he hadn't realised it either.'

Kirov turned to her. 'But of course you are. Our honoured guest from England: the whole ball was planned in your honour. Surely my brother told you *that*?'

His tone was gently satirical. There was something here between the brothers that she didn't understand. But he was offering his arm to her, and smiled down into her eyes just as he had so long ago at Hardiway House. Suddenly this ballroom was all ballrooms, this dance all dances, and every other consideration faded away. She laid her hand on his sleeve, and smiled back in a way that made Peter look abruptly thoughtful.

And then she was walking with him up the ballroom along a

238

path that opened itself magically through the crowd, like the hedge of thorns yielding to the prince's sword. On either side the beautifully dressed women and distinguished men were drawing back, laying their palms together in soft applause, smiling, nodding their heads, and she stepped like a princess, the cynosure of all eyes, knowing herself beautiful, and chosen.

The path grew into a clearing, grew larger, and now they were standing alone in the centre of the empty floor, and he turned her to face him, looked into her eyes, slid his arm around her waist. An instant's pause, and then the orchestra struck up. It was a tune she didn't know, but the three-beat throb of the waltz came up through the floor into the soles of her feet. His firm hand was at the small of her back, his strong arm bracing her, and then they were moving, dancing, flying.

Alone at first, quite alone for one circuit of the floor; and then other couples joined them, masking them from curious eyes and giving them a kind of privacy. He was smiling faintly. Suddenly Fleur felt quite simply happy. One dance, she told herself. That's all. Don't build castles out of clouds. But you may enjoy the dance – that's allowed.

During the second circuit they passed Marya Vassiliovna, sitting in a high-backed chair, like a throne, against the wall half-way along the room. She was chatting to the ladies gathered around her, but she smiled at Fleur and Kirov as they danced past.

'Shouldn't your sister have opened the ball?' Fleur asked.

'Rose doesn't dance. She's a cripple.'

The harsh word shocked her. 'Oh. I'm sorry.'

'Don't be sorry for Rose,' Kirov said, still faintly smiling. 'She isn't sorry for herself. She's the strongest person I've ever known, and "complete unto herself".'

'Why do you call her Rose?'

'It's the name her parents gave her. When she was born she was pink and white and very beautiful. But she was struck down with an illness when she was still a baby. They thought she would die, but she was too strong. She survived, but it left one leg wasted. It was a long struggle, but she can do everything now, except dance. Well, she could dance if she would, but she says people shouldn't be obliged to watch her, because it looks ugly.'

'Oh,' Fleur said again. There didn't seem to be much else to say. He looked into her eyes, reading her thoughts.

'She really meant it, when she said she wished to know you better. I understand from Petya that you are fixed here until the autumn?'

Fleur explained the circumstances.

'I never thought I would see you again,' he said abruptly. She wasn't sure if he meant it as a lament, or as a justification for his former treatment of her.

'I didn't think the opportunity would ever arise for me to come here,' she said.

'Why did you?'

He seemed to be searching her face for the answer to some question; but he should not expect it to be that easy, she thought resentfully.

'I always wanted to travel,' she said. 'One should not let opportunities pass by, so I always think.'

'Ah, do you? Do you?' The answer seemed to please him. He hummed a few bars of the music. 'This is an old Russian tune. It has words, about falling in love while skating on a frozen pond. There's a special excitement about the winter in Russia: it's a great shame you should not see it. And Russians write the best waltzes of all. It's in our blood. Don't you feel it?'

He whirled her extra fast around the corner of the room, taking her breath away. Through a gap that opened between the dancers, she saw Richard standing out at the side of the room, his head thrust forward in a posture of disappointment and anger. Fleur was puzzled, until a few moments later they passed Lyudmilla, twirling in the arms of Count Peter. Now how had he managed that?

'My brother is a very insinuating man,' Kirov said, reading the thought in her face. 'I believe he bullocked his way into your acquaintance on the ship before you had ever set foot in Russia.'

She met his eyes. 'It was pure chance that we met. He had no idea who I was, nor I him. I understand you didn't mention me to him at all?'

He looked awkward. 'No, I—' he stopped and began again. 'Was I wrong not to do so, my dear friend? We had been good friends, had we not? But I didn't think we would ever meet again, and I hesitated to speak of you, in case he misunderstood. I didn't want the memory of our pleasant meetings to be spoiled by – by his misinterpretation.'

Only friends, that's what he was saying. *We were friends, nothing more.* But every sense was telling her otherwise. Through his look, his touch, the tone of his voice, he was conveying to something wiser and more foolish in her that it was not friendship he felt for her – not friendship at all.

She was confused, happy, worried, glad, apprehensive. But most of all, she felt a blissful sense of relief at being here in his arms again, held close, at home. Enjoy the dance, she told herself dizzily. That's allowed. The dance . . .

Too soon, it ended. The music whirled and died away and settled into quiet as dead leaves do when the breeze drops. Without it, they could no longer fly. The heavy earth claimed them, and they stopped, facing each other in the middle of the ballroom, plain mortals again, bound by gravity.

'I must leave you,' he said, still holding her hands. 'We will dance again later, if you'll permit?'

'Yes,' she said, and drew back her hands. He smiled suddenly, and was gone.

Almost immediately Maxim Foskine appeared at her side. 'Before anyone you are sure to like better can get you, mademoiselle – will you dance the next with me?'

'I shall be honoured,' she said. She was certainly lightheaded now. Her feet were hot and heavy and anchored to the ground, but her head swayed emptily like an over-tall sapling in the breeze.

'No,' Foskine said seriously, as though it were a question of fact, 'the honour will be all mine.'

She didn't argue with him. Like Paget, Foskine was restfully uncommunicative. They stood in silence waiting for the music to begin, looking about them at the other dancers settling like the coloured stones in a kaleidoscope into new patterns of partnership. Through a gap, across the room, she saw Kirov and Peter standing together, apparently in the middle of a restrained but heated argument. Their bodies were stiff and inclined towards each other, and there was a little space around them, a circle whose radius was the embarrassment of people pretending not to notice bad behaviour. Peter's jaw was thrust out, and he seemed to be haranguing his elder brother, who was hearing it in silence, but with a smile that was plainly meant to be provoking.

Evidently Foskine had seen it too. 'How much they hate each other, those Kirovs,' he said languidly.

She looked at him, startled. 'Do they? But why?'

'Lord knows,' he shrugged. 'Perhaps because they're both absolutely impossible in their own ways. Fish and cheese, you know, couldn't be more different. But they've always been like it. I couldn't tell you the number of times I've seen them quarrelling in ballrooms. Damned embarrassing. Damned bad form.'

'Why in ballrooms?'

'Oh, not only there, of course. But this just reminded me. In ballrooms it's usually over a woman. Other places, it could be anything. Kirov's the Emperor's man, for one thing, and as patriotic as they come, but Petya don't care for politicking and that sort of thing. He joined the regiment simply to have a good time, and that makes Kirov rage. He thinks Petya's idle and useless – which he is, of course; but then why shouldn't he be?'

The music began and he stopped abruptly. Fleur reflected in a puzzled way over what Foskine had said, and tried to puzzle out what the brothers had been arguing about. A few moments later she thought she had the clue, for she saw Kirov dancing with Lyudmilla, while Peter was nowhere to be seen. Usually about a woman? Had Peter's object been Milochka all along, then? And was Kirov dancing with her now simply to annoy his younger brother? It was ignoble, but remembering that provoking, insulting smile, she could believe it – certainly

Milochka was too young to interest him otherwise. The impression was strengthened later when she saw them dancing together again: Milochka, like Madame Brunnow, was looking up at him as though he were being particularly fascinating.

Her own evening passed not unpleasantly, and she never lacked for a partner, being usually in the position of having to choose between several applicants for each dance. But the dislocated feeling that her head was distantly detached from her feet persisted. Since her face was wearing a pleasantly receptive smile, and her mind was elsewhere, she may well have gained a reputation that evening for being a good listener.

It was late before Kirov claimed his second dance with her; claimed it, moreover, with a pleasant lack of ceremony which seemed like close friendship, even intimacy.

'I'm sorry I couldn't come before,' he said, 'but there were so many duty dances, and so many people I dared not offend. If it were not such a public ball, I would be able to dance almost every dance with you.'

'Is that what you want?' No, she didn't say it aloud. 'Duty must always come before pleasure,' was what she did say.

It was meant part-ironically, but he looked serious, and said, 'I wish my brother could learn that; but I'm afraid he is past hope.'

'I like him as he is,' Fleur confessed. 'But I wouldn't care to have to depend on him for anything.'

'You'd be wise not to,' he said. 'But time is short – I don't want to waste it talking about Petya. What I want to ask you is whether you will come out to Schwartzenturm and stay for the summer?'

She was startled. 'I – I don't know. I don't think it would be quite fair to the Polotskis to leave them when they've—'

'Oh, naturally I would invite them, too. Or rather Rose would. She means to call formally tomorrow, and issue the invitation. What is your trouble? No one stays in Petersburg in summer, you know – the dust is beyond endurance.'

'They may have made other plans already – accepted another invitation. They may not think – they may not like—'

She couldn't visualise the Polotskis spending several weeks in another palace such as this. Madame, she thought, would probably not like to leave home at all.

He smiled gently. 'Don't worry, Rose will persuade them, if it's what you wish. That's why I am asking you first – to find out if you would like to come. If you would, Rose will arrange it all. She's wonderful at getting her way.'

So are you all, you Kirovs, she thought. Of *course* she wanted to go, wanted to see Schwartzenturm, wanted to be able to be near him; but was it not abominable that he should use his sister in that way? Would she not resent it, if Fleur accepted the invitation she had been forced to extend?

'She really does want to get to know you,' he said, reading her face easily, as on so many occasions before. 'And I'd be glad for her to have a companion worthy of her. She is so much alone.'

She thought about it. 'All of them?'

'All of them. You will come, then?'

It was unwise, wasn't it? It would be folly to put herself in the way of having her heart broken all over again, wouldn't it? Common sense, self-preservation, dictated that she refuse. 'Yes, if it can be arranged,' she said.

'Ah,' was all he said; but his smile told the rest.

In the carriage going home everyone was silent and thoughtful, and Fleur was glad not to be obliged to speak. She felt exhausted, overwrought, not entirely happy. She was afraid of what might happen, of what she might be going to feel, and at what cost. Yet she was glad at the prospect of seeing him again if they did go to Schwartzenturm. But how could that be arranged? Whatever he said, she didn't believe that Rose could persuade the Polotskis against their will.

You're a fool, she told herself grimly. Someone offers you poison in a cup, and you drink it like wine. Someone offers you the point of a sword, and you throw yourself onto it, as if it were a downy bed.

Kati was waiting for her, and seeing how tired she looked

got to work in sympathetic silence on the hooks and laces. When she was in her nightgown, she sat at the dressing-table with her head bent forward, while Kati drew the tormenting pins out of her hair. Her feet were burning, and she slipped them out of her slippers and rested them on the cool wooden floor. Her ribs ached, and there was a red and throbbing ring like molten fire round her waist and each thigh, where the blood was returning to claim the territory denied it all evening by her strings and garters. Sleep, she thought. Her bed beckoned her more enticingly at that moment than all the tall dark handsome lovers in the world.

Kati had left her, and she was just reaching out to douse the lamp when she heard the door slide open, and there came the familiar pattering of ten naked feet across the floor.

Oh no, not now, she thought. *Not tonight, Milochka!*

It must have been something important: Milochka didn't even scratch the screen or make her customary enquiry. She simply appeared, her face wreathed in a rapturous smile, and said, 'Oh good, you're still awake! Oh Fleurushka, wasn't it a wonderful ball! The best, best, best ever in the whole world!'

Fleur did her best. 'Yes, it was lovely.'

'You're tired? Well, I won't keep you awake. I don't feel as if I could ever fall asleep! I feel as if I could dance from now until next year!' Fleur regarded her with dismay, but she went on, straight to the heart of the matter. 'You know you said to me yesterday that I should wait until I met someone I felt strongly about? And I didn't think I ever would, but it's happened! I've fallen in love with the most wonderful, exciting, glorious man in the world. Oh Fleur, I'm so happy!'

'So I see,' she smiled. 'And what is the name of this paragon?'

Milochka opened her eyes wide. 'How can you possibly not know? He's so different from all the other men, he's like a god walking amongst mortals! The most handsome, the most exciting, the most romantic—'

'Obviously I'm blind to his glories,' Fleur said, stifling a yawn. 'But that's just as well, isn't it?'

Milochka laughed kindly. 'Yes, for I should never let you

245

have him! It's Count Kirov, silly! Count Sergei Nikolayevitch Kirov, and I shall love him until I die!'

If you listen, Fleur thought, you can almost hear God laughing.

Chapter Thirteen

In memory, that summer at Schwartzenturm had a dreamlike quality to Fleur, an idyllic interlude between her ordinary life and what was to come afterwards. The visit took place to begin with without the elder Polotskis, for Mr Polotski could not immediately leave his business, and Madame would not leave him. The arrangement left both Fleur and Madame feeling a little uneasy – Fleur felt it was not quite good form to abandon her hosts to go to stay with someone else, and Madame was not quite happy about allowing Milochka to go away without a chaperone.

But Mr Polotski was eager for Fleur to have the opportunity of visiting a great country estate, and cheerfully confident that the Countess Tchaikovskova was chaperone enough for Milochka.

'After all, Sophie *dushka*, it's a country estate she's going to, not Moscow or Kiev. There's not much mischief she can get up to out in the country, is there? And we'll be joining them in a few weeks.'

Fleur was surprised at his complacency, and was forced to conclude, a little uneasily, that he valued the connection for its social importance. She liked Polotski, and would have preferred to find him immune to that sort of consideration; but Russia was not England, and she had already learned that getting anything done involved either bribery or the use of influence. It was ordinary prudence for Polotski to seize any chance to extend his influence, and Kirov was, after all, close to the Emperor.

Madame's faint apprehension disappeared when she

learned that Peter Kirov would not be there – his duties would keep him in Petersburg for some weeks. Neither parent was worried about the elder Kirov: the basic laws of hospitality meant he would never tamper with the affections of a guest under his own roof, even if he could be supposed to be interested in a child of Milochka's age.

No one, of course, worried about Fleur, which amused Fleur in a mild way. It did prove, however, that the story of her embarrassment in England had not spread to Petersburg circles, and she was determined to keep it that way. Kirov's reasons for wanting her there were a mystery to her. She resolved to be on her guard, without knowing precisely what against; to enjoy his company, but to keep aloof from him. How these conflicting aims were to be reconciled was something she didn't consider too deeply.

Schwartzenturm was only about twenty-five miles from Petersburg, and the three young people travelled there in an open carriage, followed by a *kibitka* carrying the servants and luggage. Fleur never forgot her first sight of the summer palace of the Kirovs. It was an extraordinary building, a vast Palladian mansion connected by screen walls to two pavilions, one a whimsical Rheinschloss, and the other – the 'Black Tower' of its name – a grim Highland keep. She remembered Peter's comments about its architect, and smiled to herself. It squatted like an esoteric joke at the end of a most English gravel drive bordered by tidy lawns. The drive ended in a forecourt dominated by a huge white marble fountain of writhing mermen and spouting dolphins, reminiscent of Castle Howard's. It was the oddest thing she had ever seen.

Madame Tchaikovskova was waiting to greet them, her face bright with genuine pleasure. She hugged them all, apologised for her brother's absence, begged them to call her Rose, because everybody did, and thanked them for their kindness in coming to relieve her solitude.

'There are plenty of horses, and a river where we swim, and there will be company from time to time in the evenings,' she said apologetically. 'I hope you won't find it too dull.'

'By Jove, no, ma'am,' Richard said politely. 'One can never

247

be dull where there are horses. In England, after a winter in Town, it's quite the thing to go on a repairing-lease into the country.'

'Your brother will be returning soon, I suppose?' was Lyudmilla's wistful response.

'Oh yes, he's only away for a day or two on business. I expect him at the beginning of next week.'

Fleur smiled at the confidence of the statement. 'And what you expect will be fulfilled. I wish we could say the same of our father, eh Dick?'

'You haven't heard from him?' Rose asked.

'No, but we didn't expect to. However, in this case, we're confident he'll come back in time, because his passport is dated, and Mr Polotski says even in Siberia it will be checked often.'

'Yes, that's true,' Rose said. 'And he has Russian servants and guides, who'll send him back to you. Of course, for my own sake, I wish you need never go away, but you'll want to go back to your own country.'

Though she had met her only twice before, Fleur felt somehow that Rose really meant it. What was odder was that Fleur felt towards her a warmth of affection she had never felt for any female in her own country.

'Perhaps you could come and visit me, in England,' she said. 'I should be delighted to receive you.'

Rose laughed. 'Thank you! I am honoured by the invitation – but this is Russia, you know. I should never be given a passport. Travel abroad is not encouraged, particularly travel to England.'

'Why not?' Richard asked, bristling a little. 'What's wrong with England?'

'It's thought to be a haven for revolutionaries and agitators and communists,' Rose said with a disarming smile. 'We mustn't be allowed to come in contact with them, in case we catch their infection and bring it back to Russia.'

'But it isn't like that at all,' Fleur protested.

'I dare say,' Rose said. 'But when truth and dogma fight, dogma will always win.'

Later Rose showed them to their rooms. To Fleur's pleasure, they had separate bedrooms on the upper floor, in the ordinary English manner. Even so, her room was large enough to contain a sofa and two armchairs grouped around the fireplace, and a writing-desk and a reading-table, as well as the normal bedroom furniture. In one corner, as in every room, there was an icon on the wall, with a small, red-shaped lamp on a table below it. Fleur's icon was of St Sebastian – a prickly subject, she thought, to share a bedroom with.

As she had expected, a tentative enquiry revealed that there were no water-closets or bathrooms. But after all, if abroad were just like home, there'd be no point in travelling, she told herself.

'We have the bath-house, of course,' Rose said. 'Have you ever had a Russian steam-bath?' Fleur shook her head. 'Then I shall take pleasure in introducing you to its delights. Oh, I am so glad you are here!' she exclaimed suddenly. 'We shall have time to talk and talk!'

'Yes,' said Fleur, 'I'm looking forward to that. And I should like to see round the house, too. It must have an interesting history.'

'I leave that for Seryosha, if you don't mind. He knows more about it than me. But I'll show you the countryside with pleasure,' Rose said, and added, with a wry smile, 'I ride better than I walk.'

Fleur was ashamed of her thoughtlessness. Of course, walking must be no pleasure for Rose, and climbing stairs, as she had already witnessed, was a great labour to her. She felt a warm rush of sympathy with her old-young hostess, whose eyes were shadowed with pain, but who affected such defiantly youthful toilettes. Today, for instance, she was wearing white muslin decorated with knots of pink ribbon, and her hair was gathered into two bunches of ringlets above her ears. In repose, she looked slender and graceful, as though she might at any moment raise her hands and dance, like Milochka in high spirits.

But Rose would never dance, would never know the pleasure of running through a meadow, would never fly upstairs for her handkerchief rather than wait for a slow-footed servant. What must it be like to be her, Fleur wondered. Had she ever been in love, wanted to marry? What were her aspirations and desires?

But as Kirov had said, it was impossible to feel sorry for Rose, who did not feel sorry for herself. Despite the limitations set on her life, she had a kind of openness and confidence that Fleur envied. It was partly to do with being Russian, she thought, for Russian women seemed to enjoy a degree of freedom Fleur could only work for secretly at home. Well-born Russian women spoke and moved freely, went about with very little chaperonage, stated their opinions boldly, and even, for a wonder, drank glass for glass at dinner along with the men, instead of being condemned, like English women, to sipping lemonade and barley water.

There was much that Rose could teach her, Fleur thought, particularly about courage, and self-sufficiency. But most of all, she was simply looking forward to having a female friend of like mind in whom to confide. She was quite satisfied already, even on this short acquaintance, that Rose would prove to be like-minded.

The first few days passed tranquilly. Rose provided them with horses from the stables, and took them out to show them the immediate countryside.

'Once you know the best rides, you can come and go as you please, without bothering to wait for me,' she said. It was mainly directed at Milochka and Richard, and the deep roots of English propriety in Fleur made her wonder that Rose should consider a young buck like Richard a suitable chaperone for a pretty young girl. But Rose had summed them up the first evening, and put them down as being like brother and sister to each other.

Fleur wondered how Richard's pride would like that; but on observing them herself during the course of the first long ride, she saw that their relationship had changed, and that Rose was right. The calf-eyed worship in Richard's face had gone. He was seeing Milochka not as a goddess, but as a normal human girl – if a very pretty one – and they chatted to each other with comfortable freedom and the occasional sharp sibling disagreement. That was good, she thought. If Richard and Milochka kept each other amused, it would free Rose to spend her time with Fleur.

So it proved. By the third day, the young people were riding off alone, and Fleur and Rose were taking their horseback exercise in a different direction, and enjoying private conversation. Rose's own horse was a fiery little chestnut Arab, whose temperamental outbursts she handled with astonishing ease. She rode, to Fleur's rather shocked surprise, cross-saddle like a man, wearing the baggy trousers and soft leather boots of a Cossack. Fleur thought it was not only vaguely indecent, but must be extremely uncomfortable. Rose told her that on the contrary it was very comfortable, and offered to teach her, but Fleur declined, thinking there were some things a lady simply couldn't do, even in a foreign country.

'I'm still trying to get used to the vastness of everything,' Fleur said one day as they walked their horses along a white track between the seas of high young corn. 'Your sky is the biggest thing I've ever seen. It's so big it hardly seems like sky at all, in fact, just endless empty space overhead. And the land is so vast there's no horizon, just misty distances where the eye can't see any further. I understand now what your brother meant about things seeming to crowd in on him in England.'

It was an empty land, too. Even so close to St Petersburg, the villages were few and far between, and they were all the same, drearily monotonous: a wide mud track between two rows of identical wooden houses – *izby* – each with a beast-shed and a tilled patch full of cabbages behind. It struck Fleur that slavery might well endure in such a land, for even if a serf wanted to run away, there was nowhere for him to run to. Everywhere else would be exactly the same as the place he had left.

'The law is,' Rose explained, 'that if a serf runs away and can stay uncaptured for ten years, he gets his freedom, so there'll always be some who try, even though the chances of succeeding are very small. Of course they never consider how

251

miserable their life will be during those ten years on the run, or what on earth they'll do at the end of it when they are free.'

'But doesn't that simply prove that freedom is an end in itself, and valuable to all men?' Fleur asked tentatively.

'Serfs aren't men. They don't think at all. They're like cattle, following a familiar routine – you know, from the field to the byre and back again. Move the gate, and they'll line up against the fence where the gate used to be.'

Fleur was rather shocked by this, especially from someone she considered intelligent, and though she didn't wish to argue with her hostess, she felt obliged to say, 'But a human being, however stupid, is not an animal. It's our duty to improve their understanding, to educate them—'

Rose laughed. 'Listen, I'll tell you something. My mother – who as you know, was English – had the same idea. She decided out of her own money to build a school and provide a schoolmaster for the village children. At first the serfs wouldn't send their children to it, because they wanted them to work in the fields beside them. So mother made attendance compulsory, and reduced the serfs' work quota in her own fields to make up for it. And what do you think they did? Thank her? No, they burnt the school down, beat the master almost to death, and then marched on the house to burn that down too. My stepfather had to call out the army to restore order.'

Fleur listened to this, shocked and almost disbelieving. 'But why should they behave so violently?'

'Because they are violent – ignorant and violent. They're suspicious of anything new, particularly a new idea, and their one idea is to smash it, destroy it before it can change anything. Force is all they understand – that's why you have to keep a firm hand on them, and flog them when they get out of line. Seryosha's too soft with them, like his father before him. That's why they take advantage.'

Fleur shook her head involuntarily, and Rose went on, 'You are English, and don't understand, but even my mother had to learn. The *muzhiki* respect a firm master, as long as they think he's fair. But if they think a punishment is too light for the offence, they despise him. They don't expect kindness, and they don't understand it. They see it as weakness.'

Fleur was not unfamiliar with the argument: she had heard it often enough applied to the common soldier in the British army. He was a brute, and must be treated like a brute. It was firmly believed by almost everyone – yes, even by many of the soldiers themselves – that harsh discipline, provided it was fair, was respected, and clemency despised.

But she couldn't help seeing, from her own experience, how harshness brutalised people in the first place. She felt instinctively that there must be some way to break the cycle, and since the initiative could not come from the brutes, it must come from their masters. How to do it, she didn't know; and she accepted that there were enormous difficulties in the way. What she couldn't accept was that it was either impossible, or – as some of the Russians she had met seemed to think – undesirable.

The weather was fine, and they spent most of their days out of doors. In the evenings – those astonishing White Nights of northern Russia, when it never got quite dark, and the evening twilight faded gently into the faint pallor of before-dawn – they sat together in the pretty octagonal drawing-room, whose French windows opened onto the terrace over the formal garden.

There was a grand piano there, and a harp – which Rose played – and they often made music together in various permutations. There was a large library of books, mostly in French and German, a few in English and Russian, and Lyudmilla and Richard pounced on a collection of Gothic horror novels, and began working their way through them, devouring them uncritically like children given the run of a pastry-cook's.

As a result, Lyudmilla decided that one or other of the towers must be haunted, and she and Richard would often trot away together to look for skeletons and secret passages, to return dusty and dishevelled, but always disappointed. There was also a massive jigsaw which Rose had unearthed, on which they all worked in a desultory way. It was so large it had to be laid out on a board on the floor, and the picture was fiendish – a copy of David's painting of Empress Josephine being crowned by Napoleon, all crimson and gold robes and pink faces. And Fleur and Rose, of course, talked.

On Saturday Fleur was introduced to the delights of the bath-house. It was a wooden building in one of the court-yards, with a fire-house next to it where she supposed in her innocence water would be heated. She and Rose went there alone the first time, for Milochka was out with Richard walking her dogs.

'I'll show her later where it is. She won't need instruction like you,' Rose said.

They went in. Inside the floor was of stone, with a wooden partition down the centre of the room. 'The other side is the men's side,' Rose said. There was a long wooden table down the length of the room, and around it a trench was cut in the floor, and there was a range of cupboards along the wall.

'First you must take off all your clothes, and put them in the cupboard. Then you lie down on the table.'

Rose began to undress herself, and Fleur hesitated, deeply embarrassed, for she had never in her adult life been naked in front of anybody. Rose paused and looked at her quizzically, and then a surprising deep blush spread across her face.

'I understand. Don't worry, I'll leave you alone,' Rose said abruptly. It was the hurt in her voice which alerted Fleur. After a second's surprise, she realised that Rose thought she was afraid or embarrassed to see Rose's withered legs.

Fleur's hand went out in instant remorse. 'Oh, no, I didn't mean – it isn't that! It's – it's simply that I've never undressed in front of anybody before.'

Now they were both scarlet. 'I'm sorry,' Rose said, 'I should have thought. I will tell you what to do, and then you shall have your bath alone. It's just that the steam-bath is a wonderful place for conversation. It's something we Russians enjoy sharing.'

'Please – please stay,' Fleur said. 'I'm being stupid and missish. When in Rome, as the saying is—'

'If you're sure,' Rose said doubtfully, and Fleur insisted. Not for worlds would she hurt this kind creature.

Once she got used to it, Fleur made the surprising discovery that nakedness somehow increases confidence. At Rose's signal, servants brought in red-hot stones, carried on iron litters, and rolled them into the trenches in the floor. Then they threw water over the stones, and at once a great cloud of steam arose, filling the room. This process was repeated as often as requested, and meanwhile the ladies reclined on the slabs in the hot steam, and sweated, and chatted.

'Later we'll be massaged, and then rinsed off, and you will find yourself feeling cleaner and happier than ever in your life before,' Rose promised.

The extraordinary relaxation and feeling of intimacy generated by this process gave rise to conversation that would have been difficult elsewhere. Fleur found the courage at last to ask Rose if she had ever been in love.

'Oh yes,' she said at once. 'Many times. The first was the strongest, though. I fell in love with my stepfather's soldier-servant, a Hungarian mercenary. He was shaped like a barrel, with a terrible scar down his face and only one eye, but I adored him!' Fleur laughed. 'No, truly! It was he who taught me to ride, at a time when nobody thought I would ever be able to walk. He set me astride a Cossack pony, and said, "There, now you have six legs instead of two. You can go anywhere on the face of the earth." That pony was my second great love. He was clever and kind, and took care of me like a nanny. He was called Myelka – which means Little Honey – and I've called all my horses Myelka ever since, even when, like my present devil, it doesn't suit them.'

'But what about real love?' Fleur said.

'That was real love,' Rose insisted.

'Don't be mischievous. You know what I mean. Did you ever fall in love with a man?'

'Yes, that too,' Rose admitted. 'There was a young man called Felix, when I was eighteen. He was so beautiful! He danced like an angel – though not with me, of course. He wanted to get married, but his father wouldn't allow it. That was when we were in disgrace, you see, after that business with Sashka. Seryosha told you about that?'

'Yes,' Fleur said. 'What happened?'

'Nothing happened. Oh, to Felix, you mean? Well, he went off to do his military service in Georgia, and was killed in a Chechen raid.'

'Oh Rose, I'm sorry!'

'It's a long time ago,' she said easily. 'There have been others since, but none I wanted to marry. I fall in love easily, but I get over it very quickly. And I like my own company best. You have to try so hard with other people, don't you? With yourself everything's easy.'

'Yes, I've often felt that too. At home I'm alone for a lot of the time. But I've always thought that it must be possible to find the right man, the man with whom you feel as if you're alone, if you know what I mean. But perhaps I'm being unrealistic.'

Rose lifted herself on one elbow and looked at her. 'Have you ever thought you'd met such a man?' she asked.

'Yes,' Fleur said, a little unwillingly. 'Just once.'

'What happened?'

This was the perfect moment to confide, but she found she couldn't yet quite do it. 'I was mistaken. It turned out that he didn't feel the same about me.'

Rose looked at her for a long time, and then sighed and lay down again. 'Never mind. You're young yet. There'll be others. You're much too pretty to be left on the shelf.'

Thus cleansed, on Sunday they all went to church. The little squat white church with the blue enamelled cupola decorated with silver stars stood on the main road just opposite the entrance to the drive. Behind it was a cluster of wooden buildings, and beyond them, rising white into the empty blue air, the thin smoke of the village, just out of sight.

Inside the church seemed very dark, to an English person's eyes, for it was windowless, and lit only by the light from the open door, and the multitude of candles standing before the icons on the walls. There were so many of them, the walls were almost completely covered, and the candlelight reflected off the gold of haloes and picked out the rich colours of robes, giving an impression of half-hidden jewels piled up in the shadows of a pirate's cave.

Fleur had been surprised when she first went to church with the Polotskis that there were no chairs or pews, but they had explained to her that Russians do not sit down in the presence of the King of Kings, before whom even the Emperor himself bows the knee. It seemed to her further evidence of the deep sincerity with which Russians kept their religion, and it saddened her to compare it with the indifference commonly met with at home, and the deep schisms within the Church of England.

She rather enjoyed the service, though she understood none of the words: the liturgy in Russian sounded very impressive, sonorous and rolling, and the singing was very beautiful, although strangely sad, as sad as the faces of the Byzantine saints. There was none of the mediaeval jolliness of old English hymns and early religious paintings: Russian Christianity seemed to have a deep vein of melancholy to it, which went with the dark mystery of the churches and the lilac clouds of incense that numbed the air.

After the service, Rose took them to visit some of the family pensioners who lived in the cluster of buildings behind the church, and the rest of the day was spent quietly at home. Milochka and Richard worked on the jigsaw, while Rose and Fleur chatted. Later Rose read while Fleur caught up with her diary, and the young ones played a game with picture cards which involved a lot of whispering and helpless giggles.

The next day was Monday, and in the afternoon, Count Kirov came home.

'Ah, here's one I wanted you to look at,' said the Count as they paused in front of the enormous painting which dominated the first-floor landing. 'That's my mother, Anna Petrovna.'

Over a period of days he had been showing her the house, in between other activities. 'It would weary you to see it all at once,' he told her. That was of a piece with his kindness and consideration towards her since his return. He treated her like an old and valued friend; he was careful of her comfort and pleasure; he sought her out, preferred her company.

It was not quite like their old intimacy – there was a sort of tension in the air between them – but it was far from indifference. And sometimes she would turn her head to find him looking at her with an expression she couldn't quite fathom, but which haunted her imagination. She knew Rose had seen it too. She had seen Rose watching them together, had seen puzzlement and speculation in her expression, and once or twice she had thought Rose might be on the verge of speaking to her about it; but nothing happened.

Fleur had taken pains to observe Lyudmilla's reactions, in view of her passionate profession of love after the ball at the Kirov Palace, and had been reassured. She thought Lyudmilla was still attracted to Kirov, but she behaved with the greatest propriety in his presence, and even seemed rather subdued, almost as though she were a little afraid of him. Kirov treated her with the sort of grave courtesy a childless man employs towards an engaging youngster – there was no danger there. And it was certain that Milochka spent her time more often and more enjoyably with Richard, with whom she could forget dignity and romp. Fleur felt that even if the infatuation had survived this far, a few more weeks would see it off entirely.

Today, as soon as Milochka and Richard had set off on their ride, Kirov had suggested to Fleur that they looked at the paintings. 'There's a huge collection, but few of them are of any value. One or two "old masters", and the rest are family portraits – divided almost equally between horses and humans. We Kirovs have always been fond of our horses!'

They had toured the main rooms downstairs, and Fleur saw that he was right. Most of the paintings were undistinguished, though one or two were interesting because of the subject. The one they stood before now was very poor, a strange amalgam of styles, but it interested her because the background appeared to be a view of England: a rolling landscape of patchwork fields dotted with woods and snug farms, which was so different from the country around her now that for an instant she felt homesick.

'It looks like Berkshire or Wiltshire,' she said. 'Not like Russia at all.'

'It's meant to be Hampshire, my mother's home county,' Kirov said with a smile, 'but she was no great artist. She painted the background in herself, with my father's help, to remind her of home. The rest was done by the estate painter. You'll see lots of his work around. He was very good on horses, which was why he was kept on.'

'Yes, I see,' Fleur said. In the foreground was a woman in a rust-coloured riding habit mounted on a beautiful black horse. The horse was quite well done, but the woman's body was wooden and out of proportion, though her face was rather better.

'Is it a good likeness?' she asked. The woman was neither beautiful nor plain. She looked rather ordinary, except that her expression was grimly determined, as though life had always been hard for her, and she saw no reason why it should be otherwise for anyone else.

'I don't really know. That was done when I was very young, and I don't really remember her like that. She changed so much when my father died. She grew old almost overnight. But I think there is a little of her, in the eyes, perhaps, and the shape of the face.'

She looked up at him. 'I suppose you must look more like your father.'

'Yes, I'm said to be very like him. Petya took much more after Mama.'

Fleur studied the picture again. 'She must have loved your father very much.'

'She did. He was everything to her. All through the Napoleonic invasion she travelled by his side, and never minded what dangers she faced as long as she could be with him. And afterwards they were never apart. When he died, all her joy in life ended. She lived ten years after his death, and when she was dying, she told me that they'd been the longest and loneliest years of her life.'

She heard the hurt in his voice, and said quickly, 'I'm sure she didn't mean that as a slight to you.'

'Yes she did,' he said simply. 'I'm sorry, but you can't know. She had no room in her heart for me. Sashka was her favourite, always, even though he wasn't her child. When he died, and then Papa died, there was nothing left for her.' He smiled crookedly. 'I never blamed Sashka, believe me. I loved him too. But I could never take his place with Mama.'

Fleur didn't know what to say. She knew, none better, what it was like to lack a parent's love, a parent's care; but here was Kirov, a man thirteen years her senior, who still minded bitterly that his mother had not loved him. He had been married, and even that hadn't healed the wound. In the face of her own indifference to her father's neglect, she couldn't understand it. Well, perhaps it was just different for a man, she thought a little helplessly.

She looked again at the grim-faced young woman on the horse before they moved off along the passage. She must have been extraordinary to have followed the drum, as the saying was, in a country such as Russia, and against an army such as Napoleon's. Fleur had met one or two soldier's wives: tough, indomitable little women, who suffered incredible hardships rather than be parted from their men. Such a life was completely unsexing, and though that grim young woman was obviously a world away from the pipe-smoking, burden-bearing little brutes Fleur had met, there must have been similarities of temperament. Perhaps that was why Kirov was – a little strange sometimes. She could not have been a comfortable mother to have; no Madame Polotski, for sure.

They reached the landing at the other end of the corridor, which was lit by a large window. Fleur stopped to look out of it, and saw Richard and Milochka, who had collected their horses and were cantering away across the park.

'There they go,' she said affectionately. 'Off on their adventures.' Kirov came up beside her and stooped to look out. Milochka was ahead, turning back in her saddle to shout something at Richard, and despite the distance, the sound of her healthy young voice, though not her words, was carried back to them on the summer air through the open window.

'They seem to get on very well together,' Kirov said.

There was something odd about his voice, and Fleur glanced at him to see that he was frowning thoughtfully as he watched the figures diminish into the distance. Was he disapproving, she wondered suddenly.

'Yes,' she said lightly, 'just like brother and sister, I always think.'

He looked at her, faintly questioning, and then his brow cleared, and he smiled. 'As long as I don't have to entertain them all day, I'm content,' he said. 'Would you like to see the Black Tower? We're close to it now, and you've never been up there, have you?'

'I'd like it very much,' she said. 'Milochka raves about it: she and Dick have made it up between them that it should be haunted, you know! I'm sure they really believe they're going to hear rattling chains and bloodcurdling groans one of these nights. They're secretly longing to spend the night up there, and catch the spectre red-handed.'

He didn't smile at her joke. 'I don't think it is haunted,' he said. 'There's no great tragedy connected with it. It was built by an elderly princess, who went and lived up there to get away from the world, and refused to see anyone but the servant who brought her food.'

'That's a sad story, if not a tragedy,' Fleur said.

'Not really. Mama was sure she was quite happy up there, looking out over the world. The view from the top is magnificent.'

The massive bulk of the Black Tower looked grim and gloomy even in bright sunlight, and inside the air struck cold. It contained nothing but the winding staircase up to a single suite of rooms at the very top, from which another staircase led out onto the leads. The rooms were empty of furniture, but the sunlight streamed into them through the dusty windows, and Fleur agreed at once that there was nothing unhappy or haunted about the atmosphere.

'There's something here I wanted you to see before we go up on the roof,' Kirov said, and led her over to a painting which was hanging on the wall in solitary state. 'This is my late wife, Elisabeth Feodorovna. Rather better than most of the family portraits, as you see. It was commissioned from one of the best Court painters in St Petersburg, and it's very like.'

Fleur looked with surprised and painful interest. The woman in the portrait was very young, almost a child, with a little, kittenish face and a wistful expression, and soft light brown hair. She was dressed in white lace, with the gathered skirts and huge sleeves of the 'thirties, and her hands in her lap held a lace fan and a posy of white rosebuds.

'It's charming,' she said. 'But she looks so very young. How old was she?'

'That was her wedding portrait. She was fifteen years old, and I was twenty. They marry them young in the Caucasus. Life is harsh and uncertain there, and there's no time to waste.'

'The Caucasus?'

'It's a wild and mountainous region in the south – so wild, it's under military rule. That's how I met Elisabeth, during my tour of military service, holding down the tribes. I fell in love with her at first sight, and married her, and brought her home here. We were married just six years before she died.'

'I'm so sorry,' Fleur said. She looked at the tender, wistful mouth and shy eyes in the painting, and tried to imagine what Kirov must have been like at twenty. In love with her, marrying her, losing her: it must have affected him profoundly. She glanced at him, and saw that he was staring at the picture with a brooding look. 'Thank you for showing it to me. It must be painful for you to look at it.'

He seemed to come to himself abruptly. 'What? Oh, no, not really. It was all a long time ago.'

'But – I'm sorry, I thought—' She was confused. 'I thought that since you hid the picture away up here—'

He smiled. 'No, not at all. It's like your kind heart to think of it, though. No, I keep it here because it's where Lisa liked to be. She loved this tower. She used to spend hours up here, staring out of the window. Have a closer look at the picture, tell me if you notice anything.'

It was an old-fashioned and formal painting. The background was a pair of curving velvet drapes, beyond which, as through a window, could be seen the traditional 'Arcadian' landscape of rolling Italian hills dotted with little trees. But there was one difference: tucked down in a fold of the hills in the middle distance was a house whose eccentricity was unmistakable.

'It's this house, it's Schwartzenturm!' Fleur said. 'What a nice idea. Was your wife very fond of it, then?'

'No,' he said. 'No, I don't think she liked it at all, but we spent almost all of our married life here. The last year, when she was ill and failing, I took her to my estate in the Crimea, but by then it was too late. It was Mama's idea to have that put in, to make it into a family portrait. Trying to assimilate Lisa into the family, you see; but as it turned out, she never was part of it.'

'Why not?'

He hesitated before answering. 'She gave me no son. Mama held that against her – she wanted the line to continue. But in any case, Lisa always held herself apart. She was homesick for her own land and her own family. She missed the mountains. She never got used to our flat northern country. I think that's why she used to come up to the tower: it was the only way she could get up high, and see into the distance.'

Fleur waited, feeling there was more here than he had yet told her. Kirov stared broodingly at the picture for a moment longer, and then seemed to shake himself, and said cheerfully, 'The view from the roof is magnificent – come and see.'

Bemused, she followed him up the stone steps and onto the leads. The air was warm and bright, the sun falling clear and hot from the empty sky above them, the breeze singing softly and unimpeded about their ears, fluttering their hair and sleeves. All around them the broad and tidy fields of crops spread towards the horizon, dotted here and there with the tiny, brown figure of a stooping peasant or a labouring ox; and away to the west was a dark green curdle of woodland, looking almost black with the distance.

'It's wonderful,' she said.

They stepped up to the parapet and stood there side by side. Fleur laid her hands on the hot stone and stared outwards, acutely conscious of his closeness. Had he brought her here, she wondered, solely to tell her these intimate secrets, about his wife's unhappiness, and his mother's harshness? And if so, why? She had too little experience of men to know whether it was simply a thing that men did. She felt she ought to be honoured by his confidence, and yet she didn't know exactly what it was he was confiding.

'When I was a child,' he said softly, 'I used to think you could see for ever from up here: the whole of the world, all the way to the encircling sea.' She made an interrogative sound. 'The peasants believe the land is surrounded by an eternal ocean. My old nurse had told me about that. Well, perhaps they're right – who can tell?'

She glanced at him to see if he were joking, and he smiled down at her, something close to the old smile that made her quiver, made her feel that he was stepping into her mind as easily and comfortably as a man steps into his own drawing-room.

He put out his hand, and gathered hers where it lay on the parapet, and held it, stroking it gently with his thumb. It was such a natural gesture, but for her, so devastating.

'There are two sorts of knowledge in life, it seems to me,' he said. 'What we know of our own experience, and what other people tell us, that we believe. But which should we base our decisions on, *Tsvetoksha maya*? Perhaps if we judged only by what we knew at first hand, we would make fewer mistakes.'

'We should make fewer decisions,' she said, struggling to understand. 'What we can know at first hand is so little.'

'Well, perhaps that would be no bad thing,' he said. He looked at her for a long time, and though the smile didn't fade, it grew sadder, revealing that subtle brushstroke of melancholy in every Russian work of art. 'I don't think Lisa knew one happy day after I brought her here. I haven't been very good at bringing happiness to people, have I?'

'That's not true,' she began, and then realised that it was not possible to finish what she wanted to say. She didn't even know if he meant it as an apology, but his next words were clearer.

'Thank you, my dear friend. I can't tell you how it warms me to know that you have gone on liking me against all the odds. And it was a struggle, wasn't it? But I never meant to hurt you. I wish you would believe me that I never meant to hurt you.'

'I do believe it,' she said with difficulty.

He lifted her hand to his lips and kissed the tips of her fingers. *Tsvetoksha maya*. Lovely English rose. How I wish we could live our lives at the top of this tower, away from the rest of the world, like the old princess – just the two of us. But it's not possible. Other considerations have to be taken into account. And other people always will intrude on what should be a private conversation.'

He placed her hand back on the parapet and released it, as one putting away from him something he had finished with. She felt a vague disquiet that something final had been said or done without her knowing it, some decision made on her behalf that she had somehow missed. And now it was too late. He was moving away from the parapet, back towards the steps.

'We must go back, I'm afraid. I have to see my Supervisor of Accounts this morning,' he said. Now why, she wondered as she followed him, did that sound like an excuse?

Chapter Fourteen

Peter Kirov arrived from St Petersburg, bringing with him a party of young people: three officers from his regiment, one of them a married colonel, together with the colonel's wife and two of her unmarried female friends. They had come to stay for the month, and the atmosphere in the house changed at once. It was very like a house party at a country house in England, Fleur thought, except that everything was done on a more lavish scale; and the guests talked and laughed more loudly, and seemed to enjoy themselves a great deal more than her fellow countrymen ever did.

Lyudmilla reacted rapturously to the increase in company. The presence of four attractive young cavalry officers, three of them unwed, brought out the worst in her, and she languished and giggled and flirted abominably with all of them. Fleur felt sorry for Richard, who had grown used to having Milochka to himself, and now had to come to terms with heavy competition. It had the effect of reawakening his interest in her in a non-sibling way, and the more she flirted, the more he glowered and brooded.

On the first evening Fleur came down rather early, before the bell was rung for dinner, and on entering the octagon room she found Peter there alone, sitting at the piano and picking out a tune one-handed. His expression was dark. He touched the notes slowly, broodingly, and the tune hesitated sadly on the air. She stood still for a moment, watching him, and then he seemed to sense her presence. He looked up, and his face spread into a warm and welcoming smile which lit his eyes and made him look, for a moment, almost handsome.

'Miss Hamilton! There you are!' He stood up and hurried across the room to take both her hands and look down at her with such pleasure that for a dizzy moment she thought he might forget himself and hug and kiss her. And if it weren't for the conventions, she thought, she wouldn't have minded.

'Peter Nikolayevitch,' she said in the Russian form she had learned. 'I'm very glad to see you again.'

'Oh, so am I, more than I can possibly convey to you in your abominably cold language!' he laughed. 'For instance, how can I express anything but indifference when I am forced to address you as *Miss Hamilton*? How do you English manage? Is there nothing between chilly formality and the intimacy of blood-relationship?'

266

'I'm afraid not,' Fleur said, 'though I suppose you might try *Fleur Ranulphovna*.'

'Damned if I will! I'd never manage it after even a single glass of vodka, and I assure you I mean to drink a thousand toasts to your glorious eyes before this night's over!'

'You do talk such nonsense!'

'Yes, but charmingly, don't you think? How are you liking Schwartzenturm? Have you been bored to distraction?'

'Of course not. With your sister and brother to talk to, how could I be other than content?'

A shadow passed over his face; then he spoke with forced lightness. 'Rose, I grant you, is excellent company when she troubles herself to be; but my stick of a brother must have been a sore trial to you. Never mind, I'm here now, and you may consider your duty by him done. I hereby give you leave to forget him and enjoy yourself.'

She was a little puzzled how to take this, or how to answer it, but he saved her the trouble by continuing at once. 'And how has it been with the lovely Lyudmilla Ivanovna? I come charged with all sorts of messages from her parents which I shan't bother to deliver, since they all involve behaving herself, which would surely spoil her fun!'

'She is in the best of spirits, as you saw for yourself when you arrived. But have you been to visit the Polotskis? That was kind of you.'

'Yes, wasn't it?' he said frankly. 'I called in twice, which is twice more than I called on any of my relatives during that time. But I like the Polotskis – they're good, reliable people. One always knows where one is with them. Their desires and ambitions are perfectly straightforward, and openly expressed.' His voice had taken on an edge which made her raise an eyebrow in enquiry. 'They told me, for instance, almost in words of one syllable, that I am not the man for their daughter. She is a considerable heiress, as I expect you know, and though my family is good, I am only the cadet.'

Fleur eyed him with dismay. 'Oh, surely they weren't so blunt? You are joking, aren't you?'

He smiled, a better, clearer smile. 'No – but I honour them

for it. It's better to know where one stands, I always think.'

Fleur searched for comfort. 'I don't think you would have suited anyway,' she said.

He laughed, pressing her hands. 'Oh, you are so lovely when you say things like that! I wasn't serious about her, I assure you, and my heart is not broken! It's been kneaded and pummelled so often in the course of my reprehensible career, that it has the consistency of India rubber. And now, seriously, we must decide what I am to call you. I suppose you wouldn't allow Fleur, without the Ranulphovna?'

She felt a little shy, but realising she had been holding his hands for the last five minutes, considered it was rather late to be missish about it. 'As your sister's intimate friend,' she said, 'which I am proud to count myself, I think perhaps it would not be improper.'

'Bravo! Fleur it is, then.' He lifted one hand to his lips and saluted it. 'Best of creatures, may you flourish! *Floreat Flora!*'

At that moment they were interrupted by the entrance of Count Kirov, who stopped dead at the sight of them, a frown – almost a scowl – overspreading his face. Fleur at once, and most annoyingly, felt herself blush; and Peter, while discreetly letting go of her hands, looked at his brother with something like defiance. The air between them bristled with hostility, which Fleur could feel, but could not account for.

'Ah, my illustrious senior,' Peter said with an ironical bow.

'Ah, my worthless cadet,' Kirov replied in kind. 'What can have brought you from your room, fully dressed, before the bell? Was it simply to find someone other than your servants to annoy?'

'I might observe that *you* are not usually known to haunt the drawing-room when it lacks a good ten minutes to the hour. Obviously Miss Hamilton's English habits of punctuality have rubbed off on you.'

'Miss Hamilton? You were not so formal a moment ago,' Kirov said tartly. Fleur looked from one to the other like a spectator at a tennis match, feeling extremely puzzled and ill at ease.

'I wasn't sure whether she had yet given you permission to

use her given name,' Peter said smoothly. 'Or perhaps you haven't deemed it necessary to ask.'

'The question hasn't really arisen,' Fleur said quickly. 'You know how rarely one uses a person's name, when that person is present.'

'Rarely, yes – and tact such as yours is rare, ma'am,' Peter said.

'As rare as a Siberian orchid, you might say. Have you heard from your father lately, Miss Hamilton?' Kirov said pointedly.

It was an obvious warning to Peter to change the subject, for which Fleur was grateful, except that since Kirov already knew that she hadn't received a letter, she was unsure how to answer.

'Papa never writes unless there's something he wants,' she said a little blankly.

'Just like you, Seryosha,' Peter said quickly. 'And does your father always get what he wants, Miss Hamilton? My brother does – or he has done, until now.'

'What do you think, Petya – Miss Hamilton has been riding Kudlatka, and managing him very well. Better even than Rose did.' A second warning, and this time Peter heeded it.

'He's a lovely animal, isn't he? Full of spirit, but as gentle as a dove. I sometimes think the Mamelukes are even better than our Karabakhs, for intelligence at least.'

'I've never ridden a Karabakh, or at least I don't think I have,' Fleur said. 'I don't think we have them in England. We have Arabians, though. Is that what you mean by Mamelukes?'

A little stiltedly at first, but with growing fluency, they discussed horses until the bell rang and the rest of the company came flocking downstairs, releasing them from each other. Peter moved away and attached himself to Lyudmilla – perhaps to deliver her parents' messages after all – and Kirov, with one last, grave glance and bow to Fleur, went to be polite to the two unmarried females.

Soon the *zakuski* were brought in – a selection of radishes, fried sardines, hard-boiled quails' eggs in spinach nests, caviare and bread-and-butter, with the inevitable flasks of chilled vodka. Fleur had grown used to it by now, enough to be able to tell a good one from an indifferent. The conversation rose and grew general. Fleur chatted over her plate and glass to the colonel and his wife, but her mind was elsewhere.

What was the cause of hostility between the brothers? Or at least, what specifically? It was impossible, in view of some of the things that had been said, not to wonder if it were herself. And yet, that didn't seem to make sense. Kirov had made it very plain in England that he didn't want her, and though his behaviour towards her lately suggested affection, if not even sometimes tenderness, there seemed to be no serious intention on his part. As for Peter, she had never given him any cause to think she regarded him other than as a friend.

At length the double doors were thrown open, and they were led by Rose into the dining-room. It was a wonderful sight, ablaze with light, which reflected off the silver and crystal, and warmed the strawberry-red livery of the servants who stood behind each chair. The company trooped in and took their places, bare shoulders and glossy curls, bare bosoms and flashing jewels, snowy linen and embroidered waistcoats with orders and ribbons and stars. Fleur had a moment of stepping outside herself, and seeing herself amongst this glittering company: confident, tonnish, titled people, any one of whom, probably, could have bought Grove Park ten times over, for cash, and her dowry with it. Even her brother, down the table from her, who was heir to a baronetcy and what counted in England as a snug fortune, was nobody here.

And then she caught Kirov's eye on her, turned her head, and received his smile, and was part of it all again. She was his honoured guest: that was all that mattered.

It was an elegant dinner, each dish being handed and eaten separately in the Russian style, which Fleur thought so much more civilised than the English way. It began with bortsh – white soup with soured cream stirred into it, which was served with patties filled with mincemeat. Then came *blinis*, deliciously light pancakes served hot and spread with caviare, onto which whipped butter was spooned so that it melted into golden globbets over the salty fish-eggs. There was a fried white fish with slices of preserved limes; boiled fowls in a white sauce with capers and truffles; pickled peas and French beans; a tongue in aspic; a salad of leaves; spiced fried potatoes; some kind of game bird, roasted, served with sweet bilberry sauce and sliced, salted cucumbers; and then desserts of sweet cakes, an iced fruit pudding, and a stiff, creamy substance called *yoghourt* which Fleur had not come across before, but which she thought superior to the English creams.

A dozen wines were in circulation, mostly French and Rhenish, but also some Russian wines from Livadia and Massandra, and sherry and port, which were called 'English' wines. The mention of this fact turned the discussion to how sea power had given England her wines. Fleur recalled from her history lessons that England had acquired the island of Madeira from the Spanish in return for the British navy's rescuing their royal family from Napoleon.

And then Peter suddenly called down the table to his brother, 'Talking of navies, what on earth is going on in the Dardanelles, Seryosha? I always have to come to you to understand politics.'

'Nothing is going on in the Dardanelles,' Kirov said quickly. 'It's much ado about nothing.'

'But shall we have a war?' one of the ladies asked. 'I can't get any sense out of Papa about it. You're close to the Emperor, Sergei Nikolayevitch – can't you tell us?'

'A war?' Fleur said. 'With whom?'

'Why, with England, of course,' the same lady said, turning large eyes on her. 'Your country has sent a war fleet to the Straits, didn't you know?'

'Yes, and France has, too,' said someone else. 'They must mean something. You don't send ships all round the world for no purpose, do you?'

There was a clamour of comment, over which Kirov raised his voice. 'There will be no war, I assure you. It's a simple matter of adjustment between Russia and Turkey, which Russia and Turkey will settle.'

'This business of the Holy Places, and protecting Orthodox

interests in Jerusalem?' Peter said. 'But I thought that was settled already. I thought the Sultan agreed to give Orthodox Christians the same rights as the Catholics?'

Kirov set his hands flat on the table. 'It's a little more complex than that, Petya. The Emperor wants the Sultan to guarantee his ancient right to represent and protect all the Orthodox subjects of Turkey, and the Sultan is dragging his feet over signing the document. We may have to make a few demonstrations of strength to spur him on, but that's all it will be.'

'But then what are the English and French fleets doing there?' Richard asked. 'Surely it's nothing to do with us?'

Kirov turned to him with faint reluctance. 'I'm afraid your government has got it into its head that the Emperor has designs on Turkish territories, when the inevitable break-up of the Turkish Empire occurs. But nothing could be further from the truth, I assure you. The Emperor seeks only to assert his right to defend Orthodox Christians, to protect the independence of the Danubian Principalities, and to ensure that Constantinople remains a free port. As soon as England and France realise the truth, they will withdraw their fleets and go home.' He smiled around the table. 'This is what you might call a diplomatic misunderstanding – unfortunate, yes, but not serious. There will be no war, I assure you. Nobody wants a war.'

A brief silence followed his words, and then Rose stood up and said, 'We'll have coffee in the drawing-room, I think. Come, everyone.'

Chairs were drawn back, and the company rose like a disturbed flock of birds, and conversation broke out again. In the octagon room, coffee was served in heartbreakingly fragile little cups with gilded rims, frail as wrens' eggs. As soon as everyone was settled, Kirov asked Lyudmilla to sing for them all. She agreed with happy lack of self-consciousness, and Richard quickly offered to accompany her.

When the two of them had taken up their stations at the pianoforte, Kirov positioned himself nearby, standing by the open French windows with his cup in his hand, and fixing his eyes on Lyudmilla's face. She was obviously aware of his scrutiny, and acted up, singing with more expression even than usual, and making heart-rending gestures with her hands when she got to the sad part.

Fleur had hoped he would come and sit by her, as he usually did in the evening. Feeling an unreasonable pang of jealousy, she got up and drifted out onto the terrace, and stood looking out over the gardens while she tried to reason herself into a better frame of mind.

'Is this melancholy song breaking your heart?' asked a familiar voice beside her. 'Or is it indigestion that makes you look so sad?'

She turned and smiled to show she was not unhappy. Peter leaned his elbows on the parapet so that he could look at her face. He had lit a small cigar, and the aromatic smoke drifted upwards in thin blue coils.

'How could it be indigestion,' she said, 'after that delicious meal? I'm only sorry that I shall have to go back to the English way, all the dishes served at once and getting cold; half of them overcooked and half undercooked in the interests of getting them all on the table at the same time. Oh, I shall miss Russian cooking, I promise you!'

'Don't go back, then,' Peter said. 'Stay in Russia.'

'Don't be silly, how can I?' she laughed, thinking he was talking idly. 'What on earth would I do here?'

'The same as you'd do in England – get married.' There was a faintly watchful expression in his eyes. 'All men are not like my brother, you know.'

She was startled, and then surprised, and he looked away from her and said softly, 'What an abominable little show-off Lyudmilla is!'

'I thought you wanted to marry her,' Fleur said, feeling ruffled.

'It doesn't mean that I have to like her, does it?'

She frowned. 'Don't be provoking!'

'It's what I do best,' he said lightly, and then looked at her again, carefully. 'What my brother does best is breaking hearts.'

'What has that to do with me? Do you suppose mine to have been broken?'

'Oh, such a sharp frost! And I thought it would be a warm night! No, dear Fleur, not broken. I hope no more than bruised. But I know my brother very well, and I know he was pursuing you while he was in London. I can deduce the rest easily enough.'

'Who told you—?' she began in slow anger.

He lifted his hands. 'Don't bite! I mean no harm. Your brother and I were drinking-friends, remember. One gets confidential in the mess after the second bottle.'

'My brother?' she said wrathfully.

'You've stolen my next words. Brothers! Who'd have 'em? I've watched mine in action in drawing-rooms all over the country. Quite a technique he's developed. But you mustn't think too harshly of him – he really can't help it, you know.'

Fleur bit her lip, struggling with various emotions. But it was hard to be angry with Peter at any time, and harder still when he seemed to be on the verge of telling her something she had long wanted to know.

'I suppose you mean because of losing his wife in that tragic way?' she asked at last, as neutrally as possible.

Peter shrugged. 'I don't know about that. He was spoiled long before he got married. He was born resentful, if you want to know the truth! Nothing was ever good enough for him. He always had to come first, and be loved the best, and be flattered by everyone; but even if the whole world had walked past him in a column kissing his feet in turn, it still wouldn't have been enough for him.'

'Oh come, you exaggerate,' she said uncomfortably. It was hard to tell from his bantering tone how seriously he meant any of this.

He shook his head. 'There's something I know that he doesn't. Mamochka told me once: before he was born, while he was still in the womb, I mean, she rode off in pursuit of the French army, over desperate country in the depth of winter, in an attempt to find my half-sister. Not Rose, another one, my father's child by his first wife. She'd been abducted by one of the French officers.'

Fleur didn't see where this was leading. 'Did she rescue her?'

He looked put out by the question. 'What? Oh, no. She wouldn't leave him, when it came to it. But that's not the point. The point is that Mamochka risked her baby's life – Seryosha's life – for the sake of someone else's child who wasn't any kind of kin to her. She swore she'd never told him that, but I think he absorbed the knowledge somehow, from her blood, and he knew. He sucked in resentment with her milk. He never forgave her for not loving him best, and after that, all women were tainted with her crime.'

Fleur stared at him, struggled with the idea for a moment, found it impossible to swallow or even chew. Could he really believe it? She couldn't tell. His face was perfectly grave now; he didn't seem to be playing. She listened in her mind to Kirov's voice talking about his mother. 'You call her Mamochka,' she said abruptly, 'but your brother calls her Mama. Mamochka is a warmer word, isn't it?'

'He's not a warm man,' said Peter. She shook her head in protest, and he said, 'Don't misunderstand me. I love him. But there's no kindness in him – you shouldn't be mistaken about that.'

But she knew better. She had experienced warmth and kindness at his hands, as well as pain. She regarded Peter for a moment, and shook her head. Jealousy – it must all be jealousy. 'You're wrong. I don't believe it.'

She turned to look in through the French doors, to where Kirov was now leaning on the piano, his eyes fixed on Lyudmilla, and an expression of genial, almost paternal amusement on his face. 'Look at him with Milochka, for instance. If he were a cold man, an unkind man, he wouldn't take such interest in a child like her, would he?'

Peter looked, and laughed – a low laugh, and not a merry one. 'Oh Fleur, you fool! My brother takes an interest in Lyudmilla Ivanovna because he means to marry her; and just at the moment he's studying her and your brother to see if

275

there's anything between them he needs to do anything about. Don't look so incredulous! Believe me, I know what I'm talking about.'

His jealousy, she thought, plainly knew no bounds. Fleur stared at him a moment longer, and then left him and went back into the drawing-room without a word.

The rest of the evening passed in a daze, and she had difficulty in understanding anything that was said to her. It was one thing to dismiss Peter's words as the product of sibling rivalry, quite another to cope with the distress of hearing them. She felt as though she had breathed in poisoned air. She longed to have a headache and go to bed, but she knew Peter's eyes were on her, and she would not give him any reason to think his words had affected her. So she drank brandy, chatted distractedly, laughed at the wrong moment in anecdotes, and went to her chamber only when the rest of the company departed.

She held herself in rigid control until she was safely in bed and Kati had departed, and then surprised herself by bursting into tears. It was a violent storm, and soon over; but she was still swollen-eyed and catching her breath when there was a scratch at her chamber door, followed by the familiar pattering of Milochka and her dogs crossing the floor.

'Fleurushka, are you awake?'

Nothing she could do now to avoid discovery. Milochka advanced smiling, and then her face dropped in consternation. 'But you're crying! Oh, what's wrong? Tell me! What is it?'

'It's nothing,' Fleur said, and then, desperately, 'I'm worried about my father, that's all.'

Milochka climbed on the bed and hugged her clumsily, and then stroked her hair with innocent and touching affection. 'Oh poor, darling Fleur! But don't cry any more, I'm sure he's all right. Why shouldn't he be? We'd have heard for sure if anything had happened to him. I expect you're just homesick, aren't you? And your poor face is all swollen! Oh, I'm a beast to be so happy when you're miserable!'

Fleur took control of herself. 'Nonsense, don't be silly,' she said with an attempt at briskness. 'Why shouldn't you be happy? I'm just being silly – and I'm quite all right, now. What did you want to talk about?'

But Milochka obviously had a fit of remorse on her. 'I've been neglecting you dreadfully – I don't know what Mamochka would say! Oh dear, I've been spending all my time with Richard, and never thinking about poor darling you! Can you forgive me, Fleurushka? I shall devote every moment to you from now on!'.

Now Fleur laughed. 'Don't be silly! You would hate that – and so should I. I'm very fond of you, Milochka, but I don't want to spend every moment of the day with you!'

'Don't you? Oh well, that's all right then. But I shall stay with you *lots* more from now on, anyway, and Richard can look after himself. Because in any case—' She stopped and looked sly. 'Can I tell you a secret?'

'If you must,' Fleur said.

Milochka didn't notice the discouragement. 'You know I told you I'd met the man I want to marry? Well, what do you think about it now? Did you see the way he was watching me at the piano? Of course he can't do anything until Papa arrives. Oh, I wish it were next week! I can't bear to wait! Just think, to be an engaged woman – and I shall be a countess! Papa will be so thrilled!'

Fleur wasn't so sure about that, but she didn't want to attack on the strong front. Instead she said, 'Do you really like him, love? I've watched you the last few weeks, and it seemed to me that you weren't really at ease with him.'

Milchka frowned, opened her mouth and closed it again, and then said, 'Well, he's a bit – strange sometimes, isn't he? Almost frightening – like one of those gods carved out of granite, you know. Oh, but so romantic, Fleur, and handsome and thrilling!' Her face cleared again. 'And I wasn't sure if he really liked me, because he didn't seem to mind about Richard, but when he saw me flirting with Zakovsky and Pilov and Peter Nikolayevitch, it did the trick! He was so jealous, he watched me like a hawk all evening!'

'Yes, I saw him watching you,' Fleur said doubtfully.

'Well, you keep on watching, and you'll see how I manage him! You need to make a man jealous to bring him to the point – like spurring on a horse, you know! I shall flirt with all the officers every evening, and by next week, when Papa comes, he won't be able to bear it another moment! He'll be so mad for me, he'll speak to Papa before he's even taken his coat off!'

'Yes, love, perhaps, but I just wonder—'

'Don't worry, I know just how to handle it! Oh Fleur, I'm so happy. You're happy for me too, aren't you? Because I do love you, and I want you to be my friend always and always! Say you will, dear Fleur, please.'

'Of course I'll always be your friend,' Fleur said, but with dismay in her heart for what she saw would inevitably lead to disappointment.

Over the next few days, Milochka's campaign was carried on to the amusement of some and the embarrassment of a few. Fleur could detect nothing of the lover in Kirov's attitude: he treated Milochka with grave courtesy to her face, but sometimes Fleur caught him looking at her with faint amusement, as if he were watching a puppy play.

Peter said nothing more about his brother's supposed scheme, and in fact didn't refer to their conversation on the terrace at all. He behaved towards Fleur just as he always had, flirted mildly with the other women, played kind brother to Rose, and the amused older brother to Milochka. He and Kirov were polite to each other, and Peter seemed to be making an effort not to quarrel with him, but it was an obvious effort, and Fleur felt the strain of the atmosphere.

To herself, Kirov seemed kinder than ever, though he had less time to spend with her, dividing himself equally between his guests. Yet Fleur still felt she had a special status with him, that he spent time with the other women out of duty, but with her for pleasure. The longer she was with him, the closer she felt to him, and – she had reluctantly to admit it – the more she loved him. It made the prospect of returning to England in the autumn something to be dreaded.

Peter's remarks about him she had now entirely dismissed

as the product of wild jealousy, and probably now very much regretted by him. She allowed herself just a little grave reserve towards Peter, to let him know how much she disapproved of his outburst, and she saw from his subdued reaction that he had taken it to heart. Sometimes she would turn her head to find him looking at her broodingly, though the gaze was always instantly removed.

Still, the whole situation was proving rather a strain on her nerves, and her nights were often restless and haunted by large, complicated dreams in which she struggled with undefined problems. One morning she woke very early, unrested, with a headache and a feeling of oppression she could not shake off. It would be hours before Kati brought her the solace of tea, and since there was no bell to ring, she got up and dressed herself, did the best she could with her hair, and went downstairs.

Typically, because she wanted one, there was no servant to be found. The house was quiet – none of the guests would be up yet, and the servants were presumably still in their quarters. The drawing-room was empty and dusty. She crossed the hall again, and a maid came out of one of the small sitting-rooms, stopping when she saw her.

Fleur asked in French if anyone was up, and if she could have some tea, and the maid looked at her with that complete lack of expression she had grown used to on the Russian servant's face. She didn't know if she had been understood, and started again, but the servant, without a word, gestured towards the room she had just quitted, and went away. Fleur shrugged and went into the room, and found Rose there alone, seated over the samovar.

'You're up early,' Rose said equably. 'This is just ready – will you have some?'

Rose was neatly attired, but without her usual style this morning, and her hair was drawn back in a plain knot. Fleur wondered if it was simply because it was early, and then noticed how drawn Rose's face looked. Catching her glance, Rose gave a tired smile.

'I didn't sleep well last night, so at about five o'clock I

decided to give up the attempt. It's one of my bad days. I don't have them very often now, but when I do—' She shrugged.

'Are you in pain?' Fleur asked contritely.

'Yes, but don't let it upset you. The only thing to do is ignore it. I do, and so should you.'

She poured tea and handed Fleur's cup. 'Couldn't you sleep either? Is there something on your mind?'

It seemed to Fleur that the time had come to confide in Rose, and ask some questions, but she didn't know how to go about it, especially as Rose was suffering. As if she understood her trouble, Rose said, 'Don't be afraid to use me, if I can be of help. Anything that takes my mind off myself helps me to get through the day.'

'Thank you,' Fleur said. 'I would like to ask—' And she stopped, not knowing how to start.

Rose looked at her shrewdly. 'Have my brothers been upsetting you? I know you've noticed the tension between them. And I saw Petya watching you last night, like a cat at a mousehole. What has he been saying to you?'

Fleur felt herself blushing, and the automatic denial sprang to her lips. 'Oh, nothing at all. No, he hasn't—'

Rose's face grew grave. 'Ah. It's Sergei, then?'

She looked closely at her guest, and Fleur, struggling for composure, dropped her eyes and took her lip between her teeth. It was harder even than she had thought it would be to confide what she had hidden so long.

'Oh Fleur,' Rose said with deep pity, 'you haven't fallen in love with Sergei?'

Fleur hesitated a moment, and then nodded, and with the nod came the tears. Rose got up with difficulty and came over to sit beside her and put her arms round her. Fleur allowed her head to be drawn onto Rose's shoulder, and for a satisfying few minutes they both cried. Women always have tears waiting to be shed: the pains of each are the pains of all womankind.

'Now then,' Rose said at last, 'you had better tell me everything. Obviously this all started when he was in England, didn't it?'

So Fleur told her. Rose sat quietly, twisting her damp hand-kerchief absently between her fingers, her eyes never straying from Fleur's face, while the pent-up feelings of two years of silence burst over her in a flood of words.

When she had done, Fleur stopped, and looked at Rose hopefully, as though she expected her to be able to say some-thing that would make it all right again. Rose looked old today, Fleur noticed almost absently, and unlike herself, as though her features had settled into the homogeneity of age. If she had covered her hair with a peasant scarf, she could have been any old Russian woman seen anywhere in the country, sitting on a bench in the sunlight, waiting for death.

'My dear, I'm so sorry,' was what she said at last. 'I did wonder whether there was something going on. I've seen the way he looks at you sometimes, and there were times when I wondered if I ought to warn you. But you seemed so calm and happy in his company, not as if you were in danger. And to be frank with you, he doesn't behave towards you in quite his usual way – the way he does with women he wants to capti-vate. In fact,' she added thoughtfully, 'I've never seen him behave towards anyone as he does to you.'

Fleur struggled with a painful hope. 'Do you think – could it be that he—?'

It was not a question Rose could or would answer. 'How can I say?' She frowned in thought. 'I think your interpretation of his behaviour in London was right. He'd allowed himself his usual indulgence, but then realising he'd raised expectations, he tried to remedy the situation and save your reputation. It was hard, I know, but it was kinder than he's been to women of our own society. Probably he felt obliged to behave better abroad than at home. I don't know. Here he has often made women fall in love with him, and led them on in the cruellest way. He has no heart where women are concerned – you ought to know that.'

Fleur shook her head. Even from Rose, she didn't believe it. 'But why? Why should he behave like that? He's so sensitive, and kind, and – Is it because of his wife? Did he really bury his heart with her? Did he love her so much?'

Rose was thoughtful. 'I think he certainly did love her in the beginning, or at least he was infatuated with her. A young man's first passion, you know, is as much being in love with love as with the object. He brought her back like a prize of war, except that she wasn't an unwilling captive. Poor Elisabeth! She adored him, you know, but he made her very unhappy. Well, it isn't easy for any woman to compete for love with her husband's mother; and my mother was a larger-than-life character, while poor Lisa was milk-and-water.'

'He said – Sergei said – that your mother hated her because she didn't give him a son.'

'Did he say that? What nonsense. No, it's true Mother disliked Lisa, but that was completely irrational, and she knew it. Lisa came from the Caucasus, and Mother hated anything to do with the Caucasus. She did her best to hide her feelings, but Mother struggling with herself was a frightening thing to witness.'

'*Why* did she—?'

'I don't know for sure. Something terrible happened there, to her and my stepfather, which she would never talk about. And it may also have been because my stepfather's first wife, Sashka's mother, came from those parts. My mother's passions were very simple. Powerful, and not always logical, but simple.'

'He said that your mother always loved Sashka best, that she didn't have any time for him. He was very bitter about it.'

'That's nonsense too,' Rose said calmly. 'My mother loved my stepfather, first and foremost – and he loved her. It was all-consuming. Beautiful, I suppose, in its way, but not comfortable for the rest of us. The children of lovers, you know, have a hard row to till. And after my stepfather, she loved Seryosha.'

Fleur looked surprised.

'She did,' Rose affirmed. 'She adored him, but he wanted all her attention, and of course he couldn't have it. As to Sashka—' She shrugged. 'I think she felt guilty about him. Again, it was something to do with whatever happened in the

Caucasus – she felt that she had done the wrong thing by Sashka for some reason, and it haunted her. She tried to make it up to him, and when he went to the bad, she blamed herself. Then when the shock of his treachery killed my stepfather, you can imagine how that affected her – not only to lose her husband, but to lose him through something she felt she'd done, through her own fault.'

Fleur could imagine. Guilt, remorse, were grinding, biting passions. As powerful in their way as jealousy. It was not a comfortable picture of home life Rose was painting.

'Mother was a tortured woman after that. Then Elisabeth came along and brought it all back to her, reminded her all over again. Poor Lisa. I tried to befriend her, but she was such a little creep-mouse thing. In the end, you know, I don't think Seryosha loved her at all. I think he hated her in the end, for coming between him and Mother – as he thought. And it's as though he's hated all women ever since, punishing them for Lisa's fault.'

Fleur shook her head. 'With all that jealousy and hatred, how did you manage to grow up so good and kind? And Peter's quite normal too.'

'Oh, it's easier for girls than for boys,' Rose said carelessly, and in a flash of insight Fleur saw that it wasn't, that she hadn't come out of the fire unscathed, but tempered. What immeasurable suffering had made Rose as she was, Fleur could only begin to guess at. 'And Petya was so much younger. He was only a little boy when the Trouble happened; and he was only sixteen when Mother died. She never had any time for him anyway, which with our mother was a good thing. All the same, he isn't as simple a creature as he appears to be. It's easy to underestimate Petya, especially when Sergei's around.'

Fleur didn't hear the warning in the words. Her mind was still running on Sergei. 'Peter said last night – he said Sergei means to marry Lyudmilla,' she said with difficulty. 'Do you think that's true?'

Rose considered, and then shrugged. 'I don't know. All I can say is that the idea doesn't surprise me.'

'But – such a young, silly girl?'

Rose made a wry face. 'Milochka's father is very rich, one of the richest men in Petersburg. That's reason enough for anybody.'

Fleur was shocked. 'But he doesn't have to marry for money! He has all this—' She waved her hands helplessly.

'He's deep in debt, on the brink of bankruptcy. I tell you that in confidence – Petya doesn't know it. Things have been getting worse for the last five years, and he's been growing more and more worried. Marrying an heiress would be one way out of the difficulties.'

'But surely he wouldn't deceive the Polotskis?'

'That wouldn't be necessary. Come, surely it happens that way even in your own country? A title in exchange for a fortune – that's the way these things are done.'

Fleur shook her head. 'But it's Milochka! If it came to it, you surely wouldn't let that innocent child be deceived?'

'Deceived? Who's deceiving her? I've watched Sergei in her company, and he's been the soul of propriety.'

'Yes, very well, but all the same, she's in love with him.' Rose looked sceptical. 'Or she thinks she is.'

'It doesn't strike me that way,' Rose said. 'I think she's a very level-headed young woman under that frivolous manner of hers. If she has ambitions to be a countess, she'll know perfectly well how it's to be managed. She's known her own worth since the day she learned to count.'

She looked straight into Fleur's eyes. 'In any case, it isn't my affair, or yours. Neither of us has any right to interfere—'

'But surely—!'

'And it wouldn't do any good if we tried,' she went on inexorably. 'Believe me, I know what I'm talking about.' She put her hand over Fleur's and pressed it. 'The only person who is likely to be hurt in this situation is you, and it's you I'm worried about.'

Fleur's eyes became veiled. 'Oh, you needn't worry about me, I assure you. Now that I understand everything, I know exactly where I stand.'

Rose smiled and withdrew her hand and said, 'That's good.

I'm glad, my dear, because I don't want to lose your friendship.'

Fleur smiled. 'I don't want to lose your friendship either. It's very important to me. You're the only real friend I've ever had.'

She wasn't aware of how brittle her smile appeared, and Rose let the conversation pass on to talk about tea and breakfast and going for a ride and other trivial, healing topics. Rose had learned a great deal in her long and difficult life about hurt pride, and understood the importance of saving face. Fleur's English way of hiding her feelings was not her own, but she was perfectly willing to play the game with her.

Chapter Fifteen

Count Kirov was summoned to Petersburg to attend the Tsar, and was away for several days. When he returned, he brought the Polotskis with him.

Fleur couldn't help seeing how out of place they were amongst the company as it was constituted. Although Polotski conducted himself with perfect confidence, and Kirov was an attentive host, while Rose engaged Madame Polotski in comfortable conversation about domestic matters, they looked wrong, and the fashionable young people were ill at ease when they were in the room.

Fleur was glad to see them, however, and Madame's greeting of her was everything that was kind. A little later, Polotski sought Fleur out privately to give her a letter from her aunt. He was also able to tell her about the events that had taken Kirov to Petersburg.

'It looks as though we shall have war with Turkey after all,' he said. 'I can't see how it can be avoided: our troops have invaded the Danubian Territories, and the Turks won't sit down under that.'

'Invaded? Why?'

'Oh, it's supposed to be to protect them against the Turkish threat to their independence. But really it's a threat on our part, because the Turks refuse to sign our treaty.'

'Is this to do with protecting the Orthodox Christians?' Fleur asked. 'Count Kirov was talking about that. But he said that the last thing anyone wants is war.'

Polotski made an equivocal face. 'Yes, I dare say he did. But Kirov is the Emperor's man, through and through, and you mustn't believe everything he says. Oh, *he* believes it all right – and I dare say the Emperor even believes it himself. There's an honourable precedent for rulers not to let one half of themselves know what the other half is thinking.'

'But then, what is going on?'

Polotski sat down and patted the seat beside him. 'I'll tell you, because I know you won't repeat it. On the surface it is all about the Orthodox subjects of Turkey. The Sultan has agreed, at our insistence, to guarantee Orthodox Christians the same rights as the Catholics. But we are also claiming the right, based on some ancient treaty covered in cobwebs, to interfere to protect them whenever necessary, which of course the Sultan won't agree to, because that affects Turkish sovereignty. There's a great difference, as you'll see, between promising to protect, and giving someone else the right to protect.'

'Yes, I do see,' Fleur said. 'But you say that's only the surface reason?'

He winked. 'As a merchant, my dear, I can tell you that all quarrels between nations are to do with protecting trade – raw materials, markets, trade routes. Turkey commands a great deal of important territory in the Mediterranean – especially all the land around Constantinople and the Straits, which is our only warm-water trade route – as well as Egypt and the trade route to India. If the Turkish Empire were to break up – or if it could be hastened down the road to collapse – all those valuable pieces of land would be there for the taking.'

'And Russia means to do that?' Fleur said, rather shocked.

'Good heavens, no,' Polotski said, fixing her with an innocent eye. 'But that's what your country thinks Russia wants. And Turkey thinks it, too; and France pretends to think it, because it has a hot-blooded new young emperor with the name of a famous warrior, who wants some battle honours to show to his people.'

Fleur was bewildered. 'But nobody really wants war, surely? It's wasteful and destructive and – and those times are past. Since Waterloo – since the Great Exhibition – everyone is dedicated to peace, surely?'

He smiled sadly. 'If men were rational, if there were no such things as pride and greed and vanity, it might be so. Above all, if there were never any hot-blooded young men with too little to do! Boredom, I'm afraid, has a lot to do with war. After a long period of peace, the young men of every nation start to fret after some adventure in which to prove themselves and their manhood.'

'Yes,' said Fleur doubtfully. She remembered the comments of Richard's friend Brooke, about war being a catharsis. But surely it couldn't be as simple as that? If that was why wars happened, surely it would be easy enough to stop them?

'War acts like the application of leeches on overheated blood. And it's almost forty years since Waterloo,' Polotski finished.

'Do you think my country will go to war with yours?' Fleur asked in a subdued voice.

He hesitated a moment, and then he said, 'Yes, I think so – with or without the French. I don't know about them. But you needn't mind it, you know – it will all happen a long way away, too far away for you to hear the gunfire.'

She met his eyes. 'But my brother is a soldier. And a hot-blooded young man.'

He had no comfort to offer there. 'Ah yes. There is that, of course.'

Aunt Venus's letter did little to reassure Fleur. Aberdeen, the Prime Minister, was firmly against war, saying that it would be a disgraceful thing and an act of insanity to be drawn into a war which would adversely affect the peace of Europe; and there was a large anti-war party which was a powerful combination of philanthropists and manufacturers.

'But,' Venus said, 'there is the usual clamour from the drums-and-glory rabble, along with the inevitable emetic out-pourings of Tennyson and his crowd; and a lot of sentimental claptrap from the Romantics about "noble causes" and "purging the baser emotions" and "freeing the spirit from the pursuit of private gain" – which is supposed to have unmanned us and made us soft and luxurious. I'm afraid, Fleur, that it is this which will have the greater effect on the ignorant and vulgar, whom I don't need to tell you make up the majority of mankind.

'If we avoid war, it will be by the skin of our teeth, though I don't cease to hope. The Cabinet are largely against intervention, and Frederick says that in the end the public will certainly wonder what we have in common with the Turks, who are a brutal, dirty, cruel and barbaric people, besides being Infidels. Why we should go to war to defend them against the Russians is more than I pretend to understand. Let them get on with it, say I! But be on your guard, love, and be prepared to come home should things get uncomfortable. Seymour is an excellent man, and will oil all necessary wheels.'

But Fleur soon had more immediate, if not ultimately more important, things to think about. Milochka had been wildly excited ever since her parents arrived, and during the dressing-hour she came to Fleur's room, bubbling over with it.

'I'm ready already,' she said. 'Can I sit with you, Fleurushka, while Kati does your hair? Oh, you're wearing your rose-coloured silk! I do like that one. Pink suits you so well. I think blue is more my colour, don't you? Look, do you see what Papa has brought me?' She leaned forward, putting her hand to her throat. It was a large sapphire, cut like a drop of water, suspended on a fine gold chain.

'It's beautiful,' Fleur said. 'How kind of your father!'

'He is, isn't he? He's the best Papa in the world.' She glanced at Kati, and then burst out, 'Oh Kati, you must close your ears – and mind your tongue, too, or I shall have to cut it out! I must tell your mistress now or I shall burst! Papa's with the Count this minute, Fleur, what do you think of that? I saw them go into the Count's business-room before the dressing-bell, and when I went downstairs just now to look, they were still in there!'

Fleur glanced sideways at her, alarmed by her excitement. 'I don't think you ought to set too much store by it. There are grave political matters afoot at the moment. More than likely it's that they are discussing.'

'Oh pooh!' Milochka said. 'Why should Papa discuss politics with the Count? It can't be anything important – not as important as *my* business, anyway.'

'Not to you, I dare say, but—'

'No, no, I'm sure of it. He's asking Papa now, and there will be an announcement tonight. Oh, I'm so happy!'

Fleur turned to her, forgetting Kati's presence for the moment, and caught Milochka's hands. 'Are you quite sure it's what you want, love? I can't help feeling that you haven't thought enough about it. And for all I've watched him, I can't see that he really cares for you – or you for him.'

Lyudmilla was impatient. 'Oh stuff! Of course it's what I want. And I've told you a thousand times that I adore him!'

'So you have: but do you *like* him?'

She stopped dead at that, visibly taken aback. A variety of thoughts flickered through her eyes like fish swimming through a clear stream; and then some resolution stiffened her, and her eyes narrowed.

'What is it to you, anyway? Unless – unless you want him for yourself? Is that it?'

Fleur met her eyes steadily. 'I'm concerned for your happiness, that's all. I don't think you understand what kind of a man he is.'

'And you do?'

'A little better than you, I think. I'm eight years older than you.'

This consideration seemed to disarm Lyudmilla, and her brow cleared. She leaned forward and kissed Fleur's cheek. 'So you are, of course! Dear Fleur, don't let's quarrel,' she said gaily. 'I'm sure you mean it for the best, but I know what I'm about. And after all, if I find I don't like him after we're married, well, I needn't have anything to do with him, need I? But I'm sure I shall. He's so handsome and romantic and – and he's made for me! I can tell!'

The door opened, and old Nushka came creaking and puffing in like a steam-tug, scolding as she moved as though it were a natural part of motion.

'So that's where you got to, you naughty child! Bothering mademoiselle with your chatter and nonsense – and me not having finished with you. I turn my back for an instant and off you go, no more sense than a puppy! How can you go downstairs with your hair like that, tell me? Saint Nino save us, you look as though you'd never seen a hairbrush in your life! Come away this instant and let me curl you, or you'll end your days a spinster, as sure as death.'

She gathered up her charge effortlessly, and hustled her away without protest, though Lyudmilla turned at the door to make a comical face. In the silence that followed their departure, Fleur stared at her reflection thoughtfully. Kati met her eyes in the mirror, and opened her mouth to make a comment; but closed it again without speaking when she saw her mistress's expression.

Fleur went downstairs as soon as she was ready, even though it lacked ten minutes to the hour, in the hope that Kirov would be there, as he sometimes had been lately, so that she could talk to him alone. On the stairs, however, she met Polotski coming up. For once his step was heavy; instead of bouncing on his toes, he walked as though he were very tired.

He stopped at the sight of her, and smiled rather distractedly. 'Ah, there you are! Are you early, or am I even later than I thought?'

'There are ten minutes to go,' Fleur said.

'Then I shall be on time. I'm a quick dresser.' He smiled again, and was passing her, when he stopped and looked at her rather quizzically. 'I've been with the Count, you know, having a private talk with him.'

'About – about what we were talking of?'

'No, not that. About a more personal matter.' He hesitated again, and then said, 'Perhaps it's best if I tell you now, in advance of the announcement – or have you guessed?' She said nothing, and he surveyed her face carefully. 'Yes, I think perhaps you have. Kirov has asked me, in the prescribed manner, for Milochka's hand, and I've given my consent.'

She stared. Only now did she discover how completely she had disbelieved it – in spite of Peter's words, and Rose's lack of surprise, and Lyudmilla's confidence. She had thought it the merest fantasy. She could not make it real in her head. 'You consented?' she said at last, almost in a whisper. 'But *why*?'

The question seemed to puzzle him. He took a while to answer. 'It is a good match. His is a good family, and it will be a step up for her. I have given her everything wealth alone can give – only a marriage such as this can give her more.'

'But – you don't like him. You don't approve of him. You said to me—'

'He has behaved just as he ought in this matter. He assures me he has said nothing to Milochka, and done nothing to single her out. He has brought his proposals to me, her father, like a man of honour. I have nothing to reproach him with.'

In the face of his calm, and of his – to her – incomprehensible change of attitude, she could think of nothing to say. At last she said, 'Has he talked to you of – of finances?'

Now Polotski smiled. 'Do you think that I, Ivan Grigorovitch Polotski, would accept a son-in-law about whom I had made no enquiries? I've known all about the Kirovs since Count Peter first invited you to the ballet: their finances, their standing, their allegiances – why, I don't suppose the Emperor's Third Section itself, his secret police, know more about the Kirovs than I do!' He touched her hand. 'I'm grateful to you for your concern. You are acting like a true friend. But don't worry – I have accepted his proposal with my eyes wide open. And Milochka will be as pleased as a dog with two tails,' he chuckled. 'She's been hinting about him all day, and languishing like a camellia every time he passes through the room. It's her life's ambition to be a countess!'

She had nothing to say. He patted her hand again, and moved on up the stairs. 'I must hurry and get dressed. It will be announced tonight, so I'd better not blot my book by being late.'

She went on down the stairs, placing one foot before the other. She crossed the hall to the drawing-room and found it empty. On the far side, the French windows were open onto the terrace, and from outside she heard the sound of voices in altercation – familiar voices. As her feet carried her forward into the room, the words became distinguishable.

'—because you are so utterly useless!' Kirov was saying. 'You cost me money at every turn – expensive, idle and vain!'

'If you'd ever thought to tell me the true state of affairs—' came Peter's voice, high with anger. 'But no – I wasn't to be trusted with the truth. And now you have the injustice to blame me—'

'And what would you have done to remedy matters, if I *had* told you?' Kirov said sneeringly.

'You know very well!' Peter said. They must have turned away at that moment, for Fleur did not hear the next words, only the sound of them, and of Kirov's reply. Her feet had stopped her in the middle of the room, and she didn't seem to be able to go on, or to go back.

Now Peter's voice again, growing suddenly louder as if he were approaching rapidly. 'I could have won her – *and* her dowry – if you hadn't interfered!'

He appeared in the doorway of the terrace, and seeing Fleur shut his teeth quickly on the last word. Kirov's reply floated after him.

'I suppose it doesn't matter to you a jot which of us ended up marrying her?'

Peter looked hard at Fleur, as if he would have liked to reply to that but could not in her presence, and then he walked rapidly across the room, passing her without a glance, and disappeared. Kirov now came to the terrace door, his face drawn with anger, drawing breath as if bent on following up the quarrel; and in his turn saw Fleur and stopped himself short.

Fleur stood miserably, quivering with the hostility as a dog shivers at the smell of fire, her eyes on his face, her mind numb with shock. He looked at her for a long time. The anger drained from his face quickly, to leave a strangely wistful look. He seemed to understand a little of what she was feeling, for after a while he held out his hand to her, as to a child or an animal, and said in a gentle voice, 'Come, let me talk to you. It's all right. Come to me, *Tsvetoksha*. It's all right, truly.'

She moved forward. When she was near enough, he reached for her hand and took hold of it, drawing it into both of his. His eyes were full of tenderness as well as that unnerving sadness. He led her out onto the terrace, and walked with her to the parapet at the end, and there stood beside her, still holding her hand. They both stared out over the parterre to the park beyond, golden in the early evening light. The fading sky above was alive with martins, shrieking faint and far off in their long summer joy.

'You know, then,' he said at last. 'Who told you? Polotski?'

'Yes. I met him on the stairs.'

He sighed. 'I wanted to tell you myself.'

'Why? You owe me no explanation.' She hadn't meant it to sound so harsh.

'Yes, yes I do. Oh, *doushenka*, if only you and I were alone in this world!'

'Don't,' she said jerkily. 'Don't say things like that. Don't call me those—'

'You think I don't mean them?' He turned to her eagerly, his eyes glowing, almost hypnotic. 'Can you really not know, after all this time, how I feel about you? I thought – in London – and now here – we had become too close for misunderstanding—'

'You must truly have no heart, to bring that up, to talk about London now, especially now!'

'Oh, but that's why I owe you an explanation! I should have confided in you then. I thought you understood, I thought you knew why I did what I did, but it seems there are differ-

293

ences between us after all, that we think differently about certain things. Perhaps that's inevitable between a man and a woman. Knowing I had to leave you, I did what I could to protect you. But I want to be sure you understand one thing, at least – that if I had no one but myself to consider, I should never have left England without you. I was not free to act as I wished—'

She tried to draw back her hand, fixed him with a burning look. 'If you were not free, you had no right to act the part of freedom with me! You had no right to make me love you!'

He gripped her hand tighter, turning fully to her with a despairing movement of his shoulders. 'I swear to you, that it was not design on my part, to make you love me. Did you make me love you? It just happened. From the first instant I felt so natural with you, as though I had always known you. I behaved by instinct, not realising – not realising where it was leading us. Not until your friend turned on me that day and raged at me like a faithful terrier defending his mistress did I think—' He bit his lip and began again. 'It's madness to remember it now, I know, but you didn't seem to be separate from me at all. You were like a part of me, living tissue of my being. *I never thought*—!'

She stared at him for a long time. 'I don't,' she said at last, 'I don't know how to believe you.'

If you loved me, said her inner voice, you would not marry someone else for money. But below that another voice, deeper, wilder, more atavistic, said *I understand*. Loving me, you can be apart from me, because you will never be apart from me. It was not logical, it made no sense, but she sensed that it was true.

He must have seen the change in her eyes, for he said with a kind of relief, 'You do believe me?'

She didn't give him the words, but she didn't deny it. He sighed and turned away to lean against the parapet, as though the effort of speaking had exhausted him. She looked out into the shadowed garden under the paling sky, too numbed to think.

After a while he said, 'These last weeks have been a haven

to me. To be able to be with you was enough. I've felt so tranquil – I thought you did too. I knew what I had to do, but it couldn't touch that inner core of certainty. That's why you came, isn't it – to Russia? I knew. When Petya told me he'd met you, I knew why you'd come.' She shook her head, but he didn't see it. 'I thought when I left you in England that it was enough to know that you were in the world, to know that you were alive, and saw the same sun rise, and looked up at the same stars at night. But it wasn't. I needed more. I needed to see you again.'

He turned to look at her, lifted her fingers to his lips, and she saw to her amazement that there were tears in his eyes. In England, men did not cry. She had never seen a man cry, and it touched her unbearably. 'Nothing can ever part us, *Tsvetoksha maya*. Believe that, and we can live and do whatever we must do.'

It was madness. He was spinning a web of words, a shining web to entangle her, change reason to unreason, drug and drowse her into acceptance of fantasy instead of reality. But he spoke to a part of her that had no words, which was eager for the drug, which longed to believe itself to death. Drowning in honey, she thought faintly. Must resist.

And then he took her other hand too, and bent forward to place his lips lightly on hers for an instant, and the touch seared to her soul.

'I love you,' he said.

She knew it was the death-stroke, and she received it gladly, as they say the fly does, wrapped in the spider's silk.

Lyudmilla's wedding-day: *quelle pièce*! Fleur thought – but was it tragedy or comedy? The Polotskis' house had been astir since dawn, and the activity had gradually increased as the morning broadened, until it resembled an ants' nest stirred with a stick. Madame Polotski had relieved her pent-up feelings by having a fit of hysterics at eight o'clock, which had done her so much good that she now felt she could face the rest of the day with calm.

For weeks she had been contemplating with growing horror

the prospect of having to combine their friends and relatives with the Kirovs' illustrious connections, without the diverse elements causing an explosion. But after her hysterics, the happy thought occurred to her that the guests would not be mixing socially until *after* the ceremony, when it would be too late for anyone to call the wedding off.

At nine o'clock she had closeted herself with her daughter, together with Nushka and her own French maid, Sybil, a professional hairdresser, the two best needlewomen in the house, a chambermaid to fetch and carry, and The Dress; and the interesting processes that were going on inside might well have made the walls bulge.

Fleur was sitting in her room half-dressed, for Kati was so excited that she couldn't be prevailed upon to concentrate on anything for more than five minutes, and was forever running off to see how 'mademoiselle's toilette' was progressing. Fleur hardly needed bulletins. Since everyone went to that fascinating door with the slightest excuse – or without one – and in doing so must pass audibly through Fleur's room, she knew everything that had happened in superfluous detail.

The latest crisis had been the discovery by Sybil of what was thought to be A Spot on the bride's matchless chin; but was discovered by Nushka, after much panic and sendings-out for ice and witch-hazel, to be only a red mark where Milochka had been propping her face on her knuckles.

Fleur did not manage to feel deeply moved by these events. There was a strange lassitude over her which made it an effort even to pick up a hairbrush, or she would have given up on Kati long ago and begun to dress herself. As it was she sat at her dressing-table behind the bed-screens and stared at her reflection without seeing it, resting her own chin on her fist in a way that would have made Sybil feel faint.

She had, in any case, other things to think about. Only yesterday Richard had come to her looking grave, and bearing a letter from Aunt Ercy, which he offered her, saying, 'Read this, Flo, and tell me what you think.'

Fleur looked at it despairingly. Aunt Ercy not only wrote very small, and crossed her pages, but had a habit of underlining the words she would have emphasised in speech, which on average was every other one.

'You tell me what she says, love. I don't know how you make her out.'

'Practice,' Richard said with a faint smile. 'She's never got used to the idea of the Penny Post. But what she says – or the important bit – is that the Cabinet's rejected the Austrian mediator's proposals for settling this question of the Orthodox Christians in Turkey. Apparently, because the Tsar met privately with Franz Joseph, our Government's convinced that there's an Austro-Russian plot afoot to partition Turkey between them. They think the Tsar means to recreate the Holy Alliance and cut us off from the East.'

'Why is everyone so suspicious of the Tsar?' Fleur sighed.

'You know why,' Richard said shortly. 'Because he's the autocratic ruler of a country that still approves of slavery.'

'And he has territorial ambitions?' she enquired ironically.

'Well he has. It's no use looking at me like that, my girl. Facts are facts, and Russia's always pushing away at its frontiers. Anyway, the thing is that the Government's taken the plunge and ordered the fleet through the Dardanelles, and France is expected to do the same. With that sort of support hanging about outside Constantinople, it's ten to one but Turkey will declare war on Russia, if she hasn't already. I asked Petya about that, but he didn't seem to know. These Russian ministers play their cards close to their chests.'

'I see. And you think England will be drawn into it?'

'Well, we already have been, haven't we – warships through the Straits?'

'But isn't that just a gesture to make Russia back down? Aunt Venus's letter says they're still hoping to avoid war.'

Richard shrugged. 'It's got to come. I can't see how we can avoid it. We're committed to supporting Turkey, and you can't imagine Tsar Nicholas is going to say "Very sorry, didn't mean it" after all this time, can you? No, it'll be war all right.'

He was plainly relishing the prospect. Fleur thought of Polotski's words about hot-blooded young men with not enough to do; and Aunt Venus's words about Turks being dirty, barbarous Infidels. Richard had been a guest in Russia for six months, and had enjoyed the best of hospitality, the warmest of generosity; he had savoured the delights of a civilised society, got drunk with Count Peter and called him brother, and had made a dozen more friends who, if they had spoken English, would have been indistinguishable to him from his mess-mates in the 11th Hussars.

And yet he was ready and willing to go to war against them in order to protect a people he knew nothing good about, whose culture was utterly alien to him, and who didn't even share the same religion. It really was the oddest thing. Men, she concluded, were more different from women than foxes from geese.

'Well, love, what do you want to do?' she asked.

He stirred restlessly. 'You know what – go home! As soon after this damned wedding as can be arranged. I wouldn't even stay for that, except that I know you want it.'

'Weddings are women's things, of course!' she murmured. 'But how can we go home? We must wait for Papa. He'll be here any day now.'

'He should have been here a fortnight ago. Damn it, Fleur, you know what he's like! He comes and goes according to his own timetable, and that's got nothing to do with the rest of the human race.'

'But his passport is dated. He'll have to come back soon. They won't *let* him stay.'

'If he's anywhere where such things count. I don't think you have an idea about how vast Siberia is, or how wild. Petya's been telling me—'

He stopped abruptly, realising that what he was going to say was not tactful. He had long been accustomed to the idea that his father's wanderings in uncharted territories might – almost must – one day cause his death. That he might one day disappear and simply never be seen again was something Richard had prepared himself for; and since he had no love for his casual parent, and could only inherit the title and property if he did die, he saw no reason to be hypocritical about it.

But of course, women were soft creatures, and not at all

logical, and it was no use expecting them to think the same way.

To be sure, if Papa did disappear there'd be that tedious seven-year wait before he could be declared dead, which would be inconvenient, and it would be much better if he were to die properly, with witnesses, so that there was no doubt about it. But a man can raise credit on a reasonable assumption, and Richard could enjoy the property and the status, if not the title itself, in the meantime.

But these thoughts were not to be shared with Fleur. 'In any case,' he went on firmly, 'I must go back to get my promotion. If I don't take up that captaincy, it'll go to someone else – especially if there's going to be a war. Cardigan's a whale on punctuality and form and so on, and he'll expect me to apply on the day, on the spot. A captaincy in the Cherrypickers is not to be played fast and loose with, you know.'

'But without Papa, how will you be able to pay for it?'

'Don't worry about that. I'll raise the recruits all right,' he nodded. 'Uncle Markby will come up with the rhino if all else fails – you know Aunt dies to see me in pink pants again!'

Fleur sighed. 'Well, I see you are determined, and if you must, you must. But I'm not going with you. I'm going to wait here until Papa comes back. I don't know how you can be so callous as to run off home without knowing what's happened to him. Suppose he's in trouble? Who is to rescue him, if we go home?'

Richard looked faintly surprised. 'Are you gammoning me? In the first place, what on earth do you think you could do about it? Drive off to Siberia in a sledge with a rope and shovel and a spare bottle of brandy? And in the second place, since when have you cared what happens to our illustrious parent?'

'What a terrible thing to say! He's my father – of course I care.'

'Well, he's never cared a button about you,' Richard said frankly, 'so you might as well save your tears for someone who'll appreciate them.'

Fleur set her jaw, and as they stared stubbornly at each other they looked more alike, and more like their father, than at any other moment. 'I don't care what you say,' Fleur said eventually. 'I'm not going until Papa comes to fetch me, or at least until I get word from him.'

'You may suit yourself,' Richard said, 'but I warn you, Flo, I shan't stay with you. I'm not going to miss that commission.'

'As you please,' Fleur said. 'But you will stay for the wedding, at least? I insist on that.'

'I've already said I will.' He turned to go and then paused, looking at her quizzically. 'You don't mind about it, do you? The wedding, I mean. I thought you were sweet on Kirov at one time.'

She smiled inwardly at the inadequacy of the expression.

'My friendship with Count Kirov is one that can't be touched by his marrying someone else. And I'm very fond of Milochka – you know that.'

'Aye, I suppose so.' He continued to look at her for a moment, as though not entirely satisfied with the answer, and then almost visibly shrugged and dismissed it from his mind.

'I shan't see you at dinner tonight – there's a special do at the mess, and I promised Petya I'd get drunk with him. But don't worry, I'll have him in place and upright for the starter's gun. You just want to hope Kirov don't scratch when he sees the filly's native herd! He might not be so keen to breed from her then.'

'Don't be so vulgar, you dreadful boy!'

Richard grinned and departed.

Breeding. Of course, that was what marriage was about, when it came down to it. Family, genealogy. The getting of a son, the continuing of the line. As Fleur sat before her mirror, waiting for Kati to come back, her mind drifted over the problem. She didn't like to think about that aspect of it; but she had wondered, on and off, whether Milochka had considered what getting married would mean, or whether her mother would take her aside and tell her.

Of course, all girls heard tales, absorbed them without really knowing how as they grew up, of wedding nights, of brides whose hair turned stark white overnight with horror, of terrible sounds issuing from the closed door of the bridal chamber. Men had 'certain urges'. But what on earth did they *do*? Fleur simply had no idea, and try as she might, she could not imagine what it could be that was on the one hand so hideous, and yet on the other hand was obviously designed by nature and therefore must be, in the pure sense of the word, natural.

She had been in contact with many *filles de joie* (*joie*, after all?) in her life, and there had been ample opportunity for her to ask them what it was they did, but she had never quite liked to. But after all, they did it without coercion, and found it preferable to washing clothes or scrubbing steps for a living. Could it be so bad?

Her confusion and speculation had been increased last night, when Milochka came running into her bedroom, her head under her nightcap bulging with curling-rags, for what Fleur supposed must be the last of their nightly conferences. The dogs pattered after her and jumped up onto the bed, and for once Fleur didn't object. The shy one thrust its head under her hand, and she caressed it absently.

Milochka sat cross-legged, her bare toes poking out like a pink fringe from the hem of her nightgown, her face shiny with suppressed excitement. For the moment, she seemed too excited to speak.

'Well, love, so it's tomorrow,' Fleur said at last. 'Are you nervous?'

'No – well, yes. Of course I am – but – oh Fleur, have you ever thought about – well, afterwards? *You* know, after you're married – what happens then.'

Fleur felt her cheeks grow warm. 'Thought about it? Well, a little. Not very much. Of course, my mother died when I was very young, but I supposed that if I ever did get married, one of my aunts would tell me—' She stopped and cleared her throat. 'Has your mother—? I mean, did she—?'

'No,' Milochka said, 'but Nushka just has!' She rocked back and forward, almost bursting with excitement. 'When she was getting me ready for bed just now, she told me, and, oh Fleur, it's *awful!*'

And at that she had put her fingers over her mouth, gig-

301

gling, and her eyes above the stifling hand were wide open – with shock, yes, but with something else, too. Fleur puzzled at it. It was a sort of unholy glee, the expression you might see in the eyes of a child who was about to commit some extremely naughty but blissfully pleasurable act, like stealing hothouse peaches.

'Surely not awful?' Fleur had said, half hoping, half dreading that Milochka might burst out with it.

But she only said, 'I can't tell you – it's too dreadful!' And after a moment more, she had kissed Fleur on the cheek and run away, still laughing. It was odd to contemplate now that Lyudmilla knew something she didn't. *Awful*? The image kept presenting itself of Milochka cramming a stolen peach into her mouth, her face screwed up with bliss, and the juice running over her chin and down her hands.

But when the moment came, when Fleur got her first sight of the bride in all her finery as she stepped out of her chamber with her mother and nurse behind her, there was no sign of that glee. Milochka looked dead white and terrified, and held herself as rigidly as though she thought she might shatter if she brushed against anything.

The Dress was magnificent, a stunning creation of white embroidered satin and silver lace, so stiff and regal it might almost have stood up on its own. The royal impression was increased by the fact that Milochka was, of course, wearing a crown – the wedding-crown of the Orthodox ritual – from which a magnificent spangled veil fell down her back to join with the vast figured and embroidered train which would need six of her friends from Smolny days to carry it.

And inside the magnificence Lyudmilla looked so small and frail and frightened that it was hard to get away from the impression that the dress was wearing her, rather than vice versa. Fleur went up to her to murmur the appropriate compliments, and to lean over very carefully to kiss her cold little cheek. Milochka received the salute rigidly, moving only her eyes, but then, as Fleur drew back, she suddenly seized her with two icy hands and cried, 'You won't leave me, will you, Fleur? You won't go away?'

'Of course not,' Fleur said, puzzled.

'No, I mean after the wedding. Please, stay with me, say you will! You don't have to go back to England, do you?'

Her eyes flickered sideways to see how close her mother and Nushka were standing, and she lowered her voice to an urgent whisper. *I don't want to be left alone with him*! You must stay with me – you're my dearest friend! I need you with me!'

Fleur thought she was growing hysterical, and pressed the cold hand reassuringly. 'I wasn't planning on going away yet,' she said calmly. 'I still haven't heard from my father, and I don't want to leave Russia until he comes back and fetches me.'

Milochka looked only a very little comforted. 'Then I hope he never comes back,' she said. 'That way you'll have to stay with me.'

It was quite usual in England for the bride to take a female companion with her – often an unmarried sister – on the honeymoon, for it was accepted that gentlemen did not care to spend all their time with their wives, even when they had only just married them; and that a newly married woman would certainly have things she would want to talk about to a member of her own sex.

Count Kirov, however, was not taking Milochka away at once, because of the delicate political situation. They were simply to settle in the Kirov Palace, and to take their honeymoon, in the form of a trip to his estate at Kurmoye in the Crimea, at a later date, when circumstances allowed.

Fleur had assumed that she would stay with the Polotskis in the meantime, and the revelation, made to her at the wedding-breakfast, that Milochka wanted – insisted – expected her to go and live at the Palace too, took her aback.

Madame added her pleas to her daughter's. 'It would be the greatest kindness. My poor silly girl is so nervous,' she said, with a soft glance at the new Countess Kirova, 'and she knows nothing about how to go on. I've taught her all I can about housekeeping and managing servants, but you are the one who can tell her how to go on in public. You've been at Court—'

'In England,' Fleur put in.

'It's the same thing. Court is Court. And you've mingled with the sort of people she'll have to be doing with now. After all, it was you Count Peter came to call on in the first place, and that's what started the whole thing.'

'But you'll be lonely without her, and I had hoped to be able to mitigate that loneliness a little,' Fleur said. 'I must stay with you. Milochka will have her new family to advise her on protocol.'

Madame smiled warmly. 'You are the kindest of creatures, to worry about Vanya and me. But there's no need. We have each other – poor Milochka has no one. To be sure, if dear Madame Rose were to be living with her, it might be another thing, but she is going back to the country straight away. The city doesn't suit her health, so she tells me, and I can understand that, for riding is what she likes to do most, and the country is best for that. And Count Peter is going away with his regiment almost at once—'

'Is he? I didn't know,' Fleur said.

'Yes, my dear. This foolish war with Turkey, you know. He thought he would be bound for the Danube, but it seems there may be fighting in the Caucasus, too, at any moment, and he's afraid his regiment is being sent there, which he hasn't told his brother yet, not liking to upset him on his wedding-day. So you see,' she went on, keeping tenaciously to the point, 'the only members of her new family that she knows and likes won't be here. It would make such a difference to her if you would stay with her until your father returns for you.'

Still Fleur hesitated, unwilling to commit herself to what seemed to her a course of doubtful propriety – to say nothing of how uncomfortable it must be for her to be living in the same house with the man she loved and his new wife. But a little later, Kirov himself came over to speak to her.

'I understand Lyudmilla has asked you to take up residence at the Palace?'

'Yes, but I will refuse of course. It's a matter of finding a tactful way of doing it.'

'Why?'

'Why what?'

'Why will you refuse? Would it be so very distasteful to you?'

She looked up at him in surprise, and didn't answer.

'*Tsvetoksha*, it seems to me the perfect solution. The one unendurable thing to me about this marriage was the thought of being parted from you. But here is the opportunity for us to be together – to meet every day, to converse, to dine, to attend social functions together. It might have been arranged on purpose by a benevolent deity!'

She struggled with things she had no words for. 'But – but you are married now! Married to Milochka. It would be wrong—'

'Wrong? In what possible way? How can it be more wrong now than before? Now Milochka provides a chaperone for you – propriety is assured! No one can think ill of the situation.'

She only looked at him, wordless protest in her eyes.

He grew grave. 'Are you thinking of—? Yes, I see it now. You are thinking of what happens between a man and wife, thinking that that changes what I feel about you, what we are to each other. But you're wrong, so wrong! It is such a little thing, so unimportant! A dull, necessary little process like – like having to shave every day! Would you let that rob us of our innocent happiness?'

She stared, mesmerised by his shining eyes, the passion of his words.

'What is between us is much more important, and more enduring. You know why I have married Lyudmilla, and I swear to you I shall never knowingly give her cause to regret it. She will have everything she expects, and she will be happy. But she will never be to me what you are. She will never truly be my *wife*. True marriage takes place in the soul, and your soul and mine were joined long, long ago.' He bowed his head over her, and she felt the warmth of his wine-scented breath on her cheek. I love you, she said in her heart. I don't know how to go away from you.

'Don't leave me,' he said very softly. 'I need you. And Lyudmilla needs you. Don't leave us.'

His face was very close to hers, and she felt dizzy with longing. She couldn't resist him. She knew she would say yes.

BOOK THREE

Crimean Crocus

Chapter Sixteen

The soft air of the Crimean spring came in through the veranda windows, fluttering the muslin curtains for a moment, then letting them rest. There had been a storm during the afternoon – one of those brief and violent tempests that plague the Black Sea in April and October – and now at dusk the air smelled clean and damp and mossy, like fresh linen back from the laundry.

Kirov had been still a very long time, sitting back in his chair just out of the circle of yellow lamplight which lit the chessboard. Now the chair creaked faintly, and the great emerald of his signet-ring flashed a green fire as his hand came forward out of the shadows.

Here on the estate at Kurmoye, a few miles north-east of Eupatoria, he had abandoned European clothes and taken to the full-sleeved silk tunic, loose trousers and soft boots of his forebears. Fleur thought they suited him admirably: he looked to her more devastatingly handsome than ever. It was her delight to look at him – a painful delight that she paid for every night alone in her narrow, solitary bed.

She watched the hand as it descended with the delicate precision of a machine to select the knight. It was delicately carved from Indian ebony in the shape of a horse's head, a fierce little stallion with pricked ears and flaring nostrils – no poor bony Indian horse, this, but the Mameluke stallion of some desert warlord, clever and proud. As she watched, half in a dream, Kirov sprang him over a cluster of defending pawns, and there he stood, challenging her mighty queen, inside her defences.

'Check,' he said quietly.

She hadn't seen it. She sat forward hastily, drew an exasperated breath, and then looked up to see the laughter in his eyes, and smiled deprecatingly.

'You were far away,' he said. 'What were you dreaming of this time?'

'Desert warriors on Arabian horses,' she said.

'What rich and colourful imaginings you have,' he laughed. 'What of my warrior? Will your queen have him killed, do you think – or keep him captive in her tent?'

Lyudmilla, who was playing the piano quietly on the other side of the room, suddenly struck a wrong note, loud and jarring in the gently creeping dusk. Kirov turned his head with a protesting look.

'Sorry,' she said shortly.

He turned back. 'Well, *Tsvetoksha*?'

'Hush,' Fleur said, 'I must concentrate if I'm to beat you.' And she leaned forward with a rustle of black silk and rested both her forearms in their long lace mittens on the edge of the table, bending her head to study the board. It was difficult to concentrate. She could feel Kirov's eyes on her, and knew, though she was ashamed of knowing, that with her golden hair and fair complexion, she looked particularly beautiful in black.

She was in mourning for her father. The news had come just after Christmas, a message from Khatansk in the frozen Tundra, sent via the Governor of Western Siberia and the military courier to Petersburg. Young Mr Baverstock of Her Britannic Majesty's Embassy had brought the news in person to the Kirov Palace, requesting a private interview with Miss Hamilton.

Fleur had been dressing for a party, and came down to the library with her hair hastily bundled into a cap. Baverstock stood up, his clean pink face creased with concern, and she knew at once it was not good news.

'I'm sorry to call on you with so little ceremony, ma'am. I was for leaving it until the morning, but Lord Seymour said you ought to be told at once.'

There was a little silence, and then Fleur said, 'Please sit down, Mr Baverstock.'

He sat awkwardly, and Fleur took the sofa opposite him. The echoing space between them seemed a mile. In the vastness of the room, with the two-storey stacks of books rising sheer like the walls of a crevasse behind her, he thought she looked tiny and frail. Her eyes were a burning blue in her little pale face, and a curl, as yellow as a golden guinea, was slipping out softly from her cap. He wanted to protect her feminine fragility. He wanted to go out and fight dragons for her.

'It's bad news, then,' she said, bringing him back with a jerk from his dazed dreams of chivalry.

He blushed deeply; but he was a soldier, and a straight question demanded a straight answer. 'Yes, ma'am, I'm afraid so.'

She stared past his shoulder. 'I suppose I expected it, really. And it was bound to happen one day.' She sighed – he saw her smooth white breast rise and fall – and looked at him. 'Tell me what you know.'

It was little enough. Khatansk was a town on the Khatanga river, on the boundary between eastern and western Siberia, but the news had originated from wilder lands much further to the east. It came from a fur-trapper, a free peasant – there were no serfs in Siberia – who had nursed one of Sir Ranulph's servants in his hunting shack.

'These trappers go out on hunting trips for several weeks at a time, and they have wooden cabins in the hunting areas for shelter. Then when they've enough pelts, they go back to their villages,' Baverstock explained. 'It seems that your father's servant came stumbling to the hut during a snowstorm, badly injured and suffering from exposure. The trapper took him in and cared for him, but he died the following day.'

Fleur nodded, but said nothing.

'The trapper waited until he'd finished hunting before going back to his village and telling the *mir* – the local headman – about it. The *mir* took his time thinking about it, and eventually decided it was important enough to go to the nearest town for. There the local jack-in-office sent an official report to his regional superior, and eventually the message reached Khatansk, where there's a courier service. So the story, you see, has passed through many mouths – losing bits all along the way, I'm afraid.'

Fleur nodded again.

'All that's left of it says that your father's sledge went down a ravine that had been partly hidden by snow and ice. This one servant managed somehow to drag himself clear; your father and the other servants must have perished. I'm so sorry, ma'am. I wish I could have brought you better news.'

Fleur's expression was a blank. The quest for the Siberian orchid had ended, then: her father had died for love of a flower. No, perhaps not – for love of adventure and fame. 'I suppose he didn't say whether Papa found the orchid?' she said at last.

'Ma'am?' Baverstock looked puzzled.

She waved the question away. 'Never mind. So no one has seen my father's body? It still lies, as far as you know, at the bottom of a ravine?'

Baverstock bowed his head in assent. 'We have no way of vouching for the authenticity of the story, except that the wounded man gave the trapper this. Of course, he may have given him other things that we know nothing about.'

Baverstock held out his hand. Fleur expected her father's watch, but received into her hand his compass, which he had always worn on a leather thong around his neck. She looked at it closely. There were his initials engraved on the back of the brass casing: RFH. She saw there was a deep scratch on the glass of the face, from the accident, perhaps. If he had been parted from this, the most essential piece of his equipment, he must really be dead. It was true, then: he was gone, and she would never see him again.

'Yes, it's my father's,' she said.

She sounded so calm, Baverstock thought. He had expected shrieks, hysterics, tears, or at least a dead faint – but shock affected different people in different ways, he told himself. In any case, he had very little experience of women, except for his elder sisters, who were not the swooning sort. They hunted five days a week at home in Rutland, and toasted each other with neat rum when they took the brush.

Fleur appeared calm because she was calm. Later, when she

312

was alone, she tried to discover what she felt about it, but it seemed to be nothing at all. It was all so vague, so indefinite. No one had seen the body, no one even knew where it lay. He had gone away, and not returned, that was all. If she had seen him it might have been different, but she couldn't think of him as dead without being able to visualise it, and there was nothing to visualise.

When she thought about him, all that came to mind was the image of him, tall and vigorous and very much alive, dashing past her in the passageway at home to get to his study and his microscope with some fragment of moss he thought might be interesting – so absorbed in it he didn't notice he had almost knocked her over. His life had always been so utterly separate from hers that it was difficult not to believe he was living it still, somewhere out of sight, just as usual.

If anyone had asked, she would have said she loved her father, but she had no idea what that meant. If she had been at home in Grove Park perhaps she would have missed him, but here in Russia everything was different. Familiar things in her mind and heart seemed to be in different places. It was like entering your own house and finding someone had moved all the furniture around while you were out. She wanted to grieve for him because she knew she ought, but all there was where the grief should be was a blank.

The best she could do was to get on with the practicalities: telling the Kirovs and Polotskis, instructing Kati to make up mourning clothes for her, writing to Richard and her aunts, sending a notice to the English newspapers and instructing the family solicitor – she didn't trust Richard to do those things, especially since he was with his regiment, not at home. Fortunately Grove Park already ran itself. Before she came away she had left instructions for the solicitor to pay the wages of the small permanent staff, and to give Mrs Pettit a budget for the household bills, and those arrangements could continue until Richard decided what he wanted to do with the estate.

But she had to decide about her own future. On the surface of it, her reason for staying in Russia was now removed, and there was no need for her to remain any longer. Her aunts, and Richard, if he thought about it, would expect her to go home. Moreover, in January the international situation deteriorated further, as Lord Seymour himself told her when they met at a reception at Prince Narishkin's palace.

'I don't need to tell you, do I, m'dear, what the English papers have been saying about the Russians sinking the Turkish fleet at Sinope?'

Fleur nodded. They had *The Times* and the *Chronicle* every day. 'Yes, I know, they've been calling it all manner of ridiculous names – murder and massacre and so on! But it seems to me that it was a perfectly legitimate naval action.'

'And a damn' clever one on Admiral Nakhimov's part, when you consider what a rattle-trap collection of old wrecks makes up the Russian navy,' Seymour agreed with a twinkle. 'Superb tactical manoeuvre! But the mob at home has whipped itself up into a fury because the Turkish fleet was at anchor at the time, which they choose to believe wasn't fair play. And the papers are playin' it up for all they're worth, of course.'

Fleur wrinkled her brow. 'Why *do* they do that, sir?'

'Sells copies,' Seymour said economically.

'Oh.'

'Anyway, the upshot is, the pressure's on the Cabinet now to do something.' He lowered his voice. 'I can tell you this because I've already told His Majesty, but he may not decide to release it yet. So keep it to yourself until it breaks officially, won't you?'

'Of course, sir. You can trust me. What is it?'

'Our fleet and the French have been ordered through the Bosphorus, so the fat's in the fire properly. An ultimatum has been issued by our governments to the Tsar to withdraw his army from the Principalities within two months, or war will be declared.'

Fleur paled at the word 'war'. It had such a ring of finality about it. No more talking – no more hope of escape – just the grim inevitability of death.

'He won't withdraw,' she said quietly.

'I don't suppose anyone thinks he will,' he sighed. 'It's a lot of damn' nonsense, but it looks as though we're going to be drawn into this business after all.'

'Yes, I see,' said Fleur. 'Thank you for telling me.'

'Thought you ought to know, seein' the situation you're in.' He tried to lighten the atmosphere. 'Your aunt would never forgive me if I didn't keep a fatherly eye on you, y'know.'

Fleur smiled faintly. Aunt Venus's admirers were always popping up in her life. 'Do you think I ought to go home, sir? Will I be imprisoned if war's declared?'

'Good God, no! This is a civilised country. The Russkis don't do things like that. They couldn't do without the English population in Petersburg – all the banks'd close down for a start! No, no, m'dear, if you want to stay, you'll be quite safe – except of course that I shall have to go, along with my staff, so you'll have no one to pass on your letters. But I can make arrangements for your correspondence. Williams – the financier, you know – can set up something for you through his bank, if you want to stay. I just thought you ought to be fully informed, so that you can make your decision. Now your father's dead – damn' sorry about that, by the way – you may feel you want to go back home; and if you do, it'll be easier to travel before we declare war than after.'

'Yes, I see that it would,' Fleur said. 'Thank you for telling me, sir. I shall have to think carefully and make up my mind what to do.'

She consulted with both Count Kirov and Mr Polotski before deciding, and they both confirmed what Lord Seymour had said, that even if the two countries did go to war, the large English population in Russia would stay put. The diplomatic staff would have to leave, and one or two others might choose to out of patriotism, but the financiers and merchants and factory owners and engineers and nurses and governesses whose livelihoods were all bound up in Russia would stay, and no one would think twice about it. If there were eventually to be any fighting, it would not happen on Russian soil, anyway. The war, if it came about, would be very much something that happened to other people.

And Lyudmilla said, 'Please stay, Fleur! I wish you would!'

But when it came to it, she found she had already made up her mind. What was there for her in England, in any case? Only the empty house at Grove Park, and her old routines, and obscurity, and loneliness. She had no female friends in England, and Teddy and Richard and all the other young men of her acquaintance would be going away to the war. At best she might marry James Paget – and that would be loneliness of a different sort.

Here she had more freedom than England would ever allow her. Here she might live in modest luxury – her share of her father's estate would go a great deal further in Russia. In any case, she had no living expenses at the moment, and both Milochka and the Count were carelessly generous: she hadn't paid for a new dress since she first arrived in Petersburg. Here she was regarded as a distinguished foreigner whom even the highest of hostesses was honoured to receive, while at home, where an unmarried female past a certain age was an embarrassment, she was almost nobody.

And here she could be with Kirov, which until she learned to stop loving him was everything. It was not difficult to decide to stay, at least for the present – to put off the decision to leave. And perhaps, if the arrangement worked well, she might never go home.

The strange, reluctant scramble towards war continued. The politicians of each nation gave the impression of people on a precipitous slope desperately trying not to break into a run, sometimes even digging in their heels, but sliding onwards against their will. Nobody wanted to go to war – it was said again and again – and yet war crept somehow nearer.

Only the Tsar, with his mysterious and almost mystical calm, seemed to know what he wanted and where he was going. The Anglo-French ultimatum to withdraw from the Principalities he ignored entirely, according it no acknowledgement whatever. He ignored the advice of Prince Paskevitch, who warned that the Russian army was doing no good there and might at any moment be outflanked and cut off. He ignored his minister Orlov, who warned him that

Austrian friendliness was not to be relied on: Austria feared Russian territorial ambitions, and would also be quite happy to have France's hands occupied, to keep her from meddling in Austrian affairs in Italy. The Emperor continued to believe that Austria was on his side, and that his cause was just, and that the Russian army should press on towards the Danube.

Britain and France declared war at the end of March, even before the date of the deadline. The news moved the Emperor not at all. His eyes were fixed on Silistra, the Turkish stronghold on the Danube; and if the English and French fleets were cruising about the Black Sea, what of it? Hadn't the Russian fleet destroyed the Turkish fleet already? It could see off any enemy. It was invincible in a just cause.

Kirov worried about this last piece of sublime confidence. He was sure the Emperor was right in all his decisions, but he wasn't sure this time that the Emperor was in possession of all the facts. Kirov had been to England much more recently than His Majesty, and seen for himself the amazing advances in engineering – particularly in the use of steam power, and in ship-building techniques. He was afraid the Emperor might not know what a different thing a fleet of steam screws was from a fleet of sailing ships.

He hurried to the Peterhof to beg an urgent private audience. He was gone a long time, and when he returned it was to tell his surprised household that they were to pack at once. They were going to Kurmoye for the summer.

Fleur thought about their sudden departure as she studied the chessboard. (He had got her hopelessly enmeshed there – she was going to lose her queen, at least, probably the game, too. How had he got his knight inside her palisade?) Kirov had not told even her what the reason was for leaving Petersburg. She had thought at first that he had been sent on some kind of mission for the Emperor – he was, after all, one of his aides. But when they arrived at the estate he had put on a tunic and devoted himself to relaxation and country matters; and that, together with the brooding look she sometimes surprised on his face, made her guess that he was in a mild form of disgrace.

The Emperor had refused to listen to his advice, perhaps, and he had pressed it a little too strongly. She could imagine Nicholas's stern brow drawing down into a warning frown, imagine him suggesting that Kirov was in need of a holiday.

'Your honeymoon trip – you haven't taken it yet, have you? Perhaps now would be a good time.'

An Emperor's suggestion – with all the force of an order, impossible to refuse. And now Kirov waited to be recalled, to be given some task to do which would prove he'd been forgiven.

Yet, she thought, glancing privately at his face from under her lashes, he was not so very unhappy here. They'd been here a month, and lately the frowns had not been much in evidence. She thought he was actually enjoying his holiday from high politics. He was settling into the routines of a country gentleman, and surprising himself by how little he cared for the progress of the war.

It was peaceful here. Kurmoye was a beautiful place – rolling hills, lightly wooded, with meadows full of wild flowers, and terrace after terrace of neat vines; brown and violet streams chuckling over stones, and deep rivers where trout flickered in the chequered shadows; fruit trees in blossom, and young corn springing in little glebes tucked into the folds of the land.

It was a place she could easily grow to love; and it had been easy here to allow herself to slip into a dream of contentment, to forget the unpalatable fact that her own country and her adopted country were at war with each other, and that the man she loved and was happy to be with was the husband of someone else. During the daytime she *did* forget it; during their peaceful evenings together it was no more than a distant echo, like the memory of an old unhappiness. Only after they had retired to bed, as she lay awake in the dark listening to the sounds of night, waiting for sleep to come and release her, did she remember everything, and drain the bitter draught to the bottom of the cup.

But she had accepted the cup of her own free will; chosen, at least, to live with all the dangers, and *know*, rather than to be safe in ignorance, in stupid blankness and oblivion. That would have been worse – so she believed most of the time. Worse, always worse, not to know.

She must have shaken her head, for he said softly, 'What is it? What are you saying no to?'

She looked up. He was smiling at her, that particular smile that took all the bones out of her. Had he read her thoughts? She often thought that he could. It made her nervous, in a delicious sort of way.

'I see no way out,' she said. 'You have me trapped.'

His lips curled a little more. 'A willing victim, I hope?'

'I would sooner lose to you than win from anyone else,' she said.

'Now you've robbed me of my prize. Since you yield so graciously, it would be churlish of me to demand a forfeit.'

'No, no, you shall have whatever you want! You mustn't deny me the pleasure of displaying my generosity!'

'Very well then. Anything I want?'

She met his eyes steadily. 'Anything. Name the forfeit.'

'Then—' He paused, and the air between them quivered with unspoken possibilities. 'I require you to forfeit your clothes.'

Fleur, too shocked to speak, noticed in the moment of silence that followed that Lyudmilla had stopped playing.

Kirov smiled like a cat. 'Yes, your black clothes. I request you formally, Miss Hamilton, to lay aside your mourning. Four months is enough, in all reason, for a father you saw so little of. Won't you resume your normal colours? I'm sure we'd all be obliged to you – wouldn't we, Milochka?'

He turned his head just slightly to direct the last words towards his wife, but his eyes were still fixed on Fleur. Out of the corner of her eye, Fleur saw a white movement as Lyudmilla turned on the piano stool to look at them.

'You shouldn't ask it, Seryosha,' Lyudmilla replied. Her voice was light and hard. 'Let her choose for herself. We can't know how she feels about things.'

Suddenly Kirov turned right round, so hastily that his full sleeve knocked over two pieces – the castles, which were very tall and rather unstable. 'You're quite right, my wife, as always,' he said, with a mocking bow. 'Wisdom is a lovely quality in a woman, particularly in a woman so young.'

Fleur reached out and carefully turned her king onto its side, and then stood up. Neither of them looked at her: their attention seemed locked on each other.

'Nevertheless, I think I will give up mourning, if it won't offend you. I think black will prove to be too hot here, now the weather's getting warmer.' And she walked away, out through the long doors and onto the veranda.

The dusk was deepening fast. A large moth, heading eagerly for the light of the lamp indoors, blundered into her, and clung for a moment to the black silk of her abdomen, palpitating. She looked down at it – the first she'd seen here, large and pale, with a soft brown dust on its wings.

She felt confused and uneasy. What was the relationship between Kirov and Lyudmilla? He had told her that Milochka would never truly be his wife, that he was marrying her only for her dowry. Yet she saw that Milochka had some strange power over him. However difficult and contrary she was, he remained always kind and patient with her. Sometimes she seemed to taunt, even to threaten him with veiled hints that Fleur did not understand, but he bore them meekly, rarely even resorting to the irony he had used tonight.

He watched her, too, as Fleur had seen, when she was not aware of it. Fleur had seen him stare at Milochka for an hour together, with unwavering attention, while she played the piano or sewed or played with her dogs. It was hard to say what the stare portended: it didn't seem entirely like love; sometimes it seemed perilously close to hate. But it was constant – almost obsessive. Whatever it was, it was not indifference.

And it was not her business. That was what was at the very bottom of the cup. With a sigh, Fleur moved a step or two away from the door, and turned towards the shadows before gently dislodging the moth. But despite her care it fluttered away only a foot or two before veering back towards the lighted doorway.

Spring softened into the tenderness of early summer as April became May. The knotted black sticks of the vines, which had looked dead all winter, suddenly broke into miraculous, vivid green life; the meadows were glossy-gold with buttercups. Far away, where the war was, the Russian army struggled with famine and sickness far more than with the enemy, plodding towards Silistra and the Danube; while out in the Mediterranean, hastily converted sailing ships crammed with seasick British soldiers made their slow way towards the Dardanelles.

May deepened into June, and the rich green of full summer. The British army landed at last at Varna, on the Black Sea coast of Wallachia, but made no further move to engage in action – for which Fleur was profoundly grateful. Austria formally demanded that Russia withdraw from the Principalities. The Russian army crossed the Danube at last but failed to take Silistra, which was still holding out under siege.

More seriously, news came from St Petersburg that the British fleet had appeared at Kronstadt, and was visible to the Tsar and his family from the very windows of their summer palace. It cruised up and down, blockading the port and tying down the empire's crack troops, two hundred thousand of the Imperial Guard, who had remained in Petersburg in case the British tried a landing, or the Swedes took advantage of the situation to invade Finland, which they had always regretted giving away.

But at Kurmoye, it was hard to be aroused by the news. It all seemed so remote from their summer idyll. The country-estate routines of riding, walking, fishing, boating, and picnicking, and the evening rituals of dinner and music or chess or cards had a mesmeric quality. Perfect day followed perfect day, with the occasional harmless thunderstorm to clear the air and refresh the greenery.

They saw no one but themselves and the servants and estate-workers. These last were Tartars – free peasants, not serfs – and Fleur felt much more at ease with them. She felt she could behave naturally, without the oppressive knowledge that they were obliged to be obedient to her wishes. It touched off a new discussion with her companions about the nature of slavery. Fleur questioned again whether any man had a moral right to own others like chattels; Kirov concluded gravely that serfdom harmed the masters as much as the slaves; and Milochka tossed her head and said they were talking nonsense: Nushka wasn't any less contented than Kati, was she?

But Fleur was glad that here at Kurmoye she was once more able to visit the villagers on errands of mercy, and while a few were suspicious and hostile towards her, others welcomed her help and advice, particularly on medical and hygienic matters. It gave her life the dimension of usefulness without which she felt restless and unfulfilled. The occasional nervous headaches which had afflicted her in Petersburg went away, and the odd fits of nameless tearfulness or irritability she had sometimes suffered no longer troubled her. She felt calm, well, and almost completely happy.

Fleur was aware that all was not entirely well with Lyudmilla. She would go on happily enough for days, and then suddenly take a mad fit on herself. Then she would tease the dogs until they were miserable, or have a violent quarrel with Nushka, or risk her neck riding helter-skelter over the roughest country she could find, or turn the house upside down with some impractical scheme which upset the servants and annoyed her husband.

Once she cut up half a dozen fine gowns with the idea of 'making them over' and entirely ruined them. Another time she idly picked up some green dye, and took it into her head to dye everything she could lay her hands on. She started with her white muslin chemisettes and Kirov's handkerchiefs, and then got out of hand; and she only stopped when she ran out of dye at last in the middle of transmogrifying the white house-cat, Milka.

That was the only time Fleur ever saw Kirov angry with Milochka. Not only had she ruined his handkerchiefs and a shirt, but she had spilled dye over some of his books; and he disliked cruelty to animals and was particularly fond of cats. He rebuked Lyudmilla with a cold anger that was somehow more terrible than hot rage, while Milka sat by looking bedraggled and miserable, attempting to lick himself clean and desisting when he discovered how bad it tasted.

Milochka received the scolding in sulky silence, like a child before a parent, and then disarmed reproach by suddenly bursting into tears. Kirov stopped at once, seeming to be quite taken aback; and when a moment later he discovered some really bad scratches on Milochka's hands and arms, where Milka had vigorously resisted his translation, he took her at once onto his lap and petted and soothed her, and sent for borax and hot water to bathe the scratches himself.

Fleur wondered uneasily about these outbursts, and put them down eventually to boredom. Lyudmilla, she reasoned, was used to living in a big city, and hadn't the resources inside herself that came from living alone and isolated, as Fleur had done for so much of her life. She did her best, therefore, to keep Milochka amused, rode out with her, encouraged her to read and improve her mind rather than always to waste her time playing with her dogs, and even tried to interest her in her good works amongst the villagers. This last Milochka resisted vigorously. She hadn't become a countess, she declared, to spend her time binding peasants' wounds and teaching dirty children to read.

One Sunday afternoon in July, Fleur and Kirov were sitting in the shade on the veranda, talking, while Milochka played the piano inside. Fleur had persuaded her that she ought to practise a little, but her heart was obviously not in it, for she played only half of any piece before switching restlessly to another, striking wrong notes and fumbling harmonies and taking liberties with the time.

One of the servants had roused the house during the night with shrieks, claiming to have seen a ghost, and now Fleur and Kirov were talking idly about supernatural phenomena. Kirov was sitting on the swing-seat, one foot tucked under him, rocking himself by pushing at the floor with the other.

He was completely relaxed – so relaxed that Milka had curled up on his lap and was snoring softly. Fleur sat nearby, fanning herself gently, and enjoying the barbed pleasure of looking at him. Beyond the veranda's deep shade, the day was so hot that even the cicadas had fallen silent, and the short, midsummer shadows of the trees were utterly motionless.

'But you can't prove that it isn't so,' Fleur was saying. 'And what about the saints? What about the miracles? Are you to reject everything you can't catch in a net and keep in a box?'

'We have good authority for those,' he said. 'The fact is, you want life to be more than it is. You want more than it can readily furnish.'

'Well, and don't you?'

He smiled. 'Perhaps I did once. One grows tired, you know. It's a great effort to go on struggling to invest things with significance.'

'But if you stop trying, what is there then? Isn't that what we are *for*, to find more than is there? We're not animals, to live our lives in dull reality, to eat, breed and die, and leave no mark of ourselves behind.'

'Oh, but you're passionate,' he laughed, 'and it's too hot! I yield you any argument today.'

Inside the house Lyudmilla stopped playing. Ngorny appeared and bowed to his master. 'If you please, sir – there's a horseman approaching. I think it's an Imperial courier.'

'What, in this heat? The fellow must be foundered! All right, I'll come.' He removed Milka from his lap, heaved himself up, and followed Ngorny along the veranda.

Milochka came out from the house, fanning herself, and Milka gave her a reproachful look and fled. He had never forgiven her for the dye incident: his front half was still faintly green. She flung herself down in the swing-chair and pushed herself moodily with one foot, making the ropes creak in protest.

Fleur raised an eyebrow. 'What's the matter?'

Milochka continued to frown and rock. 'It's too hot, and there's nothing to *do*!'

Fleur smiled faintly. 'What would you like to do? If there's anything in particular that you want, I'm sure Sergei Nikolayevitch would arrange it for you.'

The mention of her husband seemed to annoy Lyudmilla. 'Oh would he?' she said, flinging an irritable look in the direction he had taken.

'Of course he would.'

She tossed her head. 'Anyway, there's nothing *to* do here, with just the three of us! Nobody would think the entire Tarutinsky regiment was just a few versts away at Eupatoria! But do we ever invite any of the officers to dinner? You'd think we all had the plague!'

'Is that what you want, then – more company?' Fleur asked reasonably.

Lyudmilla didn't want to be reasonable. 'Oh, it's all right for you!' she exclaimed, as if in answer to an entirely different question. 'You're quite happy sitting about here in the evenings doing nothing! Reading dull books and playing chess with Sergei – sometimes it's more as if *you're* married to him than I am!'

She could hardly have said anything that struck more sharply to the heart. Fleur laughed brittly. 'Oh don't be silly! Do you think he's neglecting you for me?'

'Well, isn't he?'

'Of course not. How many times has he offered to teach you to play chess? He'd much sooner play with you. He adores you.'

Milochka shut her fan with a snap. 'Does he?' she said sourly. Her eyes narrowed, bright with some point reached and overstepped. She had the breakneck look of one determined to embark on some dangerous piece of folly.

Fleur was sorry she had introduced a line of reasoning about which she couldn't be completely sincere. She didn't really think Kirov adored Lyudmilla; on the other hand, she no longer believed he had married her entirely for her money. He had some very powerful feeling towards her. She fascinated him in some way. Fleur wondered if it had something to do with his first wife, to whom Milochka bore just a faint resemblance.

So now she said, 'He cares very much about you. After all,' she added, twisting Milochka's knife for her, 'he married you, didn't he – when he might have had anyone?'

Lyudmilla reached the breaking point. She sat up abruptly, glanced away along the veranda, and then hissed, 'If he loves me, why doesn't he—?' she began, and stopped, reddening. 'Why doesn't he—?'

Fleur met her eyes, startled. Good God, what confidence had she unwittingly provoked? 'Doesn't he what?'

'Oh, *you* know what I mean!' Milochka cried fiercely.

Fleur felt her face grow hot and fought desperately with embarrassment. A cascade of images tumbled through her mind: Milochka giggling with her eyes shocked above her stifling hand; Kirov looking down at her with a burning gaze, telling her it was an unimportant thing, like shaving every day; Kirov kissing her lightly – fastening the invisible shackles about her wrists; Milochka cramming a stolen peach into her mouth, the juice running over her chin.

He had said Lyudmilla would never truly be his wife – *was that what he meant*? Faintly in the back of her mind there sounded a fanfare of triumph – oh, reprehensible, but sweet, so sweet!

'Yes, I understand,' she said at last, trying to sound calm and matter-of-fact. 'But surely, love, it doesn't matter, does it?'

'Of course it matters!'

'Well, a little, perhaps – but it shouldn't be so important to you. Women aren't meant to care for that sort of thing. You have the husband you wanted, and he proves he cares for you in many ways.' She remembered Kirov's words. 'That other business – it's such a little thing!'

'Oh, what do you know about it?' Lyudmilla cried, exasperated. 'You don't know anything! You're not even married!'

Fleur flinched inwardly from the careless blow. 'No, of course not, but—'

'Then don't talk about what you don't understand! Little thing indeed!' She flung herself back in the chair and swung vigorously, her lips pressed tightly together and her eyes bright with anger.

This was perilous. Not only might he come back at any moment, but whatever Milochka chose to confide in her she would have to live with, and God only knew whether it would make things better or worse in the long run. Yet there was part of her that had to know, however painful it was.

'Milochka,' she said slowly, 'do you really mean that he doesn't—?'

'No!' she snapped.

'But – not at all? Not ever?'

'At the beginning, once or twice. But after that – no.'

'Oh.' Well, it explained at least why a healthy young woman like Milochka showed no signs of increasing, even after nine months of marriage. Perhaps that was why she was unhappy – she must want children, and children didn't come any other way.

'So now you know,' Milochka said abruptly, and Fleur saw all of a sudden that the young woman's anger was only a thin veneer over a deeply puzzled hurt. It had been a confidence imparted from a desire for explanation – and she trusted Fleur's wisdom to be able to supply it. In spite of her taunts, she wanted Fleur to comfort her and make things all right.

Transfixed by the appealing eyes, Fleur racked her brain despairingly for words – almost any words – and felt an enormous relief as the sound of booted heels on the wooden veranda put an end to the privacy of their conversation, and saved her from exposing her inadequacy to the situation. She knew her cheeks were still flushed, and she looked down at her hands, struggling for composure.

Kirov appeared, with a dusty, uniformed figure behind him. Fleur looked up in surprise.

'It wasn't an Imperial courier after all,' he said. 'Or at least, it was, but only in a sense.'

Fleur's initial surprise was giving way to pleasure, but Milochka was ahead of her. She jumped up from the swing-chair and ran along the veranda to fling herself into the visitor's arms.

'Oh Petya, I'm so *glad* to see you! You've absolutely saved me from dying of boredom!'

Peter, receiving Milochka's impetuous kisses on his chin, met his brother's eyes over her head with a shrug and a faint smirk.

Chapter Seventeen

Peter came out onto the veranda and sat sideways on the rail, swinging one elegant leg idly as he lit a thin Turkish cigar. Fleur, rocking herself slowly on the swing-seat, stared past him into the dusk. It was the time of evening when the bats began to hunt, and the luminous air flickered with their moving scraps of shadow. The cicadas shrilled monotonously, drowning the bats' small cries, and the air was stifling-warm. It smelled, faintly and deliciously, of hay: one of the servants had cut the long grass under the lemon trees that morning, and it had been drying all day in fragrant heaps, destined as a treat for the horses.

Now there was the first aromatic smell of tobacco, too. Having got his cigar going satisfactorily, Peter watched a blue wreath wind upwards through the hanging swags of climbing roses which hung all around the veranda. He glanced at Fleur under his eyelashes, and then away again.

'Well, it's quite a cosy *ménage à trois* you've got going here!' he said casually. 'I have to hand it to my brother: he may be a dry stick, but when it comes to administration, the man's a genius!' He looked sidelong at Fleur again, to see her reaction. Her face was expressionless. 'Who would have thought,' he went on, 'that he could persuade *two* beautiful women to live together under the same roof with him, without murdering either him or each other? If the Emperor had only had the sense to make full use of those organisational skills, he'd have conquered the entire world by now.'

'Oh shut up!' Fleur said at last.

Peter laughed. 'At least that's better than being ignored! But why so cross, princess? Strange though it seems to an out-

328

sider, it would appear to be what you've chosen of your own free will.'

No one cares to have that kind of truth pointed out to them. She looked at him darkly. 'Why do you have to torment him all the time? Do you think he's blind, or a block? Do you think he doesn't notice?'

'Torment him? What can you mean?'

'You know perfectly well – flirting with Lyudmilla the way you do!'

'My dear girl, you have it wrong. Lyudmilla flirts with me – I merely accommodate her. The poor child needs some diversion – it can't be easy to be married to Sergei.'

'Oh, why do you keep saying these things?' Fleur cried, goaded.

Peter smiled to himself. 'In any case, I would have expected you to be grateful to me.'

'Grateful? For what?'

'For keeping the lovely Countess Kirova occupied, of course, thus leaving the field clear for you and her husband to do – whatever it is you *do* do. Though for the life of me,' he added with mild interest, as though discussing a parlour trick performed with a pack of cards, 'I can't fathom out what it is.'

In spite of herself, Fleur felt a smile tugging at her lips. 'We don't do anything, you absurd boy!'

'Come now, that's better. The worst thing I've seen since I came here is that you've become capable of going for hours at a time without laughing. Nature didn't design you to be grave – or a nun,' he added quietly.

She chose to ignore the last part.

'And that's another thing,' she said sternly, 'why did you come here?'

'But I've told you already – to convalesce from my wound! It's traditional in the Caucasus to go to Pyatigorsk, but Pyatigorsk smells of horses. Besides, it's full of *petites bourgeoises* looking for husbands, and they have no subtlety,' he said plaintively.

'You didn't come from Pyatigorsk. In fact, you didn't come from the Caucasus at all – you came from Petersburg.'

'Discovered! But how did you find that out?'

'Simple – I asked your servant. So, what are you doing here? Tell the truth, sir – if you can!'

He shrugged, 'Menshikov – Commander-in-Chief, Western Crimea – has been reporting sightings of British scouting vessels off the Crimean coast. The Emperor wants more information. So, since I happened to be hanging around Petersburg, pretending my arm still hurt me, he thought I might as well earn my crust, and sent me down here to look around for him.'

Fleur frowned. 'But surely he could have asked your brother to report? After all, he is on the spot.'

Peter looked at her quickly. 'He could have, but he didn't. That's why I didn't tell Sergei – and you won't either, if you love him. It would break his heart.'

'You mean – he's still out of favour?'

Peter nodded, and she realised that in spite of all his harsh and teasing words, he must care for his brother, or he wouldn't be so careful of his feelings. She liked him better for it. Perhaps he was allowing Lyudmilla to flirt with him in order to keep Kirov's attention away from the question of why he was here.

'But what did he do that was so bad?' she asked.

'He argued with the Emperor, and the Emperor doesn't like that. Almost told him he was wrong. Absolute and immediate obedience, that's what the Emperor likes. He doesn't enjoy having his opinions questioned, and he's slow to forget an offence.'

Fleur thought back to what he had said a moment ago. 'You said there were British ships off the coast? But surely there have been scout ships about ever since January, when our fleet came through the straits? Why is it different now?'

Peter drew on his cigar again, and the glow of the red tip told Fleur how much darker it had got since they'd begun talking. She'd grown used to the endless twilights of the north, and it still took her by surprise how quickly it got dark here, by comparison.

'Well, little flower, it's like this: we're pulling out of

the Principalities. Gorkachov has at last convinced His Majesty that his army is doing no good there, and the order went forth for them to recross the Danube at once and start the withdrawal. And since the occupation of the Principalities was the whole *casus belli* as far as the British were concerned, it means they now have nothing to stay in Wallachia for.'

'Oh, thank God!' Fleur cried. 'Then they'll go home! There won't be any fighting after all! Oh Peter, I can't tell you—'

'Whoa, steady! Not so fast. Your delight may be premature. Either they'll go home – or, according to Paskevitch, they'll mount an attack on Sebastopol.'

She stared. 'Oh, surely not! Why should they do that?'

Peter shrugged. 'There isn't anything else on the Black Sea for them to attack, is there? Sebastopol is the only thing faintly resembling a stronghold, and it does happen to be our only naval port, containing our entire fleet.'

'But all the same—' Fleur protested.

'Don't blame me! *I* don't believe it. Come to that, the Emperor doesn't believe it, and nor does anyone else in Petersburg. But Menshikov's been complaining for months about the lack of defences here, and wailing that the Crimea's in great danger, and that the whole of the Black Sea fleet might be swept away in an instant.'

'So Menshikov believes it, then?'

Peter grinned. 'Probably not. But he's responsible for protecting Sebastopol and the fleet, you see, and he can only muster about twenty thousand men, when our best reports say that the British and French together number about sixty thousand. If they were to attack Sebastopol, we'd be in trouble; and if anything happens to our precious fleet, it's Menshikov's head that's on the block. Simple precautions, my dear Fleur. In Russia it's customary to prepare your excuses well in advance!'

'Oh I do hope they go home – our army, I mean! Richard must be there with them – his regiment is, at all events. And there've been such terrible reports of sickness amongst the men – dysentery and cholera.'

331

He noted that she had somehow convinced herself that it was only the men who got sick, not the officers, but forebore to disillusion her. 'Anyone could have told them that Varna's a noted plague-spot,' he said instead. 'The Turks probably did tell them, but if your army is anything like ours, it wouldn't have made any difference. Common sense is the last thing that ever rears its head in the conduct of a war.'

'But it's Lord Raglan who's commanding our army,' Fleur said, 'and he's the sweetest man, and wonderfully efficient! He was the Duke of Wellington's military secretary at Waterloo, and the Duke always said he'd fight a war without guns or horses if he had to, but not without his secretary.'

'If he was at Waterloo,' Peter said, 'he must be the sweetest *old* man.'

'Well, all generals are old,' Fleur pointed out. 'How could they be otherwise?'

He bowed to her logic. 'Quite. You could hardly allow the war to be run by junior officers, could you?'

'Of course not,' she said, but she had the oddest feeling that he was joking when he said it. 'So will you be going back to Petersburg?'

'Not immediately. I've sent off my report, but no further orders have come for me, so I shall just lie low and hope they forget all about me. I shall stay here, and carry on my good works towards my brother and his lovely bride – unless,' he met her eyes deliberately, 'you've changed your mind, and you'd like me to rescue you, and carry you off on my white horse and marry you?'

'Your horse is a bay; and you're not the crusading type,' Fleur objected.

'How do you know? I might be hiding all sorts of propensities under my motley. The guise of the clown is designed to deceive, you know.'

Fleur smiled, though for a moment his expression seemed watchful, and she seemed to hear Rose's voice saying 'It's easy to underestimate Petya, especially when Seryosha's around . . .'

But she said, 'You'll never marry. You could never confine

yourself to one woman, when there's a whole world of them out there to be flirted with.'

'How right you are,' Peter said lightly. 'Thanks for reminding me. But I shall stay here anyway. My brother needs me to divert him and keep him from turning into a pillar of stone.' He reached for her hand and carried it to his lips. 'You'll allow me to amuse you at any rate, won't you, *chère* Fleur, even if I mayn't run away with you?'

'I shall be glad to be amused,' she said warmly.

'I would bet on that,' he murmured, and she decided diplomatically to ignore it. She retrieved her hand and sought a harmles topic of conversation.

'Did you see Rose while you were in Petersburg? She sent me such a lovely letter. I was so sorry that we had to leave so suddenly – I was expecting to spend the summer at Schwartzenturm, of course, and to have the pleasure of her company.'

The advent of Peter ended their isolation, for he was quick to ride in to Eupatoria and make friends with various officers of the Tarutinsky, whom he then had no difficulty in persuading Lyudmilla to invite out to the estate for dinner, or for longer stays when they could get leave.

Lyudmilla was at her best with these young officers, for they treated her with a grave respect, as Kirov's wife, which prevented her from flirting with them openly as she might otherwise have done. Instead, she put on a young-matronly dignity, which, though it evidently amused Peter, Fleur thought was charming. And when her youthful high spirits broke through, it was innocently, as an infectious gaiety which made the parties delightful and left the subalterns lingeringly unwilling to go back to the garrison.

As July turned to August, there was a continual stream of visitors to Kurmoye: hunting parties, fishing parties and picnics, formal and informal dinners, and once a ball, on a floor laid in the open air and lit by strings of coloured lamps. The female ranks were swelled on that occasion by garrison wives and Eupatoria's leading daughters, but the numbers were still very unequal, and Fleur and Lyudmilla were much in demand.

Once or twice the invitations were returned, and they drove or rode in to Eupatoria to visit. Fleur discovered that the town was a convalescent base for sick and wounded soldiers – there were about two hundred of them there, recovering from a variety of wounds and diseases. She was able to make herself useful by visiting them, too, and reading to them, writing letters for them, or, in the case of those who spoke only Russian, just sitting with them and giving them someone prettier to look at than the garrison surgeon.

Peter was not recalled to Petersburg, though he was away quite often during the day, making the excuse of various social engagements, which caused his brother to remark that even as a serving officer he seemed incapable of shaking off his habits of idleness. Fleur guessed that the absences were on military business, and honoured Peter for holding his tongue, even when lashed by Kirov's scorn.

He did, however, exact his revenge by continuing to flirt with Lyudmilla, who in turn did it to torment her husband – perhaps, Fleur thought, in the hope that it would make him jealous. She would see Kirov watching them both expressionlessly; but she was sure that even if the method chosen was a blunt arrow, the intention must hurt him. She did her best to deflect them by occupying Peter's attention as much as possible when he was at Kurmoye.

All through August the enduring topic of conversation amongst the men was, of course, whether the allied English and French armies would attack Sebastopol. Fleur listened to all the arguments with painful attention. It was bad enough that their countries were at war, but Sebastopol was altogether too close for comfort. It would be a very different thing if there were actually an invasion of Russian soil. She saw how that would make her own position immediately much more uncomfortable – to say nothing of the danger to her brother and his friends who so far, she believed and hoped, had faced nothing more grave than boredom and discomfort at Varna.

Opinion was much divided on the subject. Since General

Menshikov had publicly scoffed at the idea, there were plenty who merely repeated his opinions that the Allies hadn't sufficient men for an invasion, and that in any case landing them from ships on such a sea was impossible. But Menshikov no more than the Emperor had any idea how much difference steam power would make to that exercise.

Others pointed out that Admiral Kornilov, the Chief of Staff of the Black Sea fleet, was convinced that there would be an attack, and was so worried about the lack of fortifications that he had gone so far as to prepare a list of wealthy officers and civilians willing to subscribe out of their own pockets for the building of fortresses. This scheme had failed to gain official sanction, but the Admiral had persisted, and finally obtained permission for the merchant contractor Volokhov to build at his own expense at least one coastal fort to guard the Sebastopol roads. The work was going on at that very time: it would probably be finished by October.

But as August advanced and the Allies remained at Varna, confidence grew. Everyone said it was now too late in the year for anything but a short-term attack to be mounted; and the autumn storms would soon be racking the Black Sea, making it all but impossible to land an army. Besides, the Russian troops had recently trounced the Turks in the Caucasus, and if the British were so mad as to land, the Tarutinsky would trounce them too!

Menshikov's appeals to Petersburg had had their effect, however: reinforcements were arriving all the time. There was no railway south of Moscow, so the regiments had to march all the way, taking many months to cover the vast distances of Russia. The Tarutinsky, for instance, had left its headquarters last December, and had not arrived in the Crimea until April. Similarly, all supplies had to be brought by horse-drawn transport in the same way, over largely unmade roads. But, it was reasoned, the Allies would have problems at least as great in supplying their forces by sea.

On the whole, the news most confidently expected was that the Allies had embarked and were sailing for home. Fleur prayed for it nightly. Quite apart from her brother and all the young men who had been her dancing-partners over the years, and all the unknowns who yet shared her English blood, there were now the young men of the Tarutinsky to be afraid for. It was an uncomfortable thing in time of war to care for people on both sides.

On a sultry day in September, Fleur and Lyudmilla sat on the veranda waiting for news. The previous day the long-dreaded blow had fallen: word had been brought that the Allied fleet had been seen off the coast of the Crimea. There were about a hundred ships, according to various reports, moving north-easterly – transports, with a small convoy of armed ships. So an invasion was intended after all, mad as it seemed, and late in the year though it was. Another surprise was that the fleet was evidently not planning to land at Balaclava, the closest harbour to Sebastopol, but appeared to be heading for Eupatoria, which was some forty-five miles from the naval base.

Spirits appeared to be high amongst the Allies: a small landing-party had rowed ashore and captured a coastal telegraph station, solely, it appeared, in order to send the message to Sebastopol: 'We shall be with you shortly.' It was said that Sebastopol had replied 'You'll be made welcome – we have been expecting you for a long time.' Lyudmilla told the story to Fleur with relish, having got it from Nushka, who got it from Ngorny, who got it from one of the Tartar villagers. Fleur rather spoiled the effect by asking what language had been used, and how the signallers had known each other's codes – questions Milochka thought quite unnecessary, and typical of Fleur.

Kirov had ridden off early that morning for Eupatoria to try to find out what was happening. The women had nothing to do but wait, and time dragged as the hazy sun tracked slowly across the pale, hot sky.

'Why have they come so far north?' Fleur wondered, not for the first time. 'They surely can't be meaning to land here and march all the way back to Sebastopol? It doesn't make sense.'

'You'd better hope that they do,' Lyudmilla said, fanning

herself more vigorously. 'Better Sebastopol than here – you don't want them tackling all those dear boys we've dined with and danced with.'

'Better that they go home; but it doesn't look as though they mean to. Oh, if only they'd go home!'

'If they do attack Eupatoria, what about us? Will we have to evacuate?' It wasn't the first time that question had been voiced.

'I don't know,' Fleur said. 'The people on the next estate haven't gone, have they? I suppose it depends on which way the army moves.'

'They wouldn't hurt us anyway, would they?' Milochka asked in a small voice. 'Civilians – helpless women – and you're English! You can make them leave us alone, can't you?'

Fleur sighed. 'There's no point in worrying about anything until we know more.'

'Stupid,' Milochka said affectionately. 'Nobody worries because there's any point in it. You worry because you can't help it.'

They were silent for a while, fanning themselves, waiting. Beyond the veranda the grass was bleached by the summer's heat to the colour of a lion's mane, and the leaves of the lemon trees were already beginning to curl, revealing the ripening fruit, glowing like lamps in the shadowed depths of the foliage.

The invisible cicadas scissored away in the grass, but all else was still, the damp air blanketing sound. Suddenly Milochka stood up, her face intent. 'Horseman,' she said tersely, cocking her head. 'Listen!'

Fleur stood too, hearing a moment later the low thunder of a galloping horse. Milochka was up and running along the veranda. Fleur followed, and as they reached the corner they saw a bay horse and a white uniform approaching in a cloud of dust along the track.

'It's not Seryosha, then,' Lyudmilla said.

An Imperial uniform. *One of ours*, Fleur thought, and then realised that in her case both sides were 'ours'. Dear God, let there not be a battle! Let there be no fighting!

'It's Petya,' said Milochka.

In a moment he was with them, tramping along the wooden boards while a servant led his horse away into the shade. His brown face was pale with dust, his white jacket was fawn with it. Fleur found herself remembering the wings of the twilight moth that had blundered into her, on that spring evening that seemed so long ago.

'Where's Sergei?' he asked abruptly. His voice sounded parched.

'He's gone into Eupatoria,' Fleur said. 'Let me get you something to drink.'

Petya made a negating movement of his hand. 'I must have just missed him, I suppose. Damn. When will he be back, do you know?'

'Petya, what's happening? Is there going to be an invasion? Will we have to leave?' Lyudmilla tugged at his attention.

'Hush, give him time,' Fleur protested. 'Sit down, Peter. Get your breath. I'll order tea for you.'

But Nushka appeared at that moment with a tray of lemonade. She must have moved quickly for an old woman, Fleur thought, to be here so soon.

'Oh Nushka, you're an angel,' Peter said in a clogged voice, and took a glass from her with almost desperate haste.

'Galloping in all that heat,' Nushka tutted, shaking her head at him. 'Madness! Don't tell me the British are coming after all?'

Peter emptied the glass and held it out to be refilled, and emptied it a second time before replying. By this time all three women were hanging impatiently on his silence. It almost made him laugh.

He spoke at last. 'I've come to tell you that we're leaving Eupatoria – the Tarutinsky, that is. It looks as though the Allies mean to land somewhere along the beaches to the south of the town, in Calamita Bay, and if they do, there's not enough of us at the garrison to stop them. If the regiment stays where it is, it'll be cut off, so it's evacuating the whole town and marching off to Sebastopol to join up with Menshikov's forces.'

'What about the convalescents?' Fleur asked quietly. 'They can't march.'

'They'll be staying, of course, under Major Branitsky.'

'Oh, wonderful!' Milochka said. 'So we're to be left with nothing but a handful of cripples to protect us, while the brave Tarutinsky runs away!'

'Will we have to evacuate?' Fleur asked. 'Will it come to that?'

Peter looked distracted. 'That's what I wanted to talk to Sergei about. At the moment, there's just no knowing what the Allies will do. You're very close to the town here. If they make a base at Eupatoria, I'd be surprised if they didn't send out scouts at least, and there'll be foragers too. Sergei's Cossacks could probably put up a good fight, but that would only make things worse. If they were to come, it would probably be better just to let them have what they want.'

'Probably?' Lyudmilla queried.

'They won't harm civilians,' Peter said, 'but it might not be too pleasant for you. And they say the Allied army is riddled with sickness. They brought the cholera with them from Varna, and dysentery, and God knows what besides.'

'So you think we had better leave?' Fleur asked.

'I don't know. On the other hand, you see, Sebastopol's the only place you can go to, and that's probably where the Allies are going. If it should come to a siege—'

'Surely the General isn't going to let the Allies get that far without fighting them?' Lyudmilla said. 'He must come out and fight! He can't just let them walk all the way to Sebastopol unchallenged!'

'Milochka, my child, I don't know what Menshikov's going to do,' Peter said with a faint, tired smile. 'He doesn't confide in me, you know! All I can tell you is that there are Cossack messengers going back and forth all the time, so he surely knows what's happening.'

'But—'

'I wish I could stay and take care of you, but I've had my orders. I'm to report to Menshikov at once. The Staff never has enough gallopers.' He stood up, meeting Fleur's eyes. 'I don't know if I'll be able to come back. In fact, I don't know when I'll see you again. If there's anything important to report to Petersburg, it's almost bound to be me that's sent. It will be for Sergei to protect you from now on. That's why I wanted to see him before I left.'

'You can't mean just to leave us!' Lyudmilla cried.

'It isn't what I would have chosen,' he answered her, though his eyes were still on Fleur. 'But I'm under orders now.'

It suddenly occurred to Fleur that he was going to where the fighting would be, if there were any fighting – and it looked, now, as if it were inevitable. The Allies would land, and the Russians would have to resist them. Peter would be fighting against her people. Fighting? He might be killed! She might never see him again. This might be the last chance she ever had to tell him – to tell him – what? She held out her hand, and he took it and pressed it briefly. 'You'll take care of yourself?' she said.

'I'll do my best,' he said, and smiled suddenly, lighting his ordinary face into something better than ordinary, like a lamp illuminating an icon. A brief flicker of images ran through her mind, scraps of memories of him, from the first time she had seen him on the ship, to the last time she had danced with him – under the velvet night sky by the light of those absurd coloured lamps, gaudy as children's sweets. She liked him so very much. She didn't want him to be hurt. She thought she might kiss him goodbye, but the moment had passed.

'I don't want to get killed, I assure you,' he said. 'And you take care, too.'

'Yes, I will. God bless you, Peter Nikolayevitch.'

He released her hand and turned to enclose the startled Lyudmilla in a bear-hug. 'Goodbye, little sister-in-law. Look after Sergei. And if the Allies do come – I pity 'em. Caught between you and the Russian Fifth Corps, I think I'd probably prefer to face the Fifth Corps.'

Then he was gone, tramping down the veranda and calling for his horse, leaving the women in thoughtful silence.

Fleur turned at last to Nushka. 'I think it might be a good

idea to keep one or two essentials packed for your mistress, in case we do have to leave – and you might ask Kati to do the same for me.'

'Bless you, *barishnya*,' Nushka said comfortably, 'but I've had the bags packed and ready this week past. Saint Nino told me in a vision the Allies were coming.'

Lyudmilla turned. 'Did she, Nushka? Why didn't you tell me? And did she tell you what's going to happen?'

Nushka looked at her gravely. 'You'll be in great danger, *barina*, but you'll come through with a whole skin,' she said. 'You'll have to be very brave, though. There are trials ahead for you.'

It was just the right thing to say to engage Lyudmilla's interest. She forgot her fears and anxieties, intrigued by the notion of herself as a heroine. 'Great danger, eh? Well, if the Allies do come, I shall fight 'em off, of course. I'm sure I could learn to shoot a gun. I shall cut 'em down to the last man—' A sudden thought stopped her. 'Unless it's your darling brother of course, Fleur.'

'I'm so glad you thought of that,' Fleur said drily.

Kirov returned in the afternoon to say that the regiment had marched out.

'There was nothing else to be done. It'd be impossible to hold Eupatoria against such a force, and Menshikov could never have brought reinforcements up in time.'

'And where is the Allied fleet?' Fleur asked.

'Coming to anchor just off the town. They've got boats out all along the bay, looking for somewhere to land. Menshikov is going to try to hold them somewhere between here and Sebastopol – on one of the rivers, I imagine. The Tarutinsky will join up with whatever force he sends out.'

'What about us, Sergei?' Lyudmilla put in impatiently. 'Do we have to leave, or shall we hold the house against them?'

Kirov smiled, and only then did Fleur notice how tired he looked. 'I believe you would, too,' he said. 'No, it won't come to that. I suppose we may have to move eventually, but there's no immediate urgency. It will take them a couple of days to disembark.' He turned to Fleur. 'They will have to send a party to demand the surrender of the garrison. Branitsky's orders are to offer no resistance – not that he could, with only the convalescents left under his command – so the exchange should be quite civilised. It occurred to me that it might offer you the chance to get news of your brother.'

Fleur looked surprised. 'You mean – I could go there and meet them?'

'Why not? Whatever officer is sent to receive the surrender, he's bound to know your brother, isn't he?'

'Oh, yes!'

'You'll be able to get word to him at least, perhaps send a letter.'

'Oh yes, please,' Fleur said, looking rather dazed. 'That would be wonderful!' To know at least that Richard was all right – to send her love!

'We'll need to leave at once,' he prompted her gently, 'if we're to be there to meet them.'

'Yes, of course. I'll go and get changed.'

'Me too,' Milochka said. 'I'm coming too!'

'Of course you are,' Kirov said. 'Just be careful what you say if you do meet an English officer.'

'Of course I will,' she said with dignity. 'I'm not a fool, you know.'

The English officer was in dark blue dress uniform with smart scarlet facings, scarlet stripes to his tight overalls, and a drooping plume of swan's feathers on his shako. To judge by his immaculate turnout and air of languid insouciance, he might just have stepped out from his club into St James's Street, rather than from a crowded transport ship.

Colonel Lord George Paget of Her Britannic Majesty's 4th Light Dragoons had come ashore with a small party of officers with a summons from Lord Raglan for the surrender of the Eupatoria garrison. Major Branitsky had consented gravely, and at the end of the interview, as the English officers were withdrawing, he asked if Lord George would receive in private an English lady who had a request to make of him. Paget, though mystified, could only agree.

Branitsky made him free of his office, promised him tea, and left him alone. A moment later the door opened again, and Paget turned to see almost the last person he would have expected.

'Good God! Miss Hamilton! What are you doing here?'

'I know at least what you're doing here, Lord George,' Fleur said, advancing to shake his hand. 'Major Branitsky surrendered in form, I take it?'

'In form's about right – d'you know, he insisted on fumigating the Summons, in case it had infection hangin' about it? And then told us that our army must consider itself in strict quarantine from the moment it landed!'

Fleur tried not to laugh. 'Oh, but he didn't mean to insult you! It's just port sanitary regulations. He's naturally worried about his convalescents. They're just beginning to recover, and it would be terrible if they were to go down with cholera now, wouldn't it?'

'Oh, you know about the cholera, do you?'

'We heard that you had lost quite a few men in Varna.'

'A few – yes.' He sounded dazed. 'But what *are* you doing here, ma'am? Last I heard, you were in St Petersburg.'

'I'm staying with Count Kirov and his wife, on their summer estate, Kurmoye. It's a couple of miles inland from here, to the north.'

'Ah, yes, the Kirovs.' Paget gave her a sidelong look. 'Of course.' He cleared his throat. 'I was sorry to hear about your father, Miss Hamilton. Read about it in *The Times*. Are you fixed in Russia for good, now?'

'I don't know,' she said. It depended, didn't it, on what happened here? 'It's a surprise to me to see the army here. What on earth is the idea of it? I thought you would have gone home when the Russians pulled out of Wallachia.'

'So did we, I can tell you. It wasn't Raglan's idea, either. He'd as lief have gone home, but orders came direct from London, from Pam himself. Sent to say it was entirely the Old

Man's choice, but the great British public wanted to read about the capture of Sebastopol in its morning newspaper, and what was he going to do about it? And so here we are.'

Fleur looked a little anxious. 'You know, don't you, that I can't tell you anything. I'm here as a guest. And you mustn't tell me anything, either.'

'No, no, of course not,' Paget said. 'Wouldn't dream of it.' He eyed her sympathetically, as well aware of the awkwardness of her situation as she was. 'By Jove, though, it's good to see an English lady again! You're looking more beautiful than ever, Miss Hamilton! And that's an amazin'ly fetching bonnet!'

'Thank you,' Fleur said. She hesitated. 'How is your brother?'

'James? Oh, bearin' up! He took it quite hard at first when you said you weren't coming home, but he's put it behind him now. Got a new horse – big grey by Darius – a real scud! Fancies it very much for the 'Guineas.''

'And how's my brother, Lord George? Can you give me news of him? I suppose he is here with his regiment?'

She had put off asking, for fear of the answer, and now Lord George looked as though he wished she'd put it off longer.

'I'm afraid he's not terribly bright at the moment. He's been laid down with dysentery since we left Varna. It's a damned unpleasant sort, too – hangs on, you know, makes a chap feel very low. We've all had it, on and off, in varying degrees. Hamilton's got a bad dose this time, though.'

'He hasn't been wounded, has he?'

Paget looked happier. 'No, not wounded. Not a scratch! Well, of course, we haven't really done any fighting. Left that to the Turks – and they did surprisin'ly well at it, too! No, no, he's as fit as a flea, apart from his health!'

Fleur smiled faintly. 'If I write a note to him, can you deliver it?'

'Delighted to – of course! Nothing simpler. Buck him up no end.'

She paused for a moment in thought, and added, 'I know you can't tell me anything about your plans, but I'm naturally anxious to know whether we need to refuge from Kurmoye. Can you tell me if it will be safe for us to stay there?'

Paget hesitated. 'I think I'm safe in saying, ma'am, that you will have nothing to fear from us. Well, you must know already that our object is not Eupatoria, or anything in this area! We'll obviously be sending out foraging parties but – well, I think I can see to it that you're left alone.'

'Thank you,' she said gratefully. 'I can assure you, too, that you have nothing to fear from us! Indeed, if only I might, I'd ask you all out to Kurmoye to dinner.'

'By Jove, that would brighten a few faces!' Paget said. 'The worst thing about campaigning is the kind of food you're obliged to eat! I say, d'you remember Stuffy Cusworth, of Ours, Miss Hamilton?'

Fleur laughed. 'Do I not! I've met him at every table in the Shires! My uncle used to call the family the Dining Cusworths. How has he taken to camp life? Salt pork and ration biscuit must be a sore trial to him!'

'You wouldn't recognise him – the poor chap's fading away!'

The tea came in, and the chat grew lively.

The Allied fleet anchored at last in Calamita Bay, and on the next morning – the 14th of September – the disembarkation began. There had been rain during the night, and the day dawned fresh and bright, with clear golden sunshine under a blue sky.

It was not unobserved. A troop of the 57th Don Cossacks, sent by General Menshikov, arrived shortly after the landing began, and sat on the top of the cliff observing, while their officer made notes about the numbers of men, their apparent state of health, and the equipment they were carrying. They were within rifle shot, but though the toiling Allies down below glanced up from time to time, they made no attempt to drive the Cossacks away.

In the afternoon the weather changed, the sky grew dark, and the sea whipped up. A violent Black Sea rainstorm began, throwing the disembarkation into confusion and finally halting it in a jumble of half-unpacked gear and abandoned boxes. There was no shelter from the storm, and the Cossacks reported that the men who had already landed had no tents. They lay down in the rain on the beach that night, and many of them never got up again.

Hampered by the weather – burning sunshine interspersed with violent rainstorms – and by the lack of drinking-water and the fact that half the men had diarrhoea, the disembarkation took five days. It was not until the morning of the 19th that the Allied army was ready to march off. Again, it was not unobserved; but this time, as well as the Cossack scouts, there were a number of parties of civilians watching from the heights. There were Tartars from the villages, and ladies and gentlemen from the country estates who had come on horseback or in open carriages, some of them bringing picnics, for the sake of the spectacle.

And it was a spectacle worth witnessing. From the safety of a high vantage point above the grassy plain where the disembarkation camp had been set up, Fleur gazed with a tugging at her heart at the familiar colours and appurtenances of the regiments making a living kaleidoscope below them. She told off the regiments to Kirov and Lyudmilla, unaware how wistful her voice sounded.

Formed up, the whole army covered an area four miles by four miles – sixty thousand men, bands playing, colours flying, marching off under a clear blue sky in brilliant sunshine, beside a sea as calm as a lake. The French were on the right, next to the sea, with Turkish horsemen to protect their flank. Fleur pointed out the Zouaves on the far right, with their blue coats and little red caps and baggy trousers, marching with their women, trousered too, and as often as not wearing uniform coats like their men.

Right out in front went the advance guard of the 11th and 13th Hussars, with the upright figure of Lord Cardigan – Jim the Bear, as his men called him – to the fore on his favourite golden chestnut, Ronald. The famous crimson overalls of the Cherrypickers, and their swinging gold-braided pelisses and their perky busbies, were strung out in a dashing line, leading the way, looking for danger. Fleur stared and stared, hoping she might be able to pick out her brother, but the distance was too great to recognise individuals.

Out on the left flank there were the glittering lance-points and fluttering pennants of the 17th, along with the 8th Hussars. And to one side were gathered the blue jackets and scarlet facings of the 4th Light Dragoons, with Lord George Paget sitting his grey at their head, waiting to take up the rearguard. All these precautions, Fleur thought, showed that the Allies had no idea how unprepared the Russians were. They must suppose the Russian army was somewhere nearby, ready to pounce, whereas reports said it was still making its way laboriously up from Sebastopol, looking for a suitable ground on which to make a stand.

The watchers gazed at the great, impressive mass of infantry in the centre, in solid double columns: the scarlet impassivity of the Guards, marching in perfect time; the dark green of the Highlanders' kilts swinging above the twinkling of their red-and-white checkered stockings; the dull black-green of the rifle divisions, flickering with silver buttons; and the plain jackets and black shakos of the line regiments, all the way out to the left flank, where the 44th marched, distinguished by their yellow flashes.

There were horses and gun-carriages, officers and bandsmen, bearskins and busbies and shakos and the peaked kepis of the French regiments. The sunlight flashed from gold buttons and epaulettes, from brass badges on cap and valise, from steel bit-rings and lance-points and bayonets. There was scarlet and gold and green and royal blue, the dazzling white of pipe-clayed cross-belts, the fur trimming of pelisses.

Oh, it was a wonderful sight, an army marching off under the bright morning sun to the sound of 'Garryowen' and 'Scotland the Brave' and 'Lillibulero'. Larks shrilled high above them, hares got up from the grass and raced away before them, the horses snorted and neighed, the gun-carriages creaked, and the feet tramped, shaking the air.

But after a while the bands fell silent. The sun rose higher, beating down from the clear sky on men in unsuitable uniforms and burdened with their marching-kits; and as the rearguard came into view, it was plain that all was not well with the Allied army. There were so few carts, so very few baggage-horses! And already there were men staggering, men dropping their greatcoats and discarding their heavy shakos, men falling to lie still on the short, burnt grass.

Men gripped with dysentery suddenly fell out and squatted hopelessly, in the open, without shame. Men dazed with heat and exhaustion hung on feebly to the sides of baggage carts, or simply sat down, heads hanging between their knees, too stupid to go on. And even from a distance, the cholera cases could be seen, flinging themselves to the ground and writhing in agony, stepped over and round by everyone until an over-crowded hospital cart could finally reach them.

When the last divisions had passed, the plain looked like a battlefield, scattered with bodies and discarded equipment. All that was missing were the dead horses. The 4th Light Dragoons, from being the rearguard, was transformed into a hospital party, helping and directing the removal of the stricken men back to the beaches for re-embarkation onto the transports.

'We have to do something,' said Fleur at last. None of them had said anything for some time, watching with helpless pity the plight of the sick under that burning sun.

'What can we do,' Lyudmilla said. It was not a question. 'We can't help them.'

Fleur looked from one to the other of her companions. 'We must go down there. We have to do *something*. We have a little water with us – we can give them that, at least.' Still there was no response. She stared at Kirov urgently, her eyes wide. 'They're my own people!'

He sighed, knowing how hopeless it was. 'Very well,' he said. He turned his horse towards the path down from the ridge, leading the way for them.

When they reached the plain, they became aware of how overpowering the heat was without the light airs that had stirred on the high ground. What the soldiers in their woollen coats and tight stocks must have suffered! And there was no water on this plain, no water in this part of the Crimea at all. They trotted, Fleur leading, until they reached the first of the bodies, and there Fleur jumped down and pulled her water-bottle from behind the saddle. She looked round, but Lyudmilla had not dismounted. She was staring at the man with distaste and horror.

'Help me,' Fleur said simply, but Milochka shrank into herself, shaking her head.

'I'll hold your horse,' she said.

Kirov dismounted, and while Lyudmilla held both their mounts, he and Fleur did what they could. It was little – so little. Their water was soon used up. They could only straighten the bodies of the dead decently, and comfort the still-living with their presence.

'Someone's coming,' said Lyudmilla suddenly.

A horseman was cantering towards them across the hot, glittering plain. As he came nearer, Fleur saw that it was Captain Portal of the 4th Light. A moment later he halted his horse before them in a little swirl of dust and saluted, his eyes flickering over Kirov and Lyudmilla, and coming to rest on Fleur.

'Miss Hamilton, ma'am!'

'Captain Portal. We are unarmed, you know. Only civilians. We came to see if we could help.'

'Yes, ma'am,' he said, and coughed, and licked dry lips. The sun was reaching its zenith, and there was no shade anywhere. 'Colonel Lord Paget sent me to fetch you. He's at the rear, ma'am, and particularly asks that you come at once.' He turned his horse and they followed him.

'What does Lord George want with me?' Fleur asked. 'Is our help needed?'

He glanced at her unwillingly. 'It's your brother, Captain Hamilton, ma'am. The Colonel thought you would want to know that he was taken very ill this morning. He thought you might want to take him home with you, seeing that you've a place nearby.'

Fleur heard the words behind the words. Paget would not have suggested such a course, unless he thought that, taken back to the transport ship with the other sick, Richard would die. Or perhaps he thought he was dying already, and was offering Fleur the chance of seeing him for the last time.

'What is it, Portal?' she heard her own voice ask. Above her in the empty sky the skylarks still shrilled their mad joy, as if there were no death and misery on the earth below them.

'I think it's cholera, ma'am,' said Portal reluctantly.

Chapter Eighteen

Lyudmilla reached him first. 'Oh Richard! Richard!' She knelt in the dust in a tumble of hair, her tears splashing on Richard's unheeding face. 'Fleur, do something! You must save him!'

'I suppose it is cholera?' Paget asked without hope.

'Yes,' said Fleur. She recognised the pinched, shrunken look of the face, the clammy skin, the feeble, rapid pulse.

'Thought so,' Paget sighed. 'He was taken with spasms this morning, just when we were forming up. Of course, he's had the diarrhoea for days now, but then we all have. Nobody knew it was anything worse until he suddenly fell off his horse. We were going to get him back to the transports; then I saw you.'

Richard was lying on the hard-baked earth of the burning plain in the full glare of the sun, his head propped on his valise. He was in the state of deep collapse that follows the initial diarrhoea, vomiting and violent cramps. His hair was matted with sweat; his shirt was streaked with vomit, and his clothes were soiled. As well as the smell of his emissions, there was the characteristic smell of the sickness about him.

Yet in spite of all this, Lyudmilla hung over him, crooning in Russian the words Nushka had spoken to her when she was a child, stroking his hair and face, oblivious of the repellent nature of his illness.

Kirov spoke. 'How bad is he?'

'This is the critical point, the collapse after the convulsions,'

Fleur said, her fingers against her brother's jaw, feeling for the pulse. 'From here he will either die, or pass into the reaction stage.' She glanced around her briefly. 'We must get him out of this place.'

Lyudmilla jumped up on the words. 'Yes, yes, let's take him home! Oh quickly!'

'Can we?' Kirov asked.

Paget shrugged. 'Frankly, sir, I wish you would. It's hellish on those transports already, and there's no one to nurse him: his servant's down with it too.' His face contorted briefly. 'This damn' sickness! We thought we'd left it behind at Varna! There've been hundreds more cases even since we landed. You take him, Miss Hamilton, and save him if you can.'

Fleur stood up decisively. 'Thank you, Lord George.' She looked towards Kirov. 'We must make a litter.'

'There's plenty of material around here,' Kirov said.

Paget stirred restively. 'I must go on. I wish I could help you more, but there's so much to do.'

'I understand,' Fleur said quickly. 'God bless you for bringing me to him!'

She shook his hand, and he mounted his horse, called to his men, and trotted away.

They fashioned a crude litter with discarded greatcoats and the stirrup-leathers from all three horses, and set off at last slowly towards the north-west, with Milochka leading the horse, Kirov steadying the litter, and Fleur leading the other two mounts. It was a weary and anxious walk until they reached the nearest Tartar village, about four miles away. It took them two hours, and in that time Richard did not stir or open his eyes.

They soon discovered the reason for the army's pitiful lack of horses and carts: they had brought very few with them, expecting to be able to commandeer them when they landed. But Tartars have their own ways of hiding their belongings, and the Allies' scouting parties had found nothing but empty sheds and apparently starving villagers.

For Count Kirov and his ladies, however, a cart was forthcoming. Indeed, had the villagers known that the British army was ready, as always, to pay hard coin for what it commandeered, they'd have brought forth all they had.

'You may have my house, *barina*,' the cart's owner said hopefully, 'to nurse the poor sick man. A shame to jolt him miles and miles in this heat! Why not let him rest here until he is better? My family and I can go and stay with friends, and you may have the whole house.'

Lyudmilla looked at Fleur eagerly. 'Wouldn't that be better? Perhaps he shouldn't be moved?'

But Fleur considered only briefly. 'In the reaction stage, nursing is all important. Much better to get him home, where we have the resources. I would sooner move him now than later. To be truthful, he knows nothing at the moment.'

'I agree,' said Kirov. 'We're less than twenty versts from home. We can be there in three hours, and if we keep him out of the sun—'

The Tartar shrugged and provided a covered kibitka and a pair of strong horses, and came along himself to drive, saying proudly that no man could get better speed out of his horses than him. 'Then I can bring it back myself, and save you trouble,' he added.

'Very well. Let's get going,' Kirov said.

He rode behind with the three horses. The women rode in the cart, tending the sick man.

'What can we do for him, Fleur?' Lyudmilla asked again and again.

'Nothing. Only what we are doing,' Fleur said. 'All will depend on his passing this crisis, and only his own strength can decide that.'

Lyudmilla hung over him mournfully. 'He looks so very sick. Will he get better?'

'He was always strong and healthy,' Fleur said. 'He has a good chance.' But she could hear the doubt in her own voice. She remembered what Paget had said, that Richard had been suffering from diarrhoea for several days: it was a weakening condition, which must have drained his strength.

Again and again she checked his pulse, bathed his face and

moistened his lips with the water the Tartar had provided, and prayed to God to spare him. He was her little brother, all she had left now – in a way, all she had ever had. The true depth of her affection for him was only revealed to her now, when there was an even chance at least that she would lose him.

When they got near home, Kirov left the kibitka to canter on ahead and alert the house, and have Nushka make up a bed in a room on the cooler side of the house. Richard was still deeply unconscious when they brought him in, and at the sight of him the old nurse muttered something and rapidly crossed herself. Then she firmly drove Milochka from the room.

'Don't argue with me, my lady. The *barishnya* and I are going to wash him, and what help do you think you could be with that? Go on now, don't annoy me, little soul. You can come and see him later – aye, and sit with him, if that's what you want!'

Between them, she and Fleur stripped Richard of his filthy clothes, washed him, and dressed his sores with salve. He was pitifully light: a slightly-built young man in any case, he had lost all his flesh, and his ribs stood out 'like an old horse', as Nushka said tenderly.

They put him into a fresh linen nightshirt, and slipped him between the sheets, and Fleur stood by him again, her fingers under his jaw, her brows drawn together in a frown.

Nushka paused beside her on her way out with the dirty clothes. 'He's in God's hands now, *barishnya*,' she said; then, 'He has a great look of you about him, you know.'

Fleur grunted without really hearing her. Nushka touched her arm gently. 'I've put an icon of Saint Sebastian in the corner there, you see – he's the patron saint of soldiers. And tomorrow is Saint Eustathius's day. He was a soldier too, so don't be afraid – he's being well looked after.'

Fleur looked at her and after a moment gave a distracted smile. 'Thank you. Yes, I know.'

'That's right, *barishnya*,' Nushka nodded. 'I'm going to take these things away and get them cleaned up. He'll be needing them again.'

In the cool of the evening, Richard regained consciousness, and as he opened his eyes, the first thing he saw was Lyudmilla's face bent over him, framed with her soft fawn curls. He thought he must be dreaming. The white walls and the pale evening light had an ethereal air about them, and his body was as light and insubstantial as foam on a wave. No, not a dream. He must have died after all.

'Milochka?'

It was barely more than a whisper, but a symphony to Lyudmilla's ears. 'Oh Richard,' she said, and bent to kiss his damp cheek, and her tears wet his lips. He licked the salt drops gratefully. 'Nushka said you wouldn't die! She said Saint Nino had told her so, and Saint Nino is always right. How are you feeling, dear Richard?'

Dear Richard couldn't speak, but the sound of Milochka's voice had roused Fleur, who was taking a rest in the next room. She came hurrying in to lay a cool hand on Richard's brow and a finger under his jaw, and then smiled at his bewildered look, understanding his thoughts.

'No, it's not a dream,' she said. 'You're in the Crimea still, at Count Kirov's summer estate at Kurmoye. Don't you remember, I told you in my letter that we were here? You got sick on the march, and Lord George Paget gave you to us to nurse. And now I'm going to get you something cold to drink. You're thirsty, aren't you?'

Richard only nodded slightly, but the look in his eyes was avid. One of the symptoms of cholera was a torturing thirst, and he had been out on that burning plain – after five days on marching rations – and before that on shipboard all the way from Varna, where water was always in short supply . . . The nightmare of thirst was still with him, she could see.

She brought him iced champagne. 'Don't gulp, love,' she said. 'There's plenty – all you can drink. Just take it a little at a time, or you'll bring it up again.'

'Let me, Fleur, let me,' Milochka said eagerly, and Fleur

relinquished the glass, watching carefully for a moment to see that she supported his head properly and didn't drown him. But careless, impatient Milochka had been transformed by some magic into a tender nurse, and she did just as she ought.

When he was laid down again, the mere effort of drinking seemed to have exhausted him. He lay flattened against the pillows, and there seemed hardly enough of him to make a shape under the bedclothes; but he seemed to want to speak, and Fleur drew up the little stool and sat close beside him, taking his hand in both hers.

'You're safe now, Dick. You're going to get well. Milochka and I will nurse you, and all you have to do is rest, rest completely, and don't excite yourself. I'm going to give you a small dose of laudanum in a moment, to make you sleep quietly. Is there anything you want to ask first?'

She saw him assembling his words, to make the best use of his remaining strength.

'The army?' he whispered.

'We saw it march away towards Sebastopol. We've had no more news of it. As soon as I hear anything, I'll tell you, I promise. The Cossacks bring us news – they know everything that goes on. What else?'

He looked dazed, trying to think. 'Is it cholera?'

'Yes, love. But you know I've had lots of experience of that. Remember at home, when they had that outbreak at Isleworth? I know what to do. Don't be afraid.'

He moved his eyes, looking for Lyudmilla, and finding her, whispered, 'Thought I was dreaming.'

'*Not* dreaming, dearest Richard,' she said, her eyes bright with unshed tears. She took his other hand and pressed it. 'I'm really here!'

Fleur looked at her warningly. 'We must let him sleep now, Milochka. He mustn't be upset.'

'I won't upset him,' she began indignantly, and then bit her lip as Fleur frowned and shook her head.

But Richard was still looking at her, and now he whispered, 'Stay?'

Her face lit. 'Yes, I'll stay. Of course I will. I'll sit here while

355

you sleep, as quiet as a mouse, and when you wake up, the first face you'll see will be mine.'

There was the faintest glimmer of a smile on Richard's face. The champagne was doing its work, and his eyelids were drooping. Fleur decided that he didn't need the laudanum, and she sat still until his eyes closed and his breathing steadied. Then she warned Lyudmilla again not to disturb him, and to call her if he woke or appeared restless, and left her to her chosen vigil.

Out on the veranda Kirov rose to his feet expectantly.

'He came to himself,' Fleur said. 'He was rational, he knew us. He's sleeping now, and Milochka's watching him. I think he—'

That was as far as she got. Suddenly her throat closed up, and the tears welled over. Kirov crossed the small space between them and took her in his arms, and she abandoned herself to the luxury of his broad chest to weep on, and the comfort of his hand on the back of her head.

'It's not just Richard,' she said jerkily through her tears. 'It's all of them! All those dead – and the others, marching away—'

She thought of the little army marching along by the sea, small and gaily coloured as a child's toy set out on the plain below. Oh the pitifulness of men's splendour, as they marched with drums and fifes and colours flying to pit their frail, warm bodies against the cold impartial death of shot and shell. How could she explain it to him? He had not been with her when the soldier said, 'I used to be an ostler.' He was a man too: he would not understand how fragile men seemed to women – how fragile and foolish and brave.

'Why do they do it?' she said into his chest. 'Why do men do it?'

His hand moved in her hair. 'To make life more than it is,' he said.

Richard seemed a little better the following day: though he was still pitifully weak, his skin was warmer, his pulse stronger, the diarrhoea less. Simply being clean and cared for had helped, allowing his own strength to fight the disease. The crisis had passed, and Fleur expressed a cautious optimism, which inspired Lyudmilla to wild rejoicing. Fleur had to speak to her severely once or twice about disturbing the patient.

It seemed that Richard had passed into the third, the reaction stage of the disease; and from there, with proper nursing, a strong man might make a rapid recovery, if there was no relapse. It was all in the nursing, as she knew very well. A relapse could give rise to severe complications, and could carry a man off in hours.

She and Nushka soon weighed each other up, each coming to the conclusion that the other knew her job. The patient's pulse must be carefully monitored, and he must be kept warm and quiet. He must have plenty of fluids, barley water to line the stomach, and champagne to stimulate the heart and nourish the blood. Chalk and potash salts would check the diarrhoea; and, Nushka added, he must have ordinary salt to replace all he would have lost through sweating. That was a new idea to Fleur, and she wondered about it, but Nushka seemed so sensible that she felt inclined to trust her, and allowed her to add salt to the barley water.

For most of the day he slept, waking only briefly from time to time to take fluids and to pass motions. He did not speak, and seemed hardly to know where he was, though once he smiled faintly when the glass was taken from his lips. But again, when the evening grew cooler, he woke properly, and was obviously much better. Though he was very weak, the collapsed appearance and the pinched, shrunken look of the face were gone. Nushka said it was always so if they were given salt. Salt made all the difference.

Fleur had expected that Lyudmilla's devotion to nursing would wane during the day, but she stayed at her post and seemed to want nothing better than to sit beside Richard while he slept, simply to be the one who gave him the glass when he woke. Fleur and Nushka, of course, saw to his more basic needs; and at dusk both insisted that Lyudmilla should go for a walk to refresh herself.

'Or we shall have you sick next, *barina*, and where would that get us?' Nushka said, driving her charge out like an unwelcome cat in the kitchen. 'Go on, now, and see to those poor blessed dogs – they've been sitting with their noses pressed to the door all day! The young master won't get up and dance a jig while you're out, I promise you.'

So it was Fleur who washed Richard's face and hands when he woke, gave him lemon barley water, and received his first confidences.

'I must have got it on the ship,' he told her. 'I thought I'd escaped, though I'd been trotting ever since we landed at Varna – everybody had. God that was a hellish place! Yet it looked so pretty . . .'

There was a long pause. Fleur sat quietly, feeding him sips from the glass. He resumed, his voice weak, his words broken with long pauses.

'But the ship was another matter. Two hundred men in a space meant for seventy. Nine in ten of 'em with diarrhoea. No fresh food – nothing but salt pork and biscuit. Had to be eaten raw – no room to cook it, and no firewood to cook it with. Water on short ration – none to wash with, and precious little to drink. No wonder the cholera spread. It was the only thing that flourished on that hellish trip!'

He shuddered, and she gave him more barley water, propping his head with her hand. He drank, his eyes fixed on the middle distance. She decided it was better to let him talk – it might ease his mind to unburden it.

'Three days was what they'd allowed for crossing the Black Sea,' he went on, 'but those who embarked first were in those ships for seventeen days. Orders were to rendezvous with the convoys at Balchik Bay, fifteen miles south of Varna. God, I can tell you we were glad to get away from Varna! But we took the cholera with us, of course. Every day more men died. We heaved 'em overboard after dark.'

Fleur took the empty glass from him, and stroked the hair from his brow, feeling for fever. His eyes were glazed: he was very far away now.

'We were a week at Balchik. No one had any cannon-balls

358

to weight the dead bodies when they were thrown overboard. We weighted them as best we could, but it wasn't enough. When they start to decompose, they blow up with gases, you see.'

'Oh Richard—'

'So up they came to the surface again. Untimely resurrection, Brooke said. The worst of it was, the weights were just enough to keep them upright, so they floated head and shoulders out of the water, watching us – watching us.'

'No more, Dick. It's over now.'

'The sun burned the faces black, and then the flesh started to shrink away, so it looked as though they were grinning. The teeth seemed very white in those black faces, you see. They bobbed up and down in the harbour, hundreds of them, more every day; grinning at us, as if they were saying, "Come in and join us! Come on! You know you'll be with us sooner or later!" '

He stopped abruptly, jamming his teeth together and closing his eyes against the memory. Fleur felt his pulse. After a moment he opened his eyes and looked at her. 'It's all right. I won't faint.'

'I don't want you to excite yourself,' she said. 'You must stay calm and quiet.'

'Talking about it won't make any difference. It's not something I can forget. And it wasn't the worst thing. That was just imagination, after all. The poor devils were dead, even if they wouldn't lie down. No, that wasn't the worst thing. It was the voyage from England – and the horses. Oh God, Flo, the horses!'

She held his hand. 'Gently, love. It's over now. Tell me about it if it helps.'

'Horses were never meant to travel in ships. They're bad sailors. They're nervous. Why in God's name did they choose to send us in sailing ships? I tell you, Flo, I'll never say another word against steamers! Steamers at least sail pretty level, and they'd have got us to Varna in a fortnight. We were two months in that ship! Two months, the horses shut up in a foul little hold, with no light or air, and no stalls to separate them.

They were tied up by the head only, and when the wind blew up—'

He stopped, gathering himself. 'Crossing Biscay,' he went on, 'it wasn't much of a blow for us, but down below it was like a scene from hell. As the ship rolled, all the horses were thrown off their feet together. They screamed with panic, kicking out, jerking at their headstalls – *you* know! Some were trapped underneath, thrashing, others treading on 'em. Oh God! We tried to quiet 'em. Even the sailors helped, risked their lives trying to get 'em on their feet again. And then as soon as we'd got the poor beasts up, over the ship'd go the other way, and it would all start again.'

'Oh Dick, it's horrible. It's too horrible.'

'I tell you I never want to see anything like that again – eighty horses, mad with fright, all trying to break loose at once! I stayed at Pearl's head for three days, day and night. But my God, I was lucky! All of mine made it. We lost thirty out of the eighty horses. I've never cried so much in my life as I cried on that voyage.'

Fleur was fighting with her own tears. 'Is Pearl all right now?'

'She was last time I saw her, but she's very thin. They all are. I lost Kittiwake – he was new, you didn't know him – when Jim the Bear took us out on that mad reconnaissance of his, back in July. The poor little devil just dropped dead from the heat and fatigue. We lost a hundred horses that time. Brooke lost both his, so I lent him Oberon.'

'Oberon? You have Oberon with you?'

'I hoped you wouldn't mind. Better for him than trailing about the lanes with Mary Scott bumping on his back.'

'Mary Scott's a good rider. That's why I lent him to her.'

'Brooke's a good rider too. He's got the best hands of anyone I know. You needn't worry. I suppose Brooke's got them both now. I wish I knew if I'd ever see Pearl again.'

He stopped and closed his eyes, suddenly exhausted. There was a great deal Fleur wanted to know about the welfare of her horse, and much she might have said about Richard's taking him into so much danger without permission, but she resisted the desire easily. His face was looking drawn again. She took his pulse again, frowning a little.

'No more talking now,' she said. 'You must rest. In fact, you're to sleep for a while. Later, when you wake, Milochka can bring you some more champagne – as long as you don't let her tire you, love.'

He smiled faintly, his eyes closed. 'She's a trump, that girl, ain't she?' he murmured. 'Didn't I say – back in Petersburg—?' He was asleep.

When Lyudmilla returned from exercising her dogs, she was annoyed that Fleur wouldn't let her go in to sit with Richard again.

'I won't disturb him!' she protested. 'I'll just sit there, quiet as a stone. You think no one knows how to do anything but you!'

'He's not going to do anything for the next hour. I'd prefer you to leave him alone until after dinner.'

'But he needs me!'

Fleur glanced at Kirov for help, and he intervened gently. 'Hasn't it occurred to you that perhaps we need you too?'

She looked at him suspiciously. 'What for?'

'To keep our spirits up. Richard is sleeping, and Nushka will do very well to sit by him in case he wakes; but only you will do to dine with us and cheer us with your conversation.'

Lyudmilla was not convinced. 'You don't really want my company,' she said doubtfully. 'You're tricking me.'

'Yes I do. I really do,' he said, holding her gaze steadily. 'Why don't you go and put on a fresh gown? It will do us so much good to sit down to a civilised meal and have you to look at across the table.'

She allowed herself to be persuaded, though from her expression it was clear that she still suspected she was being manipulated. Fleur wondered too. He had sounded quite sincere when he said 'I really do'.

When Lyudmilla had gone, Fleur rose and said, 'Perhaps I'd better change, too, if we are to dine properly.'

'One moment,' Kirov stopped her, and she turned back. 'I

wanted to tell you alone, because I don't entirely trust Milochka not to blurt it out. A Cossack scout has come in with a report of a battle.'

Fleur paled. 'A battle?'

'It seems Menshikov made a stand along the bank of the River Alma – about twenty versts from where the Allies landed. The Allies came up to them around midday today, and the battle began an hour or so later. The Cossack said the fighting was very fierce on both sides. I don't yet know what the result was.'

Fleur nodded dumbly. At least Richard was here, was her first helpless thought, and out of it; but what of all her other friends? How many of them were now mangled corpses?

'There'll be more news later,' Kirov said. 'Until then, I think it's best to say nothing to Milochka. She's not the world's most tactful creature.' Fleur nodded again, and he reached out to touch her. 'I'm so sorry,' he said gently; but she evaded him and turned and went away. This was not something a touch could comfort.

They sat down to dinner at last rather late, but Lyudmilla, at least, was in good spirits and had made good use of the intervening time. She looked flushed and pretty, and had put on a much-ruffled gown of pale apricot silk which suited her fair colouring admirably. Kirov encouraged her to chatter, which she did amiably, about her plans for Richard's convalescence. She seemed to envisage its taking many months, for she was talking of Christmas in Petersburg when some sort of commotion at the front of the house stopped her in mid-flow and brought Kirov to his feet.

'Who on earth can that be, arriving at this time of night?' Milochka said innocently, and then noted Fleur's expression. 'What is it? What's happened?'

'Wait here,' Kirov said sharply, throwing down his napkin and leaving them.

Milochka stared at Fleur as though the answer might be written in her face. 'What's happened? You're keeping something from me, aren't you?'

'Oh hush,' Fleur said distractedly. 'I'm trying to listen.' It must be another Cossack, she thought, with news of the battle. It could not be good news for her, whatever there was to tell.

There were voices, and then footsteps, and at last Kirov appeared. His eyes went straight to Fleur, and held a warning. 'It's a visitor. Yes, it is news, but it will be rather a surprise to you.' He turned to address someone over his shoulder. 'Do come in. We're having dinner – perhaps you'd like to join us.'

A man came in, dressed in civilian clothes, but very dirty and rumpled. His face was streaked with dust, his boots white with it, his hair matted with sweat. He paused just inside the door and looked round apologetically, his eyes pausing briefly on Lyudmilla before resting apprehensively on Fleur. Lyudmilla looked at the stranger with surprise and interest, but Fleur was perfectly still with astonishment.

'Hello, Fleur,' he said, in a voice parched with dust.

It was Theodore Scott.

Dinner resumed after a pause just long enough for Scott to wash the worst of the dust from his hands and face, and to accept the offer of a clean shirt from the Count's wardrobe. Emerging looking a little less wild, he proved to be unwounded, only gaunt and very weary-looking. He gazed around the table with a faintly bemused air which told Fleur as clearly as words what he'd been living on these weeks past. She had used the interim to tell Milochka briefly the little she knew, and to beg her not to trouble their visitor with questions, but to let him speak in his own time.

'I understand from Count Kirov that Richard is a little better,' was the first thing he said as his soup was placed before him. 'Is that right? Paget told me you'd taken him. I suppose it was the cholera?'

'Yes, but he seems to be recovering – please God,' Fleur said. 'He's very weak, but I believe he's out of immediate danger. You know with cholera it's all in the nursing, so he has a better chance here than on the ship. I've good hopes for him.'

363

'Thank God!' Scott said. 'If only some of our others could have the same sort of care! Conditions on the hospital ships are appalling.'

'You shall see Dick later, after dinner, if you like,' she said. 'He's sleeping at the moment.'

He was spooning up cold beetroot soup with amazing rapidity. 'You must be wondering what I'm doing here,' he said when he had emptied the bowl.

'Yes, I did wonder. You're not in uniform, I see.'

'I've come as a civilian. Sir John Burgoyne, the engineer, was sent out to advise on the best way to attack Sebastopol. He couldn't be given a military appointment because he's senior to Sir George Brown, who's second in command, which would make things awkward. And the engineers themselves are under the command of old General Tylden, who wouldn't like his toes trodden on. So Burgoyne's here unofficially, as it were, and I'm his assistant. They thought with my civilian background and my military experience – brief though it was – I'd be a good compromise.'

'Yes, I see,' Fleur said. 'It's very good to see you again, Teddy – a face from home. How are they all?'

'Oh never mind all that,' Lyudmilla broke in impatiently, unable to restrain herself any longer. 'For God's sake, tell us about the battle! What's happened? Is it over? Who won?'

So between mouthfuls, Scott told what he knew. The Allied army had had no idea where the Russians were, or in what strength, and had marched off expecting to meet them over every succeeding ridge. They knew they had been spotted by the Cossack scouts, and advanced in fear of an attack at any moment.

It had taken them five hours to reach the first of the five parallel rivers which lay between them and Sebastopol – the Bulganek. By then the entire army was tortured with thirst. The officers could do nothing to restrain the undisciplined rush down to the water: men threw down their arms and elbowed each other aside to stagger into the water knee-deep and lap like dogs.

'All but the Highland Brigade. Old Colin Campbell wouldn't

let them break ranks,' Teddy said. 'Made the poor devils march down in formation.'

Because the men were so exhausted by then, and there were so many new cholera cases to be dealt with, Lord Raglan had given the command to bivouac beside the stream. They had spent the rest of the day and the night there, expecting to be attacked at any moment.

'The night was clear, and we could see the watch-fires of the Russian camp quite clearly. They were up on the heights above the next river, the Alma, about six miles away. It looked as though they were hanging in the sky, twinkling like golden stars. Raglan ordered the men to pile arms and sleep in order of battle, in case the Russians attacked at dawn, but they didn't, of course. They had a good position on the Alma – the best. They wanted us to come to them.'

The Allies marched the next morning towards the Alma, their numbers depleted by the cholera, which had carried off more victims during the night. The march was a repeat of the previous day's, the men tortured with thirst under the burning sun on the waterless plain. They'd had difficulty filling their water-bottles at the Bulganek once it had been trampled into a muddy morass. Men fell out, dying from heat and exhaustion, from dysentery, from cholera: the army left a trail behind it of dead men and discarded equipment.

They came around noon to the top of a grassy ridge, and saw below them the gentle slope down to the river, bordered with orchards and vineyards. The river was deep, with high, sheer banks. On the other side the ground rose steeply in a series of natural terraces to the heights where the Russian army sat waiting, guns mounted as though in a fortress.

'It was well chosen. We'd have to make our way down that long, shallow slope, cross a fast-flowing river, climb its steep bank, and then make our way uphill over bare ground, and all the time be pounded from above by the Russian guns. And if we managed all that, the last part of the advance would be made scrambling up into the mouths of heavy artillery, firing at a range of a few yards.'

He looked at Kirov. 'Your general – Prince Menshikov, isn't

it?' Kirov nodded. 'He'd picked his ground beautifully. He must have thought it was impossible for any force to make a frontal attack. I certainly thought so.'

He stopped and finished the baked fish before him. The servants changed the plates and served spiced chicken, and refilled the glasses.

'They opened fire on us at half past one. It was a hellish cannonade – I've never heard anything like the noise! When it's happening, you know, you can't think of anything – it's as if your head's filled to the brim with nothing but the noise.'

'Yes, I know,' said Kirov.

'Do you, sir? Well, Lord Raglan made the men lie down, to keep out of the fire, and requested the French to begin a diversionary attack on the right flank. There were cliffs there, going down to the sea, but there were good paths all the way up, wide enough to get carts up. I don't think your people could have known about those paths. They were so taken by surprise when the French appeared, they just turned tail and ran. But there was some muddle, and the French didn't follow it up, which gave the Russians time to rally. They brought some guns up and started pounding the French, and eventually they sent a message to Lord Raglan to say they must have support, or they'd have to withdraw.'

He took a sip of wine, and went on, 'Our men had been lying down under cannonade for about an hour and a half by then, and I think there must be nothing worse. They must all have longed for something to do, even if it was more dangerous, rather than just lie there. Perhaps Lord Raglan reasoned that way. At all events, just after three o'clock, he gave the order to attack – straight forward and up the escarpment! It was madness!'

Swept by continuous fire, the British army advanced in a line two miles long and only two men deep, down the slope, across the river – the men were so thirsty that even though the river was being raked with grapeshot, they stopped in the middle to drink – and up the other side. The thin, straggling line continued to advance through dense smoke and into the deadly fire, wavering when every few minutes a great gap was torn in it, but never stopping. The slopes became slippery with blood, were littered with bodies, but the survivors simply closed up and pressed on.

'I've never seen anything like it. I've never even heard of anything like it,' Scott said, shaking his head. 'It was the maddest, bravest, worst thing I ever saw! I don't think the Russians believed it. Our men were just magnificent; nothing shook them; and when they made the last rush, the Russians simply threw their guns down and ran for it. I can't say I blame them. What can you do against courage like that?'

So the Russian position was taken; but through some confusion or mistake, the British second line had not moved up in support. Seeing the hesitation, the Russians rallied and counter-attacked, driving the British back down the hillside.

'So it was all to be done again – the same ghastly thing, up that hellish slope, churned into mud with British blood, climbing over the bodies of the dead. But now the second line was there in support – Colin Campbell's Highlanders. You should have seen 'em! It was as if they were on the parade-ground. They formed up and advanced like a machine, never altering their pace, simply closing up every time a man fell. It was – inhuman.'

Kirov's eyes were distant, imagining it. It could not have been done, he knew, with Russian troops. Russian soldiers had to be kept in a solid mass to give each other courage. Such spirit and discipline as this – for men to advance only two deep against such fire – could not exist amongst peasants pressed for service against their will.

'They took the guns and the Russians turned and fled, and such a cheer went up! I was up on the hill right across on the other side with Roger Fenton – you know, Fleur, the photographer – and we heard it quite clearly! It was about a quarter to four – the whole advance had only taken about forty minutes.'

He stopped abruptly, and a silence fell. Then Fleur asked, 'Has the army gone on?'

'No. The order was to bivouac on the heights for the night. We have to suppose the Russians will turn and make another stand further on, and our men were in no condition to fight again. And then there was the question of the wounded. It's going to take all night – perhaps most of tomorrow, too – to deal with them, and to bury the dead.'

He sighed, a sound that seemed dragged up from some very great depth. 'The battleground is covered with them – lying in heaps in places. I don't know how many. Counting the Russians as well as the French and English, I'd say there must be three, maybe four thousand casualties lying out there. The way they moan and cry is horrible! And then there are the cholera victims. They've all to be carried back to the ships, and we're three miles from the sea there. We've so few carts, most of 'em are having to be carried on litters – it's going to take a long time.'

'So what brought you here, Teddy?' Fleur asked.

'There was nothing for an engineer to do. So I decided to ride back and find out if Richard was going to be all right, and see how you were.' He essayed a faint smile. 'I didn't think I'd get a dinner like this into the bargain. I shall be eating better even than Lord Cardigan tonight!'

'You're welcome to stay, of course,' Kirov said.

'Thank you, sir,' Scott said, 'but I mustn't. I ought to be back by morning, in case I'm wanted.'

'Then I'll send a servant with you to show you the way, whenever you're ready to go.'

'Thank you, sir,' he said again.

'You'll want to see Richard,' Fleur said. 'I'll go and see if he's awake – but try not to overexcite him, Teddy. Tell him about the battle, but not in the words you've used for us.'

'I understand,' said Teddy. 'Don't worry, I'll make it sound as tame as a tea party.'

True to his promise, Scott kept his words mild and unemphatic. Richard was obviously upset, but that was perhaps inevitable, and Fleur thought that on the whole the visit had done him good. It had comforted him to see his childhood friend again, and to have news of his companions. Best of all, Teddy was able to reassure him that Pearl was all right, and being taken care of by his friend Brooke.

'The cavalry hadn't anything to do, you know,' Scott told him. 'Raglan's keeping 'em in a bandbox – won't let 'em so much as dirty their overalls. Of course, hot-headed chumps like Lew Nolan – you know, Dick, Airey's galloper – are fretting themselves silly about the lack of action. Even Brooke said it was a dashed shame they weren't allowed to chase after the Russkis when they fled. But the Old Man knows what he's doing. The Russkis had something like six thousand sabres against our nine hundred – hardly a match, if they'd turned and stood! And our Heavy Brigade is still at sea, en route from Varna, of course.'

'You'll tell Brooke to make sure she gets water, won't you?' Richard whispered. 'And tell him to make sure she's properly rubbed down. And tell him—'

'Yes, don't you worry, old fellow. He knows what to do.'

'And tell Brooke and the others—' He swallowed. 'Tell 'em, I suppose I'll be joining 'em soon. I'm on the mend, you know.'

'Yes, I see you are. I'll tell 'em.'

'I'll be with them again soon. Very soon. I'll be back. Tell them that.'

Fleur intercepted Scott's gaze and glanced significantly towards the door. Her brother was looking pale and exhausted. He mustn't be tired any further. Scott nodded to her, and gently extricated himself from Richard's anxiety.

There was time before Teddy Scott left for him and Fleur to exchange a few words in private.

'It was good to see you again, Teddy,' Fleur said warmly. 'How are things at home? Have you seen anything of my aunt and uncle?'

'I saw your Uncle Frederick before I left London. They were all puzzled that you wouldn't come home, of course, but your uncle said to me privately that he thought you'd probably inherited your father's taste for adventure.'

Fleur smiled painfully. Yes, that was like Uncle Frederick! She suddenly missed him acutely. She could see him in her mind's eye so clearly before the fire in the drawing-room of the house in Hanover Square. Hanover Square! How fantastic, how exotic! London seemed infinitely far away; wildly improbable, like the landscape of a dream.

'And Mrs Pettit, and dear Buckley? Did you see them?' she asked.

'Yes, I dropped in once or twice when I was passing Grove Park. They keep things going, just as always. You could step in there tomorrow and find it just as you left it.' He eyed her curiously. 'I think they still expect you to come back. I must say, I never thought I'd find you here like this.'

'I never thought I'd see you out here with the army,' she countered.

'Oh, one does what one can, you know. I couldn't leave it all to Dick.' He grimaced. 'Father's mad keen on the war, so there was plenty of encouragement for me to come. There's a lot like him back home. Agitating and fulminating. Wanting to thrash the Russkis and teach Old Nick a lesson in manners – you know the kind of thing. Read it by the yard in the *Chronicle* and the *Gazette*.'

Fleur though of her aunt's words about the drums-and-glory brigade, and nodded. 'Yes, I suppose the papers are full of it.'

'They are. But of course it ain't a bit like what they say when you get here.' He frowned. 'There's a chap here, correspondent for *The Times*, called Billy Russell. He's a mad Irishman: he and Lew Nolan are like knives and forks! But anyway, he's writing down everything just as it is, not prettying it at all, and sending it all back for his paper. The people at home will know what it's really like at the war – the dirt and the cholera and the lice and the starvation. Maybe it will change things, I don't know. And Roger Fenton's taking his collodion pictures of it all. Well, I came out to do my bit, but I don't know but what Russell and Fenton between 'em won't make more of a difference in the end than the whole Brigade of Guards.'

He was silent for a moment, thinking, and then came back to earth, and sighed and looked at Fleur curiously.

'And what about you?' he said. 'You've changed, Fleur, I can see that at a glance.'

'Changed? In what way?'

He frowned, puzzling it out. 'I'm not sure. You're – more confident, for one thing and—' He paused, perhaps thinking that what he wanted to say was not flattering. 'You seem to fit in here, at any rate. If I didn't know you, I'd think you *were* Russian.'

'Thank you, Teddy,' she said gravely.

'But are you really all right?' he persisted, looking a little embarrassed. 'I mean, this is a strange set-up, isn't it? Are you really happy?'

'Yes, I'm happy.' She looked at him defiantly. 'We're friends, the Count and I. Good friends. You never did understand, you know.'

'No, I suppose I didn't.' He looked doubtful. 'Do you mean to stay? I mean, for good, in Russia?'

'I don't know. I can't see very far into the future at the moment.'

His face creased with ready sympathy. 'No, I suppose you can't, with poor Richard lying there sick, poor old fellow.'

She let him think that was what she had meant.

Chapter Nineteen

The leaves on the lemon trees were turning, and already there were a few every day, crisp and curling, blowing across the paths and collecting in the corners of the veranda. But the weather remained warm, and the sunshine fell fat and yellow as butter from a sky of creamy blue. Autumn blue – so said the marvellous fruits that were coming to the table now, melons and apricots and pomegranates, and translucent grapes, red and white, and sweet as honeyed wine.

Lyudmilla and Richard were playing with the dogs under the trees, throwing a ball back and forth to each other. The dogs coursed madly between them, jumping up every time it passed overhead. Stout Pushka's tongue was hanging out of the side of his mouth, and his tail was wagging so hard it revolved like the sail of a windmill. Zubka was wearing his right ear turned tastefully inside out over his head, and he was putting a great deal more effort into barking than jumping.

Lyudmilla waggled the ball teasingly to spur the dogs on to greater excitement, and then threw it to Richard. It was a wild shot, and he flung himself sideways in a despairing attempt to field it and fell over.

Milochka burst out laughing. 'Bravo! You should join the Maryinski Ballet – I know they're looking for a new principal dancer!'

Pushka, his eyes bulging with the exertion, was pounding off after the ball, reduced to his height at last; Zubka raced obligingly, but only as far as Richard, on whose chest he planted his forefeet, the better to wash his face for him.

Richard was laughing too. 'Get this hound off me,' he gasped. 'He's drowning me! No, you stupid creature! *Nyet*! Go away! *Dovolno*!'

'No good, he doesn't speak Russian – only French,' Milochka said, coming to the rescue. She held out her hand to help Richard up, and he took it, and then with a quick jerk of the wrist tumbled her onto the grass beside him.

'That'll teach you to laugh at an invalid!'

'Invalid, pooh! And if I've got green marks on my skirt, I'll set Nushka on you, and then you'll be sorry!'

Fleur was sitting on the veranda, watching them, and she glanced across at Kirov, reclining on the swing-seat, wondering if he felt just then as she did, almost as if they were parents watching their children frolic.

Milochka's rompings with Richard were as harmless as a child's, and her devotion to his comfort was touching. Since she had first taken up the vigil at his bedside, she had dedicated herself to nursing him. Although Nushka would never let her do anything basic for him, it was always she who brought his tray and held his glass or bowl; and from the barley water and champagne stage, through the gradations of clear bouillon, milk, soups, gruel, jellies and boiled chicken, she had brooded over his progress like a diminutive mother.

His recovery had been rapid. At the end of the first week, he

372

had been well enough to get out of bed, and was soon tottering outside to sit on the veranda, blinking in the brightness of the sunlight. While Fleur had busied herself devising a light, nourishing diet for him, Milochka had kept the patient occupied, beguiling his convalescent hours with reading to him tirelessly, and with all manner of games – card-games, word-games, guessing-games, spillikins and backgammon and even, for a wonder, chess. She had always been impatient of the very idea of chess, but when Richard offered to teach her, she not only accepted, but applied herself. To judge from the hilarity of their games, Fleur didn't think she would ever be very good at it, but at least she knew the rules and the names of the pieces.

Now, apart from his still-apparent thinness, you would hardly know Richard had been ill. These last few days Lyudmilla had been taking him for long walks with the dogs, to re-educate his legs, which he said had forgotten their business. Fleur had warned him not to overtire himself, but he evidently felt well enough to romp like a fool with Milochka and the dogs, and Fleur delighted to see it.

Now she said to Kirov, 'The children are in high spirits today, aren't they?'

'Mmm.'

It was so noncommittal, Fleur didn't know if it were an acknowledgement or a query. He was reclining on the swing-seat and was very still, only his eyes moving, following their movements back and forth. His expression was brooding. For several days now he had been in this remote, dark mood, and it disturbed her. She tried again to reach him.

'It's good to see them get on so well together, isn't it?'

'Is it?' He moved at last, turning towards her, and the unhappiness in his eyes shocked her. There seemed such emptiness there, a bottomless well that surely nothing she was or could do would ever fill. What had happened to cause such pain? Or had it always been there, hidden from her? 'But they are not children,' he said. 'I have no children.'

'No, I—' She faltered and stopped.

He turned his head away, and she felt a curious relief that

373

she need not go on looking into that darkness. 'I've been watching them,' he said, 'and I wonder at Lyudmilla's devotion. She seems to be very fond of him – perhaps too fond, wouldn't you say?'

She stared at him, aghast. Surely he couldn't be jealous of Richard? It was such an innocent affection. He and Milochka were friends, just as they had been at Schwartzenturm last year, doing their jigsaw puzzle.

'I don't think so,' she said carefully. 'I think she looks on him as a brother. And she's naturally glad he's well again. We all are.'

He looked at her again, and there was a glint of black humour in the darkness. 'Are you not fond of your brother?'

'Of course I am. I – but that's what I mean.' She grew confused under that sardonic gaze. 'I only meant that one can't be too fond of one's brother.'

'And I only meant that I am worried how she – and you – will feel when he goes back to join his regiment.'

He met her look impenetrably, but she felt somehow, confusingly, that that wasn't what he meant at all. 'But he won't go back,' she protested. 'Why should he? There's no need. And anyway, he's still convalescent. He—'

'You protest too much, my dear. You've just said he's well again. And I've seen the symptoms of restlessness in him.'

'But still—' she said stubbornly.

'He will go back. You don't understand – why should you? A woman sees these things differently. But take it from me, he wants to go back. And it will be soon. However much they have delayed so far, the Allies will know they must finish their campaign before the winter begins. There is not much time left – he knows that as well as they do.'

Fleur was silent, thinking of the confusing events which had followed the battle at the River Alma, the inexplicable actions of the Allies which had lost them all the advantage they had won at the cost of so many lives. The Cossack scouts and the villagers had kept them informed at Kurmoye of the progress of events; but they had not, of course, been able to explain them.

After the battle the Allied army had remained at the Alma for three days, picking up the wounded and transporting them laboriously to the ships, and burying the dead in two great pits – one for the Russians and one for the English and French. It was useful work, no doubt, and the Russians were glad they devoted themselves to it; for had they followed up the fleeing army, they could have taken Sebastopol without the slightest difficulty. Its defences were minimal, its troops few in number and low in morale.

But whatever the reason, the Allies did not begin their march until the 23rd of September. Since the country was otherwise waterless, they advanced slowly from river to river, from the Alma to the Katcha to the Belbek – followed, most disturbingly, by a flock of vultures. There had never been vultures in the Crimea before, as everyone knew; now, since the Alma, they were appearing, mysteriously, in large numbers, circling the army and hopping and flapping on its flanks like shabby undertakers haunting an almshouse.

Meanwhile General Prince Menshikov had not been idle. He had obliged the grieving Admiral Kornilov to empty his ships and scuttle them across the entrance to Sebastopol harbour. The crews were deployed to work on the defences and to man the battery guns. Then on the night of the 24th Menshikov marched the bulk of his army out of the city and up the road to the north-east. He was determined to protect his supply route to the rest of Russia, without which he would receive neither food, ammunition nor reinforcements; and with his army safe out of the city on the Bakchi Road, he would also be able to fall on the enemy's flank if and when it did attack.

However, during that same night the Allied army decided instead of attacking from the north of Sebastopol – which by then was defended only by the depot battalions and the reserve troops – to march in a great circle round it in order to take up positions in the south of the city. Thus, unknown to each other, the two armies were marching within miles of each other through the night. The Cossacks reported that the Allied advance guard had actually run across the Russian rearguard in the dark, frightening both sides almost equally. The Russian rearguard – a battalion of the Tarutinsky – had turned tail and fled back to Sebastopol, where it had caused more confusion by being mistaken for the enemy, and was fired upon by the defenders.

By the 26th the main Russian army under Prince Menshikov was safely established in the high ground to the north-east, while the Allies had reached the little seaside town of Balaclava, to the south of the city. But then the Allies had apparently suffered from an attack of indecision. Instead of assaulting Sebastopol at once, they had allowed the Russians time vastly to improve the fortifications. Admiral Kornilov had worked wonders, urging the soldiers and sailors to miracles of effort, and even involving the civilians, down to the women and children, in digging ramparts and filling sandbags. Every day the Russian position improved, especially as reinforcements were arriving all the time from Odessa and the Caucasus, while the Allied position could only get worse. Quite apart from the question of morale, there were the endless problems of supply, and the continuing depredations of the cholera, which had followed them, like the vultures, and settled down with them in Balaclava to finish off a steady dozen or so every day.

However, the Allies had dragged their artillery guns up into position at last, and on October the 17th, the cannonade had begun. Sebastopol was subjected to a hellish bombardment from English, French and naval guns from sunrise to sunset. The fortifications had been smashed, a magazine blown up, and over a thousand Russians killed – including the much-loved Admiral Kornilov. When the cannonade ended abruptly at dusk, the defenders had waited nervously for the inevitable swarming attack over the ramparts, which they could not have resisted – but it didn't come. The Allies, inexplicably, held off.

The defenders worked feverishly all night, dragging off the dead and wounded and repairing the ramparts, and the next morning the bombardment began again. So the pattern was established, each day the battering of the walls with cannon-fire, the hellish noise, the dust and smoke and hideous loss of life; followed at dusk by the inexplicable failure to launch an attack, and a night's frantic activity for the Russians, repairing the damage of the day.

When they were alone together, Fleur and Richard had wondered what Lord Raglan and Canrobert, the French Commander-in-Chief, were doing; and could only conclude that they were intent on wearing down the enemy, which seemed an eccentric procedure, as well as wasteful and dangerous. It was late in the year, and they could surely not be thinking of staying the winter in the Crimea? They must reduce the fortifications soon, or the campaign would fail.

Despite her protests to Kirov, Fleur also had seen the symptoms of restlessness in her brother. While she wondered academically, he wondered fretfully. What was going on? What were the plans? How was the army faring? How were his friends? How, above all, were his horses? These questions had been gnawing at him for some days now, and though he appeared to be entirely engrossed in his frolickings with Lyudmilla, he had not completely deceived either Kirov or his sister.

Two servants came out from the house with the samovar, and seeing it, Milochka got up from the grass, brushed herself down and led Richard back to the veranda. The dogs frisked past her, and then flopped down by the rail, jaws smiling and frilled pink tongues dripping as they panted briskly in the grateful shade.

'It's warm,' Lyudmilla said, throwing herself down on the old wicker sofa and pulling off her hat to fan herself with. 'I think there's going to be a thunderstorm. What do you think, Richka? Are you afraid of the thunder? Boom boom! Made you jump!'

'Don't,' he protested peacefully, waving her away. 'It's too hot.'

Kirov waited patiently until Fleur had poured everyone's tea – here in the Crimea they had it in thick glasses in the old-fashioned way, instead of in European china cups with saucers. Then he gathered their attention and said, 'We've had a pleasant summer here, haven't we? But all things have their season. Tomorrow I have to leave, and you must all decide what you want to do.'

They looked at him in surprise, but it was Lyudmilla who spoke, her eyes narrowing watchfully.

'What do you mean, Seryosha? Leave? Where are you going?'

'To Sebastopol.'

It was a bombshell, and from his expression, Fleur felt he was enjoying his effect on them. He looked around the circle of faces in pleased silence for a moment, before he condescended to explain.

'I received a letter today from Admiral Nakhimov. Menshikov, when he left Sebastopol, placed him in command of all the forces defending the town, and of course he could only obey, but he's been a seaman all his life, and he's never felt happy about commanding ground forces. Now Kornilov's dead, he's feeling more than ever isolated. So he asked Menshikov if he could send for me to be his liaison and general administration officer. I understand, reading between the lines, that there's a certain amount of confusion in the town.'

Fleur had a brief image of a town under siege and under constant bombardment – the destruction, the loss of life, the difficulty of keeping track of supplies, and of discovering the whereabouts of people whose last known address was now a heap of rubble, and who themselves might now be a heap of rags and torn flesh – and thought that confusion was probably a mild word for it.

'Menshikov has given his approval, and I've been given a colonel's commission in my old regiment. I'm to report by the 23rd at the latest – the day after tomorrow – but I shall leave in the morning. No sense in delaying, is there?'

His gaze passed around them again, and came to rest on Lyudmilla with a faintly triumphant smile. 'It's a good job I kept my old uniform, don't you think, my dear? And you, of course, must decide where you would like to go. I don't recommend that you stay here without me. Perhaps it would be best if you went back to Petersburg.'

It was the oddest thing, Fleur thought, but he said it in such a way that she was sure he was trying to provoke Lyudmilla into refusing. And yet if he wanted her to come with him to Sebastopol, why didn't he simply ask her? Then she told herself she was imagining things, reading too much into simple words. Pleased as he must be to have been recalled to duty, he would of course want Lyudmilla to go to a place of safety. Sebastopol under bombardment would be a dangerous place; no place, certainly, for a delicately nurtured female.

Lyudmilla rose to the bait with a snap. 'Go to Petersburg? Oh no! If you're going to Sebastopol, that's where I'm going. I'm not going to miss all the fun, I promise you! Besides, what would I do in Petersburg without you?'

'I'm flattered that I'm so essential to your happiness,' he said. 'But Sebastopol would be far too dangerous for you. And remember there will be few women there. It's full of soldiers and officers, but their wives and daughters will have been sent to places of safety – all but the hardy few who refuse to go.'

Lyudmilla's face glowed, and Fleur could almost see the image she was painting for herself. *You will face great danger. You will have to be very brave.* The Heroine of Sebastopol, refusing with incredible gallantry to be separated from her husband – perhaps saving the entire town through some stunning act of courage and presence of mind! Kirov could hardly have chosen words more calculated to inspire his wife to rebellion.

'I don't care if it is dangerous,' she said. 'I'm going with you, and that's final!'

'Sir—' Richard said. Lyudmilla's smile dropped from her face and her head whipped round to look at him. She had forgotten all about him for a moment.

'Yes,' Kirov said, 'I had wondered about you. You will have to think about your position.'

'I don't need to think, sir. I must rejoin my regiment.'

'No. Richard, no!' Lyudmilla's cry was low but urgent.

Kirov's lips quirked in a wry smile, as though some familiar old wound had tweaked him.

'You mustn't make it harder for him, my dear. He knows where his duty lies.'

'I have to go, Milochka,' Richard said, his face pale and his eyes bright.

'You've been ill. You're not recovered yet!' she cried.

'Yes I am. You know I am. I've been wondering for several days now how I could get back, but I've put off saying anything, because I knew how you'd hate it. But now the time's come. I have to go back and finish what I've begun.'

'But you might be killed!' Lyudmilla cried from the heart. 'Don't go, Richka! I won't go either. We'll go back to Petersburg. It doesn't matter about the silly war – let the others fight it! What does it matter? They don't need you.'

'It's my duty.'

'You've done enough. You don't have to go. Nobody's sent for you.'

'It's no good, 'Lochka. I have to go. Oh God, don't!'

Milochka burst into tears, burying her face in the pillows of the old sofa, and Richard dropped to his knees beside her and petted her head with clumsy tenderness.

Fleur had not spoken since Kirov had made his unexpected announcement. She had the curious feeling that she had been watching a play, something which had nothing to do with her, which was happening outside the frame of her life to people with whom she had no connection. Kirov was watching Lyudmilla crying and Richard trying to comfort her, with that familiar blank look in his eyes, and a faint, sour smile on his lips, but he was not outside the drama like Fleur. She had the feeling he had stage-directed the whole scene, manipulated the players into playing the parts he had written for them. *But why?*

Milochka's tears were as brief as they were noisy. Richard thrust his handkerchief into her fingers, and stood up to say quietly to Kirov, 'Can you arrange for me to go back, sir? What will it involve? Am I a prisoner?'

'The situation is rather unusual, isn't it?' Kirov said musingly, as though he were thinking it out. 'Since you came here as to a hospital, and since I was not at that time in uniform, you ought not to be considered a prisoner. But of course, since receiving this letter, I am now an officer of the Imperial army, and can place you under arrest at any moment. Curious, is it not?'

Lyudmilla stood up abruptly, gave her husband a reproachful look from behind wet eyelashes, and ran indoors.

Richard eyed him cautiously. 'Are you going to do that? I don't want to cause any trouble, sir. I just want to get back.'

'If I take you to Sebastopol as my prisoner, we could arrange a cartel of exchange with your side – if they've taken any prisoners, that is.'

'Couldn't you just let me go outside the city, and let me make my own way back?'

The Count smiled gently. 'No, I don't think that would be advisable. You might never make it to your camp. Vedettes on either side might well shoot you by mistake. Under a cartel of exchange, we'd be sure you got back safely.'

'Yes, I see. I'm sure you're right, sir. Thank you,' Richard said gravely. He bit his lip, looking down at his hands, conflicts of loyalty clearly visible in his handsome young face. 'If you'll excuse me, I'd better go and – there are things I'd better—' He muttered an incoherent excuse, and left them.

Silence fell. Kirov remained quite still for a moment; then he stretched out one elegant leg and with the toe of his boot gently massaged Zubka's ribs. The dog groaned faintly and rolled over onto its side, and its paws twitched with pleasure. Slowly up and down went the pleasuring toecap, pushing the roll of fat back and forth along Zubka's ribcage. Kirov was slumped low in his chair, his head turned away so that Fleur could not see his face. If he had been a woman, she would have been sure that he was crying.

She stood up to go indoors. She thought he had forgotten her presence, but without turning he said quietly, 'Don't go.'

She hesitated, watching him. Since she had first met him, she had felt strongly, perhaps unreasonably attached to him, as if there were invisible cords stretching between them, binding her self, her life – her soul, if you would – to him. Even now, she felt it still, though she didn't understand him, didn't understand what he was doing, what he was suffering. Yet looking down at his bent head and hunched shoulders she felt she was for him, no matter what happened. *I am for you*. As every person drew up the lines of division between themselves and the rest of the world, she was behind his line, facing outwards with him. As little as she understood why, she couldn't cross that line and remove herself from him.

Still without looking at her, he reached out his hand in her direction, his long fingers uncurling and stretching out for her. *No right*, she thought confusedly, *you have no right to ask*. But after a moment she put her hand on his, and he locked his fingers through hers tightly. Now connected to him, anchored, she wanted to ask all sorts of things about what he was doing, and why, but she couldn't sort them into any kind of order, or put them into the right words. In the end she simply said, 'What about me?'

He turned his head at last, and of all the expressions she might have expected to see on his face, it was none of them. He smiled at her, the good smile.

'Where I go, you go,' he said. 'Did you doubt that, *Tsvetoksha*?'

Kirov was given a house on Vladimir Street in the Old Town, overlooking the South Bay and the Naval Barracks on the opposite shore. It was a small house, whitewashed, with a roof of curling tiles whose soft red colour reminded Fleur of strawberry jam. It had been a wine shop at one time, and the ground floor was easily convertible into offices for Count Kirov, while the four rooms on the upper floor constituted their living quarters. It was cramped, but housing was in short supply in Sebastopol, because of both the huge influx of personnel, and the destruction of so much property by the bombardment.

Old Sebastopol had been a pretty town of piled white houses with pink roofs, neoclassical public buildings, and churches with copper domes painted gold and blue. It was laid out in a grid, with two handsome boulevards running parallel from Theatre Square to Nikolaevsky Square; most other streets were narrow and unpaved, and led off these two boulevards. It had been a favourite holiday resort – witnessed by the large number of taverns and inns – to which the huge naval dock-yard and careenage was a later addition and perfectly possible to ignore. There was also a large modern suburb on the north side of the main harbour, but Old Sebastopol had always ignored that, too.

It was a holiday town no more. On every street there was something to remind the onlooker of the presence outside the walls of a besieging enemy. Down by the quayside the activity was most intense, for ships brought supplies down the river, and boats crossed from the Old Town to the North Shore all day long, loading and unloading goods and personnel. The Grafskaya seethed with grey-clad soldiers and black-clad sailors, and civilian drivers and porters in various shades of dun. There were peasant women, too, in bright-coloured scarves, selling rolls of bread and tea and hot wine; and officers in greatcoats left open to show a flash of green or sky-blue or white, stepped fastidiously as cats over puddles and dung in their polished boots.

There were great heaps of supplies, jumbled together without apparent order: sides of beef, sacks of coal, heaps of firewood, iron bars, fascines and wickerwork gabions, boxes and barrels and bags of flour and bales of hay. There was litter – broken wood, rags, spilled oats, rusty cannon-balls, flotsam from the sunken ships – like a scum all along the exposed grey mud of the shore. There was a dead horse, slowly decaying, washed up by the sluggish tide, which it was no one's business to remove.

There were horses and waggons, gun-carriages, field pieces, stacks of muskets, boxes of ammunition; there were rough peasant carts loaded high with bloody corpses creaking up the hill towards the cemetery; there were litters and stretchers bearing wounded coming down from the bastions to the handsome old Assembly Hall, which now served as a dressing-station.

At the top of the town there were whole streets which had been reduced to rubble; others where individual houses had been smashed, leaving a gap like a missing tooth. Windows were gone here, a roof caved in there, an upper floor made uninhabitable, a wall shored up with timber. There were craters filled with water in the middle of the road from the mortar shells; cannon-balls and lumps of shrapnel embedded in walls. And all day long, punctuating conversation and thought, there was the booming of the cannonade, and the intermittent whine and thump of shells.

Kirov was kept busy, and when he was away from his ground-floor office, it gradually silted up with messengers and petitioners who could not be dealt with by the subaltern and two clerks he had been given to help him. The subaltern was a very shy man with the rosy, downy cheeks of youth, which glowed with painful self-consciousness whenever either Fleur or Lyudmilla appeared. He didn't seem to be much help to Kirov, though he tried very hard, furrowing his clear brow earnestly as he listened to some incomprehensible request from a veteran sergeant who'd been working the army to his own benefit for fifteen years, and who could ease saleable commodities out of the system with the dexterity of a gourmet slipping steamed mussels from their shells.

The first thing that Kirov had to arrange was the cartel for Richard, but it turned out to be easier than they had expected. A night sortie on the night of the 20th–21st had resulted in a young officer of the Vladimirskys being taken prisoner. He was only a cornet, so Richard was more than a fair exchange for him: the staff officer from Balaclava who came to negotiate seemed surprised and delighted with the offer.

Richard had nothing but his valise to pack, but the farewells were hard. Lyudmilla dissolved into tears, raised streaming eyes and wet cheeks to him, hung round his neck, begged him incoherently to take care of himself and to take no part in the fighting. He made vague and soothing promises in return.

'It's not our quarrel,' she said. 'Afterwards, when it's over, you'll come back? Promise me!'

Richard seemed to remember what she had plainly forgotten, that she was a married woman. On what terms was he to return? 'I'll write to you. And when the war's over, I'll come and visit,' he mumbled, and she accepted the tone of his voice, crying too much, probably, to distinguish the words. He detached her gently from around his neck, and turned to his sister.

Fleur wasn't crying, but her face was grave. She reached up and laid her lips against his cheek. 'Keep yourself safe, little brother,' she whispered into his ear. 'And don't forget, we're not on opposite sides.'

He hugged her briefly and let her go. Their eyes met. *Oh but we are*, his said. *From now on, we are.* He wanted to ask her to come with him, but how could he do that without hurting Milochka? And in any case, he knew she wouldn't come. The complications of love, loyalty and duty were too much for him. He picked up his valise and turned away from them, wanting only to be gone.

It had never looked like this from a distance, when they practised field manoeuvres on Hounslow Heath, galloping flat out in their cherry-pink pants, cheering, with their sabres glinting in the sun, light of heart as if they were chasing foxes over the Leicestershire Wolds. But foxes didn't make you love them. Foxes didn't look at you with drowned, tragic eyes, sawing at your heart as you went away.

The exchange took place at the bridge over the River Tchernaya by the Inkerman ruins, at dusk on the 23rd, shortly after the cease-fire for the day. Kirov was there to see it done, and exchanged friendly words with Calvert of Raglan's staff, whom he had met in London – he had come to translate and was pleasantly surprised to find it unnecessary. They chatted about the Carlton and a dinner they had both attended at the Mansion House and mentioned various common acquaintances; and then Kirov shook hands with Richard, and rode back to Sebastopol. If he had divided loyalties, he was an old enough soldier to know how to deal with them.

On the morning of the 25th Lyudmilla came flying into Kirov's office from the street, her bonnet slipping off the back of her head, her hem muddy, her expression wild. Kirov was dictating letters, and looked up with mild enquiry.

'Why didn't you tell me?' Lyudmilla demanded furiously.

'Tell you what?'

'You know very well!' Her head jerked round to the elderly clerk. 'Get out,' she snapped.

'You may go, Bezhkov,' Kirov translated. Lyudmilla barely waited until they were alone to turn on her husband.

'This morning when I asked you why the guns weren't firing, you said that perhaps the Allies had thought of something else to do,' she said fiercely. 'But I've just met Varkhin in the street, and he says that we're attacking Balaclava. He says that Liprandi's out there with our whole army, and there's a battle going on *now*!'

'Is that what he says?' Kirov said mildly, as though Varkhin had predicted a spell of wet weather. 'How interesting.'

Lyudmilla's fingers curled into claws. '*You knew!*' she cried out. 'You've known for days that it was planned!'

He shrugged. 'Menshikov was hardly likely to keep the army standing by idly while we were being bombarded. Anyone could have guessed he would attack Balaclava. It's the enemy's sole lifeline. Capture that, and we've got them.'

'No!' she shouted. 'You didn't have to guess – you knew! They've been moving into position for the last week, since the 18th, since before we left Kurmoye! You knew what they were going to do, and you sent him back on purpose! Now there's a battle, and he'll be killed, I know he will! You planned it all!'

She burst into tears. Kirov got up and came round the table. He put a hand on her shoulder, but she shook it off furiously. 'Don't touch me!' she sobbed.

'Milochka, you must calm yourself,' he said gently. 'Hush, stop crying. Just think what you're saying.'

'I know what I'm saying. You want Richard to be killed. You could have kept him here until after the battle, but you sent him back on purpose, and I'll never forgive you.'

'You're talking nonsense, my darling. In the first place, I didn't send him – he asked to go back. You *know* that's true. In the second place, how could I have known about the timing of the attack before I left Kurmoye? Do you think Prince Menshikov confides in the scouts? Do you think he confides in me?'

'You knew, all the same,' she said sullenly, wiping tears on the back of her hand, unwilling to be persuaded out of her suspicions.

'As I said, anyone could guess that there would be an attack on the harbour. It's basic common sense. But as to knowing *when*—' He shrugged. 'Besides, do you think even if I'd told Richard what was planned, he'd have agreed to stay here? He's a hot-blooded young man, and a patriot. He'd have *demanded* to be allowed to go and fight for his own people.'

'Then you should have kept him here without telling him.'

'But that would have been to cheat him,' Kirov said gravely. 'How could I do that? How could I prevent him from doing what his courage and loyalty, his sense of duty, dictate? Don't you want your young friend to live honourably?'

'I want him to *live*,' Milochka said, but the fire was gone out of her voice. She was only tearful now, not angry.

He touched her shoulder, and this time she didn't pull away. He took her in his arms and stroked her head. 'Whether he lives or dies is not in our hands. It's a matter between him and God. And there are many ways of dying, apart from being in a battle. He might stay back at the camp, out of harm's way, and die of cholera, or fall in the harbour and drown, or be kicked in the head by a horse. You can't protect someone from all accidents. What happens will happen.'

Lyudmilla felt there was a flaw somewhere in his argument, but couldn't put her finger on it. She removed herself from his arms, but not violently. 'All the same, you should have told me,' she said. 'This morning, when I asked.'

'I didn't want to upset you,' he said.

She looked at him suspiciously, chewing her lip. 'How bad will it be?'

He shrugged. 'God knows. We have no intelligence about their numbers. We don't know what force they've left to garrison the village. All we know is that this is our best chance to break the siege. Cut off their supply base, capture the road that leads from Balaclava to their camp on the Heights, and they must surrender. Then it will all be over – you should be pleased about that, at least.'

'If we win,' she said shortly. Then, 'Does Fleur know?'

'If she doesn't now, she soon will,' he said.

During the day, the most extraordinary reports filtered in of the ferocious fighting spirit of the English: of wild men in women's dresses who fought with devilish screams that chilled the blood; of horsemen armed only with sabres who attacked Russian heavy artillery head-on. 'They are mad, the English,' one young officer said, limping down the hill to the dressing-station. 'How can one fight madmen? It's not fair.'

The firing stopped at four in the afternoon, and some time later a triumphant battalion dragged into the city seven British naval guns, captured from the redoubts which had been set up to guard the Woronzov Road. Soon the church bells began ringing, signalling a victory. Excited crowds turned out to see the guns dragged down to the waterfront, and a rumour went round that Admiral Nakhimov was to give a victory ball that evening, with fireworks.

But later reports were more modest, and the claims were gradually whittled down as more eyewitnesses made their way back. The result of the battle, it was generally agreed at last, was a draw. The Russians had failed to take Balaclava, which everybody had guessed was the objective; but the English had failed to hold the road, and half the redoubts on the Causeway Heights had changed hands.

It was later still, after dark, in fact, when the English soldiers who had been taken prisoner were brought in from General Liprandi's camp, where they had been taken immediately after the battle for questioning. Most of them were wounded, some very badly, it was said that no single Englishman, however serious his wounds, had surrendered, which was considered much to their credit.

'We shouldn't be fighting the English,' said Lyudmilla's friend Lieutenant Varkhin. 'They are like us. We should be allies, fighting the Turk together.'

Fleur, who had hurried up to the top of the town to meet them, noticed at once that the prisoners were nearly all cavalrymen. They came in under guard, marching – or rather shuffling – two abreast, the walking wounded to the fore and stretchers bringing up the rear.

Fleur addressed the officer of the guard, who stopped and saluted her politely. 'Captain, you must allow me to accompany these men, and do what I can for them. I have medical supplies in this bag, and a docket here from Colonel Count Kirov which gives me permission.'

The captain looked doubtful. 'Very well, ma'am, if it's what you want. But we'll be fetching a surgeon up to 'em from the dressing-station, as soon as there's one free, and it's no job for a lady.'

'Never mind it,' she said firmly. She had an idea how long it might take a surgeon to get through his own casualties. 'Where are you taking them?'

'To the Old Admiralty Building, ma'am. There's a casemate there for the men, and rooms for the officers.'

'Very well. Thank you, captain.'

She stood aside to let the men go past her, searching for any face she knew. As they passed a torch on a street corner, she caught a glimpse of a pair of pink overalls, and fell in beside a trooper with most of his head roughly bandaged.

'You're a Cherrypicker, aren't you?' she said.

The trooper turned his head to peer at her with his one uncovered eye.

'You an English lady, miss?'

Other heads turned eagerly to the words – bloodied faces, pale in the darkness; dark shapes of bodies, striped white with bandages; bandages blotched dark with blood.

'Yes. I'm the sister of Captain Hamilton of the 11th. Do you know what happened to him? Is he all right?'

The trooper shook his head. 'I dunno. He was with us when we charged the guns, miss. I ain't seen him since.'

'Charged the guns?'

He reached up and touched his bandages. 'That's where I copped this packet, going into the battery. Coo, you never seen nothing like it, miss!'

'We heard some rumour that cavalry had charged a Russian

battery, but we thought it must be a mistake. We didn't believe it,' Fleur said, perplexed.

There was a murmur of assurance from the men nearest her.

'Neither did we, miss,' the trooper said with grim humour. 'The whole blessed Light Brigade! Straight into the mouf of 'ell we went, guns blazing away on all sides of us, miss – and Jim the Bear riding out in front, steady as a church, like it was 'Ampstead 'Eath on a Sunday.' He shook his head, but cautiously.

'Was he killed?'

'Lord Cardigan? I dunno, miss. Soon as we broke through the guns, I got 'it on the 'ead with a rammer by a Russki gunlayer, and that's the last I knew, till I woke up in the Russki camp.'

'He wasn't killed, miss,' said another man – one of the 17th Lancers. 'Last I saw him, he was riding back down the valley, just like he rode up it – straight as the Bank of England. I was on the ground with this 'ere leg, and he went right past me with a face like a stone stachoo.'

'But why did you do it? Who ordered it?'

'Lord Raglan, miss,' said the lancer, and then, 'That Russki general what questioned us—'

'General Liprandi?'

'Is that his name, miss? Well, he thought we were drunk. He says to us, he says, "Now then, boys, what spirits did they give you to make you charge us in such a mad manner?" And Wightman – that's him, miss, on the stretcher, with the smashed knee – Wightman says, "By God, sir," he says, "if we'd of 'ad so much as a smell of liquor, we'd of taken 'alf of Russia by now".'

There was a murmur of agreement and praise for Wightman's boldness. The trooper went on, 'The truth was, miss, we'd been standing to since before dawn, when Lord Lucan turned us out, and we 'adn't 'ad bite nor sup since the night before. And when we told him so, the Russki General said, he said, "You are noble fellows," he said, "and I pity you." And he sent us all up some vodka miss – a big tot each – and I can tell you we needed it!'

'I believe you,' Fleur said. 'But what a strange thing – the cavalry to charge guns. The destruction must have been terrible!'

'It was,' said the lancer soberly. 'I never seen so many men fall. When they took me, miss, it was nearly the end, and Ours was down to no more than thirty men. There was dead men everywhere. And the horses—'

He didn't finish the sentence, and no one else finished it for him. Troopers, as Fleur knew, grew very attached to their horses. Someone in the darkness sniffed audibly, and the Cherrypicker had a tear trickling from his one visible eye.

'That's how they got me,' another trooper said, 'when they shot my mare out from under me. She was eleven years old, miss, a light bay with a white star. I'd had her since she was four. I used to keep her star white with chalk, and she always—' He stopped and swallowed hard.

'I'm so sorry,' Fleur said helplessly. The trooper nodded, biting his lip. 'I'll come and visit you all in the casemate,' she went on, 'as soon as I've seen the officers. Are there any from the 11th here?'

'There's Captain Brooke, miss,' said the Cherrypicker, jerking his thumb over his shoulder. 'He's hurt pretty bad, though. Most of the officers took was too bad to move. They're still up at the Russki camp. They only brought Captain Brooke, and Lieutenant Chadwick of the 17th, and Mr Clowes of the 8th, and they're all in a bad way, miss.'

Brooke, of all people! she thought as she stood aside and searched for him in the passing column. Poor dandy Brooke, with his tight corsets and fine whiskers! Hurt badly? She could guess what that might mean. But he at least ought to know what had happened to her brother.

Chapter Twenty

She almost missed him, for he went by on a stretcher, and it was only at the last moment that she saw the fur-trimmed pelisse thrown over his chest and realised it was he. His face was covered with blood, some of it fresh, and some hardened to a crust, and his pink overalls were blackened in many places. He was deeply unconscious, and breathing stertorously, and she wondered despairingly if he would reach the Admiralty alive.

She was glad to discover, when the prisoners reached their temporary prison, that there was a Russian surgeon already there, together with two orderlies and a nursing nun. Fleur made herself known to them, and asked if she could help in any way. The notion of ladies nursing was not as unknown or as abhorrent in Russia as it was in England. The surgeon asked if she had ever worked in a hospital, and she told him briefly of her experience with the sick, upon which he welcomed her gladly.

He assigned her to tend to the less seriously wounded of the troopers. Understanding the importance of obedience, Fleur did as she was asked, and the next two hours passed without her being able to find out anything about her brother. The men were all garrulously eager to tell of their experiences, but none had noticed Richard specifically.

At the end of that time, Count Kirov appeared and took her aside.

'I think you've done enough,' he said. 'You had better come home to dinner or you'll exhaust your strength. Have you found out anything about your brother?'

Fleur shook her head. 'There's a wounded officer, a friend of Richard's, from his regiment, but I haven't had a moment to speak to him yet – if he's awake. He was unconscious when they brought him in.'

'What's his name?'

'Brooke. Captain Brooke.'

'I'll go and see how he is, while you finish here.'

'How's Lyudmilla?'

'Frantic. She's begun to wish she'd come with you.'

Fleur shook her head. 'It's no place for someone like her.'

'I wouldn't have let her come. And it's no place for someone like you, either. Finish what you're doing, and be ready to come away.'

He went out, and she returned to the bandage she had been applying to a leg wound. 'Was that your husband, miss?' the trooper asked her, with a sympathetic look.

'What? Oh, no, I'm unmarried,' she said vaguely.

'Oh, your father then,' the trooper nodded. 'I could tell by the way he was telling you off. Just like our old Sergeant Smith – you know, kindly, like, but stern. He was right, too, miss – you shouldn't of come here. But me and the lads is right glad you did, and no mistake.'

'Thank you, trooper. I shall come back tomorrow and see how you're all going on.'

Kirov returned and beckoned her away. 'He's asleep. You can come and see him tomorrow. His injuries are severe, but not grievous. Piragov doesn't think there's any immediate danger.'

'What will happen to him? To all of them?'

'The fit men will be marched up to Simferopol, probably tomorrow. The three officers are all seriously wounded. They'll stay here until they're well enough to exchange – or until they die. You know as well as I do the chances are about even.'

'Yes,' she said.

He led her towards the door, and made a curious grimace. 'The most serious problem facing us at the moment is what to tell Lyudmilla when we get back.'

Brooke was awake the next morning, but weak, and in a state of shock. He was amazed to see Fleur, and clutched her hand and began to weep. She had great difficulty calming him. It didn't seem the right time to question him, but remembering Milochka's tear-stained misery of the day before, she felt obliged at least to ask him, very gently, if he had seen her brother during the charge of the Russian battery.

'Right beside me,' Brooke whispered. 'Good old Dick! We broke through the guns, and he was there beside me, slashing away. The Russkis ran, and we chased 'em, like foxes. Then there was a terrible explosion. Must have blown me out of the saddle. Don't remember any more.' He closed his eyes. He was very pale, and his recent agitation had brought a cheesy sweat to his face. 'Dick was there. Good old Dick—'

'It's all right. Rest now, Captain Brooke. You're in safe hands.'

She sat with him until he fell asleep again, and then visited the casemate, where the men who were too badly wounded to march were lying. She asked if there was anything she could do for them. They all said that they had been very kindly treated, and seemed to want only to talk. Over the next few days, from them and from Brooke, she gradually pieced together a picture of the extraordinary events of the battle for Balaclava.

The problem had been that the harbour of Balaclava was far from suitable for the purposes the British army had put it to. It was half a mile long and at best a quarter wide, an almost landlocked lagoon surrounded by steep cliffs, like a tiny fjord, with the pretty little seaside village climbing the slopes in a charming tangle of gardens, vineyards and gay little villas with green-tiled roofs.

From there a steep and narrow road led through a gorge up onto a plain, two miles away, and above that the land rose steeply again to the high plateau before Sebastopol. The main army was camped on the plateau, the cavalry on the plain; and Balaclava, from which every bullet, blanket and scrap of food the army required must be brought, was down below them as though at the foot of a castle wall, isolated and inaccessible.

The French were camped well to the west of the English, out on the headland, and served much better by two open bays – Kamiesh and Kazach – through which they were well supplied. Having got themselves comfortable, they were very reluctant to disturb themselves, and General Canrobert so continually refused to support Lord Raglan's plans that he earned the nickname of Bob-Can't.

This aggravated the second problem that had faced Lord Raglan from the beginning of the expedition: he was horribly short of men, particularly of cavalry. The losses at Varna and at the Alma, together with the slow but relentless depredations of the cholera, had worsened the situation. He could spare no more men to garrison Balaclava than one regiment, the 93rd Highlanders, numbering about five hundred, together with a hundred convalescents and some Turks, who were an unknown quantity.

The English infantry camp was up on the plateau before Sebastopol, where Lord Raglan also had his headquarters. The plain below, where the cavalry – both Light and Heavy Brigades – had their camps was like a natural amphitheatre, an oval enclosed on all sides by steep hills. It was bisected longways by a ridge – the sort that in England would be called a hog's back – which divided the plain into two parallel valleys, known as the North Valley and the South Valley, and along the top of it ran the Woronzov Road. The English therefore called the ridge the Causeway Heights.

Six redoubts had been built along the Causeway Heights to protect the road and the approach to Balaclava. They were armed with naval guns and manned, since there was no one else to spare for the job, by Turks.

How much of this was known by the Russians it was impossible to find out. They had begun to assemble a large army to the north-east of the plain several days before, but Raglan had had no men spare to send out, and the Russians had therefore been allowed to assemble their whole army undisturbed. It numbered about 25,000 foot and 6,000 horse, together with horse artillery and a Don Cossack battery of heavy field guns.

On the morning of the 25th, Lord Lucan had turned out the cavalry an hour before daybreak, as was his practice. It was misty and bitterly cold, and the men stood-to in the dark, tightening girths with chilly fingers and grumbling comprehensively about Lord Look-on's unnatural habits. Lord Cardigan, on the other hand, was still tucked up in his cosy bunk aboard his private yacht, the *Dryad*, moored down below in Balaclava Bay. Lord Cardigan had been given permission to sleep on his yacht because of ill health, and as he disliked getting up early, it was usually left to Lord George Paget to deputise for him at this unpopular hour.

It was said to be Lord George who, doing the rounds with Lucan, spotted in the half-light that No. 1 Redoubt was flying two flags. It was the traditional signal that the enemy was approaching. No sooner had he mentioned the fact than the guns in the redoubt opened fire with a tremendous crash, shattering the quiet of dawn – the first shots fired in what was to become the Battle of Balaclava.

As the light grew stronger, the grey mass of the Russian army could be seen approaching in two columns, marching towards the Causeway Heights and the redoubts, which were manned only by the Turks. The English foot was two hours' march away up on the heights, and the only fighting force – Sir Colin Campbell's Highlanders – were drawn up across the gorge which formed the entrance to Balaclava itself, committed to defending the base camp.

There was little anyone could do about the redoubts. Lord Lucan tried a feint with the Heavy Brigade to draw off the Russians, but they were not to be deflected. The Turks quickly took flight, and within a short time the Russians had occupied four of the six redoubts. They dismantled No. 4, the one nearest the British position, and established themselves in the other three, commanding the Woronzov Road.

Now all that stood between the Russian army and Balaclava was the 93rd. The chilly mist cleared as the sun rose, and the morning brightened into a golden autumn day of crystal clarity. Down below, the harbour of Balaclava lay like a sheet of silver, reflecting the green and purple cliffs, and beyond it the lovely blue sea was calm as a lake. All around the plain the heights rose, long-shadowed in the morning sunshine, to the dark blue sky, and the air was so still and so clear that every sound travelled for miles, every shout, every clink of bit-ring, every stamp of hoof.

The mass of the Russian cavalry began to move slowly along the North Valley; and then a large force detached itself and came galloping over the Causeway Heights to bear down on the Highlanders. There was no time to get the men into squares, the usual way for infantry to receive a cavalry charge. Five hundred Highlanders in kilts and red coats and bear-skins, together with the hundred convalescents, formed up in a line only two men deep, to face three thousand Russian horsemen.

The story went that old Sir Colin Campbell, veteran of the Squares at Waterloo, went down the line saying to every man, 'Remember there is no retreat from here. You must die where you stand.' The men of the Light Brigade, watching from the western end of the Causeway, where they'd been sent in reserve, were adamant that the line was rock-steady, and never flinched as the grey-clad mass of horsemen bore down on them.

Perhaps their sheer imperturbability upset the Russians – it wasn't reasonable, after all, for such a thin line of infantry not to be afraid when they were outnumbered six to one by heavy cavalry. At all events, the Russians checked, and then halted as though uncertain; and then the Highlanders opened fire. Their minie rifles were far better than Russian muskets: every shot told. Horses and men went down, and the Russian line wavered for a moment, then advanced. A second volley. More Russians fell, and the thin red line yelled and surged forward eagerly, longing to get to grips with the enemy. A third inexorable volley cut down yet more horsemen – and sud-denly the Russians wheeled and retreated, to a wild, trium-phant cheer from the Highlanders.

Meanwhile, a detachment of eight squadrons of the Heavy Brigade – about five hundred troopers – under old General Scarlett had started across to support the Highlanders. They had only got halfway when the rest of the Russian cavalry came over the Causeway. There were about three thousand of them, and on seeing Scarlett's force, they halted and closed up into a dense mass, ready to charge downhill and engulf the smaller force. General Scarlett formed his men up, taking care to dress the lines as though they were on parade, clearly intending to charge the Russians *uphill*.

This extraordinary tactic, and the unhurried care with which they dressed their lines, so unnerved the Russians that they did not sound their own charge, but remained halted at the top of the slope, seeming unsure of what was to happen next. They were not left long in doubt. The English trumpets sounded the charge, and the Heavies went galloping up the slope, with old red-faced, white-moustached General Scarlett in front, riding so hard that he disappeared into the mass of Russians, whirling his sword like a dervish.

The Inniskillings and the Scots Greys galloped stirrup to stirrup, the Skins yelling their blood-curdling Irish howl, the Greys their fierce growling moan. They crashed into the Russian force like a wave hitting a rock, and fought ferociously, hacking away with their swords to left and right until their arms ached. Even when their swords broke they didn't yield, but clawed at the bearded enemy with their bare hands like madmen. To the watchers, the locked mass of men and horses seemed to sway back and forth like a huge beast; and then it began to surge backwards, up the hill. The Russians were yielding; then they were running, wheeling away to gallop over the ridge, fleeing up the North Valley towards their comrades at the eastern end.

Now was the time for the Light Brigade to join the battle and pursue the fleeing Russians, and put their cavalry out of action completely. But the Light Brigade did not move. Lord Cardigan would do nothing without direct orders from Lord Lucan; Lord Lucan would do nothing without direct orders from Lord Raglan; and he was up on the plateau, 700 feet above the action. He was watching as though from a grandstand position, but in touch only by the tenuous method of sending staff gallopers down with messages. The path down from the plateau was precipitous, narrow and crumbling, and a galloper with care for his own neck and his horse's legs could take half an hour to reach the bottom.

So the Light Brigade sat and waited as they had waited all morning, seeing others win glory while they were allowed to do nothing. Lord Cardigan sat before them in his gaudy, perfectly pressed uniform, mounted on chestnut Ronald, who was groomed to gleaming copper perfection. The men lounged by their horses, smoking their short pipes and grumbling to each other, the officers smoked cigars or ate hardboiled eggs and biscuits, and muttered about the pusillanimity of their leaders.

The advantage won by the 93rd and the Heavies had been lost. The Russian cavalry was safe at the eastern end of the North Valley, behind the battery of heavy artillery which had been set up. The Russians had also moved field pieces up onto the north side of the North Valley, and as they were holding Nos. 1, 2 and 3 redoubts, they could sweep both North and South Valleys with fire from the Causeway Heights, too.

Suddenly the Light Brigade saw a staff galloper appear over the edge of the plateau and start down the path. Lord Raglan was sending further orders.

'I said to Richard, "Who the deuce is that?" ' Brooke remembered, 'and he said, "It's that mad Irishman, Lew Nolan. Who else would ride like that?" You should have seen him, Miss Hamilton! That path was practically vertical, and he came down it as if his horse had wings. We all held our breath, watching him slithering and sliding and sending down showers of loose stones. I said to Dick, "It must be something important", and he laughed and said no, that was the way Nolan always went about things.'

Having reached level ground, Nolan spurred into a gallop, and pulled up at last, his horse trembling and sweating, before Lord Lucan.

'We saw him hand him a note, and Lucan read it over three or four times in that maddening way of his. It mustn't have made sense to him, because he shook his head and asked Nolan something, and Nolan answered – well, we couldn't hear what he said, but we could see even from that distance that he was being insolent. Of course, Nolan hated Lucan – utterly despised him. We could see he was talking to him in

399

that arrogant way of his, as though Lucan was nothing but a grimy subaltern!

'Lucan looked furious. He read the message again, and looked all round him, and then asked Nolan another question; and Nolan tossed his head in a sort of contemptuous way and flung out his arm, pointing down the North Valley.

'We couldn't make it out at all. I don't think Lucan could, either. He sort of shrugged up his shoulders, and then turned round and came trotting over to Lord Cardigan. Well, Miss Hamilton, I don't need to tell you about those two, do I?'

Fleur smiled and shook her head.

'They hate each other like a cook hates mice,' Brooke went on, 'and all through the campaign they'd been snip-snapping at each other like two pairs of scissors. But they're always perfectly polite in public, of course. Lord Lucan halted before Lord Cardigan and held up the paper Nolan had given him, and said, "Our orders are to advance at once down the North Valley. You are to lead the way with the Light Brigade, and I will follow up in support with the Heavy Brigade."

'I thought Cardigan's eyes would start out of their sockets. I can tell you, Miss Hamilton, mine were bulging a bit. They were the craziest orders I'd ever heard! We had no infantry support, no guns. Everybody knows – it's the first rule of battle – that you don't send unsupported sabres against artillery like that. Well, it was Cardigan's way to obey orders without question – and to see we did too – but this must have been just too much for him. He gave a sort of bark, and said to Lucan, "Certainly, sir. But allow me to point out that the Russians have a battery in the valley in front of us, and batteries and riflemen on both sides."

'Lucan just shrugged his shoulders. "I know," he said, "but Lord Raglan will have it, and we have no choice but to obey." And Cardigan said nothing more. He just saluted and rode over to tell Paget what was on.'

'But what do you think the orders meant?' Fleur asked. 'Surely from up on the plateau Lord Raglan must have been able to see how dangerous it would be.'

'That's what I thought. Richard said, "Raglan can't mean us

400

to ride against those guns. He's kept us in a bandbox all the way from Eupatoria. He can't mean to throw us away now." And I said Raglan must be able to see what was what from up there. And Dick said, "If you ask me, he can see no more than we can. There's something going on that we don't know about."'

'And was there?'

'I don't know. Down there, what with the Causeway Heights, and all the hummocks and hillocks and cols, you couldn't really see anything that wasn't right in front of you. I don't know what the Old Man was thinking about. There was some sort of a mistake made somewhere – and if you ask me, it was Lew Nolan that made it! He was a hot-headed devil, and he'd been fretting for action since before the Alma. He was full of mad-brained notions about what the cavalry could do in battle. As far as he was concerned, cavalry was all that mattered, and there we'd been, sitting all day doing nothing. It's my belief Raglan's orders weren't clear, and when Lucan asked what they meant, Nolan put his own gloss on 'em. Riding straight at the guns is just the sort of bottle-brained scheme he'd like. It's a certain fact that he asked to be allowed to ride along with us, anyway, and he went over and sat beside Morris of the 17th, who was a particular friend of his.'

The Light Brigade was formed up with the 17th Lancers and the 13th Light Dragoons in front, the 11th Hussars and 4th Light behind, and the 8th Hussars to the rear. Lord Cardigan took his place all alone out front, two lengths in front of his staff and five lengths in front of the first rank. He raised his sword, the trumpet sounded, he gave the order in a calm voice, and the Light Brigade moved off at a steady trot towards the guns and massed cavalry of the Russian army.

Sickness had reduced the numbers of all five regiments. There were only about seven hundred men in all, and the 17th and 13th had so many officers sick that they were led that day by captains. The brigade moved off in dead silence, trotting over the short turf, and the day was so still that you could hear the jingling of the bits and the creaking of the saddles, the soft thudding of the hooves and the occasional sharp clink of a shoe hitting a stone.

Out in front of them rode Cardigan, the living embodiment of cavalry pride. Tall, slender still in spite of his years, with his huge cavalry whiskers, his tight pink pants and his dark blue pelisse aglow with gold lace, he sat stiff and straight in the saddle, looking neither to left nor right.

'Even when the guns started crashing out on both sides, he never looked anywhere but ahead,' said Brooke. 'He might have been a mutton-headed old booby, but by Jove, he was as brave as a lion!'

Fifty yards down the valley, an extraordinary thing happened. Nolan, who was riding beside Captain Morris in the front rank, suddenly kicked his horse into a gallop, and slewed out of line, diagonally across the front.

'Captain Morris shouted at him to steady,' Private Michaels told Fleur, 'but I saw he was kicking his horse on deliberately. He cut right across in front of Lord Cardigan, which made me lord mad as fire, and then he waved his sword, looking at us and shouting, like as if he was trying to tell us something.'

'What could that be?'

'I dunno, miss. We couldn't hear, on account of the noise of the guns. And next thing a shell bursts on the ground right in front of Lord Cardigan, and a fragment near rips Captain Nolan in half, right across the chest. He lets out a 'ell of a shriek, and his horse whips round and starts to gallop back between us. It was 'orrible, miss! He'd dropped his sword, but his arm was still up in the air, and we could hear this terrible shriek coming out of him, right above the noise of the guns. But it's my belief he was already dead. Soon as his horse had passed through the 4th, it stops, and he tumbles out of the saddle like a stone.'

On they rode, the tiny band of sabres, kept to a steady trot by their general out in front of them, moving down towards the band of white smoke which marked the Russian guns at the end of the valley. The crossfire from the valley sides was cutting them up. When a man or horse dropped, the riders on each side of him opened out, and as soon as they had ridden clear of the obstruction, closed up again, just as they would have done on the parade-ground in manoeuvres. While death showered down on them, they kept perfect formation, but the body of horsemen was growing smaller and smaller all the time.

Halfway down the valley they came in range of the guns at the end, too. Round-shot, grapeshot, case-shot – now the men and horses were falling not singly, but in swathes, as screaming metal tore great gaps in the lines. Their pace began to quicken, in spite of anything Cardigan could do.

'When you're in that situation, you don't want to hang about,' Michaels explained. 'You want to get to grips with 'em, and the quicker the better. We cantered, then we started galloping, and there was no more lines. In any case, there was so few of us left by then, we couldn't keep formation any longer.'

'The 17th ahead of us started to gallop,' said Brooke, 'so we increased pace to keep up with them. Then someone let out a yell, and suddenly we were all yelling like madmen. Well, I suppose we *were* mad by then. It isn't a thing you could do sane. Men and horses were falling on every side. We in the second line were riding over the casualties of the front line. You had to keep swerving to avoid them. And then there were the loose horses.'

Cavalry horses remain surprisingly calm in battle, even when wounded, provided they can feel their trooper on their back and his hand on their rein. But once they lose their rider, they go mad with terror. A horse's instinct, when it is afraid, is to run, but to stay with the herd.

'So they don't run away, out of danger,' Brooke said. 'They keep trying to force their way back into line, or to get as close as they can to some other horse with a rider. Even the wounded ones – they just keep going, trying to get back into their place. There was one moment when there must have been five or six riderless horses galloping with me, their eyes bulging with fright, pressing as close as they could to old Oberon, spattering us with blood from their wounds. The poor beasts—'

He stopped abruptly, remembering who he was talking to.

Galloping towards the guns. So close now, the smoke was a pall, like twilight, and the guns' flashes were visible, dark orange against the darkness, a bellowing flame. And then they were through, the few survivors, through into the battery, and slashing through the dusk of smoke at the bearded Russian faces.

They slaughtered the gunners, and then plunged at the cavalry beyond them, who were so astonished at the whole business that they gave back. Some of them turned and fled, and the first line cheered their victory and pursued. But not for long: back behind the guns was the whole of the Russian cavalry, and of the front line of the Light Brigade only about fifty men had survived the ride up the valley. The Russians turned and reformed, and a mass of Cossacks came down from the flanks to support them. Then the second line of 11th Hussars and 4th Light arrived.

'Nobody knew where Lord Cardigan was,' said Brooke. 'We'd seen him disappear into the smoke right at the beginning, but we never saw him again. Maybe he was dead. Lord George Paget formed us up. We were going to attack the Russian cavalry again, and then we saw that their lancers had outflanked us and were closing round behind us, blocking our retreat. The horses were exhausted, and most of us were wounded, one way and another. Our only chance was to smash our way out immediately, before the Russkis had a chance to think about it. Lord George gave us the order, and we charged. And that was when I went down.'

'What happened to you?' Fleur asked.

'I don't know for sure. There was a terrific explosion nearby, and I was hit by the blast. I felt Oberon running out from under me, but I couldn't keep hold of him. I went down and hit the ground, and everything went black.'

'And Richard?'

'He was still in the saddle the last time I saw him. After that, I don't know, of course. But he wasn't captured, that I do know.'

So she still didn't know if her brother was alive. The odds, of course, were against, for even having survived all the way down the valley to the battery, they would still have had to ride back, on foundered horses, running the gauntlet of those same terrible guns.

And what of poor Oberon? The accepted wisdom was that a loose horse stood more chance of being hit than a ridden one. She would have liked to know, at least, that her dear, good horse had met with a quick end, and not suffered horribly.

The word was passing round that five hundred of the seven hundred men and horses had been killed, and even allowing for exaggeration, the Light Brigade must have virtually ceased to exist. So it was for this that she had nursed Richard through the cholera, for this that he had returned to his regiment: the maddest, bravest, most glorious, gallant, most stupid cavalry charge in the history of the world. And had it all been a mistake after all? She wondered if she would ever know.

She paid a daily visit to the men in the Old Admiralty, but there were so few of them she felt her services were wasted there; so she asked the surgeon Piragov if she might come down to help at the dressing-station. He looked a little doubtful, but Fleur knew that help was always desperately needed, and she pressed him gently.

'Please, sir. I am very used to bad smells and horrible sights. I have visited pauper hospitals in my own country.'

'Yes, I know – but battle wounds are different from disease and sickness. What you have seen here is nothing. There are sights at the Assembly Hall that chill even me.'

'You are chilled, but you go on doing your duty,' Fleur pointed out.

He shrugged. 'It *is* my duty.'

'Mine too – everyone's, who cares.' She smiled slightly. 'To be truthful, even I don't know if I can bear it – but I think I can. Let me try. If I can't be useful to you, I will go away without fuss.'

He gave her a weary, distracted smile. 'Very well – a trial, then. God knows I can use all the help I can get, and you seem a sensible, level-headed young woman.' He hesitated, looking at her curiously. 'These are your own people – the men you visit here. Do you care so much about the Russian wounded?'

'Russians are my people too, now,' she said. 'Yes, I care.'

'Then, by God, I pity you,' Piragov said quietly.

After that, her days were full. She walked down the hill to the dressing-station every morning, and in the evening visited the Old Admiralty on her way home. The sights she witnessed in the Assembly Hall were so dreadful that at first she did not think she could bear it. It wasn't so much the blood and mangled flesh and shattered limbs and hideous wounds, but her own pity for the men's suffering which almost overcame her. They were so brave – so ludicrously brave – and so grateful for anything that was done for them; and yet they had given all in the service of their country, not as free men, but as slaves pressed against their will. The first day she had continually to step aside and lean against a wall for a moment until her legs stopped trembling and the tears could be swallowed down. They didn't need that sort of pity from her, as she very well knew. They needed her to be cheerful and confident, so that they might have something to trust, to weigh against their own knowledge of their grievous mutilation.

Her dealings with the likes of the Blacks at home in England had inured her to bad smells – which was just as well, since the stink of blood and pus and corruption filled the rooms of the Assembly Hall so thickly you might almost have sliced it up with a knife. For the rest, she soon learned what to do to be useful, and to release more experienced orderlies for more skilled tasks.

She was not the only woman there. There were nursing sisters too, nuns who brought the comfort of religion to the suffering and dying. They were very well thought of, by both the men and the orderlies, though Fleur sometimes felt irritated by the fact that they put spiritual responsibilities before medical, and would pray with a man rather than change his bandage. But she told herself that Russia was a much more devout country than England, and tried to hold her tongue.

More to her liking were the civilian women – mostly soldiers' or sailors' wives – who helped out. They were tough, unsentimental and practical, and they understood the men's needs very well. Fleur soon had a very good understanding with them, and they treated her with a shy friendliness which delighted her.

The worst thing was how short they were of supplies of all kinds. Laudanum was so scarce that operations took place without it, and the screams and moans that came from the inner room, where the surgeons wielded their knives and saws, were harrowing, especially to the men on stretchers waiting their turn to be taken in there. Bandages were scarce, medicines of all kinds, invalid food – for many of the badly wounded men were incapable of chewing the coarse ration food which was all that was issued – even basic necessities like soap, nightshirts, blankets, bowls and spoons were hard to come by in the besieged city.

Fleur, along with the other helpers, toiled and made do; and in the back of her mind was always the thought: if it's like this for us, what must it be like in the English camp?

One evening a week or so after the battle, Fleur was walking home from the Old Admiralty, tired and depressed. Another of the seriously wounded English prisoners had died, and she was beginning to be afraid that Captain Brooke was going to die too.

His wounds were many and serious. He had multiple slashes to both thighs – the most exposed part of a cavalryman's anatomy when he was fighting men on the ground – and a deep sabre-cut in one shoulder. The blast which had knocked him from the saddle had embedded pieces of shrapnel in his left side and hip, and a larger fragment had smashed several bones in his foot. He also had lacerations to his scalp, perhaps also caused by flying fragments, and a large cut and contusion on the right side of his head. The surgeon supposed he must have sustained that when he fell, either by hitting his head against a stone or some other solid object, or by being kicked on the ground in the mêlée.

The more superficial cuts were healing well, but the deep

shoulder wound was not looking quite right, and Fleur feared that mortification was setting in. If that were the case, it would be extremely serious, since the position of the wound made it impossible to fall back on amputation as a last resort. Not only that, but last night Brooke had complained of a headache and a feeling of nausea, and today the headache had worsened, and was accompanied by episodes of double vision and delirium.

Piragov thought it likely that Brooke was suffering from bleeding inside the skull at the site of the contusion. Fleur asked him what the prognosis was if that were the case, and the surgeon had merely shaken his head.

Fleur had sat with Brooke for most of the day. She had grown quite attached to the cavalryman over the last week, for stripped of his mannerisms and his ambition to lead fashion, he was a kindly man with simple affections, the adored hero of a mother and two sisters, very fond of horses and dogs and keen on all field sports.

It upset her very much to see him enfeebled by pain, lying pale against his pillow, clutching her hand as though it were all that attached him to the world. He talked, during his lucid periods, of home, telling her about the orchard and the stream, his younger sister's wedding planned for the spring, the thoroughbred colt given him by an uncle which he meant to break in the following summer. Seeing his drawn face and wandering eyes, and the look of pain that crossed his features when he moved, she feared very much that he would not be seeing home again.

She reached the top of the hill and turned into Vladimir Street, and hearing horses behind her, stepped to one side to let them pass. It was a Cossack soldier, in his round fur hat, with rifle and cross-belt over his sheepskin *tulup*. He was riding a shaggy Cossack pony, and leading another horse behind him. Fleur stared in surprise, for it was a good-looking chestnut, no native pony but unmistakably an English thoroughbred, the sort that an English cavalry officer might ride.

Then she started and jumped out in front of the Cossack.

'Pearl!'

The mare pricked her ears and whickered. The Cossack, whose hand had gone immediately towards his rifle, pulled up with what was evidently a curse.

'That's my brother's horse,' Fleur cried in French. 'What are you doing with her? Where did you get her?'

The Cossack narrowed his eyes suspiciously, and answered her in Russian. Fleur had learned a little in the past year, but only enough to give simple instructions to servants; besides, the accent and dialect here were very different from the north. She didn't understand him.

'That horse,' she said firmly in Russian, 'is mine.'

The Cossack said something in Russian which Fleur had no difficulty in translating as, 'No, it's mine.' He then offered her a lengthy sentence ending in a question, and when she looked helplessly at him, shrugged and proposed riding on.

'No, no,' said Fleur desperately, 'you don't understand. Look, you must come with me – *come with me.*'

She fumbled in her reticule, and brought out a coin. She held it up to show him, and then pointed at the mare again, and then made beckoning gestures. He shrugged again, and nodded, and with relief she set off along the street, checking over her shoulder that he was following her.

Reaching the house, she ran inside.

'Sergei Nikolayevitch, you must help me. Please come outside. There's a man out there with my brother's mare. I must know how he came by her, but he doesn't speak French and I can't manage enough Russian.'

'What sort of a man?' Kirov said, getting up at once. Thank God, she thought, for a man of decision, who didn't waste time in useless expostulation.

'A Cossack scout,' she said, leading the way.

Out in the street the Cossack was leaning against his pony in an attitude of complete relaxation, but his black eyes were alert and wary under lowered eyelids. Kirov nodded to him civilly.

'You're sure it is your brother's mare?' he asked Fleur quietly.

'Positive.'

'Very well. Wait here.'

The Cossack straightened up as Kirov approached, and saluted. They began to converse, the Cossack respectfully, Kirov in an easy, friendly way, like a popular officer talking to a trusted colour-sergeant. The conversation seemed to be going well, both men having plenty to say, with gestures. Fleur watched, frantic with impatience and frustration, not understanding a word of it.

Then they both went back to look at the mare. To Fleur's surprise, Kirov examined her carefully, looking at her teeth, feeling over her legs and lifting her feet as though he were a prospective customer at a horse fair. Then they began talking again, and from the gestures it looked as though they were arguing over price. Finally they touched hands, and Kirov came back to the house while the Cossack began to untie Pearl's rope.

'I've bought her. I'll tell you all in a moment,' Kirov murmured as he passed. 'I must pay him first. He's a hard bargainer – I had to pay a good price for her.'

A few moments later the Cossack had ridden off down the road, and Kirov had summoned the long-suffering Bezhkov to find a safe stable for Pearl. She seemed fit and unharmed, only rather nervous. The only sign of her having been in the battle was a cut on her stifle, shallow and already half healed. Fleur made much of her before Bezhkov led her away, and then she was at liberty to ask Kirov what the Cossack had said.

'It's the usual story,' he said. 'After the battle there were loose horses everywhere, of course. The Cossacks round them up and sell them for whatever they can get – to them they're findings, legitimate spoils of war. This fellow had been on picket duty up on Cossack Mountain, above the Inkerman Bridge, and this was the first chance he'd had to come into town with his prize.'

'But what about Richard? Did you ask him about Richard? How did he come by Pearl in the first place?'

He placed one hand on her arm as though to steady her. His face was grave. 'Yes, I asked. I asked him what had become of

410

the mare's previous owner, and he shrugged and said, "He's dead, master, and has no more need of her." '

'How did he know? Did he see Richard? *Tell me!*'

He closed his fingers about her wrist. 'He found her all on her own, halfway between the North Valley and the Bridge. He said he thought at first that she must be lame, because she didn't try to run away when he approached. Then he saw she was standing over a fallen rider. He went to examine him, but found he was dead, and so he led the mare away. "She's a good horse, master, very faithful, like the Cossack horses," he said to me. "She wouldn't leave her master".'

Fleur heard, but could not comprehend. She searched his face for the truth. 'I don't believe it,' she said. 'Richard dead? I don't believe it.'

'It's true,' he said. 'I'm so sorry, *Tsvetoksha*. I wish I could make it otherwise for you. But it's true.'

And of course, she knew that she had been expecting it, that nothing was more likely. She bowed her head, and took a breath, and found her chest was aching. 'I don't believe it,' she said again, but she did. It was only defiance.

Chapter Twenty-One

Captain Brooke slipped into a coma and died. Fleur was very upset, much more so than she had expected to be.

'I hardly knew him, really,' she sobbed when she told Lyudmilla about it on her return from the Old Admiralty. 'I don't know why I can't stop crying.'

'It's for all of them,' Lyudmilla said with surprising acumen. 'Not just for Brooke, but for all those dear, good, brave men.'

'It's another link gone, with home; with Richard—'

Lyudmilla patted Fleur comfortingly. 'At least he died peacefully – not like some of the poor wretches.'

Lyudmilla, too, had been helping at the dressing-station. On the day after the news of Richard's death, she had come quietly to Fleur and asked to be taken down there and presented to Piragov. Fleur was doubtful at first. The cannonade was still going on every day, and the casualties in the bastions were horrific. Every day a procession of wounded came down the hill, walking or on stretchers, to enter the bloody jaws of the dressing-station and face the surgeons' knives and saws; and every day cartloads of corpses were taken to the cemeteries.

God knew, any help was welcome, but Fleur doubted whether Lyudmilla, who after all had no experience at all of hospitals or nursing, could stand it, and said so; but Lyudmilla was quietly insistent. In the end, Fleur said to her what she had said to Piragov about herself.

'A trial, then – but if you can't be helpful, you must go away without making a fuss. If you feel faint or want to be sick, you must take yourself outside, for no one will have time to attend to you.'

And Lyudmilla said, surprisingly meekly, 'Yes, Fleur. I promise I won't get in the way.'

To Fleur's surprise, Milochka had not only stuck it out, but had proved very useful and efficient. She did turn pale many times on the first day, and, like Fleur, had to take herself off for a few minutes every now and then to compose herself. But she went quietly about her work, not flinching from even the most horrible tasks. She proved wonderfully popular with the men, with whom she joked and even flirted in a mild way, raising their spirits far better than Fleur and the nuns ever could. She also proved to have an unexpectedly inventive mind, and contrived many expedients to overcome minor problems, inconveniences and shortages that everyone else had simply put up with.

Nushka was at first horrified, then angry, then sulky at what her little lady was subjecting herself to, but Milochka merely brushed her off like a bothersome fly, and when she encroached too much, told her off so sharply that the old nurse dissolved into tears. And when Fleur commented on her endurance and ingenuity, she shrugged and refused to be praised.

'The men are so brave,' she said. 'It's the least one can do.'

When she was not at the hospital, Milochka was usually to be found being very gay in the company of the convalescent Lieutenant Varkhin and a group of officers from the Vladimirsky and the Tarutinsky, promenading in the public squares, or sitting under the awnings of the cafés drinking tea. Her demeanour with them was not exactly flirtatious – she behaved almost in a sisterly way – but still it drew eyes, and some whispers. And it was evident that the men did not all regard her as a sister. Varkhin was a gentleman, and knew how to behave himself, but the others were not always so respectful.

Fleur was surprised that Kirov had not forbidden either of Lyudmilla's occupations, or even attempted to persuade her out of them. She felt sure that he didn't like it, yet he did nothing to stop it, only watching Lyudmilla sidelong with a small, grim smile. Fleur wondered if it had anything to do with the exchange she had witnessed between them over the report of Richard's death.

Ever since the morning of the battle of Balaclava, Lyudmilla had been in a state of miserable anxiety, saying over and over again that she was sure he must have been killed. Yet when she heard about Richard's horse, and Kirov told her what the Cossack had said, she became calmly convinced that it was not true, and that Richard was still alive.

'I don't believe it,' she said. 'You know what these people are like – they'll say anything. Isn't there a saying – to lie like a tribesman?'

'But why should he lie?' Kirov said.

'Because he'd been caught with Richard's horse, of course. He knew Fleur had recognised her, so he was bound to make up some kind of a story.'

'Then if his story was only a story, what do you suppose is the truth?' Fleur asked, perplexed.

'I don't know,' she said irritably. 'I expect Pearl was just running loose and he caught her.'

'He would have to have quite an imagination, surely, to make up all those details,' Kirov said.

413

Lyudmilla looked at him with narrowed eyes. 'Oh, I know *you'd* like Richard to be dead! But I know he's alive. I can feel it.' Kirov tried to reason with her, and she cut him off. 'In any case, no one spoke to your precious Cossack but you. For all I know, you made the whole thing up yourself. Yes, that rings true! It has all the hallmarks of your devious mind.'

Kirov's lips whitened, and his eyes glinted angrily.

'Lyudmilla!' Fleur said, shocked. 'You can't know what you're saying.'

She glanced at Fleur. 'Can't I?' Her expression became veiled. 'Oh well, maybe you're right. I didn't mean it, Seryosha. All I know is that Richard's alive, and I know that as absolutely as I know this hand. So you might as well save your breath, both of you.'

Fleur glanced at Kirov. He had assumed his most enigmatic look, but his eyes were dark.

'If it helps you to think so,' he said, 'then I would be the last to try to persuade you otherwise. But you might consider how Fleur must be feeling.'

Lyudmilla was at once contrite. 'Oh, I'm sorry! I didn't mean to stir it all up for you. But I can't help it. I just know what I know.'

On the 5th of November there was another great battle. There had been a great deal of criticism, ever since the Battle of Balaclava, of Prince Menshikov. It was felt he was not doing enough to bring about the end of the siege. He had an army – why didn't he use it? It was particularly resented that he didn't share the hardships of the townspeople, but lived in safety and comfort fifteen miles away up the Bakchi Road, well out of the shell-fire.

The criticism seemed to have goaded him into action at last. Before daybreak on the 5th the army assembled on the high ground by the River Tchernaya, just over the Inkerman Bridge, because scouts' intelligence had suggested that it was in this quarter that the English were weakest. The idea was to attack the French and English separately to prevent their joining forces, and to capture a position from which they could sap all the way up to the English camps, thus forcing them to abandon the siege.

The first reports that came back to Sebastopol were of a great victory. The Allies had been completely routed, and it was rumoured that the Emperor himself was going to come down from St Petersburg to give out medals. But as survivors from the various units began to make their way back, a very different story was told. The English, though outnumbered, had fought with their usual courage and ferocity, and had driven the Russian army all the way back to the Inkerman Bridge. There had been huge slaughter – ten thousand Russians were dead, maybe fifteen thousand, and hundreds taken prisoner.

There was panic and dismay in the town that night. The siege was not lifted. The siege, it seemed, would never be lifted. Many people thought that the English would storm the walls during the night; and if they did, many people thought they ought not to be resisted. Weeks of bombardment had worn down resistance, and the slaughter had been terrible. Of the fifteen thousand sailors who had been deployed about the bastions at the beginning of the siege, there were now less than seven thousand on their feet. The rest had been killed, had died of disease, or were lying wounded in the hospitals. Together with two defeats in battle, it made people wonder if the game were worth the candle.

But when daylight came and there had been no storming of the walls, no demand for surrender, spirits rose a little, and resolve steadied. After all, they were still here, the town was still untaken. And winter was coming – a hard one, by the signs. Already the nights were bitingly cold, and the rain must be making life difficult for the besiegers, out on the open plateau. Food and firewood might be short in Sebastopol, but at least they had a roof over their heads. The fortifications were strong. They could hold out for ever if necessary.

On the evening of the 6th, Fleur and Lyudmilla were in the upstairs sitting-room, chatting quietly while they rolled bandages – an everlasting task for the hospital. Kirov had gone to headquarters and was not expected back for hours. One of Lyudmilla's admirers, grey-haired Major Stepanobsky, had sent round a cord of firewood with a note begging her not to enquire where he had got it from. So they had a good fire for once, which was cheerful – except that it made them both think of the English army with only their flimsy tents between them and the chilly rain.

There was a sound of boots on the stairs, and both women looked up. It wasn't Kirov's tread. Then the door opened, and a greatcoated, muddy-booted figure stooped in and pulled off his cap. Pushka and Zubka jumped up, growling, and then changed their minds and rushed at the newcomer with revolving tails of delight.

'Well, this is very nice! I see you have every luxury here!'

'Petya!' Milochka threw down her bandage and ran to him.

'Steady, little sister, I'm as wet as a water-spaniel! There, give me a kiss! And now you, *petite* Fleur! Oh, it's good to see you!'

'And you, Peter Nikolayevitch!'

Fleur received his embrace gladly, though his unshaven chin scratched and his wet coat smelled horrible. She and Lyudmilla helped him take off his gear, and installed him in a chair close to the fire, so that he could dry his damp stockings.

'What a snug little place you've got here,' he said as they ministered to him. 'I don't know that I don't like it better than Kurmoye, or that cathedral of a house in Petersburg! When you've been in camp for as long as I have, you start to fine down your notions of comfort. And what a delight to see someone wearing a dress! I've got so desperate for the sight of a pretty face lately, I've started fancying my horse. Well, at least he smells better than most of my companions.'

'Oh do stop talking nonsense,' Lyudmilla said, bringing him a glass of vodka, 'and tell us what's been going on.'

'Just a minute, Milochka – first, are you hungry, Peter? It's a while before dinner, but we've bread and meat—'

'*Meat*? Not sausage? Fleur, I love you! Will you marry me? Oh well, bread and meat then, if you please. And if you, Milochka *maya*, can find one of my illustrious brother's cigars for me, I shall be a happy man. I'm pining for a smoke. Where is he, by the way?'

When the women had supplied him with his requirements, they settled down again, Fleur in the chair opposite him and Milochka on the floor, hugging her knees, with the dogs sprawled beside her, bellies to the flames.

'Were you in the battle?' she asked.

'I was indeed.'

'And did we win or lose? Everyone tells a different story.'

'That's not surprising. Everyone fought a different battle. I suppose you have to say we lost. We didn't achieve our objective, and we were driven back – if it hadn't been for the Vladimirsky covering the retreat, it would have been a rout. We took heavy losses, too – I don't suppose anyone has exaggerated that, at least.'

Between mouthfuls of bread and cold beef, he told them what he knew about the battle. It had poured with rain all through the previous night, and they had moved up into position in the dark before dawn, hoping that the enemy's vedettes would be less alert after such a miserable, wet night. The day, when it came, was one of those chilly, murky November days when the cloud is so low it catches on the high ground like fog, and the light is never better than grey.

The terrain over which the battle was fought was high and rough, with steep ravines and rocky outcrops; partly wooded, partly scrub and gorse, with tussocky heather and sudden hollows to trip a man. Together with the fog, it made it impossible to assemble or manoeuvre large bodies of men – something the Russian command didn't seem to have taken into account. The battle quickly developed into a number of individual and unconnected skirmishes, which largely negated the Russian advantage of numbers.

Communication in such conditions was almost impossible. Nobody knew where anybody else was, or what was happening, or what to do next. Figures popped up out of the chilly murk, fired, and disappeared again. Groups of soldiers, lost from their units, stumbled about in the mist, their fingers red and stiff with cold, the moisture dripping dismally from their noses, terrified that every bush might conceal an enemy.

'You could hear the guns, but you couldn't tell which direction the sound came from. You know how things echo in a fog? You thought every minute the mist would roll back and you'd find yourself standing right in front of an enemy battery, the perfect target with nowhere to hide.'

Smoke from the guns added to the confusion, as did the fact that the English were fighting, for the first time, in their greatcoats. 'Of course, they're grey, which made it almost impossible to distinguish them from us until they were at close quarters. No friendly red coats to shoot at – you practically had to call "friend or foe?" before you fired.'

But most of all, it was the fighting spirit of the Allies which told against the Russians.

'I tell you, it's frightening. They just come at you like madmen. They don't seem to care how badly they're outnumbered. You could have a single English soldier standing there all alone: throw a whole platoon of ours at him, and instead of running away, the bloody fool would stand and fight – yes, and probably win! There's nothing we can do against spirit like that. Our men won't stand unless they're sure they're winning, and they just won't fight at all unless they're all pressed together shoulder to shoulder like a flock of sheep. And if one runs, they all run.'

He held out his glass for Fleur to refill. 'One can't blame them, of course. What's in it for them, poor fools? Pressed for service against their will for fifteen years, and if they survive, what does that get them? Their freedom! What a gift!'

'What will happen now?' Lyudmilla asked.

'We bury the dead,' Peter said. 'Our losses are appalling – twelve thousand men, it's reckoned, nearly all our regimental and battalion commanders, and God knows how many senior officers. It's going to take days to bring them in off the heights. There's a body under every bush, and round the gun-sites they're piled up in heaps. And after that – who knows? Menshikov has simply given up – he said this morning he has no hope of wiping out the enemy, unless the winter does it for him. We're short of ammunition, short of food, short of clothing for the troops. We're unlikely to get any more reinforcements before spring, and morale is as low as it can be. If it weren't for the sailors and their officers, we'd have no hope of holding Sebastopol at all.'

'Oh Petya, then we're doomed!'

He looked blankly at Lyudmilla for a moment, and then smiled, a little bleakly. 'Doomed? Lord, no, little one! We'll just sit tight and see what happens. And after all, what's at stake when it comes down to it? If we're forced to surrender Sebastopol, if the Allies win the war, what then? There'll be some kind of treaty between the sovereigns, and everyone will go home. It won't make any difference in the end. That's the sad thing about it all – that when it comes right down to it, it's all for nothing.'

Fleur saw that it was true. She thought of Richard, of Brooke, of the troopers in the casemate who had marched away, and those she'd seen die, of all the pitiful wrecks of humanity she watched suffering every day in the dressing-station – and felt such a sense of hopelessness and desolation that for a moment she wanted just to lie down and weep. *Why do men do it?* She remembered her question, and Kirov's answer – *To make life more than it is.* Oh, the pity of it! And yet it was so beguiling, that dream of glory and gallantry and splendid, noble death.

Into this thoughtful silence, Count Kirov returned home early.

'Well, I see you've made yourself comfortable,' he said from the doorway.

'Seryosha!' Peter stood up and came forward with his hands out, looking really pleased to see him. 'Congratulations on your appointment! I hear you're making all the difference to the distribution of supplies—'

'You've heard that? What a lot of liars there are in the army,' Kirov said with a sour smile. 'When Menshikov tolerates – even encourages – corruption amongst the contractors, what hope have I of making any difference, let alone all the difference?'

'Well, I hear nothing but praise of you,' Peter said determinedly. 'And I'm damned glad to see you in uniform again.'

Kirov eyed him critically. 'You look and smell like a Turkish porter. I take it you were involved in the battle?'

Peter grimaced. 'You take it right. I'm looking forward – if such a thing is to be had in your little dovecote – to a long, hot bath.'

'I expect we can manage that for you. When are you going back?'

Peter laughed. 'Ever my hospitable brother! I have leave for five days, as it happens, but I can go and put up at an inn, if I'm in the way here.'

'Don't be a fool. Of course you can stay, if you want to. I'd be glad to have you.' He looked thoughtful. 'Actually, it might be very convenient. Nakhimov wants me to go up to Simferopol to sort out some problems at the depot there. I'd have to be away for a couple of days, and I'd sooner not leave the ladies unattended, especially when the bombardment begins again. If I can arrange to go while you're here—'

'Have no fear! I'll take your place with the greatest of pleasure,' said Peter.

'Yes, I'm sure you would,' said Kirov enigmatically. Then suddenly he smiled, and laid a hand on his brother's shoulder. 'Well, shall we see about that bath?' he said cordially. 'I'm sure you'd like to clean up before dinner.'

'I haven't smoked your cigar yet. Never mind, I'll save it for after dinner.'

'Have it in the bath, if you like. You can have another one after dinner. You'll want a shave, too. Did you bring your servant with you, or shall I lend you Ngorny?'

'Ah, the faithful Ngorny! What would you do without him! D'you remember the time he rescued you from that naked Armenian dancer in Pyatigorsk—?'

Talking comfortably, like brothers for once, they went out.

The cordial atmosphere survived the period until dinner, and the four of them sat down at the tiny table to a simple meal by candlelight with an expectation of pleasure. Peter talked and laughed and joked, Lyudmilla was at her spirited best, Fleur smiled and responded to them both, and if Kirov was silent, he did at least appear to be enjoying the conversation. He sat back in his chair and smiled genially, his eyes going from one to the other, shining and unfathomable in the wavering candlelight.

When the dessert had been cleared, Peter jumped up and said, 'I've a treat for you all in my kit.' A moment later he returned with a black bottle, which he placed on the table with a flourish. 'English wine,' he said. 'Or as you would call it, Fleur – port!'

'So I would,' she laughed. 'Where did you get it?'

'It was a bribe. One of the English prisoners gave it to me to let him go. Where he'd got it, I didn't care to ask. Stolen, in all probability.'

'Oh Petya,' Lyudmilla said reproachfully, 'you didn't?'

'Didn't what?'

'Let him go.'

'What, you'd have me take the bribe and then not perform the deed? Shame on you! How would our noble empire survive if you couldn't even trust a man you'd bribed?'

Lyudmilla looked confused. 'No, I didn't mean that—'

'Don't tease her, Peter. She has a refined sense of honour which you'd do well to emulate,' said Fleur.

'Oh, I'm pretty refined myself. I decided that since I'd caught the man unfairly, through the merest accident, I ought to let him go anyway.'

'And the port?'

'I knew I'd do it more justice than him. I believe he knew it too – that's why he offered it in the first place.'

'There's no doing anything with you,' Fleur said. 'You're utterly unscrupulous.'

'Well,' he said fairly, 'I told you that the first time I met you. We're all manipulators, we Kirovs. The difference is that I know it.'

It was a pity, Fleur thought in the small silence that followed. The words once said could not be taken back, and the atmosphere changed just perceptibly. Peter knew he had put a foot wrong, and tried to cover his tracks.

'Have you heard anything from your side, Fleur? Any news of your brother?'

Fleur told him about Pearl, and the Cossack's story. Peter was obviously sorry to have brought up the wrong subject, but said at once what Lyudmilla had said at the time.

'Oh well, I don't think you need to set too much store by that. After all, since you'd obviously recognised the horse, he was bound to say that her master was dead, wasn't he? Just to avoid trouble.'

'That's what I said,' Lyudmilla said eagerly. 'Anyway, even if he did find her standing over a dead soldier, there's no saying it was Richard. It could have been anyone. And that's two chances to one that he's alive.'

Fleur kept silent, not wanting to raise her own hopes pointlessly. Peter looked from her to Lyudmilla, and said, 'Well, why don't you find out? Even if it's bad news, it's better to know than not to know, isn't it?'

'Find out? How?' Lyudmilla asked quickly, her expression sharpening.

'Send a letter under flag of truce.'

'Send a letter to the English camp? Is that possible?'

'Of course it is. Letters are going back and forth all the time – especially after an action. We took a letter in this morning asking about English prisoners. And everybody's going to be out on the battleground picking up the dead for the next few days, so it'll be easy enough to send a messenger out there.' The two women were silent, and he looked a little puzzled. 'I don't understand why you haven't done it long ago. Surely Seryosha must have suggested it?'

'No,' said Lyudmilla. 'No, he didn't suggest it.' She looked at her husband slowly. 'I wonder why that was?'

Kirov answered without hesitation. 'I didn't want you to raise your hopes for nothing. The Cossack was quite clear about his story. There's no doubt that Richard is dead.'

'*I* doubt,' Lyudmilla said, her voice rising, 'I doubt – that's enough!'

'It's not enough. Letters pass under flags of truce, yes, but from commanders to commanders, not from civilians to individual soldiers. It's a war they're running out there, not a post office.'

422

'I don't see that it really matters—' Peter began, but Lyudmilla interrupted.

'If the letter has to be from a commander, you could get Admiral Nakhimov to ask for me. He's a sweet man, he'd do it willingly. But I don't believe you anyway. You're just trying to stop me contacting Richard.'

'He's dead, I tell you,' Kirov said impatiently.

'He's not dead! And I'm going to prove it! I'm going to send a letter, and Peter will take it, and I'll get a reply, you'll see!'

'Milochka, don't—' Fleur begged quietly.

'Oh hush! You've got no faith – but *he*, he knows I'm right, and he still tries to stop me! Don't you want to know why?'

'You're hysterical,' Kirov said calmly. 'I suggest you leave the table until you've regained control of yourself.'

'Yes, you'd like that, wouldn't you! You'd like me to go away while you think up more excuses and get people on your side! But I'm not hysterical. I know exactly what I'm saying. You're just insane with jealousy, that's all.'

'Have I reason to be?' Kirov asked in a deadly voice. His eyelids were lowered dangerously, leaving only slits of gold, hard and shining.

'You should know! Richard and I were friends, if that's something you want to be jealous of.'

'Yes, but how *good* friends, that's what I wonder?'

Fleur sat paralysed with shock at the things that were being said. It was evident that they had both forgotten the presence of anyone else at the table.

'Friends, good friends, what does it matter? I shouldn't think you know the difference anyway. Friendship's a closed book to you, isn't it? But I can tell you one thing – he's shown me more love than you ever have! And kindness. And I care more for him than—' She stopped abruptly, biting her lip. There were tears in her eyes.

'Yes? More than me, were you going to say? Or more than any of the others? Varkhin, for instance. Or Stepanobsky. Or Mirakov. Oh, the list is endless, my wife! Yes, I've let you go your length since we've been here, on purpose to see how far you'd go. But even I was surprised to discover what a slut I'd married.'

'Slut?' Lyudmilla said. She was white with rage, but Fleur could see the hurt behind it. To hear her husband say such cruel, unjustified things – her husband whom she loved—

'Well, whore, if you prefer,' said Kirov indifferently, as though they were discussing brands of coffee.

'Sergei, don't,' Peter cried, and his hand came up as though Kirov had offered to hit her.

Neither of them heard him. Lyudmilla's rage became reckless. 'If I'm a whore, who made me one?' she demanded lividly. 'If you'd ever been *half* a man to me, I wouldn't have had to look elsewhere, would I?'

Kirov flinched as though he had been slapped. His eyes opened wide, and for an instant he looked like a man waking from a sleepwalk to find himself balancing on the roof parapet. 'Not—' he said, but his voice didn't seem to be working properly.

Lyudmilla was looking at him like a desperate child, half defiant, half terrified, who has done something terrible to draw attention to itself. Some long struggle was going on inside her husband, and all three witnesses at the table were held shocked and immobile, unable to do anything but wait for the outcome of it. The silence was sickening. Fleur couldn't bear to look at anyone's face, and looked down instead at the table. And then from the corner of her eye she saw Kirov's clenched right hand slowly, deliberately, relax and uncurl.

'We mustn't forget we have guests, my dear,' he said in a voice utterly without expression. Then, 'I wonder if your English wine will be drinkable, Petya? I suppose it's been jogged about in your kitbag. Perhaps if we decant it carefully—'

With a choking cry, part fury and part pain, Lyudmilla got up from the table and ran out. Fleur started up from her chair to go after her.

'*Sit down!*' Kirov snapped so sharply that Fleur sat, hard, and looked at him. He smiled – or at least, it was meant to be a smile, but it was all to pieces, and the pieces hurt her, like broken glass. 'It would be better,' he said very gently, 'to leave her for the moment.'

And then he addressed a remark about a military subject to Peter, who answered as though out of a dream. Slowly, painfully, Kirov put together a conversation; and hardly knowing what it was they had witnessed, they let him, responding, as shocked troops do, to the calm voice of their officer.

Fleur woke the next morning with the hollow, oppressed feeling that shock leaves behind. She dreaded meeting the protagonists again, but when they all sat down at the breakfast-table, everyone seemed to be trying to behave normally. The atmosphere might be a little strained, but everyone was being extremely polite to everyone else, and no one was saying anything shocking or wounding. Conversation was carried on – a little haltingly – over the coffee-cups. Life could go on.

Cutting short his breakfast, Kirov went off to Nakhimov's headquarters to arrange for his trip to Simferopol, and Peter walked out with him to seek out some friends who were on sick-leave in the town, leaving the women alone to finish their coffee. It was very quiet – unnaturally quiet – for there was no bombardment that morning, and the absence of it, after so many weeks, made them jumpy. It was possible to hear all sorts of things that were usually drowned out: Bezhkov's voice, for instance, droning away downstairs as he dealt with the morning's influx of petitioners; a servant singing somewhere at the back of the house; a rustling, scuttling noise above the ceiling which must have been mice or birds under the roof.

'I wonder why they're not firing?' Lyudmilla said, not for the first time. 'They can't have gone, can they? We'd have heard if they'd gone?'

'Perhaps it's a cease-fire, because of having to bring in the dead from the battleground,' Fleur suggested.

'Yes, I suppose that might be it.'

'We shall be busy this morning. We ought to be off, you

know,' Fleur said a moment later. Lyudmilla was deep in thought, staring at the wall, her brow buckled with concentration.

'Mmm?' she said vaguely, then, 'Oh, I shan't be coming with you today. Didn't I tell you? Piragov asked me to go up to the hospital today to help there. They're short-handed.'

Fleur was puzzled. 'But surely they'll need you more at the dressing-station? I mean, with the injured coming in from the battle—?'

Lyudmilla shrugged. 'I don't question orders. Piragov knows what he wants.'

'Yes, I suppose so,' Fleur said. 'I'll walk with you part of the way, anyway.'

'No, don't wait for me, I've some things to sort out first – things to take with me. You go on ahead. I'll see you at dinner.'

They left the room together, going to their respective chambers, and at the door of hers, Lyudmilla turned suddenly to ask, 'What would you suppose the officers are most in need of?'

'In need of? What do you mean? What officers?'

'In the camp, I mean. I suppose luxuries are pretty hard to come by. I wonder what they're missing most?'

Fleur stared. 'What a strange question. I've no idea. Men usually like brandy and cigars, don't they? Why do you want to know?'

'Oh, I just wondered,' she said vaguely, and went into her room and shut the door.

When Fleur arrived home in the evening, she found Peter comfortably ensconced in the armchair by the fire, with the dogs lying at his feet. He was smoking a cigar, blowing the smoke out luxuriously and watching it climb to the ceiling.

'Where does Seryosha get these from?' he asked. 'The only ones we seem to get out there smoke like old horse-blankets.'

'The Turkish deserters bring them in, I think,' Fleur said

vaguely. He looked at her with quick sympathy, and heaved himself up.

'Here, you look as if you need this chair much more than me.' He obliged her to sit down, and loosened her bonnet strings with his own hands. Fleur was too tired to protest even when he knelt before her and began to take off her boots. 'Has it been bad?' he asked shortly.

'Yes,' she said. 'The casualties are coming in too fast – we can't cope with them. I wish Milochka had been there. We really needed her today.'

Peter gave an enigmatic grimace. 'Sergei's left for Simferopol,' he said. 'He went just after noon – said he might as well get as far as Bakchi today. He expects to be gone four days. Shook my hand and entrusted you both to me, sent you his regards, but not a word to his darling wife.'

Fleur looked uncomfortable. 'That dreadful quarrel they had—'

He lifted his hand. 'Not our business. Married people quarrel all the time. It's part of the fun.'

'Fun!'

'It's never as serious as it sounds to an outsider. In any case, there's never anything to be gained from worrying about married people's relationships with each other. My brother and his wife must work out their own salvation. Let me pour you a glass of wine. I suppose we can't have dinner until Milochka gets back.'

He brought her a glass of wine and brought up another chair and chatted to her pleasantly; but all the time a faint feeling of unease was wandering about inside her head, looking for something to attach itself to.

'It's probably the absence of the guns,' Peter said when she mentioned it to him, and she thought he was probably right. However, when it grew dark enough to light the lamp, and Lyudmilla still hadn't returned, the unease began to direct itself towards her.

'I expect there's a great deal to do,' Fleur said, trying to convince herself. 'But she shouldn't be allowed to tire herself out.'

Peter stood up. 'I'll walk down to the hospital, if that will

427

set your mind at rest, and make her come home to dinner.'

'Oh Peter, will you? Thank you. I'm sorry if I'm being a nuisance.'

While he was away, Fleur walked about the room, her feeling of unease growing, though she really had no idea why it should. Nushka looked in, and seeing the curtains hadn't been drawn, came in to do it herself.

'Is my lady still at that dratted hospital, *barishnya*?' she asked, shuffling across to the window.

'Yes. But Count Peter has gone to make her come home.'

'Well, I'm glad of that. It's not right, ladies doing such things. I wonder the master doesn't forbid her.' And she gave Fleur a reproachful look, for she blamed her for putting the idea into Milochka's head in the first place. Fleur made no comment. Nushka rattled the curtains across and went over to stir up the fire and put some more faggots on, and then shuffled out.

Fleur heard her go into the main bedroom, which was next door. Through the thin walls she could hear her opening and shutting drawers, but her attention was directed towards the street, listening for Peter's return with Lyudmilla. Yes, there they were at last! She heard Peter's voice, muffled, speaking to someone downstairs. He sounded angry. Then Nushka in the next room made a sharp exclamation, and began banging cupboard doors in an agitated way.

Peter was running up the stairs. He burst into the room. 'She wasn't at the hospital. She hasn't been there all day. She wasn't even expected. And Mikhal says—'

Nushka ran in through the other door, her hands twisting in her apron, her eyes wide. 'Gone! Her clothes are gone! Her things! My little lady's run away! Oh *barishnya*, whatever shall we do?'

Fleur's unease fell with a thud into the space prepared for it. 'Run away? Oh my God, Peter—!'

'I was just about to tell you,' Peter said grimly, 'that Mikhal downstairs says that when she went out this morning she was carrying a big carpet bag, and had a blanket folded over her arm.'

'But why didn't he say anything?' Fleur cried. 'Why didn't he stop her?'

'Why should he?' Peter shrugged. 'It's not his business to pry. I dare say he thought it was just things for the hospital.'

'But where could she have gone?' Nushka asked, bewildered.

Fleur remembered something. 'She asked me this morning what I thought the officers in the camp would be most in need of. I thought it was an odd question. Oh Peter, you don't think she could have gone to the army camp, do you? But why would she do that?'

'What did you answer to her question?'

'I said I thought brandy and cigars—' Their eyes met, and they both ran to the corner cupboard. 'The brandy bottle's gone!'

Peter opened the cigar box. 'Empty! The little wretch! She might have left me one, at least.'

'Peter, this is no joking matter! We can't just let her go off to the camp like that. It's dangerous – and it isn't proper, even if she means it for the best. Sergei Nikolayevitch would be furious.'

Nushka interrupted them. 'But if she's only gone to take comforts to the soldiers, why should she take her clothes, and her jewellery, and her icon of Saint Sebastian? It doesn't make sense, *barishnya*.'

Fleur stared, and her hand went up to her mouth. 'Not the Russian camp,' she whispered. 'Oh Peter, she hasn't gone to the Russian camp at all. She's gone to the British camp to find Richard!'

Peter groaned. 'My God, yes, you must be right. That's just the sort of feather-brained thing she would do. All that fuss yesterday about sending a message – now the cat really is in the pigeon-house! What can the little dunderhead mean by it? Oh Lord, it's all my fault for mentioning it! Seryosha will skin me alive!'

'We must go after her,' Fleur said. 'If she's gone on foot we might still catch her up—'

'She couldn't be on foot. It's much too far. She'd never make it, carrying a bag as well. She'd know that.'

They both thought of the same thing at the same time. 'Pearl,' Fleur said flatly. 'She's taken Pearl.' Yes, that would make perfect sense to Lyudmilla, not only to go and find Richard, but to take him back his horse as well. But if she gave Pearl to Richard, how would she get back? Would she expect Richard to find her a horse in exchange?

Peter said, 'Right, first I'll check whether she's taken the horse, and then I'll try and pick up her trail. I'll send Seryosha's clerks out, too, to alert the pickets. She's had the hell of a start on us. We'll never stop her now, but at least we can find out which way she's gone, and make sure she hasn't met with an accident on the way. The damnable thing is there'll have been a change of guard since she left. It won't be the same men on duty.'

'But Peter, would they have let her through? Without a permit or anything – a young woman, alone?'

'In normal circumstances, perhaps not. But as I told you, everyone's out there collecting up bodies and bringing them in to the burial pits. There's so much coming and going, and only half the pickets that are usually on duty. She's only got to spin them a story: it's not as if anyone can suppose she's a deserter. And there's always bribery as a last resort.'

Nushka was already weeping. 'Oh please, master, please bring her back! My poor little lady, out there all alone, in such danger—!'

'I'm on my way,' said Peter.

'I'll come with you,' Fleur said.

'You will not. What use do you think you'd be? You'll stay here – and if she should come back by any remote, heavenly chance, for God's sake tie her up and lock her in a cupboard until I get back!'

Chapter Twenty-Two

No one had seen her – or at least, no one would admit having seen her.

430

'Which is not so very surprising. We don't know what she may have passed herself off as, but no one's going to confess they allowed the Countess Kirova to pass them, now they know who she is.'

Fleur sat down, clenching her hands together in her lap. 'We must think,' she said. 'Are we sure she's gone to the English camp? Is there anywhere else she might have gone?'

'It seems unlikely to me. Where else is there? She'd hardly have followed Seryosha. And she couldn't have been intending a long journey on horseback like that. Besides, we know she's taken Pearl. Why would she do that, unless she meant to take her back to Richard?'

'Yes, that's true. But why did she take so many clothes, and her jewels and personal things? Even if she thought it would take her a whole day to get to the English camp, she wouldn't need all those things.'

Peter looked at her gravely. 'You know the answer to that, don't you?'

Fleur looked up. 'Surely not,' she said slowly. 'Surely she can't mean to—'

'She doesn't intend to come back. She's not going to see if Richard's still alive – she's going *to* Richard.'

Fleur shook her head in bewilderment. 'But she can't be – not like that! Not what you're suggesting! They're just friends – like brother and sister.'

'Oh Fleur!'

'But I've seen them together, playing like puppies. I know Richard was mad for her right at the beginning, but—'

'You are a simpleton,' Peter said kindly.

'Richard wouldn't do a thing like that,' she said stubbornly.

'He might not, I grant you, but she would, and he's hardly likely to turn her away if, as you say, he was mad for her. Besides, you never know what story she'll spin for him, of cruelty and unhappiness. She's quite likely to do that,' he answered her protesting look. 'Lyudmilla's tough. She'll do what it takes to survive – it's in her blood.'

'But she loves your brother!'

'Do you think so?'

'Yes. Yes, I'm sure she does. She told me once—' She swallowed. 'She told me he was the only man she'd met who excited her, who was different from all the others. She said she'd love him till she died.'

A peculiar look of distaste had passed briefly across Peter's face. 'Yes, a lot of women have said that about Seryosha.'

'I love Richard dearly, but he isn't exciting,' Fleur went on. 'He's a nice boy, but absolutely ordinary.'

'Well, perhaps after a diet of pepper and spice, the palate may welcome a little blandness,' Peter said in a flat voice. 'In any case, whatever you and I may think about it, it seems on the evidence that Lyudmilla has gone to the English camp to find Richard, and that she doesn't intend to come back again.'

'What if Richard really is dead?' Fleur said.

'I don't know. I suppose in that case she might come back. On the other hand, having taken such an extreme step, she may not feel able to retract.'

'Then we must go after her, and persuade her. Tell her we'll keep it from Sergei – that he'll never know.' She met Peter's eyes urgently. 'He mustn't know anyway, Peter! It would kill him to think that she'd run away from him. That awful quarrel they had—!'

He took her hands and folded them together, closing his own around them. 'Don't think about that. This is an order I'm giving you, little flower – you mustn't think about what they said to each other, or what they feel about each other. That's not our business.'

She looked up at him, eyes wide. How could she not think about it, knowing what she knew? Peter probably thought Milochka's outburst was just irrational, but she knew better. That little thing, she thought bitterly – why had Milochka made it into such a big thing, big enough to ruin her life and break her husband's heart for?

'All right,' she said at last. 'But we must bring her back.'

Peter was silent a long time, chewing his lower lip, struggling with some reasoning. At last he sighed and gave her back her hands, sat down opposite her, resting his forearms on his knees, dangling his hands between them.

'Yes. Yes, I suppose we must. I wish to God we might just leave her to her fate, the little nuisance, but we don't know for sure that your brother is alive, and if he isn't, we can't just leave her out there.' He looked up. 'The thing is, Fleur – and this is another reason that I'm reluctant to interfere – I won't be allowed to go. I can take you as far as the English picket line, but I can't take you into the camp. If you go, you'll have to go alone.'

'Oh!' She hadn't thought of that. She'd assumed that she would have his support and protection. But only a moment's thought told her that she had no choice. 'Still I have to go,' she said with a sigh. 'For his sake, if not for hers, I can't leave her to her fate.'

'I thought you'd say that,' Peter said, not sounding entirely happy about it.

He arranged everything for her: a letter of accreditation from Admiral Nakhimov, a white flag, and a trumpeter from the Tarutinsky, who tootled briskly and nervously every few yards once they got within range of the famous English rifles. He had also insisted that she take supplies with her – a blanket rolled behind the saddle, and food, brandy and some medical supplies packed into saddle-bags – in case she should be delayed or meet with an accident. He was plainly very unhappy about the whole thing, but whether it was because he anticipated some harm to her, or because he was thinking about Lyudmilla's crime, Fleur didn't know.

There was no trouble about passing the English pickets. Fleur offered the letter from Nakhimov, but they barely glanced at it – she was indisputably an English lady, and their sympathy was quick when they learned that she didn't know if her brother was alive or dead. Besides, they had other things on their minds.

'I wish you could have a word with your side, colonel,' the sergeant said frigidly to Peter. 'There are thousands of dead out there to be brought in – and still some wounded, too. But your side keeps firing at our working parties. It's not right,

433

you know – after all, it's your dead and wounded we're bringing in as well.'

'If I had any influence with our higher command, I would certainly bring it to bear,' Peter said, 'but you know what generals are like. They never listen to common soldiers like us.'

'Too true, colonel!'

'War is hell, isn't it? Do you fellows care to smoke? These cigarillos are nothing special, but a smoke's a smoke, when all's said.'

'Thank you, colonel.'

'Very civil of you, colonel.'

They'll be eating out of his hand in two minutes more, Fleur thought with distant amusement.

'I'd better send a man with you, miss,' the sergeant said. 'It's not fitting for a lady like you to ride alone out here. Besides, you might not find the way.'

'Thank you.'

'The Light Brigade camp isn't far off. They moved it over after the last battle – what's left of it. I hope you find your brother, miss.'

'Thank you.' Fleur turned to Peter to say goodbye.

'You may be faced with some unpleasant sights,' he said. 'I want you to be prepared for that. Your way lies through the battlefield. You aren't going to like what you see.'

'I'll be all right,' she said. Now it came to it, she didn't want to leave him; and his smile, too, was looking rather bleak in the dull November light. 'I'll be going, then.'

'Yes. I wish there were some other way. Don't stay too long. Do what has to be done and come away.' He took her hand and held it a moment. 'I hope you find good news of your brother. And when you come back, wait here with these good fellows and let them send for me. I'll wait for you back at our picket line. I don't want you getting shot by mistake at the last moment.'

'Yes. All right.'

She began to turn away, and he said suddenly, 'Fleur, you won't stay there, will you? You wouldn't let anything persuade you to stay?'

434

She shook her head. 'I'd come back, whatever happened, to tell you. I know what it's like to live with uncertainty.'

'Yes. I suppose you of all people know that.'

She was gone two days. Peter had perhaps the worse part, waiting with nothing to do but worry about her: not just her physical safety, but her mental well-being too. He knew what hideous sights she might witness, and that though she had been working at the dressing-station every day, a battlefield was another thing. When the day reached its warmest point, the stench of carcases was plain on the air, and the carrion birds came flapping down to dine.

He worried also about the possibility that, despite her promise, she might not come back. If her brother were alive and well, she might find herself tempted to remain amongst her own people. If he were wounded, she might well feel obliged to stay and nurse him. And even if he were dead, might she not feel that if she were to be useful anywhere, it might as well be amongst the English as the Russians?

He waited, smoked his foul cigarillos, and cursed Lyudmilla comprehensively for pitching them all into this situation. About his brother he would not think, keeping a rigid barrier between himself and any speculation about Seryosha or his future. One thing at a time, he told himself. A soldier's life had always been one of short intervals of hideous danger, interspersed with long periods of boredom, and no soldier survived who did not learn how not to think of the one during the other.

As it happened, it was not necessary for him to be sent for when Fleur returned, for he saw her from far off. He had been sitting on his horse at a vantage point for some time that day, watching the road. The cannonade had not been resumed since the battle, and all was quiet. The day was cold and grey, and he'd been watching the swathes of misty cloud pulling in from the south-west, knowing it was going to be a soaker when it came, and thinking idly that he ought to seek shelter soon.

Then suddenly he spotted two riders approaching far away down the post-road. He knew it was her before he could possibly recognise her; but soon afterwards he was sure. A woman riding side-saddle makes a different kind of movement on a horse, even from a distance. He was so glad to see her returning, that it was a moment before it registered that Lyudmilla was not with her – the other rider was a trooper, an escort. Closing his mind to speculation, he dragged out the white flag, which he had poked into his blanket-roll behind the saddle, and trotted down to meet her at the English line.

The pickets turned to him with relief when he arrived. 'Oh, there you are, colonel!' the sergeant said, lowering his voice to add, 'Miss has had a bit of a shock by the look of her. I'm glad you're here. She ought to be got home as soon as possible.'

'I'll do that. Don't worry, sergeant.'

It was more than a bit of a shock, he thought when he saw Fleur's face. She had a white, skinned look, and her eyes were wide and dark-shadowed.

'Peter,' she said blankly, and then stretched a hand out to him.

He took it, and it gripped his hard. 'Did you find her?'

'Yes. She was there, with Richard.'

'He's alive then. I'm glad for you.'

'Yes. She was right about that all along. The Cossack must have been lying after all.' A pause. 'She wouldn't come back.'

'No,' he said gently. 'I didn't think she would.'

She shook her head wearily. 'I don't understand. I don't understand anything.'

'Not now,' he said. 'Don't think about it now. First we must get you out of the cold. It's going to rain hard any moment.' He nodded his thanks to the pickets, and turned his horse, and she followed him blindly.

'He had my horse, Oberon, too – the one Captain Brooke had borrowed, do you remember?'

'Yes,' he said. The rain was catching up with them, was going to overtake them. He saw it approaching in a soaking swathe: the heights had already disappeared under it, and the light was as flukey as dusk.

'He offered to give him back, but I said he had more need of him than me. He was all right, though – not wounded.'

The horse or the brother? Peter wondered. Yes, here it came. He hunched into his collar, and his horse flinched and laid back its ears as the cold soaking mizzle overtook them. In that instant he decided not to take her immediately back to the city. They were about equidistant at present from the city and from the evacuated Tartar village where he and some other officers were camped. He had a cottage there which he shared with a major of the Tarutinsky. At the house in the city there would be too many people fussing and exclaiming and asking questions.

He would take her to the cottage, at least for tonight. The major would find himself another billet for one night, and there would be food and brandy and tea and a fire – all they needed. Fleur would be able to sit quietly and talk to him in her own time and at her own pace. Tomorrow would be soon enough to face up to the future. Tonight she needed to escape.

She rode beside him in silence, seeming not to notice her surroundings, her eyes blank, deep in thought. She followed without question when he turned off the post-road onto the track that led up towards the Old City Heights, where the village was. She didn't even seem to notice the rain, though soaked strands of hair were conducting the water over her face like rivers of tears. As they climbed, they rode into the low cloud, and it closed about them in a white fog. It was unnaturally quiet, except for the sodden thud of the horses' hooves on the soaked turf, and the occasional yark of a crow hidden from them in the mist – a chilly, upland sound.

Only when they were challenged by the Cossack sentry did she come to herself, and gaze about her with startled eyes. Catching Peter's look, she refrained from speaking until they had passed on. Then she said, 'Where are you taking me?'

'To my billet. I've a place here – a peasant's cottage, hardly more than a hut, really, but it's shelter. We can get warm and dry our clothes.' She seemed about to question further, and he added quickly, 'I could do with some hot tea, couldn't you?'

437

'Oh, tea!' she said, as though it were some rare dream of heaven, and said no more.

The major had accommodatingly removed himself and his gear, though the fire was bright in the tiny, two-roomed cottage and he had already taken off his boots in anticipation of a quiet night. But no one could mistake the evidence of shock in Fleur's face, and she was wet through and beginning to shiver. What the major thought of the situation he didn't vouchsafe, and Peter didn't think it necessary to offer much explanation.

The important thing was that within half an hour he had got Fleur installed before the fire, with her outer clothes and boots off, her feet propped up on a log to present the soles of her stockings to the flames. He had unpinned her hair and rubbed her head briskly with a towel, and had got a first cup of hot tea into her. She was now sitting, steaming lightly, with her hands around her second cup, looking much less white, if somewhat more puzzled.

'Why did you bring me here?' she asked at last, and he thought it prudent to lie.

'It was closer. The rain came on, and it was getting dark. I wanted to get you to shelter before we both drowned.'

She accepted his explanation, though he suspected it was mainly because she was thinking of other things. After a moment she said, 'I wish they had as much comfort as this in the English camp. The conditions there are appalling, Peter. The tents are so flimsy, and some of them are just worn into holes, and the troopers have no winter clothes – they simply haven't arrived. And the horses have no shelter at all, and they're so thin! What's going to happen when it gets colder? They'll die if they're left out there like that.'

He had no answer, of course.

'There were so few of them left! I know Brooke told me about that charge against the guns, and of course we'd heard about the terrible slaughter, but numbers don't really mean anything like that, in isolation. It's when you see the pitiful

438

remnant that you realise. The Light Brigade has almost ceased to exist. Richard was lucky,' she added quietly. 'Of his troop, only two men came back.'

'How was he?' Peter asked after a moment.

She looked at him suddenly, her eyes widening. 'He has *lice*,' she said in a shocked voice. 'He warned me off, when I went to embrace him. They all have them – they have to pick them off every morning – and bugs, and fleas. But Milochka didn't seem to care. She said there were some things you just had to put up with.'

She shook her head. 'I just don't understand her. It's cold, and wet, and the mud is a foot deep already in some places. The latrines won't drain properly, and they have nowhere to dry their clothes. They have nothing, no comforts – hardly even the bare necessities. Yet she wants to stay with him. She says she can help him. She's going to show him how to build a shelter out of stones and mud. How would she know that?'

Peter smiled grimly. 'The Tartars do it that way. Probably a villager told her. I told you she was tough.'

'Yes, she is,' Fleur said thoughtfully. 'I've been wrong about her before. I didn't think she would be able to stand the sights at the dressing-station, but she went on quietly day after day doing her work there without flinching. And now she's preparing to take care of Richard, even though it means living in the mud like a pauper. With *lice*, Peter! What would her father say?'

'And your brother's willing to let her?'

She sighed. 'He seems just happy to have her there. I was wrong about that, too. There is something – very strong between them. Richard's arm's in a sling: he hurt his shoulder in the charge when a shell exploding knocked him out of the saddle. It was sprained quite badly, and he's been managing one-handed, but now Lyudmilla means to do everything for him.'

He gave her some more tea, with a good splash of brandy in it. After a moment she went on, 'But if he loves her, surely he can't want her to live in conditions like that?'

'What's the alternative? For her to go back to her husband?

If he's in love with her, that would be even worse. And besides, from what I know of both of them, it will be Milochka who makes the decisions, not Richard.'

'I think you're right. She's organising the whole camp. Her energy is astonishing, and the way she sees round problems. She's already got the men to pool their rations and take turns at cooking, to save firewood. Nobody thought of that before. They've all been trying to cook their own in separate billycans – except that more often than not it was too much trouble, and they just ate their pork raw.'

'She's quite a woman,' Peter said with a private smile. He could imagine Lyudmilla's impatience with muddle and discomfort. 'There's a lot of her father in her.'

'But what are we going to tell your brother?' Fleur said, coming to the heart of her trouble. 'When he comes back from Simferopol, expecting to find her there – how do we tell him she ran off to Richard the moment his back was turned?'

'We just tell him,' Peter said, watching her carefully. There were things he hoped would not occur to her. 'How he copes with it is his affair.'

She was thinking. 'Perhaps she may change her mind. Perhaps after a few days of cold and wet and awful food, she might find she wants to come home. Or Richard might send her back, rather than let her suffer those conditions. Oh Peter, it's terrible! How can they let our men live like that? They don't even have enough water to wash with. Richard lies down in the same shirt he's worn all day, and the day before! Well, perhaps Milochka may find it's not so glamorous after all. And yet—'

'And yet what?'

'I keep wondering, what could it have been that drove her to it? She had everything: she married the man of her choice, she had wealth, position, a title – any woman would have given her hair to be in Milochka's shoes.' Peter looked a little wry at that. 'And if she doesn't come back, she loses it all.' And how could it be worth it, for that one little thing?

'We can't know how things seem to other people. I've never

had the impression that her relationship with Seryosha was a particularly happy one.' He paused and went on carefully, 'He isn't an easy man to live with.'

She looked shocked. 'But he is! He's kind and clever and sensitive—' She stopped, the thoughts passing quite visibly across her face. Her eyes filled with tears, and he felt angry that she should feel pity for everyone else sooner than herself, when it was she, most of all, who had been duped and exploited. 'Everything's as bad as it can be,' she said at last. 'I don't know what to do.'

'For the moment,' he said, 'you'll do nothing. For the moment, you are going to take off that damp dress and get into bed there, and I'm going to make you a hot toddy to send you off to sleep.' He saw the doubt in her eyes, and smiled. 'Don't worry, I shan't offend your modesty. I shall stay here by the fire and keep my back firmly turned. You just call out to me when you're safely under the blankets.'

She hesitated a moment longer, and then said, 'Yes, all right. Thank you, Peter. You're very kind to me.'

'Not at all,' he said firmly. 'Off you go, get out of those wet things.'

He pushed the kettle back over the flames and built up the fire underneath, and when it began to boil, made the toddy. And all the while he listened to the maddeningly indistinct sounds she made behind him, the quiet tide of her breathing, and the soft susurrus of falling garments. His every sense was painfully heightened, his nerves stretched taut, his mind filled with images of her. He heard her climb onto the cot, heard her naked feet leave the floor, heard the creak of the straw in the mattress as she lay down, heard her draw the blankets up over her. Yet when she called his name softly, he jumped and bit his tongue.

He turned painfully. She had pulled the blankets up to her neck, but one bare arm was outside them. Her hair was damp and tangled, brown-gold like seaweed, on the canvas pillow. A lightning visual inventory of the discarded clothes told him that she had got down to her shift, and he felt hot and cold at the thought of her near-nakedness.

441

Her pale face looked more apologetic than anxious. 'Everything seemed damp, in the end,' she said.

'Yes,' he managed to say. 'I'll fix something up, prop them up near the fire somehow. They'll be dry by the morning. You drink this, now, while it's hot.'

'But what about you?'

'What about me? Oh, don't worry, I'll do very well in the chair.'

He came over to her with the tea-glass, and she got up onto her elbow to take it, somehow keeping the blanket over her other shoulder. He smiled. 'You look about twelve years old,' he said. 'A little tangle-haired brat.'

'I didn't think to bring a brush with me,' she said meekly. She sipped the toddy, and coughed a little, making him laugh softly.

'Just like the first time you tasted vodka, do you remember? And you were too proud to admit you hated it. You insisted on drinking it all!'

'Yes, I remember.'

'I have a comb with me, in my housewife. Will you let me untangle your hair for you? You'll sleep better for it, I think,' he said.

She didn't say yes or no, but her eyes were consenting. He fetched the comb and sat on the edge of the bed behind her. Below her bare shoulders, her white shift disappeared into the shadows of the bedclothes. He discovered his hands were trembling, and had to pause a moment to control them. Then he put one hand on the back of her head, and she tilted it forward obediently, and the wet hair slid away from her neck, exposing the bare, tender nape of it.

Oh God! he thought, and swallowed. 'Tell me if I hurt you.' He took up a wet hank, and concentrated hard on getting the comb through its tangles without pulling at her scalp; and gradually his heart slowed down to its normal rate, and he even found the process soothing. With her back to him, she had found the courage to let go of the blankets, the more easily to manage her glass; and when she finished the drink, she drew up her knees and clasped her arms round them lightly, resting against them. The little room was warm now, the firelight making it a rosy cave, and the only sound was the spitting and crackling of the fire, and the occasional spatter of raindrops blown against the window. The sense of safety and intimacy was almost tangible to him. Did she feel it too? he wondered.

'Can I ask you something?' she said at last. Her voice sounded easy, relaxed.

'Of course,' he said.

'It's about the Cossack, the one who found Pearl.'

'Yes?'

'I keep thinking about it – seeing the incident in my mind's eye over again – trying to work out from their expressions what was said. And I keep wondering—'

'Yes?'

'Well, whether there was any truth in what Lyudmilla suspected. If she did suspect it – of course she may only have said it to torment. But she said she wouldn't be surprised if Sergei had made the whole thing up.'

'I think nothing is more likely,' Peter said calmly.

She turned her head a little in surprise, and he pushed it back gently. 'No, don't move or I'll pull you.'

'But – really? Do you really think so? Why would he do that?'

'To goad her. To see what she would do. And I think she did exactly what he expected.'

'No, surely not,' she said appealingly.

'Why do you think he let her go about with that group of officers, if not to tempt her into indiscretion?'

'How did you know about them?'

'When I came to the house the other day, it wasn't the first time I'd been in Sebastopol. I've seen her myself, to say nothing of the rumours I've been hearing up at the camp.' Soldiers were crude beasts, he thought. There was more than one who speculated coarsely on why Kirov's young wife ran around with other officers closer to her own age. 'And believe me, if I'd been hearing them, so had he. Why do you think he went away like that? He's been bending her like a twig, to see

443

if she'd snap. And the thing about a twig is that, however sappy it is, if you bend it far enough, it will always eventually break.'

'But *why* should he?' she insisted, puzzled.

Oh, how to explain to her, who was so innocent, the nature of sexual jealousy? And yet, of course, it was not only that. 'I've told you before, my brother's a strange, unhappy man. He could never have enough love and devotion from anyone. Whoever it was, he always tested them, and when they passed the test, he'd set a harder one, and then a harder one; until at last they either failed, or refused to be tried any more. And then he'd shake his head sadly at them and say, "There, I knew it all along. I knew you'd fail me."'

She was a long time silent. 'I can't believe that. It can't be true,' she said.

What do you think he's been doing to you since you first met him? But he didn't say it aloud. Instead he laid the last hank of untangled hair on her neck and said, 'There, it's all done now. And the little bits here, by your ear, are already dry. They're even beginning to curl.'

He took a fine frond of hair and wound it round his fingers and released it a pleasingly springy corkscrew. She kept very still. Her bare shoulder was made rosy by the firelight. He could hear her breathing, light and rapid. He leaned closer and laid his lips to the involuted shell of her ear. He placed his hands on her shoulders, and let his lips drift to her cheek, and then the warm and throbbing place under her jaw. He felt the tension of her body through his hands, but it was not a rejecting sort of rigidity. It felt more like curiosity, as though her body were listening to an unknown language and trying to make sense of it.

He kissed her neck, her shoulder; lifted the damp hair and kissed the nape of her neck, and she shuddered. He reached round her and took away the empty glass still clutched in her fingers, and then with gentle steady pressure, made her lie down. Now she looked up at him, faintly apprehensive, yet, on the whole, trustful. She watched his face like someone waiting to be taught by an instructor something new and rather dangerous, like tightrope walking.

'Fleur?' he said. He hadn't meant it to come out as a question.

'Yes,' she said, and it sounded like an answer, like consent.

He drew his fingers down the side of her neck and over the fragile bones at the base of it. She watched him, her lips slightly parted, breathing lightly. He bent and kissed the hollow of her collar-bones, and then her cheek. He saw the enquiry in her eyes, and smiled to it. 'Fleur,' he said again.

'Yes?' she whispered.

Then he kissed her, very lightly, feeling the quality of surprise, the hesitancy of the lips under his that didn't know what they were supposed to do. He kissed again, and again, softly, accustoming her. Never kissed before? one part of his mind asked, surprised. So beautiful, and still unkissed? Oh Seryosha, what a lot you have to answer for!

He felt her beginning to like it, beginning to grow confident. He let one hand brush as though accidentally against the side of her breast, then gently, carefully move to cover it. She gasped against his mouth; her nipple hardened against his palm and by an immense effort of will he kept quite still. When he lifted his mouth from hers a moment later, her lips lingered regretfully. He lifted his head, and she looked up at him with drowned, questioning eyes.

'What is it, my love?' he asked her tenderly. His hand was still over her breast. He moved it slowly, and she drew a little breath against her teeth, like a child who had recently been crying. He saw she was not afraid, only dubious, and he wanted her so badly he dared to go on. 'It's cold out here,' he said, smiling, making it almost a joke – two good friends, comfortable together. 'May I get in with you, under the covers? For comfort?'

She looked at him searchingly, and yet he saw she had already consented. The question was hardly needed. She trusted him. She wanted the answers she guessed he had for her.

Quickly, quickly now, almost in a panic lest he lose the moment, and thanking God he had taken his boots off earlier,

445

he shrugged off his coat and waistcoat, removed his overalls and stockings; and in his shirt only, slid into the bed beside her. She was rigid under the blankets, though he guessed it was more with surprise than resistance. He was rigid from quite different causes. He forced himself to hold her quietly in his arms until the warmth that built up under the covers made her relax. He put his lips to her cheek, and to his gratification she turned her head to give him her lips with every appearance of pleasure. *All right then*, he thought, almost weak with relief; *it's all right.*

He kissed her, and with his free hand, caressed her shoulder and breast, and this time she turned into the touch, seeking the sensation that was so new and extraordinary to her. He sensed that she wanted to speak, and was glad of it – he had never given and taken love in silence. He was a man who needed words, too. He said, 'What is it, then, Fleur? Tell me? Is it good? Does it feel good to you?'

'Yes,' she whispered. Not ashamed, only shy. Her nipple was stiff and eager under his fingers, and her unaccustomed mind didn't know how to think about that. 'Is it—?'

'Is it what, my darling?' He anticipated for her. 'Is it all right? Is that what you want to ask?' Nod. 'Of course it is. You can tell, can't you? Your body knows it's right. *You* know, don't you?'

'Yes,' again, still a little doubtful, but not resisting. It was so pleasant, she wanted it to go on for ever, and when his hand left her breast she felt only disappointment.

But it was at her waist now, spanning the smooth nakedness of her waist and belly. 'You're so beautiful,' he told her, almost in agony. He caressed her slowly, and her skin seemed to flutter in the wake of his firm, warm hand. She thought of the way a cat arches up under stroking fingers, understanding perfectly now. Only when his delicately trailing fingers reached her most private place, the forbidden place, she felt obliged to protest, albeit reluctantly.

'Peter! Don't!'

'No, no, be still!' he said, his mouth to her ear, his fingers moving softly. 'Let me.'

'I can't. Please. I can't.'

But he felt the enquiry under the words. He laid his hand innocently over the soft mound and kept it still. 'You can. Let me. Just let me. I will make such pleasure for you, my dear love.'

It was forbidden, that place, not even to be thought about, far less spoken; so forbidden it had no name in her vocabulary; unseen, folded away in darkness, blind as something born in darkness and never brought into the light. She knew nothing about it. She wanted to protest – or rather felt she ought to protest – but he laid his lips on hers again, and she felt she could never have enough of the warm, astonishing pleasure of kissing him. And so when the still hand in the darkness moved again, she let it.

Then she drew a sharp breath, pulled her mouth away from his, the better to consider what was happening to her. He lifted his head and looked at her, and she searched his face. My teacher, she thought inconsequentially.

'Is it pleasant?' he asked her tenderly.

She nodded, though 'pleasant' seemed to her an utterly inadequate word for what was happening to her – exquisite, maddening, extraordinary: a melting, melting pleasure that seemed to be turning all her bones to rubber; but at the same time was hardening some central core of her, making it *want*, making it *ask*, making it lean towards him as the fount of it, as the source of whatever was to come next. Because there had to be a next. The whole quivering sensation of her body was a forward momentum, a clamouring demand for sequence.

But his words held her in the present, with the present moment, like a rider holding back a horse that wants to gallop. 'Yes, my flower? Do I give you pleasure?'

'Yes. Oh yes!'

'Then it's all right. Yes, let it happen. It's good. My dear, my love.'

'Peter,' she said. Could it really be him that was doing this? She looked into his familiar face, and it seemed so dear, so safe; and now, part of something different and wonderful. She felt a huge, overwhelming gratitude towards him. He saw it in her eyes.

447

'Would you like to give me pleasure, too?'

'Oh yes.'

'Give me your hand, then.'

He stopped caressing her, reached for her hand, drew it downwards, folded it about smooth, warm hardness, smoother and warmer than anything she had ever touched before, except perhaps the place behind a horse's ear where the great vein carries its lifeblood. With his hand still over hers, he guided her movement, and she felt his whole body respond to it. Ah, that was the forbidden part of him, then! – stinging-hot with life's heat.

'Is that you?' she said wonderingly.

'Yes, it's me,' he said. His hand returned to her, caressingly. The questioning pleasure was renewed, but with urgency now. Her breath came more quickly, and she could hear him panting too, as though they were both running. It was a demand, an urgent demand. She heard herself moan, like someone in pain.

'What is it?' he said into her ear. 'Tell me. You want something? What do you want, my love?'

'I want more,' she managed to say.

'*What* more?'

'I don't know.'

'You want me? Tell me, then. Say you want me. Say it, my flower. Tell me.'

'I want you,' she said, and it was true. She still didn't know what she wanted of him, but it was *him*; that at least was clear.

'Then you shall have me,' he said. His hand left her, and she felt an almost piercing sense of loss. But then he moved, stretching his whole body over her, touching her again, but differently. Her eyes widened as she understood. It was shocking, but it was what she wanted, what her body was demanding. *Was that how it was done*? Why hadn't she guessed? He propped himself above her with his hands, and she touched his body and felt how rigid he was in every muscle. It's not just happening to me, but to him too, she thought. He feels as I feel.

Then he pushed himself into her. A moment's shocking,

448

burning pain that made her gasp; then he bent his head and took her nipple between his teeth, and something inside her seemed to clench like a fist, and it wasn't pain any more, it was astonishing, unbelievable sensation.

'Oh it's good!' she said.

'Yes,' he said, and it was his own pleasure he was speaking of. He moved, and she found she could move too, and that when she did, it was even better; so she butted against him as a nursing lamb butts against its dam to make her give it more, more. Yes, this was sequence. Something was going to happen. She held her breath, following in the darkness inside her body the pinpoint of extraordinary sensation.

'Oh Peter!' she said.

'What is it, darling?'

She didn't know, but it didn't matter. He knew. It came – a silent explosion in the red and black darkness inside her body, and somehow inside her head, too. She held on to him as if she might be snatched away. And then it was over, and they were gasping like landed fish, and every nerve-ending in her body seemed to be jangling with surprise and pleasure.

Faint and far away the thought came to her: *So that's what Nushka told Milochka.*

Close to her was Peter, and the smell of his body, which was such an intimate thing that she felt a great surge of affection and gratitude, and tenderness, too, that made her want to hold him close to her and protect him. Now she would always know the smell of him. If I were struck blind this instant, she thought, I would always be able to single you out by it – delicious, desirable smell.

Far away, and questioning: *But how could Sergei call it a little thing? It's the biggest thing in the world!*

Peter was kissing her, different kisses now, fond, belonging kisses, asking no questions – all questions answered. 'You've taken to it like a duck to water, my darling,' he said, his voice full of happy laughter. He adjusted their bodies in the bed with casual dexterity, so that she was lying in the crook of his arm, which was divinely comfortable. 'And to think that you'd never done it before. What a waste of a talent all these years!'

She felt shy. 'Was I – was it all right?'

'Didn't you think so?'

'Oh, for me, yes – but I meant, for you. You must have done it so often before.'

He kissed her to silence. 'No comparisons,' he said sternly. 'That's not etiquette. And besides, with you every time would seem like the first time ever to me.'

That seemed to her a lovely compliment. 'It was good,' she said wonderingly. How could that be, when they had never done it before? How could their bodies get on so well together? She felt how hers folded perfectly into the curves of his like a mouse in its own nest. 'It *is* good.'

He seemed to hear the unasked question. 'It's good because it's meant to be,' he said. 'It's good because I love you.'

And I love you, also. The words presented themselves instantly, and lying here, held in the circle of his arms, the feeling presented itself too. But it couldn't be, she thought. How could it? She loved Sergei – she had been in love with him for three, almost four years. And if she loved Sergei, she couldn't love Peter, could she? Glamorous Sergei, ordinary Peter. Peter who knew the answer to her most secret question. Confusion made her silent, and Peter, hearing the silence, held her closer, as if she had offered to get up and go away.

Chapter Twenty-Three

She woke in the darkness to the extraordinary sensation of being in bed with another person. She was still curled in the crook of his arm, her head on his shoulder, and it felt so blissfully comfortable, warm and protected, safe and loved, that she thought she might easily die of sheer contentment. This, she thought, must be the best feeling in the world.

It was pitch-dark in the room. The air was cold, and the fire had burned down to red embers, lighting nothing beyond itself. Outside there was silence, no sound of rain, no bird-song. It must be the middle of the night, she thought. Under the covers it was warm, however. It was the first time in the whole of her life she had shared a bed. From being placed alone in her crib on the day of her birth, she had walked alone and slept alone, always. What a sad thing that seemed now, now that she had tasted the alternative. Two mice in a nest, two creatures in a burrow. *Mated*, she thought – the simplest, most basic concept of life.

His arms tightened around her and he turned his head to kiss her brow.

'Mmm?'

'Are you awake?' she whispered.

'Yes,' he said, stirring. Awake in more ways than one, now. 'What is it?'

'Peter?'

'Yes, my love?'

She couldn't find the words, so he had to guess. He stroked her neck and then laid his hand over her breast, and she shivered.

'Do you think we could do it again?' she asked humbly.

Laughter surged up in him in sheer joy. 'We certainly could, my love,' he said turning over to her. 'Almost as often as you like.'

They did it again, and afterwards they fell asleep, and so she forgot to pursue her enquiry about the 'almost'.

She woke again when he left her in the morning. The grey light was filtering in, and he had got up in his shirt to make up the fire. She turned quietly onto her side to look at him. He was crouched at the hearth, feeding the small flames with twigs, letting them grow gradually. They were pale and clear as crocuses – easy to swamp and kill with too much wood too soon. But he was patient, she thought, with the fire as with her. Kind – a kind man.

But he was a man, after all, and all men were strangers. She looked at the hard muscles of his bare buttocks as he crouched there, and his pale, knuckly feet, and the long curve of his back under the shirt, and his hair, roughened every way from sleep. This was intimacy, she realised, knowing a man like

451

this, seeing him in this vulnerable posture, without the disguise of his clothes and his rank and his social manner. She felt uneasy. It was all wrong, this, wasn't it? Such a degree of intimacy shouldn't come this easily.

The fire rose to a businesslike blaze, and satisfied, he stood up and turned towards her. His legs were long and bare, and between them and his shirt were the parts she shouldn't see. Shocked, she snapped her eyes shut, pretended to be asleep, but the image of them was painted there too, behind her eyelids. Dangerous and ugly – men were. Holding her breath, she heard him come across the room to her. Would he get back into bed? He was still so long she wanted to peep to see what he was doing, but dared not.

How would she ever get out of bed? she wondered unhappily. How could she get up and dress herself without seeing him, without his seeing her?

The mattress bent as he sat down on the edge of it, and his hand rested lightly on her shoulder. 'What is it?' he asked gently. 'What's the matter?'

No escape. She opened her eyes reluctantly and looked up at him. Of course, he was going to want to talk about it. There would have to be explanations. But his face didn't seem threatening. Unshaven, it was, surrounded by spiky hair – young-looking in its untidiness – but still friendly, ordinary Peter. And he knew that she was troubled, and wanted to soothe her. Well, perhaps he had the answers to the new questions as well.

'What's troubling you?' he said, and then he smiled faintly. 'Things seem rather different in the cold light of day, is that it?'

How did he know? She nodded gratefully, and then said, 'It's wrong, isn't it? It was wrong, what we did.'

'Why?'

It was the last question she had expected. 'Because – well, only married people are supposed to.'

'But you know, don't you, that it's not like that. Probably more unmarried people do it than married! Why is it wrong? Whom does it hurt? We have given loving pleasure to each other – how can that be wrong?'

452

She didn't pursue that line, because another question had crossed her mind. 'Peter—' she frowned.

'Yes, darling?' He was smiling, as though he could read her thoughts, and found her problems light.

Well, if she couldn't ask him, there was no one she could ask. 'Why do they tell us that it will be so dreadful and painful? All those stories, of brides whose hair goes stark white in the night with horror? They make us dread and fear it, but it isn't like that at all.'

He forced himself not to laugh, for really, it was pitiful rather than funny. 'Do they tell you that? Well, sometimes it is painful at first, for young girls. But you are older, and your body is more flexible. And you wanted me, and you weren't afraid, which makes a difference. Also some men can be rather clumsy and thoughtless.' He sought for a simile for her. 'You know how some riders are naturally heavy-handed, and hurt their horses' mouths, and thump about in the saddle, while others ride lightly, so that the horse is comfortable and happy?'

'Yes, I can see that it might be so.' Just a skill, then, like riding?

'But there's more to it than that,' he said, watching her face. 'We suit each other. That's a special thing.'

She was silent. He saw that there were other things on her mind, and he was afraid of what they might be. But she wasn't able to tell him the thoughts that were pouring through her mind in a tormenting flood.

Sergei – did he really think it was only a little thing? Or did he mean that with Lyudmilla it was unimportant, whereas with her—? He didn't do it with Lyudmilla. Why? Because he didn't love her? Because he loved *her* – Fleur? Was it something, then, that you were only supposed to find pleasurable with the person you loved? She thought that yes, it would be bliss to do it with Sergei, as his love, his wife, his own for ever. But what about Peter? She didn't love him, did she? And yet it had been wonderful with him. Cyprians did it with men they didn't love, and some of them claimed to enjoy it – did that mean she was a Cyprian at heart? Cyprians did it for money, too, and she knew that many of them, most perhaps, were indifferent to the deed itself. How *could* one be indifferent? Such extraordinary pleasure – and then curling so safe and warm in Peter's arms afterwards – Peter – but it was not Peter she loved. She was fond of him, yes, she liked him – but she loved Sergei, wholly and for ever.

She looked up at Peter with troubled eyes, wanting to ask him to untangle this skein for her, too. But she had at least enough sense to know that for her to talk about Sergei now would hurt him; and she didn't want to hurt him. She thought fleetingly about that precious intimacy, and the vast tenderness she had felt for him last night, but it was receding fast in the growing daylight. She couldn't get back to it – she couldn't get back to him. She felt embarrassed and ill at ease. She had done something wrong that she ought to be ashamed of, and the fact that she didn't seem to feel ashamed of the thing itself, shamed her.

He felt her conflict, and had a fair idea what it was – the English, he knew, were very strict with their young females, and the quality of Fleur's surprise last night had told him how utterly ignorant she had been. It made him feel humbly grateful that her innocence had been entrusted to him. He had loved her consumingly since the first moment he had seen her, but the passionate desire to devour was now inextricably wedded to an equal desire to protect and cherish. She seemed to him at once fragile and strong, like a harebell that grows on a wild cliff edge; and the unfettered warmth of her response to him, made from the depths of such crystal innocence, was almost unbearingly touching.

With all these feelings, passionate and tender, surging about in him, he asked her again, 'What troubles you, my love?'

She struggled in vain to find the right words, and in the end blurted out, 'I'm a loose woman!'

And he laughed.

He couldn't help it: to hear this person, who hadn't even the worldly wisdom to display false modesty last night, who had responded to him from an equal ignorance of both prudery

and lasciviousness, so apostrophise herself, was laughable –
and he laughed, fatally. He recovered himself instantly, but it
was too late. Hurt, shock and suspicion passed through her
eyes, and then she closed herself in with pained dignity.

'Oh my darling, I'm sorry! I wasn't laughing at you – not the
way you think.'

'I should like to get dressed now, if you please. Would you
have the kindness to pass me my clothes, and turn your back?'

'Fleur don't. Don't be cold with me, not after last night.'

Her eyes filled with tears and she turned her face away so
that he shouldn't see them. 'I should have thought you'd have
the decency not to mention last night. After you took advantage of me in that way—'

'Oh, I forced you, is that what you're saying now?' he
grinned. 'Why you abandoned little wretch—!'

'I don't want to discuss it. Please give me my clothes.'

'Darling, don't—!'

'I'm not your darling. And we've delayed here long enough.
We must get back to the city – can't you imagine how your
brother will feel if he gets back and finds us missing too?'

Peter's mouth turned down. 'Oh yes, my brother. That's
what this is all about, isn't it? I should have realised. And I
suppose you'll tell me now that all last night you were imagining it was *his* arms around you instead of mine?'

It was close enough to something she had thought, at least,
and suddenly the tears spilled over from her eyes, tears of hurt
and self-reproach and bewilderment. Peter was instantly
contrite.

'Oh God, why did I say that? I didn't mean it. Fleur, forgive
me.' She made a gesture of mingled negation and apology. He
caught the hand in mid-air, and after a moment's resistance,
she allowed him to hold it. He bit his lip, seeking for neutral
words to carry them over the present difficulty. 'Let's not talk
about it any more now,' he said at last. 'We've always been
such good friends – let's just remember that for now.'

She nodded, and after a moment said, 'Yes, friends.'

She sounded despondent, and he wanted to say more, but
was afraid of making things worse. She was gentle and shy,

and her embarrassment was likely to be his worst enemy at the moment. 'Friends, then,' he said at last. 'Good. And now while you get dressed, I'll make us both some tea.'

He brought her clothes and then went back to the fire, turned his back, dressed himself quickly, and made tea, thinking, wondering, planning. The miracle of last night remained untouched and inviolate in one shining place in his mind. It would be all right in the end – it must be, after that. All that could not have been for nothing. Perhaps it had been the wrong way to go about it; perhaps he should have wooed her first and ravished her later; but on the other hand, he was sure no words he had could have spoken to her as eloquently as their actions. He had made her his – now he only had to convince her of the fact.

Kirov was already there when they arrived back at the house in Vladimir Street. Peter was not surprised. He had been half expecting that his brother would return early in order to catch them out at something. Well, he thought grimly, he was welcome to all he caught this time.

'What the deuce is going on?' Kirov demanded as soon as they came in. His eyes scanned them critically, and Fleur blushed instantly and deeply wondering if her altered status was evident to other people. 'I come home to find no one here, and the servants spouting some hysterical gibberish—' He seemed very angry, but there was an underlying stratum of fear in his voice. 'Where have you been? And where's my wife?'

It was Peter who answered. 'I don't know what the servants have told you, but I'm afraid you must brace yourself for a shock. Lyudmilla's gone. She—'

'Gone? What are you talking about?'

'I'm trying to tell you. She packed a bag and left the city, to go to the English camp, to be with Richard.'

Kirov's eyes blazed. 'And you just let her? You just allowed her to walk out of the house—'

Even at such an upsetting moment, Fleur noticed that he

didn't query Richard's being alive. Had he really, then, made up the Cossack's story?

'Of course I didn't "just allow her",' Peter said. 'She'd hardly ask my permission, would she?'

'I left her in your charge. I left them both in your charge!'

'You didn't tell me to keep them under lock and key. She left the same day that you did, saying she was going to the hospital, and it wasn't until she didn't return in the evening that we had any idea anything was wrong.'

Kirov looked wild. 'I don't understand. Why didn't you go after her? Why didn't you bring her back? For God's sake, Petya—!'

'By the time we knew she'd gone,' Peter said patiently, 'she was well away. With such a start, she'd have been at the camp before we even knew she'd left. But we did try to get her back. Fleur went – at considerable personal risk, I might add – to the camp to try to persuade her to come back, but she refused.'

The terrible eyes came round to rest on Fleur. 'You saw her? In the camp?'

Fleur nodded unhappily. 'It's true, what Peter said. I begged her to come back, but she wouldn't. She wants to stay with Richard. I don't understand it. I don't understand why she would—'

'No-o-o!'

She broke off, because Kirov had made a terrible sound, an inarticulate, wounded cry. He turned around and struck both his fists against the wall above his head in a futile gesture of pain. Cracks ran out like the rays of a star from the two dents he made, and fragments of plaster fell around him.

The other two stood frozen with distress and embarrassment, not knowing what to do. Kirov cried again, but more quietly, and allowed his forehead to drop with a soft thump against the battered wall.

'I want her back. I want her *back*!' he cried.

'Sergei – Seryosha—' Peter began in a reasoning tone.

Kirov hit his head against the wall again. 'It was *you*! You let her go! You let her betray me! Now you get her *back*!'

'She won't come,' Peter said quietly.

He turned, glaring. 'Make her!'

'What use would that be? Talk sense, Seryosha. She'd only run away again. You can't make her stay if she doesn't want to.'

'But what does she want with that – that – puppy? That – *nothing*! That *reed*!'

Peter's voice was deadly with reason, with pity. 'It's her choice, that's all. He suits her.' Kirov quivered as though Peter were striking him. 'There's no rule about these things,' he went on gently. 'And you goaded her – you know you did.'

The Count began to break down, and Fleur, who had flinched from his anger, would rather have seen him rage. His shoulders went first. 'Only because she plagued me. I didn't mean – I was testing her, that's all.' His hands dropped to his sides, and he sat down heavily in the chair behind him. 'I love her. And she betrayed me,' he said.

'Don't think of it like that—' Peter began, and the anger flared, just a little, like the spurt from a kicked log.

'How else should I think of it? Betrayal – you should know all about that! She betrayed my trust, betrayed me with that – that *toy soldier*!'

Fleur thought of all she had heard about the charge of the Light Brigade, and the pitiful remnant she had seen left from the fearful slaughter; and the fact that no single man had flinched before the killing guns, no single man, however grievously wounded, had surrendered. Toy soldier? She felt a brief rage. Her brother was the equal of any man, and if Lyudmilla preferred him, then she was entitled—

She stopped dead in the middle of that thought, shocked with herself. Oh but she wasn't entitled. She was a married woman; she *had* betrayed – and Richard too. And for the sake, she supposed, of that *small thing* which was not, after all, so small.

Kirov put his head down in his hands, and Fleur felt as though she had struck him herself. He does love her after all, she thought, and the realisation was cold as death. All the time – all the time she had been deceiving herself that it was really her he loved – but it was Lyudmilla he had married after all, and she had never believed it was entirely for her fortune.

But loving him, she couldn't see him suffer without trying to comfort him, though her own heart was aching. She flung herself down beside him, catching at his hands, trying to pull them away from his face.

'No, Sergei, no, don't. She didn't mean to. She loves you, really she does. It was a moment's madness. When she's had time to think about it, she'll change her mind. She'll come back to you. Only give it time. You've seen her with Richard – they're like children playing. It doesn't mean anything. She told me she'll love you till she dies.'

He looked at her abruptly. 'She said that to you?'

'Yes – yes.'

'Just now? In the camp?'

Fleur bit her lip. 'Well – no. Not then. It was before – but she meant it. She'll come back, I'm sure she will.'

He folded his hands about hers, gripping them so hard that he hurt her. But she endured it, for his sake. 'Oh *Tsvetoksha*, thank God for you! You're such a comfort to me. I don't think I could face it if I hadn't you here beside me.'

'It's all right,' she said. 'I'm here. I won't go away.'

His eyes kindled suddenly. 'Promise me!' he said. 'Promise you'll stay with me! Oh Fleur, I need you, I need you so much. My dear, dear friend. Say you won't leave me.'

'I won't leave you,' she said, and to Peter, who couldn't see her face, she sounded shocked, not as if she had just decided something, but as if she had just realised something.

'Never,' Kirov insisted, crushing her hands yet more fiercely.

'I'll never leave you,' she said, in that same, blank voice.

Later that evening, Peter came into the room to find Fleur alone. 'A moment, then, to say goodbye,' he said.

'You're leaving?'

'My leave is up. I have to be back in camp tomorrow morning.'

'You could go tomorrow morning.'

He shrugged. 'It's moonlight. I might as well go now. Neither of you needs me.'

'Oh Peter!'

He picked up her hand and looked at it carefully, as though he had never seen one before, ran the tip of a finger around the shape of her nails. 'I suppose I should have expected that you'd choose him. After all, you did before, and under less propitious circumstances.'

'What do you mean?' she asked painfully.

He looked up. 'If she doesn't come back, he can divorce her, don't you know that? And then he'll be free to marry again. Don't tell me that hadn't occurred to you?'

'No, it – I didn't—' She stopped, confused. 'I didn't think about it like that. That isn't why—'

'Why you choose him instead of me?'

'Peter, he needs me. Now more than ever he needs me. I can't leave him.'

'You don't want to.'

She met his eyes steadily. 'No, I don't want to.'

'There it is, then.'

But he was still holding her hand, as if that were not, in fact, it. His eyes were down again, and she studied his face with a sense of newness, as if she had never seen him before. Now clean-shaven, his hair neatly brushed, his clothes immaculate as always, he was in his familiar form, the way she had known him from the beginning; yet there was a sense that just under the surface there was another him that she knew as well, or perhaps even better – the tousled, naked, vulnerable person in whose arms she had known such deep and perfect comfort.

She had felt that, hadn't she? It was not imagination. So what did it mean? She knew this man better than any other man in the world, and that must count for something. They must be, in some sort of way, attached. Oh, but she was confused! She didn't know what she ought to be thinking or feeling.

And then he looked up suddenly, surprising her, and she blushed deeply. It seemed to please him. He smiled, an infinitely understanding smile.

'In the Ancient Church, you know, we'd be considered married!' he said playfully. 'What we did would be enough to constitute matrimony.'

'Oh Peter, I'd be a monster if I didn't appreciate you!' she said contritely. 'I suppose I'm being a fool, or worse. But I can't seem to help it.'

'I know. He has that effect on people.'

'Only let me get over my – infatuation, if you want to call it that—'

He touched a finger to her lips to stop her. He didn't want her to make any promises. Nothing between them that she might ever regret. 'Let's call it an infection,' he said lightly. 'You got sick with my brother.'

But you'll be well one day, he thought, more with hope than certainty. I can wait, little flower. A good thing's worth waiting for.

'If you need me, send word to the camp, and I'll come. Don't be afraid. I won't be far away.'

'Thank you. And – Peter—'

'Yes?'

'You'll take care, won't you?'

'Always. This is my favourite skin, and I prefer it without holes.'

The cannonade wasn't resumed. There seemed to be an unspoken agreement between the two sides that only specific shots were replied to, and as soon as one side stopped firing, so did the other. The horrific level of casualties fell somewhat; but the deaths from disease rose at the same time, so there seemed little abatement in the numbers of corpses going up the hill.

The weather worsened. Heavy rains fell almost every day, and it was bitterly cold. Stories came in from outside the walls of English soldiers freezing to death in the deep mud of the trenches overnight. Observers on the Russian side said they had seen them carried out in the mornings, rigid as wooden dolls. If the Russians were suffering a death-toll from pneumonia and cholera, it was certain that the Allies must be: Fleur, remembering the worn-out clothing and inadequate shelter of the men in the English camp, suffered agonies of anxiety for them.

Then on the 14th of November a storm blew up. The gale-force winds which began the day quickly rose to hurricane force, accompanied by deluges of rain; and when the wind finally moderated towards the evening, the rain turned to snow, covering the ground an inch deep. In the city things were bad enough, with roofs ripped away, and houses already damaged by shells collapsing under the battering force of the wind. But the next day, which dawned clear and sunny, though freezing cold, and still with a brisk and bitter wind, it was known that the English fleet which had been anchored outside Balaclava harbour had foundered and been driven onto the rocks.

Two days later the first deserter from the English camp came in to Sebastopol – a private of the 790th Highlanders. He had managed to pass his own sentries without being seen, and though they caught sight of him afterwards and fired several rounds at him, he managed to get away unhurt. His testimony was soon being circulated around the town as an encouragement to the defenders, and though it probably cheered the men freezing up in the bastions night after night, it was nothing but desolation to Fleur.

The storm had wrought the most fearful havoc. The camps had been all but destroyed, the tents ripped to shreds, the equipment broken and scattered like matchwood. The rain had brought tidal waves of mud down from the higher slopes, and turned the road from Balaclava into an impassable quagmire. Horses had been blown off their feet by the hurricane, tossed in the air like pieces of paper. And then the freezing rain and snow had finished the job. Twenty men had died in the night from the cold, and many more had been taken down to the hospitals with frozen limbs; twenty-four horses of the Royal Artillery, and thirty-five of the cavalry had died also.

The harbour of Balaclava and the rocky shore outside it were littered with the precious equipment and supplies that had been on board the foundered ships – broken, spoiled, sodden, unusable; and five hundred men had lost their lives in the wrecks. Since the day of the storm, it had not been possible to carry a single mouthful of food for man or beast up to the camps: the road was like a mud glacier, and littered with dead and dying horses, oxen and mules, half sunk in the mire. Since the army was now lying without shelter of any kind on an open plain a foot deep in mud, some impassable miles from any source of supply, it was to be assumed that many more must die very soon.

'They must go home now – surely they must go home,' Fleur said to herself again and again. What had happened to Richard and Lyudmilla? Were they alive? If alive, were they starving? She racked her mind again and again for some scheme to send them relief, and could think of nothing she could do. Her position was invidious – her own people were nominally her enemy, and she would not be allowed to aid or comfort them.

Kirov was roused at last from his brooding grief. Since his return from Simferopol, he had hardly stirred out of the house, and had even left the work of his office largely to his clerks, while he sat by the fire, staring into the flames in silent thought. Now, however, the news of the devastation brought him the hope that Lyudmilla would be forced to return. He had hardly been able to believe that such a child of luxury would willingly live in the mud and stench of an army camp – but that she would stay when the camp was no more was beyond belief.

'She'll come back now,' he said to Fleur with a confidence she found painful to witness. 'She'll come back to me. You'll see.'

But the month of November dragged on, and Lyudmilla did not come home. The next news they heard was that, notwithstanding the terrible troubles and deprivations, the Allied army was not going to withdraw from Sebastopol. Reinforcements were being sent out from England; ships had been sent off to gather supplies from Constantinople. The siege was to go on. To withdraw now would mean that the siege equipment must be left behind, and the Government didn't care to see that happen.

Fleur could bear it no longer. 'You must do something,' she said to Kirov. 'At least send a letter – you can do that, can't you? You have the influence. A letter under flag of truce. Write to her, beg her to come home. You can't let her die out there for want of a letter.'

'And what about him?' Kirov said. He wouldn't speak Richard's name.

Fleur shook her head painfully. Even if there were any way of asking him, Richard wouldn't come. It would mean surrendering to the enemy, to become a prisoner of war, and he would die in his own camp sooner than that. He must take care of himself. Lyudmilla must be saved, if at all, alone. 'Write to her,' she said.

He did write, not once, but several times; but as far as Fleur knew, there was no reply. The weather continued bad, heavy rain day after day, with occasional falls of snow; the siege continued in a spasmodic way, with continual exchange of fire between the English trenches and the Russian rifle-pits, and the occasional brief tit for tat from the big guns; and the cholera continued to claim a steady trickle of victims.

Kirov was at last given something to do besides brood: there was a new initiative for improving the defences, and for building abattis in front of three of the batteries. Nakhimov and Todleben both needed his services, and he was called out to liaise between the engineers and the sailors, and to co-ordinate the supply of materials.

He was out all day, every day, and came home at the end of it tired out and chilled through. He was no happier, but at least he was too weary to lie awake all night, or to pace his room as Fleur had heard him at many a midnight since Lyudmilla left him.

On the 2nd of December, when Fleur was returning to the house towards sunset, she was startled by an old soldier who stepped out of the shadows of the doorway to the next house, and hissed at her.

'What do you want?' she said nervously. He was from one of the bearded regiments, and with his greatcoat and cap as well, there was not much of him visible from which to judge his intentions.

'Are you the English *barishnya*?' he whispered in strangely mangled French.

'Yes. What do you want?' she asked again. The man glanced both ways, and then started feeling in his pocket. For a moment she thought he meant to bring out a cudgel or knife to murder her, but her interest sharpened when she saw it was a piece of paper in his hand.

'I've a letter for you,' he whispered. 'Wants an answer. And you were to pay me two silver roubles for it.'

'Who gave you that?' she asked sharply.

'A female. Do you want it or not?'

'Yes. But I have no money with me. I must go into the house for it. Give me the letter and I'll read it there. Come,' she said impatiently when he hesitated. 'Do you think I'll cheat you?'

He passed it across to her. 'Read it private. Don't let anyone see you,' he said hoarsely. 'I'll wait here. Only be quick.'

He hardly needed to tell her that. She thrust the paper into her pocket and hurried indoors. Count Kirov was out, and she managed to avoid the servants and get to her own room, where she pulled out the letter and unfolded it.

It was not sealed: just a piece of paper, damp and rather muddy here and there, with a thumb-mark on one corner and the ink smudged in several places.

'Dearest Fleur – I must speak to you. The man who brings you this will conduct you to me. Come at once, and bring with you any money you have, also my fur tippet and muff, black boots, and any linen you can spare. But hurry, and at your peril tell anyone or let them see you leaving with the things. I told the man you'd give him a rouble for the letter and one to bring you to me. He looks vile, but you can trust him.'

It wasn't signed, but she recognised Lyudmilla's sprawling handwriting and her direct style. But what did it mean? Was she wanting to come back, and needing a go-between? It didn't sound like it – more as though she wanted fresh supplies for staying where she was. But a chance at least to speak to her, and thank God, thank God that she was well enough to be imperious!

She put the letter away in her pocket, and thought. She hadn't much money about her, but she would bring all she had. Her own linen of course presented no problem. She ransacked her drawers and quickly made a selection of what she thought would be essentials. Now for Milochka's furs and boots.

She left her room and walked quietly down the passage to the chamber Lyudmilla had shared with Kirov. Her hand was actually on the doorknob when she heard a sound from inside which made her start. She listened, her heart beating, and the sound resolved itself into Nushka's voice singing one of her mournful Georgian ballads. The old nurse spent a great deal of time in that room when the Count was out, dusting and tidying over and over again, and fondling the things Lyudmilla had left behind, as though they could tell her about their mistress.

Trust Nushka? No, Fleur thought regretfully. Nushka didn't approve of the present situation, and believed to the bottom of her heart that Richard had abducted her little lady. If she knew Lyudmilla was within seizing distance, she'd raise the alarm – and then, presumably, Lyudmilla would slip away. Fleur meant to have the opportunity of talking to her, at least.

She reversed and walked quietly back to her own room, and got out instead a fur scarf of her own, and her biggest muff. She thrust the linen and the money, all but two silver roubles, into the muff, and added some knitted stockings and a pair of gloves, and at the last minute, a small vial of perfume she saw on her dressing-table. Boots she could do nothing about – her feet were smaller than Milochka's.

She put the scarf round her neck, put on her fur hat, draped her cloak over the whole, and holding the muff under the cloak, stepped out of her room. All was quiet. She walked along the passage to the staircase door, listened a moment, and then slipped out.

She hadn't been very long, but the early December dark had fallen. She couldn't see the soldier anywhere, and for a moment wondered if she had dreamt the whole thing; then she saw the mist of his breath rise out of a doorway further along the road, and simultaneously heard his hollow cough. He stepped out as she approached, and she held out one silver rouble.

'One now, one when you take me to her. It's in her letter,' she said firmly.

The man shrugged and pocketed the coin. 'Come on then, *barishnya*. Step close, and keep up.'

'Where are you taking me?'

'Up the top of the town. Near the Fourth Bastion. Don't worry,' he added with a grin at her automatic start at the name of that grim site of carnage. 'It's not dangerous now, not unless *he* starts firing again. Then we'll have plenty to worry about.' The soldiers, she had discovered, always referred to the enemy as *he* or *him*.

He stepped briskly, and she followed in his wake, keeping her head down in case they should pass anyone they knew. But as they were going further up the town, the streets were quiet, for they were mostly deserted now, ruined by the enemy shells. Now that the sun had gone down, the air was getting colder, and the cobbles were slippery with something that was not quite frost, and not quite ice. In the sky to the west there was still a faint red light, and she wondered whether it was the last of the sunset, or the glow from the French camp, which was in that direction.

The road was so broken up here that she had to pick her way, following the soldier round craters and over potholes. Now she could see the shape of the bastion up ahead, a darker darkness against the sky, and a pin-prick of light as someone with a lantern walked along the foot of the wall. And here was what had been a row of cottages, and was now a ruin, walls standing to half their original height, gaps where there had been doors and windows, and a few jutting spars of what had once been the roof.

The soldier stopped at a doorway, glanced up and down the

467

street, and beckoned her in. She followed him, a little apprehensively, and started when he grasped her arm.

'Mind the hole in the floor,' he whispered, tugging her to the left. 'Step where I step.'

Things rattled away from under her feet, and clutching the muff tightly to her, she saw that there was a huge crater just beside her, surrounded with splintered floorboards, and with a glint of water at the bottom. It was hard to keep her footing, and she found she was holding her breath, expecting at any moment to be pitched down there. But then they were past it, and he was leading her out through the remains of another doorway into what had evidently been the garden of the house.

There was a smell of greenness, black slippery grass under her feet, long and tussocky with neglect, and a creeper of some sort growing over the broken walls. The frost was falling now, glinting on the stones of the garden path, whitening the dead leaves of the creeper. Under the far wall there was a fine drift of yesterday's snow which had never melted.

A figure waiting a little way off – a peasant woman, one would have said, in a peasant's sheepskin *tulup* over a bulk of clothes, and a peasant scarf around her head. The white face turning as they approached; the whisper, taut with anxiety: 'Fleur?'

'Milochka, is it you?'

'Oh Fleur!'

They were embracing; and then Lyudmilla pushed her back. 'Better not,' she said with astonishing calm. 'I'm still lousy. But, oh God, it's good to see you again!'

The soldier spoke up. 'Don't be long, *barina*. I've got to get you back. And keep your voices down. You don't want a sentry coming to investigate.'

'All right – five minutes,' Lyudmilla said. 'Wait over there, and keep watch.' The man withdrew, and Lyudmilla turned to Fleur, her voice low and urgent. 'Did you get out without being seen?'

'Yes, of course. But how did you get here?'

'Bribed a lot of people. Used names. Told stories. It doesn't matter – I had to do it, and it's only just the once. Did you bring the things?'

Fleur gave her the muff. 'Linen and money in here. I couldn't get into your room, so no boots, I'm afraid. But you can have that muff, and this scarf of mine – wait, let me unwind it. Oh, and I put a little bottle of perfume in there, I thought it might be something you'd miss.'

Suddenly Lyudmilla was crying. 'Oh God, Fleur! Oh you darling fool – perfume! You can have no idea—!' She took hold of herself, wiped her eyes, and then her nose with her fingers. She saw Fleur's shocked look. 'Sorry,' she said briefly. 'A handkerchief's a luxury out there.'

'Never mind,' Fleur said with an effort. 'Tell me quickly, how's Richard?'

'All right. His shoulder's better now, though he has to be careful for a while longer. The thing is, he's sending in his papers.'

'What?'

'Yes, that's why I had to come. It's no use here now. After the storm – you remember the storm?'

'Of course. We had it too.'

'Not the way we had it,' she said grimly. 'You never saw anything like it. I can't describe it to you.' She paused a moment, then went on, her voice quick and light in the darkness. 'But after that we had no food. They couldn't bring it up from the harbour, you see, because the roads were too bad for horses or carts. We asked to be allowed to bring the horses down to feed there, but they wouldn't let us, in case the enemy attacked – though what use we'd have been I don't know, with the horses so weak from hunger they could hardly stand. They were eating each others' manes and tails in desperation. Then they started dying. They lay in the mud, dying of starvation, and we weren't allowed to do anything about it.'

'Oh Milochka—!'

'The only way out was to leave altogether. Your friend Paget went home ten days ago. He'd simply had enough of the muddle and inefficiency. We hear thirty-eight other officers have gone, too. But Richard wouldn't go, because it meant taking me away. He didn't want me to have to make the final decision, you see, the dear fool! And also, he felt it was letting the side down, to go while he still had a horse.'

'Pearl survived?'

'Pearl and Oberon. Both of them. I made sure of it,' she said grimly. 'That's what I've been doing day after day – just finding them fodder – and us, of course. It broke my heart to see the others die. I couldn't save them all. I could only just find enough for our two.'

The soldier interrupted them. 'Hurry *barina*!'

'All right!' she called back softly, then turned back to Fleur. 'Anyway, yesterday Lord Lucan told Lord Raglan officially that the Light Brigade was no longer fit for duty. It barely exists, as a matter of fact – but what there was left of us was moved down to Kadikoi yesterday, and we were able to feed the horses properly for the first time.' She lifted her face, and Fleur saw there were tears. 'They were so weak, some of them, we had to feed them a handful at a time. Oh, but have you ever fed a really hungry animal? They're so grateful, it would break your heart.' She sniffed the tears back and went on.

'This morning, Richard and I talked about it, and he decided to hand in his papers. The other lord did, too – Cardigan – but I suppose no one will miss him: he's hardly been off his yacht for a month! So we're going on the first boat we can get, back to England.'

'We? You said we?'

'Yes, Fleurushka, I'm going too. Is it very shocking of me? Do you hate me?' she asked in a small voice.

Fleur stared at her through the darkness, trying to discover what she did think. 'Do you really care for him?' she asked at last.

'Would I have stayed there with him if I didn't?' Lyudmilla said simply. 'Yes, I care for him, you idiot. I think I always did – only Sergei distracted me, like a false path, you know, leading in the wrong direction. But I'm on the right path now. Richard suits me, and I suit him. I don't like the idea of leaving Russia, but this war won't last for ever, and then I suppose we can come back. But most importantly, I must stay with Richard. That's all that really matters.'

Was it? All? Fleur felt bewildered. 'Didn't you care for Sergei at all?' she asked helplessly.

'Oh yes, of course I did. I loved him – I do love him still, in a way. But it was always like a dream, somehow – exciting, romantic, all those things, but it wasn't real. It was – like syllabub, you know, frothy and delicious, but it's not enough. No,' she added more grimly, 'you need something more solid to live on, when it comes down to it. Dreaming's all very well, but you have to wake up in the end, and he would never have understood that.'

There was a brief silence. Someone went past on the road, whistling, cracking the thin ice on a puddle as he tramped. It was beginning to freeze. Their breath smoked between them, and Fleur felt the clammy cold of the long grass creeping up through the soles of her boots, numbing her feet.

'How is he taking it? Is he very upset?' Milochka asked.

'He's heartbroken,' Fleur said briefly.

'Oh.' A pause. 'I really am sorry. But you know, you have to save yourself. That's what it comes to. He was killing me slowly. I had to get out.'

'And you're sure this is what you want? You won't leave Richard and come back to him?'

'No. I'm sorry if you don't like it, Fleur, but I'm not coming back. Even if there were no Richard, I wouldn't go back to him.'

'I don't know how I'm going to tell him,' Fleur sighed.

Milochka touched her arm. 'I'm sorry to leave it to you. But you're the only one I can trust.'

'It would have been better if you'd told him yourself.'

'I've got a letter here for him – that may make it easier for you. And one for my father – will you see that it goes for me?'

'Yes, I'll do that.'

'Thank you. You're a good friend. Dear Fleur, I knew the first time I saw you that I should love you!' She handed over the letters, and watched in silence as Fleur put them away.

Then she said, 'What will you do? Will you go back to England now?'

'I don't know. I don't know what I shall do.'

'Well, I'll write to you when I get to London – oh the excitement of travelling! Just think, I shall actually see London! And either in England or in Russia, we'll meet again, when the war's over. We're sisters now, remember – we can't be parted. Richard's going to take me to Grove Park, where you grew up. Do you remember telling me about it, the garden and the river and everything?' Fleur only nodded, and Milochka bit her lip and went on, 'Are there any messages you want me to deliver?'

'To Richard, of course—' Fleur began, and then thought, what to Richard? What was there to say to him now? 'Just my love, if you please. And – take care of my horse, won't you, Milochka?'

'Yes, of course! And you – will you take care of my dogs?' Her eyes were bright with tears again. 'I miss them so! I wish I could have taken them with me. But they'd have died out there on the plain. Love them for me, Fleur.'

There was a meaningful cough from the shadows. 'I must go – my escort's getting impatient. He's likely to get a flogging if they discover his part in my little escapade!'

'Wait – I meant you to have this hat, too.'

'Oh bliss! A fur hat! I can't tell you how cold it's been. Thank you a million times! And now, I really must go. God bless you, darling Fleur! And tell Seryosha – oh, tell him I'm sorry.'

She was gone, walking swiftly over to where the soldier was hovering anxiously against the broken rear wall, pulling on the hat as she went. And then she turned to call back softly in a voice full of mischief. 'You can marry him now, you know – with my blessing! You always did want him yourself, didn't you?'

And then she really was gone.

Chapter Twenty-Four

Fleur was carrying away the Count's luncheon-tray when Ngorny appeared from the sitting-room and took it from her hands, saying, 'I'll do that, *barishnya*. There's a visitor for you.'

'Who is it?' Fleur asked, smoothing down her apron, but Ngorny had gone on down the passage, and didn't answer. She sighed and walked the other way, into the sitting-room, and found Peter in the process of taking off his greatcoat.

'Peter!'

'Hullo, little sister of mercy! And how's the patient?'

'Oh Peter!'

'Hey, hey, what's all this?' he said, kissing her hair, which was all he could reach, and folding his arms round her. She clung to him, her face buried in his shoulder. 'I wasn't expecting this kind of a welcome!'

She released herself, a little embarrassed at her own lack of control, and he gravely produced a handkerchief and dabbed away the trace of tears on her cheeks. 'Well,' he said, 'it seems as though you've missed me.'

'It's been such a long time. You know that your brother's been ill?'

'Yes, I heard. How is he? That was my first question, by the by.'

'He's been very sick,' Fleur said, taking his handkerchief absent-mindedly and blowing her nose. 'We thought we were going to lose him at one point, but he's over the crisis now.'

'What brought it on?'

She shrugged. 'Being out in all weathers on the fortifications. Not eating properly. Not changing his damp clothes.'

'In short, giving you a great deal of trouble. But he's better now, you say?'

'He's still in bed, but he's recovering – though not as quickly as I'd like. He's very low in his mind, you see, and that holds him back.'

'Still grieving for Lyudmilla?'

'I suppose so. He never speaks about her – not to me, anyway.'

Peter surveyed her face carefully. 'And you've been doing too much, and worrying too much, and making yourself fit to be ill too. I suppose you've been sitting up at nights watching at the bedside?'

She wasn't sure how sarcastic he was being. 'I've been worried, naturally. But Nushka and Ngorny have shared all the nursing with me. It hasn't been so bad, except—'

'Yes? Except what?'

Except that I've been lonely, was what she thought, but she didn't say it. Instead she said, 'I'd have thought you'd have called before, even if only to see how he was doing.'

'I didn't want to interrupt your idyll. After all, here you were, cosily tucked up in domestic bliss – it has been domestic bliss, hasn't it?'

She looked up, and saw that he was being serious. There was an intent, waiting look in his eyes. She looked away again, and sighed. 'It's strange – in some ways it's just like before—'

'Before Milochka went away?'

'Before Sebastopol, even. When the three of us were together, I often felt – oh, I know it's silly, and probably wicked – but I felt as though Sergei and I were the ones who were married. It was so comfortable, you see. Life went on – the little daily things we did – duties and pleasures. But it was exciting, too. Now Milochka's gone, we do many of the same things – you know, eating together and talking and playing cards and chess – but it's different. I don't understand why.'

'If he's been ill, it would have to be different, wouldn't it?'

'Yes, of course,' she said doubtfully, 'but it isn't that.'

She didn't think she could tell him what it was, for she hardly knew herself. She would have expected that doing things for him, washing him when he was very ill, sitting with him, giving him his medicine, bringing his meals, she would have felt that sense of intimacy that she had once had with

474

Peter. After all, she was seeing Kirov in his vulnerability – could a man be more your own than when he depended on you for everything?

When he was very ill, he had wanted her there all the time, had grown fretful if she left the room for more than a moment. Through the worst time she had sat for hours holding his hand, hardly able to move to ease a stiff neck or a cramped foot without his clutching at her desperately. And when he was over the crisis, and too weak to move or speak, he would lie against his pillows, his eyes following her wherever she moved.

Now he was almost well again, only very pulled, as was the nature of the sickness – a little listless and depressed – and there was not much nursing to be done. She spent time with him now almost as if he were up and about, taking her meals with him, reading to him and discussing what they read, playing cards, sometimes just sitting sewing while he stared at the fire, deep in thought. But it was not like before. She didn't feel the sense of belonging she had once had.

Ashamed of her own thoughts, she said briskly, 'Well, he'll be up and about soon, I hope.'

'And then what?' Peter asked.

'I'd like to get him out of this place,' she said. 'It's no place for a convalescence. It's hard to get decent food, and there's never enough firewood, and there are so many diseases lingering in the air I'm afraid every time he takes a breath he'll catch something else. I'm hoping to persuade him to go back to Kurmoye—'

'That's out of the question, I'm afraid,' Peter interrupted. 'The Allies have got quite a force at Eupatoria now. They've been landing the victorious Turkish army from the Danube, and there are rumours of fresh troops from France, too. A large army there is a serious threat to us – it could cut off our supply line and completely isolate Sebastopol and our army. So our brave General Menshikov is planning a new offensive there – an all-out attack with just about everything we can muster.'

'Oh, I see.'

'Kurmoye will not be a nice safe retreat – if it hasn't already been taken over, it soon will be.' She nodded thoughtfully, and he added, 'If I were you I'd try and persuade him to go back to Petersburg. It may be cold there, but it's a dry cold, and you'd have every luxury and convenience to nurse him with.'

'But that would mean resigning his commission.'

Peter made an enigmatic grimace. 'I'll tell you this in confidence, little flower: there are going to be very big changes around here before long, and Seryosha will be wise not to get mixed up in them.'

'Changes?'

He sat down on the sofa and patted the seat beside him. 'Sit – that's right. Well now, you have no doubt heard a lot of grumbling and gossip about our beloved Prince General?'

'Menshikov? Yes, of course. No one seems to like him.'

'Quite. And it isn't just here that he's reviled. In Petersburg there's quite a party that's opposed to him – Nesselrode, for one, and Paskevitch, and Lieven – a lot of influential people, who have the ear of the Emperor.'

'How do you know that?'

He smiled rather grimly. 'I have my spies. It's a basic rule of campaign to keep open your lines of communication.'

She looked at him with new respect. She had not thought this light-hearted, frivolous man would be so efficient a schemer.

'At any rate,' he went on, 'the fact of the matter is that Menshikov has almost reached the end of the line. Whatever the result of his new offensive at Eupatoria, he'll be replaced very soon, and more than likely brought back to Petersburg in disgrace. That's why it's important for anyone closely associated with him to detach themselves as soon as possible.'

'What about you?' Fleur asked. 'You're more closely associated than Sergei – he's Nakhimov's aide, after all.'

'I've been recalled,' Peter admitted. He noted the dismay in her eyes, and went on, 'That's mainly what I came here to tell you both. Oh, don't worry – I'm not going back in disgrace. I'm the Emperor's man. I was sent here by him to keep an eye on things, and now I'm going back to report.'

'By things, you mean Menshikov? Is it you, then, that's caused his downfall?'

'No, little one, he's caused that himself. Don't look so upset – it's the way things are done in Russia. And it isn't happening behind his back: Menshikov has his own spies at Petersburg – in fact, they probably dine with my spies, and tell each other everything!'

'Oh Peter, don't joke. It's horrible.'

He took her hand and patted it. 'No it isn't. It's just the way things are. Everyone knows the rules; and in any game, it's always possible to win, if you're quick and clever. But Sergei may not have had his eye on the ball lately. What with one thing and another, he may not be aware of the pitch things are come to, and I think it's important for him to send in his papers and get back to Petersburg as soon as possible. When do you think he'll be fit to travel?'

'In a week, I suppose, as long as he can keep warm and get proper food and shelter at night.'

'Very well. I'll speak to him, and see what I can do to persuade him. You'll find travelling in winter is much better and quicker on the whole than any other time of the year: sleighs are faster than carriages.'

Going back to Petersburg, she thought. She would be very glad to get away from this place, but she dreaded meeting the Polotskis, as she supposed she must do in the capital. They had been so very kind to her, and it was her brother who had led Milochka astray, and had finally whisked her away to a foreign land, out of their reach. Their dream of glory for her was shattered: she was a shamed woman, a social outcast. They must wonder if they would ever see her again; and they would not be human if they did not curse the day they took Fleur and her brother into their house.

Peter had been watching her face, and now said, 'What about you, Fleur? What will you do?'

'Do?' she said, startled, coming back to the present.

'If Seryosha goes back to Petersburg. Will you go with him?'

'Of course. Where else could I go?'

He hesitated, and then said, 'You might go home.'

'Home? Back to England, you mean?'

'Hadn't it occurred to you?'

'No. No, it hadn't. I haven't really thought about it as home for some time now.'

'Then where is home?'

She looked down at her hands. 'I don't know. Where Sergei is, I suppose.'

There was a silence. Looking down, she didn't see his reaction to her words. After a moment she added, 'I couldn't leave him now – not now when he needs me.'

'And you don't want to,' he said, as he had said once before.

She didn't answer that. Instead, after a moment, she said, 'Will I see you in Petersburg?'

'No doubt,' he said shortly. She looked up and met his eyes, and felt an unexpected longing to be held in his arms again, the way she was on that wonderful night in bed together – to feel safe and close and loved as she had been then. I've never had a person all of my own, she thought – someone whose business it was to make sure I was happy and cared for. She wanted to tell him that she was lonely; but it didn't seem to be something she had any right to say to him.

Instead she said, 'I suppose you'll want to go in and see him now. Had I better warn him you're here?'

'Yes,' Peter said. He gave what was almost a sigh as some tension went out of him. 'Yes, perhaps you'd better.'

In the end, it was not to Petersburg they went, but to Schwartzenturm. Rose was there, smiling calmly as though they had only been out for the day, welcoming them home.

'Oh, I am so glad to see you again,' Fleur said, as Rose helped her off with her cloak.

'I'm glad to see you, too. It will be pleasant to have someone to talk to again,' was all Rose said, but her voice was warm; and later, when Fleur was in her room, using the time before dinner to write up her diary, Rose sought her out.

'You will have seen many strange things,' she said, looking

at the book on Fleur's knee. 'I'm sure there are stories in there stranger than any fiction.'

'It's been hard,' Fleur said. 'I wouldn't have guessed before-hand how hard it would be to love people on both sides.'

'Yes. And this business with Lyudmilla and Richard must have shocked you. For them both to be so unprincipled, so selfish—'

'Is that how you see it?'

'How else is there to see it? Lyudmilla was a married woman. However little the married state lived up to her expectations, she had duties and responsibilities. She chose instead to follow her appetites.'

The 'little thing', Fleur thought. How much did Rose know about that, she wondered? And in any case, was it – could it be – only that? She thought of the conditions Milochka had endured, the unceasing labour she must have had to find food for them and the horses on that frozen plain, the dirt and the lice and the creeping, relentless cold. It had only been for a month or so, certainly, but every day must have seemed like a week – and she might at any moment have chosen to go home instead. Would anyone have gone through all that; and in the end given up home, family, credit, name, country – everything in fact – simply for the sake of appetite? She might so much more easily have satisfied appetite amongst the convalescent officers, like Varkhin.

'I think she really does love Richard,' she said mildly.

'What has love to do with it?' Rose shrugged, and Fleur thought that not so very long ago, she might have answered in the same words, and in the same tone. What had changed her was perhaps not so much her brief experience with Peter, but the more prolonged deprivation of the siege. It was necessary, she thought, to have satisfactory access to hot water and clean linen and enough to eat, to keep metaphysical concepts such as honour and duty to the forefront of one's mind.

Being at Schwartzenturm seemed to revive Count Kirov. When he had got over the immediate weariness of the journey, he became much more like his old self. He busied himself about estate duties, went out riding with his sister and his guest, and was genial, even amusing at dinner. The weather was fine. It was very cold – dropping to as much as 23 degrees below zero – but it was such a dry cold, under brilliant blue skies, that it was exhilarating rather than troublesome.

Fleur felt rather guiltily glad that, not being in St Petersburg, she had avoided the necessarily distressing meeting with the Polotskis. Her relief was premature, however.

One day, when they had been at Schwartzenturm about a week, she and Kirov returned home from a ride, and tramped into the ground-floor ante-room to remove their outer garments. Their cheeks were bright from the cold air, their noses and fingers tingling, and the exhilaration of the ride had left them in high spirits. Kirov was telling her an amusing story about an old dowager on whom he had played a trick in his cadet days, and Fleur was laughing and thinking how like his old self he was – better than his old self!

'Of course, she had no idea that the bear was following her, and she walked along the line, nodding and smiling and being so gracious. I don't know why she thought everyone was gasping – probably thought they were gasps of admiration for her *ensemble*. And the bear padded along behind her, showing his teeth to everyone, and gradually getting closer and closer, and Pavelasha and I were bringing up the rear, almost helpless with laughter.'

'Oh, but what happened? Did it catch her?' Fleur asked, slipping her arms out of her coat, which the servant was holding for her.

'Well, just as she got to the end – yes, Ngorny? What is it?' Kirov broke off as his servant appeared silently in the doorway.

'Visitors, master,' he said briefly, flicking his head in the direction of the house. His eyes held some urgent message. 'They're waiting for you in the drawing-room.'

'What visitors?'

'Your brother, master. And—'

'Yes – and?'

'And Mr Polotski.'

Fleur felt her heart lurch, and put her fingers to her mouth. Kirov showed little reaction. The smile slipped slowly from his face, that was all. He seemed to be considering the information.

'Did they arrive together?' he asked at last.

'No, master. Count Peter came after the old gentleman.'

'You mean after him, or *after* him?'

Ngorny nodded just perceptibly. Kirov stared at nothing, thinking; then he caught Fleur's eye, and a change came over his expression. His mouth became grim: he looked angry rather than thoughtful.

'Very well, we'll go up and see the old gentleman. Come, Fleur.' He removed his underjacket, threw it to the servant, and followed Ngorny upstairs. Fleur followed unwillingly, her mouth dry with apprehension, wondering what fresh awfulness was going to come of Lyudmilla's actions.

The three of them – Rose, Peter and Polotski – were in the octagon room, and that it was not an ordinary social visit was evident at once, for no tea or other refreshments had been brought. Rose was sitting on the sofa, her face expressionless, watching the other two; Peter and Polotski seemed to have been arguing, for they broke off as Kirov entered and turned to him, and both were flushed and bright-eyed. Peter stepped forward and opened his mouth to speak, but Kirov silenced him with a gesture, fixing his eyes on Polotski.

'Well, sir,' he said coldly, 'I'm surprised to see you here.'

'I don't doubt it,' Polotski said grimly. 'You made good sure not to come near Petersburg, I notice – for fear of meeting me somewhere, I don't doubt.'

'My brother's been ill,' Peter said quickly. 'I told you he's only just out of danger—'

'He can speak for himself, I imagine,' Polotski said, surprisingly mildly, considering the way he was looking at Sergei.

'I certainly can,' Kirov said. 'I would scorn to avoid you, sir, but I say again, I'm surprised you have the audacity to come here, considering the way your daughter has behaved.'

Polotski crimsoned with indignation. 'And you blame me for that, do you?'

481

'Certainly. If you had brought her up properly, she would have been better suited to her new station in life. But I hadn't been married to her for more than a week before I began to have doubts about her.'

'Sergei—!' Peter tried urgently to interrupt him, but Kirov ignored him. They both ignored him, in fact, squaring up to each other like massively unequally matched prizefighters. But this was no prizefight: this was deadly. The air almost crackled with unleashed resentments.

'Doubts, was it?' Polotski retorted. 'Doubts? You hadn't too many doubts when you were trying to get your hands on her dowry.'

'I didn't know her then. I'd had opportunity to observe her manners, but I knew nothing about her character. That, however, was soon revealed to me. I have to tell you, sir, that I would not willingly bring shame on my family's name for any sum of money. I would be sorry to have to tell you that your daughter was a slut, if it weren't that the blame for what she is must be laid wholly at your door.'

Polotski was panting with rage. 'Slut? By God, sir, you'll pay for that word! How dare you, sir? How dare you?'

'How dare I? Dare to tell the truth? Her own actions condemn her!'

'And who drove her to those actions, tell me that?' Polotski cried. Fleur, rigid with shock and distress, made a movement to go, not wanting to witness any more rending of flesh, but Polotski turned on her. 'No, don't you go! You of all people must hear what I've got to say, I warned you about him, didn't I? Yes, long ago, back in London; and I should have taken my own medicine! But even I didn't know the whole of it.'

He turned on Kirov again, and in a low voice, like a growl of rage, he said, 'I know all about you now, Kirov! You thought I was just going to let things be, didn't you, because I hadn't come here before to call you to account? Well you were wrong! I was making sure of my facts, asking questions, finding out everything there is to be found out about you. My daughter left you, and I'm as sorry as I can be at the *way* she did it, because it's taken her out of my reach. But I'm not sorry she did it – oh no! She had every right to leave you, and find herself a man who was a man, a man who'd be a proper husband to her. Because you never were!'

Kirov's face drained of colour. His lips parted as though he might speak, but no sound emerged. He stared at his tormentor in a white, bleak fury.

'Aye, I know about you now!' Polotski went on with relish. 'Milochka told me in her letter how you'd neglected her, and it occurred to me to wonder why your first wife had no children either. You were wounded, weren't you, before you left the Caucasus? Aye, well may you start!' he added to Peter. 'He made sure to keep it very quiet! Pretended he was coming home because he'd got married and wanted to settle down with his new young wife on his family estate.'

He turned to Kirov again. 'But you hadn't meant ever to leave the Caucasus. You'd meant to stay there with your wife's people for ever – until you got your wound. And that changed everything, didn't it?'

Peter stared at his brother, puzzled. 'Is any of this true, Seryosha? He's talking through his hat isn't he? Just say the word, and I'll throw the beggar out.'

Kirov didn't answer, only stared at Polotski in that same white, blind way. It was Rose who spoke – quietly, as though to herself. 'Mother knew. That must have been why—' She stopped again.

Polotski looked from one to the other, and then resumed. In the absence of resistance his anger was failing, and something else was showing through – the exposed bones of a desperate hurt and humiliation.

'I managed to trace the surgeon you consulted after you got back to Petersburg – one of the Emperor's own. I may say! He wouldn't tell me anything, but I bribed one of his clerks to look in the records. But I'd begun to guess anyway. You can't get children, can you? That's what he told you. You're sterile!'

He whipped up his anger again, clenching his fists to aid himself on, to hold back the hurt.

'You're no better than a bloody mule! And what's worse, you knew it, you knew it before you married my little girl! For the sake of getting your hands on her money, you were willing to condemn her to a lifetime of childlessness, like that first wife of yours, poor pitiful lady – and we all know what happened to her, don't we? You broke her heart, and she pined away and died. But my Milochka had a bit more red blood in her, and a bit more spirit, and she had the wit to save herself, before it was too late.'

Kirov found his voice. 'For God's sake, that's enough,' he muttered. Polotski didn't even seem to hear him.

'You cheated her, and you cheated me, and you lied to us both – lied to the whole world! So I'll tell you what's going to happen now, my fine friend. I'm going to get her a divorce from you, and you're going to pay back every penny of her dowry – every last penny! And if you try to stop it, if you make trouble of any kind, I'll make sure everybody knows the truth about you. You'll never hold up your head in Petersburg again, do you hear me?'

He paused a moment, panting, his fists raised. 'By God,' he went on suddenly, 'what I'd really like to do is to kill you, Kirov, for what you did to my little girl! But I reckon this way you'll suffer longer; and I want you to have plenty of time to regret that you ever tried crossing swords with Ivan Polotski!'

There was a silence when he stopped, the most horrible silence of Fleur's life. She stood rooted to the spot with shame and distress, and she had the dreadful feeling that no one was going to speak, that they would all be condemned to stand there like that for ever.

But in the end it was Kirov who spoke, and his voice sounded light, remote, almost detached, as if it proceeded out of another world. 'You are wrong in almost every one of your assumptions,' he said. 'But I will release your daughter, if that is what you want.'

Polotski seemed taken aback. 'On my terms,' he insisted, and he sounded loud and blustering by contrast to Kirov's quietness.

'On whatever terms you choose. I will not resist you,' Kirov said in that same transparent voice. He seemed about to add something else, then changed his mind, and without another word or look, he turned and went out.

Now Fleur was able to move at last, but not very far. One step to the nearest chair, and she could allow her trembling legs to let her down.

Peter turned to Polotski. 'For God's sake, did you have to?' He looked rather green. Rose said nothing, avoiding all eyes, staring straight ahead like a statue.

Polotski looked round them, licked his lips a few times, passed a hand over his brow. 'Aye,' he said at last. 'It had to be said. He had to be stopped.' No one looked at him. He was pariah now, he was embarrassment. They wanted him to go.

He turned to Fleur. 'I want you to know that we don't hold anything against you, Sophie and me. I want you to know that we still feel the same towards you as we always did. You've had a bad time, the worst maybe, and none of it your fault. If you want to leave here, if you want somewhere to go, we'd love to have you to live with us, for as long as you want.'

Fleur could find no words. He tried to smile at her, but the muscles of his face wouldn't hold it in place. He looked, in spite of his righteous anger, badly shaken.

'We've lost our daughter, though I hope not for good. But there's a place for you in our hearts, no matter what happens. You could make your home with us. Think about it.'

Fleur looked down at the floor. Polotski looked around them once more, and then sighed.

'Aye,' he said. 'Well, I'll be going. I'm sorry it had to be this way.'

Nobody seemed willing or able to speak, even to bid him goodbye, and in the end he had to turn and leave on his own. They heard him say something to a servant out in the hallway, and then the echo of his footsteps receded.

'I tried to stop him,' Peter said at last. 'I called at their house – I thought someone should – and madame told me where he'd gone and why. It was just chance – half an hour earlier, and I'd have caught him. It was damned bad luck.'

'You wouldn't have stopped him,' Rose said. Her voice was so calm that Fleur glanced at her in surprise. 'He wanted

485

someone to be hurt for his pain. But Seryosha was right – he was wrong in his assumptions. Still, I suppose a merchant is bound to see things in terms of trade.'

'But what about Sergei?' Fleur said, outraged that they could be so indifferent to his suffering. 'Isn't someone going to go after him? He must be—' She couldn't think of an adequate word.

'I don't suppose he'd welcome either of us at the moment,' Rose said.

'Best leave him for a bit,' Peter said. 'I thought he handled it pretty well, but he'll be feeling pretty embarrassed all the same—'

'Embarrassed!'

'Wouldn't you be?' Rose said.

Fleur got up and ran from the room.

It took her a long time to track him down, though when she finally did find a servant who knew where he was, she felt she ought to have guessed.

By the time she was halfway up the Black Tower, she was wishing she had stopped to put on a coat, for the air coming in through the arrow-slits was icy. But when she emerged into the tower-room it was better – the windows were glazed, and the winter sunshine pouring in had warmed the atmosphere above freezing, at least.

He was in the countess's room, standing at the window. She paused in the doorway, unable, now she had found him, to think of anything to say. She had no idea how he was feeling – angry, hurt, shocked, indignant? In any case, what could she do or say to comfort him? Perhaps she should not have come – but she could not bear to think that no one was to offer him any support at all.

After a moment he said, without turning round, 'She died looking at this view, you know, the old countess – according to legend, anyway. She had her bed pushed up to the window, and had her maid prop her on her side so that she could look out. And that's how they found her, dead, with her eyes open.'

He turned his head a little – not to look at her, but to invite her closer. She crossed the room and stood near him, pulling her shawl round her. He continued to look out of the window. 'It's surprising how many people die with their eyes open. You'd think the eyelids would close automatically, wouldn't you? It makes me think that probably death isn't anything like sleep after all.'

Now he looked at her. His face seemed quite calm. 'I've walked across battlefields, and so many of the dead look really quite surprised, as though death wasn't anything like they expected.'

He turned away from the window. 'Has he gone?'

'Yes.'

'And Petya?'

'No, he's still here.'

'Ah.' He looked at her, his eyelids drooping a little, so that he seemed watchful, almost cunning. 'And what did you think of that little outburst?' Fleur couldn't answer. The watchful eyes probed her. 'Come, you must have thought something, or why are you here?'

'I came to see if you were all right,' she said, a little stung. 'I thought you must be – upset.'

'Did you?' He seemed to consider that, and then said, with a little chuckle, 'Upset! Yes, that's the word. Upset!' He put a hand on her shoulder. 'Thank you, my dear friend. Thank you for minding whether I was upset or not. I haven't deserved so much of you.'

'You have! You've been everything that's kind to me!' she protested, tears coming to her eyes.

'No I haven't,' he said gently. 'But never mind it now. I've never been very good at making people happy, it seems. I made *her* very unhappy.' With his hand on her shoulder he walked her across to the portrait of his first wife, and stood before it, looking at it thoughtfully.

'What he said was true, you know,' he went on quietly. 'I did suffer a wound – and concealed it. And it's true that I can't – breed, as he puts it. It made Elisabeth very unhappy. I suppose every woman wants a child.'

487

It seemed to be a question, but she didn't know how to answer it. Instead she asked, 'Why did you come back? If – if it didn't make any difference?'

'To consult the surgeons, of course. He only traced the one – but there were others. They all said the same thing. Well, when it came to it, I didn't care. I loved her, you see. But she—' His mouth turned down bitterly. 'He didn't know the whole story, you know – no, though he prided himself on having found out *everything*. He didn't know – because I made very sure it would never come out – that my wife, when she learned that I could not give her the child she wanted, decided that someone else might as well do it for me. And she didn't particularly mind who it was.'

'Ah, no,' Fleur protested softly. His hand dug into her shoulder, making the bones creak.

'Ah yes! That delicate, sweet creature, so mild and milky that everyone thought she was as innocent as a newborn lamb – she went a-whoring after any man she thought might service her. Having viewed me in a purely agricultural light, shall we say, and found me lacking, she simply looked for another ram to breed from. I offered her everything I had – my devotion, my loyalty – but all she wanted was a full belly. She scorned my love—'

He stopped, his face working with emotion. Fleur could bear the pain of her shoulder no longer, and tried gently to unlatch his fingers, but he only gripped harder. 'She even tried my brother – yes, my own little brother Petya! – thinking, I suppose, that his blood was the closest to my own.'

'But he didn't – he wouldn't—?' she stammered, afraid of what he might tell her next.

'I don't know,' he said, and his voice was raw with pain. 'I'll never know.'

'But – not Peter!'

'I never asked him. How could I? And don't you see, whatever anyone says, you can never know for certain? I only know what she was, and that he has always had everything he wanted.' He paused for a moment, his expression bitter. Then he sighed, a little wearily. 'But I kept silent, about my doubts, as about everything to do with her – weakness. I protected her as best I could. But Mother knew. Rose was right about that. She guessed – everything! There was never any keeping anything from Mother.' He stared at the portrait, and it stared back, meek and fragile. 'Her death was a release for us all,' he said abruptly.

He let her go at last, turning away to walk to the other side of the room, and she sighed and rubbed her shoulder tenderly. What *was* it he was telling her? she wondered. Was it madness? It seemed like madness.

'What about Lyudmilla?' she asked at last.

The question didn't seem to disturb him. He answered quietly as though of his own thoughts, his back turned to her. 'Lyudmilla reminded me of her, just a little. She was so young and innocent, as Elisabeth had been. But she was playful and high spirited – I liked that. Elisabeth was always afraid, of everything and everybody, flinching at every loud voice and sudden movement. God, how that irritated me! I thought Milochka would be stronger; and I thought, coming from that background, she would be truer.'

'Did you tell her,' Fleur asked, 'about your – about – that she wouldn't conceive?'

'No,' he said. 'No, I didn't. But what then? She had married me, not my loins! They make such a fuss about it, these women! As if that's all a man is. Such a little thing – ! So after the first week of our marriage, I simply – didn't – do it. That way, I thought, she would never know. But it turned out that that was what she wanted above all else. *That* mattered more to her than I did. She was a beast, like other women. Just a base little rutting animal.'

'It wasn't like that,' Fleur protested, and he turned sharply, and looked at her with those strange and burning eyes.

'Ah, my *Tsvetoksha*! But you at least were different! I hold that to me as comfort – your pure, untainted love!'

'How – how do you know I was different?' she said tremulously.

He stepped across to her, taking her by the arms, gazing down at her as though he meant to devour her. 'Don't you think I know you? Haven't I lived with you in purity all these months? If you had been like other women, would you have delighted in the love of the spirit, the love of the mind which we shared, without taint of carnality? You were happy just to be with me, to devote yourself to me, to share my company, my days, my life. No matter how you were tested, you remained true.'

He is mad, she thought; and the thought was pity. It was sad and frightening. Probably none of this was true. Probably that pale, meek girl in the portrait had been no more unchaste than Lyudmilla when she did jigsaw puzzles with Richard on the drawing-room floor. But she saw how it was, that once a thought was planted, for whatever reason, it grew without reference to fact or even probability. *Whatever anyone says, you can never know for certain*. That was the essence of it.

Rose's words came back to her: *The children of lovers have a hard row to hoe*. She imagined him as a young child, burning with love for his mother – a mother who would never return that love on his own terms. He had wanted to come first with his mother, and he never could, because his mother loved his father. Was that where it all began? His mother chose his father and loved him – perhaps to a young boy's view – carnally. And after that, all women must bear the taint.

'You're wrong,' she said, calm and sad, looking up into his handsome face, his strange, feral eyes. 'I didn't love you like that. I wanted to marry you. I was jealous when you married Lyudmilla. I believed you when you said it was an unimportant thing, because I didn't know any better. But now—'

His hands dropped from her shoulders, and she stopped, seeing where that sentence led her.

'Yes, now?' he said, the eyes hooded, watchful again.

No, she couldn't tell him. It was not his to know, what was between her and Peter. 'Now I think you're wrong.' She returned his gaze steadily, unflinching. 'Either you're wrong, or the whole of the rest of the world is, and I can't believe it's that.'

He stared at her for a long time, and then he closed his eyes and turned away, drawing an unsteady sigh. 'I see.' He walked away from her rather blindly, stopping just short of the doorway. 'I suppose, then, that you'll be going away from me now, to seek a better life, to find yourself a man who'll love you carnally?'

She bit her lip, hearing the pain he was trying to conceal from her. 'No,' she said. 'I gave you my promise. I told you I would never leave you.'

'Yes,' he said, and he sounded surprised to remember it. 'Yes, you did. Well, it's good to know that you are willing to honour your promise. But if it's irksome to you, I will release you from it.'

'For heaven's sake, Sergei,' she said, trying to lighten the atmosphere just a little, '*I* will tell you if it becomes irksome!'

He still had his back to her. 'Yes,' he said, but it didn't sound as though it were an answer to her, rather to his own thoughts.

He walked out through the door into the tower-room, and then turned his head slightly to address her over his shoulder.

'I'd like to be alone for a while. Thank you, though, for coming to me.'

'Are you all right?' she asked doubtfully.

'Yes,' he said. 'I'll be all right now.'

And so she left him.

She had barely regained the octagon room – she had had no time even to speak to Rose and Peter – when Ngorny came running in. His face was white, and his eyes were round and blank with panic, staring like two gun muzzles.

'Quick! Oh come quickly! There's been a terrible accident! My master – he's hurt. Oh quickly!'

'Good God,' Peter said, jumping to his feet, 'what's happened?'

But Ngorny's blank stare had found Fleur, and she felt her stomach sink away from her with the anticipation of disaster. She knew what had happened.

He was lying at the foot of the Black Tower. It was on the lee side, and the snow there was only a couple of inches deep. On the other side, it would have been deep enough to bury him. He was lying on his back, his legs curled, one hand on his chest, the other flung back, almost as though he had lain down to sleep; but there was a horrid, spreading red stain in the snow underneath him.

Ngorny was whimpering. 'I saw him fall. I was taking the short cut to the stables, and I saw him fall like a big bird. He must have been leaning over the edge, and slipped on the ice. Dear Mother of God, I saw him coming down!'

Peter knelt down beside him and lifted his head, and then made a dry, clicking sound in his throat as he tried to swallow. One side of Sergei's face, the side that was uppermost, was quite untouched and perfect; the underside was just a red pulp. He pulled back his hands and began to cry.

'Oh no, Seryosha,' he said pleadingly. 'Oh no, please no.'

He released me, Fleur thought. She felt quite calm, though she thought it was probably shock, and that quite soon she would begin to shake and cry, like Peter – though perhaps not with his simple grace.

And then she thought, he released himself, from a torment of his own making that had grown more intolerable with every passing year. And now he lay at the foot of the Black Tower, staring up at the sky with one questioning golden eye. He had died with his eyes open; and he looked, she thought, more than anything surprised, as though death wasn't anything like he expected.

The funeral was beautiful, at once sumptuous and glorious and sad and consoling, and Fleur found herself thinking that if she stayed in Russia, she might well decide to take instruction and have herself received into the Orthodox Church. While standing in the little church, lit with candlelight and misty with the lilac fumes of incense, it was perfectly possible to believe in the immortality of the soul, and to feel glad that Sergei's had escaped the tormenting imperfection of mortality and flown free at last.

What would happen to her now was something she had wondered on and off over the past week. To go back to

England seemed the obvious step, and yet she felt no tug towards it. It no longer seemed like home to her. To go back would seem like stepping back into a prison cell. Well, she might stay here, after all. Even without the Polotskis' kind offer, she had sufficient of an income to be independent; and Rose might welcome a companion to live with her, at least for part of the year.

She cried at last at the graveside. Here was the other side of death – the poor, sad clay, laid aside and forgotten; the earthly shape of the man she had loved, and would never see again. She cried, and was glad to cry. No mortal ought to pass without that simple tribute. And when it was all over, and everyone turned away to go back to the house, she lingered; standing in the cold sunlight, watching the gravediggers filling in the hole. The grave had been dug next to his mother's. It was a sheltered corner of the burial-ground, and the crocuses were already pushing through the thin snow on Anna Petrovna's grave. Fleur lifted her face to the sky, letting the tears dry in the bright, hard air; remembering, so many things; saying goodbye to Sergei. Gone. Gone for ever.

And then Peter was beside her. She looked up at him, and he smiled, a little tremulously. He had loved his brother, in spite of everything, and she liked that in him, that simplicity of affection. She gave him her hand, and he smiled more easily, and carried it back with his own into his pocket for warmth.

After a while, when the diggers were nearing the top, he said, 'What will you do now?'

'I don't know.'

'*Will* you go back to England?'

'No,' she said, finding her answer in his question. 'You can never go back. I've learnt that much.'

She felt some tension go out of him, and glancing sideways at him, saw that he looked pleased.

'What is it, Peter Nikolayevitch?'

'I was just thinking, that if you're not going back to England, you had better marry me.' Surprised, she didn't speak, and he squeezed her hand encouragingly. 'Well, you can't really marry anyone else, you know. That would be a sin.'

'Is that all?'

'No. You'll be happy with me.'

'How do you know?'

'Because I love you.'

'You've never told me so before. Or is it a new departure?'

'Not at all. I loved you from the beginning, but you were in love with Seryosha. Oh, I felt sure I would win you in the end, but I had to go carefully. I always knew it would take a lot of hard work.'

She smiled in spite of herself. 'Such confidence. He said that you always got what you wanted.'

'He said that? He must have been talking about himself.'

'Oh no. I don't think he ever got anything he wanted.'

'You may be right,' he said sadly, looking down at the brown, naked earth. She looked up at him, seeing him all over again as for the first time: his ordinary face – except that his eyelashes were long and silky and rather beautiful; and his chin had a slight, exquisite dent in it, too shallow to be called a cleft, but just deep enough to press a fingertip into; and his mouth was long and subtle—

She had a sudden vivid memory of the feeling of his lips on hers, kissing her while his hand caressed her breast. It hit her in the base of the stomach like an electric shock. She had shared that with him, and it was very precious; and more than that, he was telling her now that it made him her own, the one person of her very own that she had always wanted, whose business it would be to see that she was happy and cared for.

She didn't want to go away from him. She wanted to be with him always. When it came to it, it was so simple, she wondered how she could have missed it. Oh Peter, she thought, what a lot of time I've wasted.

His thoughts had been elsewhere, of course. As she looked at him in that revelatory moment, he said, 'I think he did love you, you know. I think he loved you as much as it was possible for him to love anyone other than himself. But it would never, even in ideal circumstances, have been a comfortable love.' He looked at her carefully. 'Now I love you much, much more. I can make you comfortable and I know how to make you happy. But of course, I'm not romantic or exciting – I'm just ordinary.' He brooded for a moment. 'It's funny how women always seem to be mad for men like Seryosha, who treat them badly, and really love themselves most of all.'

She turned to face him, and put her other hand in his other pocket. 'Perhaps it's just a part of growing up,' she said. 'We all believe in fairy stories when we're children.' *Trying to make life more than it is.* But there were other ways, if you looked for them. 'It was all just a fantasy, you know, loving Sergei. Not real at all. Now this—' She tugged at him, rocking him towards her, and he grinned shyly, pulling his hands out of his pockets to balance himself. 'This is real! Not as exciting, perhaps, but oh, so much more sustaining!'

She had misjudged him, this man, in many ways. She had thought him light, but she saw now that his frivolous ways disguised a basic seriousness, just as Sergei's outward seriousness hid an underlying lack of substance. And that, really, was what Peter was saying, when he said he could make her comfortable, and happy. She would have the substance, and not the shadow. *Syllabub*, she remembered Lyudmilla saying. You couldn't live on syllabub: this was good, wholesome bread and butter. Oh Sergei, I'm sorry! But I did love you as you wanted to be loved, in a way – in a way.

They left the grave, turned and began walking back towards the house, arms intertwined, already comfortable in the assumption of closeness. They had got the difficult part over with already, of course – now all the sweets were to come, of being lovers as well as friends, of curling up together every night in the same nest, safe and warm and loved.

'That's all very well,' Peter said suddenly, complainingly, 'but I want to be exciting to you as well.'

She smiled up at him. 'None of us can have everything in this life.' But she didn't say it out loud. Peter was to be her dear husband, and his feelings were her responsibility from now on. So she didn't say it.

Afterword

Menshikov's attack on Eupatoria failed, and he was dismissed and replaced by Gorkachov in February, 1855. The letter of dismissal was amongst the last dictated by Emperor Nicholas: he died on the 2nd of March, of influenza – though it was said of a broken heart – to be succeeded by his son Alexander.

But the war dragged on for another year, in muddle and suffering and sad, avoidable death. Sebastopol held out until the 8th of September, when after a full-scale attack by the Allies, General Gorkachov ordered his troops to evacuate to the northern shore, and set fire to the city. It burned for two days, and the Allies did not enter the ruins until the 10th of September. The last assault cost the Allies eleven thousand men, and the Russians thirteen thousand.

Having taken the Crimea, the Allies found they could do nothing with it. It was impossible to invade Russian heartland from there, and the French began to tire of the game. Negotiations were resumed with Emperor Alexander in January 1856, and the peace was finally signed on the 30th of March. Russia retired from the world scene for a while to concentrate on more pressing internal problems: the building of railways and the freeing of the serfs.

The last of the Allied troops left Russian soil on the 12th of July 1856, to return to a rejoicing nation which had never really understood what it was all about, but which was always happy to celebrate a victory. Soon it had passed from the minds of most of the populace entirely, and the thousands who had died were commemorated only by the odd ephemera of the war: balaclava helmets, woollen jackets called cardigans, Crimean crocuses, and, in new industrial towns, a dozen grimy streets called Alma.

Of the great hopes and popular idealism that had brought forth the Great Exhibition of 1851, there was left no trace.

London, 1851: all the world flocks to the Great
Exhibition, where beautiful, independent Fleur
Hamilton encounters the enigmatic
Count Sergei Kirov.

When they meet again in St Petersburg, she
knows that her fate is entangled with this vibrant
man, whom she cannot understand, and yet who
stirs her like no other.

But England and Russia are on the brink of war;
Kirov is on the brink of a marriage of
convenience; and Fleur finds herself trapped in
an agonising triangle of passion and betrayal.

From the magical splendours of St Petersburg to
the peril and squalor of besieged Sebastopol,
Fleur follows her love; and through danger and
suffering seeks to unravel the mystery of Kirov's
tragic past, and find her destiny.

*FLEUR is the second volume of the splendid
Kirov saga. The first volume ANNA is also
available in Pan Books.*

Cover design by Slatter-Andersen

FICTION

UK £4.99
$6.99 CAN excl GST
$12.95 Australia

ISBN 0-330-31791-1

90000

9 780330 317917